THE WORLD
of the
AENEID

Black Sea

THRACE

MACEDONIA

• Aenus

○ Acroceraunia

Simois River

• Buthrotum

Xanthus River
Troy

• Antandros

GREECE

Aegean Sea

PHRYGIA

• Actium

Sea

○ Delos

Pergamum •

CRETE

The Aeneid

TRANSLATED BY
DAVID FERRY

THE
ÆNEID

VIRGIL

The University of Chicago Press
Chicago and London

The University of Chicago Press, Chicago 60637
The University of Chicago Press, Ltd., London
© 2017 by The University of Chicago
All rights reserved. No part of this book may be used or
reproduced in any manner whatsoever without written
permission, except in the case of brief quotations in
critical articles and reviews. For more information,
contact the University of Chicago Press, 1427 East 60th
Street, Chicago, IL 60637.
Published 2017
Printed in the United States of America

26 25 24 23 22 21 20 19 18 17   1 2 3 4 5

ISBN-13: 978-0-226-45018-6 (cloth)
ISBN-13: 978-0-226-45021-6 (e-book)
DOI: 10.7208/chicago/9780226450216.001.0001

Endpapers: Lauren Nassef, *The World of the "Aeneid"*
(2017).

Page 2: A sculpture by Dmitri Hadzi in the collection
of David Ferry. Courtesy of the Estate of Dmitri Hadzi.
Photograph by Stephen Ferry (www.stephenferry.com).

Library of Congress Cataloging-in-Publication Data

Names: Virgil, author. | Ferry, David, 1924– translator.
Title: The Aeneid / Virgil ; translated by David Ferry.
Other titles: Aeneid. English
Description: Chicago : The University of Chicago Press,
    2017.
Identifiers: LCCN 2017002329 | ISBN 9780226450186
    (cloth : alk. paper) | ISBN 9780226450216 (e-book)
Classification: LCC PA6807.A5 F47 2017 | DDC
    873/.01—dc23 LC record available at https://lccn.loc
    .gov/2017002329

♾ This paper meets the requirements of ANSI/NISO
Z39.48-1992 (Permanence of Paper).

TO MY FAMILY
FOR ALL YOUR HELP

CONTENTS

PREFACE

Aurora rose, spreading her pitying light,
And with it bringing back to sight the labors
Of sad mortality, what men have done,
And what has been done to them; and what they must do
To mourn. King Tarchon and Father Aeneas, together
Upon the curving shore, caused there to be
Wooden funeral pyres constructed, and to which
The bodies of their dead were brought and placed there,
In accordance with the customs of their countries.
The black pitch smoke of the burning of the bodies
Arose up high and darkened the sky above.
Three times in shining armor the grieving warriors
Circled the burning pyres, three times on horseback,
Ululating, weeping, as they rode.
You could see how teardrops glistened on their armor.
The clamor of their sorrowing voices and
The dolorous clang of trumpets rose together
As they threw into the melancholy fires
Spoils that had been stripped from the Latins, helmets,
And decorated swords, bridles of horses,
And glowing chariot wheels, and with them, also,
Shields and weapons of their own familiar
Comrades, which had failed to keep them alive.
Bodies of beasts were thrown into the fire,
Cattle, and bristle-backed swine, brought from surrounding
Fields to be sacrificed to the god of death.

And all along the shore the soldiers watched
The burning of the bodies of their friends,
And could not be turned away until the dewy
Night changed all the sky and the stars came out.

Over there, where the Latins were, things were
As miserable as this. Innumerable
Scattered funeral pyres; many bodies
Hastily buried in hastily dug-up earth,
And many others, picked up from where they fell
When they were slain, and carried back to the fields
Which they had plowed and tilled before the fighting,
Or back into the city where they came from;
Others were indiscriminately burned,
Unnamed, and so without ceremony or honor.
The light of the burning fires was everywhere.
On the third day when the light of day came back
To show the hapless scene, they leveled out
What was left of the pyres and separated what
Was left of the bones, now cold and among cold ashes,
And covered over the ashes and the bones.

⸢ ⸢ ⸢

Aurora interea miseris mortalibus almam
extulerat lucem referens opera atque labores.

This beautiful two-line sentence with which Virgil's Latin introduces
this passage from book 11 is definitive. It defines for us how we are to
experience the telling of this heartbreaking scene; it is also, I believe,
the definitive declaration of how to read the whole continuing enter-
prise of the poem, the accounting of what men have done and what
has been done to them and what they must do to mourn, here and in
every episode of the work.

I love the way that opening line in the Latin ends with "almam,"
which I translate as "pitying," and the line therefore seems almost to

embrace with its pity those sad, those suffering, those miserable mortals; and then after that embracing line, "extulerat" follows; the light is spreading, bringing forth still more about the wretchedness of the scene, bringing back to sight what the scene looks like, exposing it to our eyes in the pitying morning light, into which and against which the black pitch smoke rises and darkens the sky; and it's by the light of the fires burning the bodies that we see, demanding a pity beyond pity, the tears on their armor, and hear their ululating cries of mourning.

And over where the Latins are, the fire of the burning of the bodies is everywhere. The Trojans and the Latins are paired in their distress, though to be sure there are differences between the two scenes. Doleful, heart-struck as it is, the burning of the bodies of the Trojans and their Arcadian allies is also mournfully glorious, a desolate celebration of Pallas's deeds. Here young Pallas is sent down to the Underworld with all the spoils his skills and his filial piety, piety owed to his father and to Aeneas as well, have earned. The trumpets' music and the music of the soldiers' ululation are sounding their praises; you can see the tears on their armor but the armor is shining; there is ceremony. Over there with the Latins there is almost none, and the pity that's invoked is even more thoroughgoing in its implacable account of their haplessness. Mortals, alike and different, in the condition of their mortality.

The terms, the vocabularies, in these great two lines—"miseris mortalibus," "referens," "opera atque labores"—in the grammar of the great sentence, tell us that what this wretched scene, so marvelously particularized, what the light of the morning and the light of the fires, showed on the particular moment is not just what's true of these soldiers and these dead bodies, but also instances of what's true of them, and of mortals, all of us, always. And so I believe these lines, this sentence, constitute a definition of Virgil's poem and a demonstration of how it goes about its work.

Miseris mortalibus

"Mortals," meaning "subject to death," therefore means "creatures," and therefore as created beings subject to chance, to the fates, to the favor and disfavor of the gods, and to the condition of not knowing for sure when they are favored by the gods and by which gods and when they are not; subject to winds, to floods, to plagues; and subject also to the rights and wrongs of their own natures, their loves, their kindness, their faithfulness to their fathers, their confusions and forgetfulness, and their own sometimes savage rage and their bloodlust. And so I translated "miseris mortalibus" as (taking the phrase from Shakespeare's Sonnet 65) "sad mortality," the name of the condition itself, of being subject to death, to the partialities and contingencies and constraints of being human.

Opera atque labores

It is no accident that this phrase deliberately recalls the Latin title of Hesiod's *Works and Days* (*Opera et dies*), or that Virgil says in his *Georgics* that he's singing the songs of Hesiod in Roman towns, and is doing so again in the *Aeneid*, or that both poems narrate the dogged pursuit of their mortal aims within the contingent partializing powers and limitations of being mortal. Jupiter saw to it that the way should not be easy, and he did so, so that mortal men would develop arts to make their way with *Labor omnia vincit*: "And everything was toil, relentless toil, urged on by need." David West excellently translates "opera atque labores" as "their toils and sufferings," and I've translated it as "what men have done, and what has been done to them." The relentless toil and sufferings are definitive of the condition of being mortal, in the *Georgics* as in the *Aeneid*.

Referens

The light is at sunrise, bringing back not only this terrible scene but also, not "ferens" but "referens," bringing *back* to mind the stories that have been told before: for example, that other, so like this one, in book 23 of the *Iliad*, the burning of the body of Achilles's Patroclus, with the bodies of the twelve captive Trojan young men, and the beasts offered up to the god of death. The consequences of the deaths of Patroclus and of Pallas are referentially there to the end of both poems and play their part in the imponderables of the conclusion. Of course, Virgil's lines and the lines brought back from Patroclus's funeral bring back many other things in both poems, but here they also bring back the crucial lines at the end of book 6 of the *Aeneid*, the lines about young Marcellus, the hope of Rome, in Anchises's prophetic account of Augustus's triumph and its promise of a stable, persisting city; and Marcellus dies a natural death, as if by chance or fate, unchallengingly, unexplainingly showing that he is mortal, that hope is mortal—"Could it have been that you could have broken through / The confines of your unrelenting fate?" So Rome itself is a mortal thing, as was Troy.

And the pitying light brings the mortal scene back to sight, and doing so it brings back to sight all those other scenes in the *Aeneid*, and, referentially, all those in the *Iliad* and the *Odyssey*, which constitute the telling of the works and days of mortal men in the condition of their mortality. And I believe we are also meant to hear in "referens" the poem's awareness that the scene is being brought back to the sight of the *reader*, who is in the condition of mortality and knows it, but knows it more vividly in the terms of the great sentence.

ON METER

As in my other translations from the Latin, I have not sought to use a dactylic hexameter instrument. In my view, the forward-propulsive character of English speech favors iambic pentameter, in which iambic events naturally dominate, with anapestic events as naturally occurring. One reason for this is that in English there are often so many articles and frequent prepositional structures; and also because, in English speech and grammar, adjectives normally occur before the noun they modify, and so their relationship is normally iambic or anapestic, even in prose. Iambic pentameter has relatively few trochaic events; dactylic events, almost never.

Iambic pentameter arises most naturally from the characteristics of English grammar and syntax, and so I am using it here. Virgil's dactylic hexameter and iambic pentameter have in common that they have (not by accident) histories of being instruments of heroic writing, and that the internal structure of their metrical lines is capacious and welcoming—though responsive to different rules—to all sorts of expressive individuation. There is room for syntactical manipulation, room for—and a susceptibility to—tonal variation, variations in the degrees of pressure or emphasis on the "weak" syllables in the iambic feet and on the "strong" syllables as well, often subtle, sometimes introspective, while continuing to be regular iambic pentameter events. And at the same time, the amplitude and continuous regularity of the line is suitable to the grandeur of the sovereign rhythm of the whole, the lines in their regularity triumphantly reiterated across the twelve books, as its essential rhythm; and each new individual line is a new metrical event in the exploration of how the poem is to be heard. What is told in the poem is deeply moving and important, and it is a creation of the way it is told, in the metrical play of its meanings. That's what's true of Virgil's metrical lines; the translator can only hope it can be true of his own.

John Dryden, in his translation of the *Aeneid*, used rhyming couplets, the so-called "heroic couplets." He did so for the music of the rhyming, but he also provided markers at the ends of the lines to make it clear that a new line was a new metrical event, as the line before it had been, and as the line after it was going to be, each line having its own way of having its own music, its own play of meanings, like and also different from the lines around it, though all of them were regular iambic pentameter. William Wordsworth said that there's always something like a pause after each line in unrhymed verse, marking the fact that a new metrical event is conceding, and another new metrical event is beginning to happen. Readers should hear it this way. As they read the lines, their imagination should hear that this succession of events is going on. Maybe not exactly a pause, but an alerted active awareness that this is happening, as in listening to measured music, all in the play of meanings. As Samuel Johnson says, "All the syllables of each line co-operate together . . . every verse unmingled with another as a distinct system of sounds."

The black pitch smoke of the burning of the bodies
Arose up high and darkened the sky above.

One sentence, two lines, both iambic pentameter, telling a continuous story; in the first syllable the character (and the content) of the smoke, and the second, third, and fourth syllables are very strongly stressed, with an effect of concentration, perhaps horrified, and certainly pitying, concentration; "black pitch smoke," "black" and "smoke" off-rhyming, and "pitch" contained within them in their rising column, a dark viscous substance, here perhaps ingredient of the bodies themselves. "The *black pitch smoke*," strongly concentrated, but in that second foot, "pitch smoke," it's still iambic, "pitch" being the adjective, "smoke" being its noun. And the last three feet, "of the burning of the bodies," want us to hear with a kind of insistence that, yes, this is the case, the smoke is of the burning of the bodies; and "burning" and "bodies" alliterate intensifyingly with the "b" of "black."

The verb "arose" is the beginning of the second line, and it weirdly reminds us of the first line of the passage: "Aurora rose, spreading her pitying light"; this new line says, by its sense and by its structural similarity, that this is opposite, authoritatively bringing on the darkness, so that the pitiful story is now told by the light of the burning of the bodies. And the vocabulary of the line—"arose" and "up" and "high"; and "high" rhyming with "sky," sky high, a distinct system of sounds—is continuous of the line before it, but with a variant music. Two iambic pentameter lines tell, in their continuances, the same story, the rising of the smoke, but each of them with a distinctive individuated truth-telling music.

ON THE TRANSLATION

Let me echo a statement I have made in connection with my earlier translations from Virgil's Latin. I have tried to be as faithful as possible. English is, of course, not Latin, and I am most certainly not Virgil. Every act of translation is an act of interpretation, and every choice of English word or phrase, every placement of those words or phrases in sentences (made in obedience to the laws and habits of English, not Latin, grammar, syntax, and idioms), and every metrical decision (made in obedience to English, not Latin, metrical laws and habits), reinforces the differences between the interpretation and the original. This is true, however earnestly the interpretation aims to represent the sense of Virgil's lines and, as best it can, some of the effects and implications of his figures of speech, the controlled variety and passions of his tones of voice. It is my hope that this translation, granting such differences between English and Latin, is reasonably close.

Reasonably close, of course, is still far away, but the effort is to achieve a representation, in the lines as they move forward, line by line, telling the tale, some kind of kinship not only to the sense of the Latin but also to the expressive complexities of implicated discernment and emotion in the lines. As I've said in the "Note on Meter" above, Virgil's explorative dactylic hexameter meters cannot be imitated, one-on-one, in English—at least not by me. The laws of his Latin syntax and grammar are too different from the laws of English grammar and syntax in my iambic pentameter meter, though it too is explorative by nature and capable of many subtleties and variations of discernment. Dryden himself said of his translation of the *Aeneid* that he had done great harm to Virgil. Every translator does, and should say so.

But I think it is not out of order for me to say that "completing" this translation of the work of such a great poet means a great deal to me personally, since I have previously translated his *Eclogues* and his *Georgics*, and I am in love with his voice as I hear it in all these poems, telling how it is with all created beings, the very leaves on the trees, the very rooted plants, the beasts in the fields, the shepherds trying to keep their world together with song replying to song replying to song, the bees in their vulnerable hives, doing their work, the soldiers doing their work of killing and dying, the falling cities, and the kings and fathers, and their sons, and Dido, and Palinurus, and Deiphobus, and Mezentius the disrespecter of gods, and the mortal son of Venus, the creature Aeneas, carrying his household gods to build a city, heroic and vulnerable, himself subject to monstrous rage, himself not always unconfused. All of them, all of us, creatures, created beings, heroic and vulnerable, and Virgil's voice telling it as it is, in his truth-telling pitying voice.

The Aeneid

The black
Breath of the war has breathed on them;
Shields gleam, and helmets, in the memory.

Book One

I sing of arms and the man whom fate had sent
To exile from the shores of Troy to be
The first to come to Lavinium and the coasts
Of Italy, and who, because of Juno's
Savage implacable rage, was battered by storms
At sea, and from the heavens above, and also
By tempests of war, until at last he might
Bring his household gods to Latium, and build his town,
From which would come the Alban Fathers and
The lofty walls of Rome. Muse, tell me   10
The cause why Juno the queen of heaven was so
Aggrieved by what offense against her power,
To send this virtuous faithful hero out
To perform so many labors, confront such dangers?

Can anger like this be, in immortal hearts?

,   ,   ,

There was an ancient city known as Carthage
(Settled by men from Tyre), across the sea
And opposite to Italy and the mouth
Of the Tiber river; very rich, and fierce,
Experienced in warfare. Juno, they say,   20
Loved Carthage more than any other place
In the whole wide world, more even than her Samos.

Here's where she kept her chariot and her armor.
It was her fierce desire, if fate permitted,
That Carthage should be chief city of the world.
But she had heard that there would come a people,
Engendered of Trojan blood, who would someday
Throw down the Tyrian citadel, a people
Proud in warfare, rulers of many realms,
Destined to bring down Libya. Thus it was   30
That the Parcae's turning wheel foretold the story.

Fearful of this and remembering the old
War she had waged at Troy for her dear Greeks,
And remembering too her sorrow and her rage
Because of Paris's insult to her beauty,
Remembering her hatred of his people,
And the honors paid to ravished Ganymede—
For all these causes her purpose was to keep
The Trojan remnant, who'd survived the Greeks
And pitiless Achilles, far from Latium,   40
On turbulent waters wandering, year after year
Driven by fates across the many seas.

So formidable the task of founding Rome.

꙳ ꙳ ꙳

Sicily was still in sight behind them
As, with joyous sails spread out, their brazen prows
Sped through the foaming waters, and Juno said,
Obsessing in herself over her grievance,
"Am I, then, I, defeated, to be prevented
From keeping the Teucrian king from Italy?
Is it because of the Fates? Pallas was able   50
To burn the Argive ships and drown its sailors
To punish the offense of one man only,
Ajax Oileus' son; Pallas herself

Was able forthwith to hurl the fire of Jove
Down from the clouds above, and from below
Raise up the ocean in tempestuous surge
And carry Ajax in a whirlwind off,
His breast aflame, on fire from the lightning bolt,
And fasten him impaled to a craggy rock.
But I who walk as queen of all the gods,   60
I, the sister and wife of Jove, must wage
Year after year my war against one people.
In time to come will there be any to pay
Due reverence to me, and at my altars
Worship with sacrifice and supplication?"

Thus, burning with resentment, in her mind
Turning these matters over and over, the goddess
Made her way to the spawning place of storms,
Aeolia, the cyclones' Berecynthian country.
There Aeolus the king in his huge cavern   70
Uses his power with fetters and chains to hold
The struggling winds and howling tempests in.
The mountain moaned with the noise of their prisoned outrage.
They blustered against the bonds he bound them with.
There Aeolus sat, scepter in hand, in his
High stronghold, he, to mollify their fury
And quiet them down; if he did not do so
Then they without a doubt would carry away
All seas and lands and the starry heavens themselves,
Sweeping them all to the nothingness beyond.   80
Therefore it was that all-knowing all-powerful Jove,
Fearing that this might happen, hid them away
In the darkest night of caverns and piled up huge
Mountains above them and gave to them a king
Whose charge it was to use his regal skill
To loosen or tighten the reins when so commanded.

➤ ➤ ➤

So Juno said to Aeolus, entreating,
"Jove, the Father of Gods and King of Men,
Has, Aeolus, given you the power either
To calm the ocean waters into peace 90
Or cause the winds to make them rise and surge.
Right now there is a race of men I hate,
Sailing upon the Tyrrhenian Sea to bring
The defeated household gods of Troy to Latium.
Shake their fleet with the raging of your winds,
Sink them, overwhelm them, scatter their broken
Bodies everywhere upon the waters.
There are fourteen beautiful nymphs in my retinue;
The most beautiful of them all is Deiopea;
I'll give you Deiopea as your reward, 100
To be your wife and be your own forever,
And be the mother of your beautiful children."
Aeolus answered: "O queen, it is for you
To discover what it is that you desire;
It is for me to do what you command.
I owe my kingdom and my scepter to
Your favor and the favor of Jupiter.
Because of this I have my rightful place
At the banquet of the gods; because of this
I am the potentate of clouds and storms." 110

＞ ＞ ＞

Having said this, Aeolus takes his spear
And with its blunt end bashes open a hole
In the hollow mountain's side, and then, at once,
The doors give way and like an army the winds,
The mob of pent-up winds, rush out and whirl
Down on the ocean and with seismic force
Heave up the waters from the lowest bottom—
All winds together, Notus and Eurus and Africus, and
Southwest, East, and South, teeming with tempests,

And vast tsunami roll toward helpless shores.   120
And then were heard the cries of terrified men,
And the shriek of the vessels' cables; all light of day
Was suddenly ripped away from the Trojans' eyes;
Black night upon the ocean waters, thunder
From pole to pole and sheets of shaking lightning
Tell of the mariners' deaths now there at hand.
Aeneas's limbs gone weak and chill to the bone,
Groaning raised up his arms to heaven and cried,
"O those others are three times, four times, blessed,
Whose privilege it was to meet their fate,   130
Watched by their fathers as they died beneath
The high walls of their native city, Troy!
Alas, Tydides, bravest of the Danaans,
That by thy hand I could not fall and pour
My life out on the fields of Ilium, where
Fierce Hector, helpless, fallen, lies, brought down
By the spear of Aeacides and where the great
Sarpedon lies, and where the river Samois
Carries away the bodies of so many
Heroes and their tumbling shields and helmets,   140
Turning over and over in its waters."

As Aeneas cries out thus, a sudden violent
Burst of wind comes crashing against the sails,
The prow of the ship turns round, the oars are broken,
The ship is broadside to the waves and then
A mountain of water descends upon them all;
Some of the men hang clinging high upon
The high-most of the wave and others see
The very ground beneath the sea revealed
As hissing with sand the giant wave recoils;   150
Three of the ships are spun by the South Wind onto
A huge rock ridge that hulks up out of the sea
(The name the Italians call it is The Altars);
Three other ships the East Wind runs aground

And carries them into shallows, a wretched sight,
The sand heaped up around them. Aeneas himself
Saw how a monstrous devouring wave rose up
And struck the stern of the ship the Lycians and
Faithful Orontes rode in, and the ship
Turned round and round in the whirlpool whirling waters.　　　160
He saw the helmsman head-first over the side;
He saw the scattered cast-out soldiers swimming
Hapless in the vast abysmal flood;
He saw the detritus floating on the water,
Troy treasure, weapons, pieces of wood; he saw
The ship of Ilioneus and the ship
Of brave Achates, Abas's ship, and the ship
Of old Aletes, all of them overwhelmed,
Their seams split open, letting in the sea.

　　　　　　　　　　❧ ❧ ❧

Then Neptune, god of the sea, became aware　　　170
Of the loud commotion of the waves upsurging
From the still foundations down below; and deeply
Troubled within raised up his placid face
Above the roiling waters and looked across
And saw Aeneas's scattered ships and saw
The Trojans overpowered by the waves,
And by the heavens collapsing down upon them.
The brother of Juno knew whose work this was,
The work of his sister Juno and her wrath.
He summoned the East and West Winds and he said:　　　180
"Are you so confident of who you are
That you have dared, without command of mine,
To collide the heavens and seas and cause such trouble?
But first it is my task to quiet the waves.
Your punishment comes later. Now, East Wind,
Speedily fly to tell your king: 'The power
To wield the trident and to rule the seas

Was given to me by lot and not to him.
Aeolus is the warden of the rocks;
Of that vast prison let him be the king,   190
And hold the winds in chains within that cavern.'"
He speaks, and as soon as he speaks, the waves are calmed,
The gathered clouds disperse, the sun comes out;
Triton and Cymothoë together push
The ships away from the rocks they are stranded on,
As Neptune uses his trident to lever them free,
And opens for them the Syrtes quicksands too,
His chariot gliding upon the quieting waters.
It is as when of a sudden, in some city,
Violence erupts, the rabble enraged,   200
Stones and firebrands thrown, but then, if the mob
Should see a man whose piety and strength
Are known to them, silent they stand and listen,
As with measured speech he calms their rage; just so,
When their creator appears to them, the rage
Of the raging waters is appeased, as he
Goes on his way, under a now clear sky.

⸎   ⸎   ⸎

Exhausted by the terrible storm at sea,
Aeneas's followers seek whatever land
Lies nearest, and so they turn toward Libya's coast.   210

There is a long deep inlet there that is
A port and shelter in whose mouth an island
Breakwater pacifies incoming waves,
So that their force disperses into ripples;
Around the sides great cliffs and peaks rise up,
And tower over the waters of the bay,
And high upon these cliffs dark overhanging
Foliage, and, above and behind, the leaves
Of trees in a black grove glimmer as they move

And stir a little in the breezes' changings. 220
Under the jutting ledge of the cliff that faces
Out as the innermost wall of the cove, there's a cave,
With seats that look as if carven out of stone,
Fresh water in basins, a domicile for the nymphs.
This port is a place where ships can rest; there is
No need for anchors, so peaceable are the waters.
Here is the sheltering place Aeneas has come to,
With seven ships, all that is left of his fleet.

His followers get themselves onto the welcome beach,
To lie there, stretching out their sea-soaked limbs 230
On dry land they so long have longed to be on.
Achates sets about making a fire by striking
Flints together to get a spark, then using
The spark to make a flame of leaves and wave them
Over the wood-chip tinder so that it catches,
And lights the dry driftwood he had found on the beach;
Weary, despondent, because of what had happened,
The Trojans take out the water-spoiled grains of Ceres,
In order to parch them in the crackling fire,
And, using stones, to crush them into meal. 240

⸝ ⸝ ⸝

Meanwhile Aeneas climbs to a high cliff, so
He can look far out, over the open ocean,
To see if there is any sign at all
Of Antheus's storm-tossed Phrygian biremes,
Or of Capys, or the heraldry of Caicus.
There is no ship in sight. But he sees three stags
That wander along the shore, and there's a herd
That follows behind, and farther still, he sees
A troop of others grazing in a valley.
So Aeneas takes the bow and arrows that faithful 250
Achates carries for him in battle, and first

Brings down those leaders, with their high branched antlers,
And then with his arrows he drives the common rout
In their confusion into the leafy woods,
And he doesn't stop till there are seven great
Conquered bodies lying on the ground,
One for each of his seven ships. Then he
Returns to the port, and divides the seven deer
Among his comrades, and shares with them the wine
From the jars magnanimous Acestes gave   260
The Trojans on the day they took their leave
From the Trinacrian shore. And then Aeneas
Speaks to his people, in order to ease their sorrow:

"O my companions, O you who have undergone,
Together with me, worse things than this before,
The gods will bring this also to an end.
You who were there so close to Scylla's frenzy,
Right in under her howling wailing cliffs,
And experienced the Cyclops throwing rocks,
Remember how brave you were. Be of good cheer,   270
Send fear away. Perhaps there will come a time
When you will remember these troubles with a smile.
Through many perils, through whatever mischance
We may encounter, our journey is toward Latium,
Where Fortune offers us a peaceful home.
There Troy will rise again. It is ordained.
Therefore endure, and expect a happier time."
These were the words he used, though sick at heart;
His face simulates hopefulness and he
Endeavors to suppress his deep distress.   280

The others ready the prizes for the feast to come:
They strip the hides from the flanks and lay bare the meat;
Some cut the meat into pieces and pierce them with spits;
Others set out the cooking pots on the beach,
And start the fires. Thus they restore their strength,

Lying along the grass and feasting on
Rich venison and Acestes' given wine.
And when they had satisfied their hunger, and
The remains of the supper were cleared away, the Trojans
Talked together about their missing fellows,   290
Not knowing whether to hope they were still alive,
Or fear they had suffered the final separation,
No longer able to answer when they are called.
More even than all the others, pious Aeneas
Grieved in his inmost heart over the loss
Of Amicus and of valorous Orontes,
And over the cruel fate that came upon
Lycus and valiant Gyas and brave Cloanthus.

                              ✦   ✦   ✦

And now the day was coming to its end.
Jupiter from his place on high looked out,   300
And over across the sea, with its many ships
And far-spread lands, its shores and peoples, and as
The god looked down upon the Libyan realms,
He thought about the troubles that he saw,
And, as he did so, Venus spoke to him
In sadness, her bright eyes shining with tears, and said,
"O you who for eternity govern, with power
And with your lightning bolt, both men and gods,
What crime could my Aeneas have committed,
How have the Trojans so offended you,   310
That after so much suffering they are kept
From every land and kept from Italy, where,
According to your promise, from their line,
The line of Teucrian kings, there would come Roman
Leaders to govern all nations and all the seas?
Why is it, Father, that your purpose has changed?
Indeed it was your promise that consoled me
For the terrible ruin of my Troy, your promise

Of a glorious fate in spite of those fatal events.
But after so many calamities, now the same   320
Bad fortune follows these people everywhere.
Great king, when will you grant my Trojans relief?
Antenor, having gotten safely away
From the very midst of the Achaean foe,
Surrounding him in the battle, could journey unscathed
Past Illyrian gulfs and through the innermost far
Country of the Liburnians and beyond
The springs of Timavus, from which the river bursts
From all nine mouths of the roaring mountain and buries
The fields below, under the tumult of waters.   330
It was here he founded Padua, raising on high
The arms of Troy, establishing a home
And a name for his Teucrian race, and now he's tranquil,
And rests. But we, your children, to whom you've given
The privileges of heaven, have lost our ships
(Oh shameful!) and are kept from Italy,
All for the sake of placating the anger of one.
Is this how faith is honored? And is this how
Our scepters are to be given back to us?"

The father smiled upon her with the look   340
That clears the sky of storms and brings fair weather.
He kissed his daughter, and this is what he said:
"Be not afraid, my lady of Cythera.
The promise I made to your children of what their fates
Would be is what it was. You are to see
The fortress walls of Lavinia's city, and you
Will bring great-hearted Aeneas to his high
Destined rightful place in the starry heavens.
I have not changed my mind. Because your worry
About your dear son gnaws at you, I will   350
Unroll the scroll of Fates and tell the meaning
Of the secrets written there. Your son shall wage
Great wars in Italy against fierce tribes,

And crush them utterly, and raise up cities,
And give his people laws to govern them.
The Rutulians having been conquered, after three winters
And summers spent in the field, he'll rule in Latium;
The boy Ascanius, now called Iulus—he
Whose name was Ilus before the Ilian fall—
Shall govern in Lavinium for thirty
Cycles of rolling months, and after that
Shall build his founding city, Alba Longa;
There for three hundred years the line of Hector
Will reign until the royal priestess Ilia
Shall bear twin sons of Mars. Then Romulus, wearing
A she-wolf's tawny hide, and proud to wear it,
In honor of that wolf who was his nurse,
Will build the city of Mars and call his people
Romans, after Romulus, his name.
For them I ordain no limits of time or space;
I grant dominion to them, without end.
Juno, who in her bitterness and dread
Has wearied earth and sea and sky, will change,
And listen to wiser counsel, and we, together,
Will lovingly foster the Roman people, they
Who wear the toga, the lords of all the nations.
It is commanded thus. The day will come,
As the appointed season comes to pass,
When Phthìa and famed Mycenae will submit
To Assaracus's house, and Argos too.
And to this noble lineage will be born
Our Trojan Caesar, glorious as far
As to the ocean, and high as to the stars,
Julius, from Iulus taking his name,
And you, your cares dispelled, will welcome him
When he ascends triumphantly to the skies,
Bringing the spoils of the conquered Orient,
And offerings will be made to him as a god.
Then wars will come to an end and savage ways

360

370

380

Be pacified and civilized under the law,　　　　　　390
By venerable Faith and the goddess Vesta,
By Remus and by his twin, Quirinus, and
The iron gates of Janus will close at last,
And in a cage impious Fury will sit
On a pile of broken useless weapons, hands bound
Behind his back by a hundred knots of brass,
And roaring hoarsely from his bloody mouth."

ʼ　ʼ　ʼ

It is thus he speaks, and sends the son of Maia
Down from the place of the gods to make it so
That Carthage, with its streets and towers, should open　　400
To let the Teucrians in, and so that Dido
Would grant them gracious welcome to her lands,
Not knowing what her fate was going to be.
Sculling upon his wings across the sky
He quickly settles on the Libyan coasts,
And there he straightaway does as Jove commanded,
And the ferocious Phoenician hearts are, by
The will of the god, at once made gentle, and
The heart of the queen of Carthage, beyond them all,
Is made most kind and open to the Trojans.　　　　　410

ʼ　ʼ　ʼ

But pious Aeneas, who has not slept all night,
His mind so full of so many cares, sets out
To explore, as soon as the morning light was given,
This strange country the wind has brought him to,
To find out who the inhabitants might be,
Whether men or animals—all he could see
Was wilderness—and to return to tell
His fellows whatever it was he might have found.
He has hidden his fleet in the quivering shadows of

Encircling hiding trees within the vault 420
At the base of a concave cliff. Alone, attended
Only by Achates his companion,
Aeneas steps forth, carrying in his hand
Two steel-tipped javelins, when suddenly,
Directly in front of him, there is his mother,
Looking as if she were a young Spartan huntress,
And with the weapons that such a maiden might carry,
Or else she looks like Harpalyce of Thrace,
Who races alongside horses and tires them out,
And runs with the winged East Wind, ahead of it. 430
Like a huntress, her shoulder carries a tight-strung bow,
Her hair is free to the wind, her knees are bare,
Her flowing dress is gathered up by a knot.
Before Aeneas has a chance to speak,
She cries, "You there, young men, have you seen my sister
Wandering anywhere near here, or shouting intent
In the chase of a foaming wild boar she's sighted? She's clad
In the hide of a dappled lynx, and wearing a quiver."

Thus Venus spoke; then Venus's son spoke thus:
"I have not seen your sister nor have heard 440
Any voices. O—but, maiden, what is your name?
Neither the face I see is that of a mortal
Nor is the voice I hear—O goddess, surely
Phoebus Apollo's sister? Or one of those
Who are called the nymphs? Whoever it is you are,
Have pity on us, tell us, what is the sky
We wander under, what are the shores of the world
The winds and giant seas have driven us to,
Not knowing what country it is we wander in,
Or among what people? Tell us, we will make 450
Glad sacrificial offerings at your altars."

Then Venus: "I am not worthy of that honor.
It is the custom of Tyrian maidens to wear

Such hunting boots and carry a quiver and bow.
This is Phoenician country, of people from Tyre,
Descendants of Agenor, who have settled here
In Libya, a race unconquerable in war.
Dido rules here as queen, who fled from Tyre,
A fugitive from her brother. The story of this
Is long and intricate, a story of wrongs, 460
But I will tell it briefly: Dido's husband,
Whom she loved with all her heart, was named Sychaeus,
The richest of all Phoenicians; Dido's father
Had given him his daughter with all the high
Felicitious solemn auguries of wedlock.
But Dido's brother Pygmalion came to power,
And ruled over Tyre; he was beyond all others
In brutal savage criminality.
Then there was frenzy and the treacherous king,
Blinded by love of gold, killed the unwary 470
Sychaeus before the altars, and then concealed
His crime from Dido as long as possible,
Tormenting his stricken sister with specious hopes,
Until one night, as she was sleeping, in
Her dream her unburied husband's ghost appeared.
Its face was ghastly pale beyond all wonder;
The vision showed the dagger in his breast,
And the altars that he met his death in front of;
The unspeakable crime in the house was thus revealed.
The ghost advised her to flee and leave the country, 480
And told her where there was a hidden treasure,
A hoard of unknown gold and silver to help her.
She was persuaded, and she and her companions
Got themselves ready; all those who hated the tyrant
Because of his tyranny, or feared him for it,
Led by a woman came together to act
In this enterprise. Ships in the harbor that were
Already rigged for sailing were seized and loaded
With treasure, Pygmalion's wealth. They sailed away

And came to the place where now you can see the great   490
Walls and the towering fort of Carthage the New.
They bought the land and called it Byrsa because
They bought as much as could be measured by
The hide of a bull. And now they are choosing judges,
Establishing laws, and putting together a senate.
But who are you? What are the coasts you have come from?
What is the journey you are going on?"
After she asked him these questions Aeneas replied,
Drawing his words from deep within his breast:
"O goddess, if I were able to tell the whole   500
Story of our afflictions from their beginning,
And if you had the time to hear it all,
I could not finish before it was the time
For heaven to close its doors and for Vesper to
Compose the day for rest. We come from Troy,
If you by chance have heard of ancient Troy.
The storm, as we were sailing across far seas,
Drove us ashore onto the Libyan coast.
I am the pious Aeneas. In my fleet
I bear with me my household gods I seized   510
And rescued from the hands of the enemy.
The heavens above know who it is I am.
It is Italy, for fatherland, I seek.
I am descended from the race of Jove.
My goddess mother showing the way, pursuant
To what the Fates had said, I set forth on
The Phrygian sea with twenty ships in my fleet.
Now, overwhelmed by violent winds and waves,
There are scarcely seven left, and I myself
Unknown, in need, wander the Libyan wasteland,   520
Driven away from Europe and from Asia—"

But here the goddess Venus broke in to say,
Preventing him from telling his story further,

"Whoever you are, I think you are favored by
The heavens, since here you are, at the Tyrian city,
Alive and breathing. And I can tell you that,
Unless the divination my parents taught
Is false, and unless the auguries mislead me,
Your fellows and their ships are found and well,
By changing winds driven to safety intact.   530
For, look!—that joyful line of twice six swans
That the bird of Jove was swooping down upon
And harrying—they now in order either
Settle already or else look down at those
Already settled where they will settle too.
And just as they, returning, joyfully play,
Ruffling their wings, and singing their joyful songs,
As they have circled down from the sky in safety,
So will, already, some of your ships and comrades
Have safely reached the harbor, and others now   540
Under full sail are coming to safety too.
Now go, and follow that path where it will lead you."

She spoke, and turned away, and as she turned
Her graceful neck shone roseate; from her hair
Divine ambrosia breathed; her gown ungathered
Flowed full length to the ground; and, as she stepped,
Her step revealed that this was truly the goddess.
He knew that she was his mother, and his words
Followed her as she fled: "Why is it that you,
As all the others do, so cruelly mock   550
Your son with images, false images?
Why cannot I hold hands with you, my mother,
And hear true words and speak true words to you?"

Thus he complains, and walks on toward the city,
But she surrounds him, he and his companion,
In darkling air and covers them with a cloud,

And thus the goddess protects them so that none
Might see or touch or hinder them on their way,
Or question them to ask about their coming.
And she herself departs across the sky, 560
And joyfully returns to Paphos where
The place of her temple is, and its hundred altars,
On each of which the Sabaean incense fumes,
And there are always fragrant garlands there.

, , ,

Meanwhile they hastened along the path she showed,
Until they climbed a hill that rises high
Above the city, and from that height looked over,
And saw the fortress towers. Aeneas marvels
At the great buildings where once there were only huts,
The pavings of the streets, the city gates, 570
The sight of the Tyrians busy at their work,
Some building walls, rolling up stones in wagons,
Some marking out with furrows dwelling plots,
Some dredging the harbor to make it deeper for ships,
Some putting down the great foundations on which
The theater would be built, and others cutting
Into the hills to get huge columns from them,
To ornament the future theater stage.
It's just as when the bees in the flowering fields,
When summer is new, are going about their work, 580
Under the sun, or filling the cells of their hives
With liquid honey until they distend and almost
Burst with the loaded nectar; or when they welcome
Into the hive the bees returning home,
Carrying what they're bringing from the fields;
Or when, as an armed patrol, they drive away
The lazy crowd of drones from the busy stalls.

The community is glowing as it works;
The honey is fragrant with the scent of thyme.

"O fortunate they, whose city is already rising!" 590
Aeneas says, looking up at the roofs of the city.
He enters, wonders to say it, hid in a cloud,
And mingles with the people, unseen by all.

                 ❜ ❜ ❜

In the center of the city there is a grove,
Solemn and deeply shady, where the Phoenicians,
Who had come there, beset by waves and winds,
Dug up from the earth (at the place where Juno showed them),
The head of a spirited horse, a symbol, an icon,
A sign that theirs would be for centuries
A people famous for their warfare prowess 600
And for the richness of their way of life.
Sidonian Dido was building a temple here,
Opulent in its votive offerings and
In the numinous presence of the goddess Juno.
The threshold at the top of the great staircase
Was bronze, the lintels of the roof were bronze,
The hinges of the resonant doors were bronze.
This is the place where Aeneas first began
To dare to hope there would be safety here,
And a turn for the better in his afflicted state, 610
For, waiting in the great temple for the queen,
And looking at all the beautiful objects in it,
Wondering at the good fortune of the city,
And admiring all the things the makers had done,
The workmanship of what was told on the walls,
Suddenly he saw depicted there,
One after another, the scenes of the Trojan War,

Famous through all the world, the sons of Priam,
The sons of Atreus, and savage Achilles
Raging against both houses, as he did.   620
Aeneas stopped, and weeping at what he saw,
Said, "Is there, Achates, anywhere on earth
That does not know the story of our trouble?
Look, there, there's Priam pictured on the wall!
Even here they praise his worth and tell our story.
These are the tears of things for what they were,
And what has become of them; the story of
The mortality of men strikes to the heart.
Nevertheless, Achates, do not fear.
In the fame recorded here there is some safety."   630

So saying, his hungry spirit feasts on the pictured
Unsubstantial scenes, as, weeping and sighing,
He gazes, his visage flooded with tears, for there
He sees the citadel of Pergamum,
And the Greeks in headlong flight from the Trojan youths
Pursuing them, hot on their heels; he sees
The panicked Phrygians fleeing from plumed Achilles'
Chariot pressing close upon them; he sees
The snow-white tents of Rhesus, and he weeps
As he sees how bloody Tydides broke in on them,   640
And slaughtered them wholesale, where he caught them sleeping,
And how he stole the fiery horses of Rhesus,
And took them back to his camp before they had
The time to forage on Trojan fodder, or drink
From the waters of Xanthus. Aeneas sees
How Troilus, unlucky boy, having lost his weapons,
So much outmatched by Achilles, has fallen out,
Down flat on his back and dragged along by his horses
And empty chariot, still holding the reins,
And bumping along the ground by the neck and hair,   650
And his spear, reversed, trailing, trundling along,

Inscribing in the dirt his wretched story.
Aeneas sees there too the Trojan women,
Their hair unbound and streaming, beating their breasts
And with gestures of supplication bearing the robe
In the temple of the goddess Athena, who
Averted her eyes and would not look at them.
He sees Achilles there, after he thrice
Dragged Hector around the walls of Troy and now
Was putting his lifeless body up for sale. 660
Aeneas groans from the depth of his being when
He sees the spoils, the armor and weapons, and
The chariot, and the corpse itself of his friend,
And Priam stretching out his weaponless hands.
And Aeneas sees his own self pictured there,
In combat with Achaean princes and
The chiefs of the Eastern tribes, and Memnon, swarthy
Leader of the Ethiopian cohort,
And there was Penthesilea, bellatrix,
Breast bared above the golden cincture she wore, 670
Furious in the battle, leading her thousand
Amazons with their crescent shields to war,
A warrior maiden in combat among the men.

, , ,

As Aeneas gazes in rapturous wonder, transfixed
By the images he sees upon the walls,
Dido the queen, marvelous in her beauty,
Surrounded by a company of youths,
Ascends the temple stairs to enter in.
It is as when on Eurotas's banks or on
The highest ridge of Cynthus Mountain, the goddess 680
Diana leads her throng of lovely nymphs,
A thousand Oreades in dancing lines
Moving to right and left as the music asks;

Diana is tallest of all the goddesses,
And wears the huntress's quiver over her shoulder;
Latona, her mother, watching, is filled with pride—
This is what Dido was like, as in their midst,
She joyfully went about her queenly work.
At the door of the shrine of the goddess, beneath the dome,
She took her regal place high on a throne,   690
From which she promulgated laws, defined
The rules of civic order, and assigned,
By lot or by division to each his share
Of the proud labor of building their city of Carthage.
Aeneas is watching this, when suddenly
He sees, making their way through the crowd, Sergestus,
And with him Antheus, and brave Cloanthus
And the other Trojans from those other ships
The black storm wind had dispersed and scattered and driven
To somewhere else, maybe to other coasts.   700
Aeneas was astonished, and so was Achates;
Both were joyful, and strangely fearful too.
They were ardent to seize the hands of their comrades whom
They thought had been lost to them, but, also, their hearts
Were bewildered by the strange unknownness of
These things they were seeing, and so they kept themselves
Hidden unseen inside in the cloud, and listened
To hear what had been the fortune of their friends,
What shore their ships had come to, after the storm,
And what was their mission, what were they seeking, in Carthage,   710
For now from their ships their delegated men
Were coming to the temple, amid the clamor
Of their petitioning cries and their beseeching.

When they had entered the temple and been granted
Permission to speak, Ilioneus, the eldest,
Calmly and gravely said: "O queen, to whom
Jove has given the right to build a new city,
And to establish rules of laws so as

To restrain the arrogance of unruly tribes,
We Trojans, wretched, driven from sea to sea 720
By tempestuous winds, we pray to you that you
Will keep the unhallowed fire away from our ships.
We are a god-fearing people; we pray that you
Will look on us and our fortunes with gracious favor.
We have not come with swords to raid your houses.
There is an ancient land, called by the Greeks
Hesperia; it is powerful both in arms
And in the abundance that its soil brings forth.
The Oenotrians were its first inhabitants,
And then, so we are told, there came a people 730
Who called it Italy, after their leader's name.
It is the land toward which we had steered our course
When suddenly stormy Orion and all his bursting
Storm winds scattered our ships among unseen shoals,
Uncharted rocks, and giant crashing waves,
Till we were carried, broken, onto these shores,
We few. What kind of people *are* they, here,
So barbarous that they behave like this,
Denying us the welcome of the beach,
Attacking us, keeping us off their land? 740
But if you have no fear of mortal arms,
And no regard for the claims of humankind
On one another, remember that the gods
Will remember what was right and what was wrong.
Aeneas was our leader, no one more just,
No one more righteous, and none more glorious
For valor and for skill on the field of battle.
If the Fates have kept him alive, if he still breathes
The air of the upper world and not yet lies
In the cruel darkness, then we have nothing to fear. 750
There would be no reason for you to be sorry to vie
With him in the rivalship of courtesy.
In Sicily there are cities, and lands to be plowed,
And their leader is famous Acestes, of Trojan blood.

Permit us to bring our storm-beaten ships to the beach,
Where we can fashion planks and oars from the forest,
So that, if it be granted that our king
And our companions have been saved, then we
Can sail, together with them, to Italy.
But if it's not so, if you, Aeneas, the best   760
Of Trojans, are gone beneath the Libyan sea,
And Iulus lost, the hope of our nation lost,
Then we, at all events, will seek the straits
Of Sicily, from which we came, and where
There are places for us to live, and where there is
Acestes to be our king." And thus it was
That Ilioneus spoke, and all the sons
Of Dardanus shouted together their loud assent.

Then Dido, bowing her head, spoke thus to them:
"Banish your cares; free yourselves from your fears.   770
My kingdom being new, and vulnerable,
Harsh measures have been needed to be used
To guard my borders all around from strangers.
Who is it, though, who has not heard of Aeneas,
His warriors and their deeds, and of Troy's burning?
Our Tyrian hearts are not so obtuse, nor does
The sun harness his steeds so far from our city.
Whether it's great Hesperia and the fields
Of Saturn that you go to, or the lands
Of Eryx that you seek, and Acestes as king,   780
I'll send you forth in safety, and treasure with you.
Or do you wish to make this kingdom your home?
This city I am building will be yours,
On equal terms. Bring in your ships to shore.
There will be no discrimination made
Between the Tyrians and the Teucrians here.

Would that Aeneas were here. Perhaps the storm
Has also driven him, like you, to these shores,

I will send scouts along the coasts and to
The farthest extremes of Libya's land to see
If he is wandering anywhere there,
In forests or in towns, shipwrecked and lost."

                              ❜ ❜ ❜

Excited, as they listened, by these words,
Pious Aeneas and brave Achates burned
To be free of the cloud that they were hidden in.
Achates, first, urgently says to Aeneas:
"Goddess-born, what thought is in your mind?
You see that all is safe, our ships all safe,
Our comrades safe, except for the one we saw
With our own eyes, drowning in the waters.   800
Other than this, all is as your mother foretold."
No sooner has he spoken than the cloud
Around them that had hidden them is parted
And vanishes as it clears away on high,
And shining Aeneas in the clear air stands there,
In shoulders and in countenance like a god,
For his mother had endowed him by his birth
With that grace of youthful beauty, that's like the beauty
Ivory has to the hand that has fashioned it,
Or the grace of silver or Parian marble set   810
In yellow gold. Aeneas, revealed to all
So suddenly, addressed the queen, and said,
"It is I whom you seek, I am here, Aeneas of Troy,
Having survived the storm and the Libyan waves.
O you who have been the only one to pity
The Trojans for the unspeakable misfortunes
That they have suffered from, exhausted by
Catastrophes on land and on the sea,
Destitute, remnant of what the Greeks had done,
That you have offered to share your city with us,   820
To be our home, there is no way that we,

Nor any Trojans, anywhere in the world,
Scattered wherever it is they are, have power
Commensurate to your kindness, to give you thanks.
I pray to the gods, if there be those who value
Goodness, and if there's justice anywhere,
May they reward you fully as you deserve.
What happy people is it that you come from?
Who are the parents so wonderful as to be
The parents of such a child? As long as rivers   830
Flow down to the welcoming sea, as long as over
The slopes of mountains the shadows move along,
As long as the stars pasture on heaven's fields,
So long will your name be ever honored and praised,
Whatever will be the country I am called to."

So saying, he turns, and with his right hand grasps
The hand of Ilioneus, his dear friend,
And with his left the hand of Sergestus, then turns
To embrace the others, brave Gyas, and brave Cloanthus.

Sidonian Dido was astonished by   840
The sudden appearance of this man before her,
And awestruck by the story he had to tell,
Of such distress, and so she said: "How is it,
Goddess-born, that you have suffered such
Misfortunes? What is it that pursues you so?
What power has driven you to these barbarous shores?
Are you Aeneas, he who was born beside
The Phrygian river Simois to Dardan Anchises,
By gracious Venus? I remember the time when Teucer
Came to Sidon, exiled from his own country,   850
Seeking help from my father, Belus, in
His effort to find a new kingdom for himself.
It was just when Belus was laying waste to Cyprus,
And in triumph holding it, victorious.
It was then I learned from Teucer the story of

The fall of Troy, and knew of you, and of
The Pelasgian line of kings. Though he was one
Of the enemies of the Trojans, he praised them highly,
And he was proud to claim that he himself
Was of Teucrian descent, from ancient days.   860
Therefore, O youths, come in, under our roofs.
I have been driven through many such misfortunes,
And Fortune has willed that I should settle here.
I have learned to come to the aid of the distressed
Because I am one who has also known distress."

　　　　　　　　　, , ,

Thus Dido spoke, and then forthwith she led
Aeneas into her royal house, commanding
That there should be at once, to honor him,
A sacrifice at the altars of the gods;
And, not forgetting them, she sent the Trojans   870
Still waiting back at the shore some twenty bulls,
A hundred great bristle-backed hogs, and with them a hundred
Fatted lambs along with their mother ewes.
The interior of the royal palace was
Opulently adorned with regal splendor,
And in its halls a banquet was being readied,
With royal purple coverlets laid out,
Elaborately embroidered, and massive silver
Plates engraved in gold with images
That told ancestral stories of the deeds   880
Of brave heroes back to dark antiquity.

His fatherly heart unable to rest for a moment,
Aeneas tells Achates to go at once
And find Ascanius, his son, and bring him,
As quickly as he can, to the royal palace.
All his parental care is for his child.
And also it is his will that Ascanius

Should bear them gifts saved from Ilium's ruin:
A mantle stiff with golden enwoven figures;
A beautiful veil with a yellow-acanthus fringe,   890
A gift her mother Leda had given to Helen,
Who brought it from Mycenae and later wore it
When leaving for Troy and her illicit nuptials;
A scepter that Ilione, Priam's eldest
Daughter had carried; a necklace of pearls; a crown
Encircled with double rows of gems and gold.
Achates obeyed and swiftly went to the ships.

                    ▸ ▸ ▸

But the Cytherean, over and over again
Was thinking what schemes and stratagems might be
Devised for Cupid, disguised, to substitute   900
Himself for sweet Ascanius, and use
His talents to enflame Queen Dido with love,
And implicate its fire in her very marrow.
She fears the treacherous double-tongued Tyrian house,
And every night she is scalded by the thought
Of Juno's rage and what it could cause to happen,
So this is what she says to wingèd Love:
"My son, my soldier, my only one, my power—
O son, you are the only one to scorn
The Typhoean arrows of the mighty Father.   910
I flee to you and supplicate your godhead.
You know how your brother Aeneas was tossed from shore
To shore by the anger of vengeful Juno, and
You have joined us in deploring it. Now Dido
The Phoenician holds him with her blandishing words.
And who knows what is going to follow from Juno's
Hospitality? At such a moment,
Juno is not likely to do nothing.
Because of these considerations I

Have thought about a way to go about it.   920
I will enthrall the queen with tricks, and circle
The flames of passion around her, so no power
Will have the power to change her, and she'll be held,
My captive in her love for my Aeneas.

Now listen to my thought about what it is
That you can do: the young prince, my dearest care,
Summoned there by his father, is going to
The Sidonian city carrying precious gifts
That were salvaged from the sea and from Troy's fire.
So I will cause the child to fall asleep,   930
And then I'll carry him off and hide him away,
In my sacred shrine at Idalia or else high
In the hills of my isle of Cythera, where he'll slumber
Knowing nothing at all about my tricks.
You are a boy and, being a boy, you will,
For one night only pretend to be this boy,
So that when Dido, amid the royal feast
And the flow of Bacchic wine, and full of joy,
Takes you up, and folds you in her embrace,
And kisses you and kisses you, you'll breathe   940
The secret fire of love into the queen,
And bewitch her with its poison."

                              Then Cupid divests
Himself of his wings, obedient to his dear
Mother's instruction, and joyously walks with the very
Gait and manner of Ascanius.
But Venus pours gentle sleep over the real
Ascanius and nestles him in her arms,
And carries him off and up to the high groves
Of Idalia where he slumbers fast asleep   950
In the sweet embrace of marjoram flowers and in
Their softly breathing fragrant shade. So Cupid

Obeys his mother, and, happy to follow Achates,
Goes forth to the city, bearing the royal gifts.

, , ,

When Cupid enters, the queen is already there,
Reclining upon a golden divan amid
Magnificent drapery. And now Aeneas
And all the Trojan youth come into the hall
And take their places on couches covered in purple.
Cool water is brought for them to lave their hands,   960
And smooth-shorn napkins are brought, and baskets of bread;
Fifty maidservants are busy preparing the feast,
And maintaining the hearth fires, a hundred more
Maidservants and an equal number of pages
Are setting out the dishes and drinking cups.
The Tyrians are thronging into the hall,
And taking their places on the festive couches.
They are full of wonder when they see the gifts
Aeneas had commanded to be brought,
Full of wonder at Iulus, the little child,   970
His glowing beauty, his charming feigning words,
The words of the little god pretending he's him.
They marvel at the mantle and the veil
With its yellow-acanthus fringe.

                                      But more than all,
The doomed Phoenician's soul cannot be sated
With gazing upon the gifts and upon the boy,
Taking fire more the more she gazes, thrilled.
And he, the boy, having lovingly clung to Aeneas,
Embracing him and hanging upon his neck,   980
And, having satisfied the father's love,
Seeks out the queen. The queen, her eyes and heart
Enamored by the boy, embraces him
And takes him upon her lap, and fondles him,

And folds him in her arms protectively,
Poor Dido, who does not know how great a god
Is settled in her lap to bring her grief.

And Cupid, to please his Acidalian mother,
Begins, little by little, to erase
From Dido's mind the image of Sychaeus,   990
And to substitute a living passion in
A heart and soul long unaccustomed to love.

                    , , ,

Then when the feasting is over and the dishes
Are cleared away, the servants bring great bowls
Of wine, festooned with garlands, and the noise
Of festive voices rolls through the ample halls;
There are lights suspended from golden ceiling panels,
And flaming torches holding back the night.
The queen calls for the jeweled and golden cup
That Belus used and all of Belus's line,   1000
And all the company in the hall are silent:

"Jupiter, it is said you give the laws
Of hospitality, so may you grant
Happiness today to Tyrians and
To the voyagers from Troy, and may our children
Remember this day that is a day of joy.
May Bacchus, giver of happiness, be here,
And generous Juno, and, you Tyrians,
Favor this company with your joyful welcome."

It was thus she spoke, and after that she poured   1010
A libation on the board, and after that
She was the first to taste the wine, and then
Passed it to Bitias challengingly, and he
At once accepted the challenge, drinking deep

From the foaming golden cup, and after that
The other lords in order drank. Long-haired
Iopas, taught how to do so by great Atlas,
Sang, and the sound of his golden lyre resounded
Throughout the hall, and what he sang was of
The wandering moon and the labors of the sun,   1020
And where the first men and the first beasts came from,
And the origins of rain, and fire, and of
Arcturus and the rainy Hyades,
And of the Great Bear and the Little Bear,
And why it is that the sun in winter hurries
To plunge itself into the sea, and why
The winter night is so slow to come to an end.
With shouts redoubled and redoubled both
The Tyrians and the Teucrians applaud,
And unfortunate Dido, drinking deep of love,   1030
With dazzled questioning prolonged the night,
Inquiring what the Trojan could tell her of Priam,
Of Hector, and of the armor worn by Memnon,
The son of the Dawn, and of the wonderful horses
Of Diomedes, and of Achilles' greatness.

"And more than this," she says, "tell us, my guest,
From the beginning, about the treachery of
The Greeks, and about your people's calamities,
And the wanderings that you have undergone,
Over lands and over the seas, for seven years."   1040

Book Two

The hall was quiet, and everyone who was there
Was rapt in the silence in which they gazed at him,
Who from his place of honor thus replied:

"Unspeakable is the story of woe I must,
By your command, bring back by telling it,
The story, O Queen, of how the Greeks destroyed
The wretched Trojan kingdom and all its wealth.
I am the man who saw what happened there,
And played my fated part in what took place.
Where is the Myrmidon or Dolopian or   10
Hard-hearted Ulysses' soldier who could keep
Himself from weeping, telling such a story?
Now dewy night is departing from the sky;
The stars as they set are telling us it's time
To go to sleep; but if you desire to know
What our calamities were, and the circumstance
Of the final agony of Troy, then though
My mind is shuddering at the memory,
And shrinks away from the story in its grief,
I will begin: 20

＞　＞　＞

Broken by savage war,
Disdained by the Fates, after so many years,
The Danaan leaders by the art of Pallas
Build a gigantic Horse, as big as a hill,
Its ribs constructed out of fir-tree limbs.
The chiefs pretend it is intended for
A votive offering to the gods, to ensure
The safe return of the Greeks to where they came from.
This is the tale they cause to be spread abroad.
Then secretly they hide, within the huge   30
Cavernous belly of the Horse, a host
Of armed warriors waiting in the dark.

Not far from the mainland there's a well-known island,
Called Tenedos, that once was prosperous
When Troy was prosperous, but now is only
A desolate unsafe mooring place for ships.
The Danaans sail to those deserted shores
And hide themselves from us, so that we think
That they are gone for good and that the wind
Has carried them away to their Mycenae,   40
So Troy at last is free from its long trouble.
All the gates of the city are opened wide.
What joy to go and see the empty camps,
And the deserted port where the ships had been.
'Here's where the Dorican soldiers had their camp,
And here's where the Myrmidons were; here's where
Cruel Achilles was; here's where the fleet;
Here are the fields on which we fought with them.'
Some of the people are stupefied by the virgin
Minerva's fatal gift, they are lost in wonder   50
At the gigantic Horse. Thymoetes is
The first of us to urge that the Horse be brought
Inside the walls to be a monument
In the citadel itself. This either is

His treachery, or else the doom of Troy
Is of its own accord at work in his language.
But Capys and other wiser counselors
Urge us either to hurl this dubious gift,
This Grecian trickery, off the cliffs headlong
Into the sea below, or build a fire 60
Beneath its belly and thus destroy it, or
Use spears to pierce its hollow sides and probe
To find what might be lurking there inside it.
The confused uncertain crowd is split into factions
Of people not knowing which way to think about it.

, , ,

Then Laocoön comes running, followed by
A throng of others, and as he runs cries out
In an anguished voice, 'O my poor fellow Trojans,
What is this madness? Do you really think
The enemy has gone? Do you really think 70
The Greeks give guileless gifts? Do you really think
Ulysses is such a man? Either Achaeans
Are hiding inside this Thing or else this is
Some kind of war machine against our walls,
Or it's designed to look down over them
And see into our houses, or else it's made
So they can descend upon us from above,
Or there's some other trickery inside.
Trojans, don't trust this Horse. I'm afraid of Greeks.
Beware of gifts from Greeks.' This said, he turns 80
And with great force he hurls his mighty spear.
It strikes the beast in the belly and shaking stays,
And when it stays, there is, from deep within,
A reverberating hollow moaning sound.
And had the Fates permitted us to do so,
And had our minds not been so self-deluded,

We would have used our steel to open it up,
And see into the Argive hiding place,
And Priam's citadel, Troy, would still be standing.

But at that moment a loudly shouting crowd 90
Of shepherds from the countryside appears,
Bringing into the presence of the king
A youth whose hands they'd tied behind his back.
This stranger, who is resolute in his purpose
Either to die or else to bring about
The opening up of Troy to the Achaeans,
Had so contrived to situate himself
That the guileless shepherds, encountering him, would seize him.
From all around a mob of Trojan youths
Come running here to see this captured Greek, 100
Reviling him, pressed close around him, taunting.
Now listen and hear what treachery the Greeks
Are capable of, by hearing what this Greek
Was capable of, for, as, unarmed, he stood there,
Looking helpless, looking desperate, looking around
At the Phrygian crowd that was gathered looking at him,
He cries: 'Alas, alas, what land is there
Where I can go where they will take me in?
What will become of me? I have no place
Among the Greeks; and the Dardanidae 110
Cry out on me for vengeance, seeking my blood!'
Hearing him wail like this, our impetus
For violence against him is quieted down.
We urge him to tell us who he is and what
Information he has, to give to us:
'You are our prisoner now, what is your story?'
After awhile, seeming less fearful, he speaks:

❟   ❟   ❟

'O king, whatever it is that happens to me,
I'll tell the truth, nor will I deny that I
Am Greek by birth; I tell you this at once.   120
Though Fortune has fashioned Sinon for misery,
She cannot make Sinon a liar. The fame
Of Palamedes, son of Belus, may
Have reached your ears. Because of his refusal
To participate in the Ilian adventure,
He was, though innocent, by false report
Brought down to death by the Pelasgians—
Who mourn him now that he is lost to the light.
My father was his kinsmen, who, though poor,
Sent me when I was young to serve with him.   130
While he was powerful still, a prince whose voice
Was respected in the councils of the king,
Our family's standing and repute were strong;
But when, because of Ulysses' subtle contriving
(As is well known), he left the upper air,
Then I was left alone to labor through
My shattered life in the darkness of my grief
And anger over the things that had been done
To my innocent friend and patron. I did not keep
My anger to myself, or my vows that if   140
I ever returned in triumph to my Argos,
I would exact revenge. My words were heard,
And I was feared and distrusted by many who heard them.
This is how it began, and it is how Ulysses
Contrived against me by spreading dark rumors about me,
And seeking confederates in his conspiracy
To bring me down. He didn't rest until
He enlisted Calchas as his instrument.
But why am I telling this story to ears to which
It is unwelcome? What are you waiting for?   150
If you regard all Greeks as all the same,

And if it's enough for you to know I'm Greek,
Then take your revenge on me, have done with it,
For this is what the Ithacan would desire,
And what the sons of Atreus would prize.'

Then we are ardent to hear his story and
To understand it, ignorant as we were
Of such Pelasgian wickedness and deceit.
And so the dissembler continues the story, trembling,
And speaking with dissembling deep emotion: 160

'The Greeks were weary of protracted war,
And anxious to weigh anchor and depart,
Longing to find their homes. Would they had done so.
But too many times there were great storms at sea
That kept them back from going. And, just at the moment
This horse you see, built out of wooden planks,
Was finally completed. From great clouds loud
Thunder sounded all across the sky.
What could this be? They sent Eurypylus
To consult the oracle of Phoebus, and   170
When he returned from the shrine he brought these words:
"Danae, when you set sail for Ilium,
You pacified the winds with the blood of a virgin,
Slain as a sacrifice. When you aspire
To return from there, you must pacify the winds,
With the blood of an Achaean sacrifice."
A cold shudder ran through the hearts of all
In the listening crowd when they heard the oracle.
"Who is it for whom the Fates are readying death?
Who is it Apollo calls for?" And then there's tumult,   180
When Calchas the seer is dragged into their midst
By the Ithacan demanding that he tell
What the gods desire. In the crowd there were many who said
That it was I whose death had been foretold,

And silently they waited for what they knew
Was going to come to pass when the seer spoke.
Five days the seer is silent in his tent,
And five more days; and would not say the words
That would send someone to death; and then, at last,
Yielding to the Ithacan's loud insistence,   190
He ended his silence with words that spelled my doom.
It was I who was to be sacrificed at the altar.
The crowd received his utterance with approval,
Each one of them accepting the exchange
Of another's death for his own relief from fear.

And now the day too horrible to imagine
Had come upon me. They were preparing the rites,
The salted meal to sprinkle on my head,
The fillets to bind my brow, making me ready.
But there was a moment when, being left alone,   200
Somehow I broke my bonds, and got away,
Escaping from my death. I hid myself
In the sedgy mire at the edge of a muddy lake,
Hoping to be unseen till they sailed away,
If that was going to happen. I knew I had
No hope of ever seeing my country again,
Or seeing my father again, or my sweet children
I so desired to see once more. I knew
That it might come to be that the Greeks would exact
Retribution, by their deaths, oh wretched ones,   210
For the crime I had committed by my flight.
But I beg, in the name of all the gods on high,
The powers who know the truth and will sustain it,
If anywhere in the world among mortal men
There's an unstained purity of faith, have pity,
Have pity on one whose sorrow is undeserved.'

＞　＞　＞

In response to his tears we spare him, and, more than that,
We pity him. It is Priam, the king, himself,
Who commands that he be freed from his constraints,
And speaks to him with welcome and with kindness: 220
'Whoever you are, now you are one of us;
Forget the Greeks; now they are lost to you.
But you must answer to the questions I ask:
What is the reason they raised this giant Horse?
Who is it who made it? Why was it made? Is it
An offering to supplicate a god?
Is it a war machine?' And when he ceased,
The other, who had been so well instructed
In Pelasgian deceit, raised up to the heavens
His hands now free from their bindings and cried out,   230

'Witness, eternal inviolable fires above,
You stars, you altars, and you evil swords,
You fillets of the gods I wore when they
Prepared me for the sacrificial altar,
Grant me the right to be released from all
My sacred vows of allegiance to the Greeks,
Grant me the right to hate them, the right to bring
All secret things that are hidden in the dark,
Out into the light. I am no longer bound
By any laws of the country that I came from.   240
If what I have to tell you keeps you safe,
Then keep me safe as you have promised me,
In equal exchange for what I bring to you.

The hope and confidence of the Danaans
Depended on Pallas's help. However, impious
Tydides and Ulysses the contriver
Together ravished the sacred shrine of Pallas,
And slew the guardians of the citadel,
And with their bloody hands seized her holy image,
Touching the fillets of the virgin goddess.   250

It was from that time and act that the strength of the Greeks
Was broken down, their hopes collapsed, and they
Were angrily dispelled from the heart of the outraged
Goddess. Hardly had the sacred image
Been placed in the camp it was brought to, over the seas,
Than Tritonia showed the signs that this was so.
Fire blazed out from the effigy's upraised eyes,
Sweat poured over its limbs, and, *mirabile dictu*,
In lightning flashes the goddess herself three times
Was seen with spear and shield, and vanished again!   260
The prophecy of Calchas from his shrine
Was that these signs are signs that they must take
To the sea and go, that Pergamum can't be conquered
By Argive weapons unless they return to Argos
To find new omens, carrying back with them
In their curvèd ships the effigy they had stolen
And brought with them from there. And now as they
Are gone before the wind to their Mycenae,
They go to recover their forces and their gods,
And after they have done so, then, unexpected,   270
They will return. Thus Calchas reads the omens.
Because of Calchas's admonition the Greeks
Have made this giant effigy to atone
For the insult to the gods and in penance for
Their disastrous unholy sacrilegious act,
The violation of the Palladium.
Calchas told them to make the effigy
Enormous, to raise it up to the skies so high
That it couldn't be gotten through the gates and drawn
Within the citadel walls where it would be,   280
According to their ancient sheltering faith,
Guardian of the safety of the people.
If by your hands there should be any harm
To this offering of Minerva, utter ruin
(O may this omen turn back upon the seer!)
Would then come down on Priam and the Phrygians;

But if by your hands the effigy could ascend
Into the citadel, then Asia would
Be able to take the war to the walls of Pelops,
And doom would then descend upon Greek children!'   290

Thus, by the guile and art of perjured Sinon,
We believed him, and therefore we became his captives,
Under compulsion of his tricks and tears,
We whom neither Tydides nor Larissean
Achilles, nor ten years, nor a thousand ships,
Could ever bring to our knees.

                         , , ,

                              But then there is
An event more frightful still, that comes upon us
Unprovided unforeseeing souls.
Laocoön, chosen by lot to be   300
The priest of Neptune, was in the act of performing
The sacrifice of a great bull at the altar
When, lo, I shudder to speak it, over the tranquil
Quiet sea that lies between the island
Of Tenedos and the mainland, there comes a pair
Of giant serpents swimming toward us, their
Immense coils writhing as side by side they make
Their steady way through the waters and head for shore,
Their breasts held high, impelling the waves before them,
Their blood-red crests held high, the rest of their bodies   310
Following along on the surface of the water,
Their great sinuous backs coiling behind them;
We can hear, as they come, the sound of the foaming water
Their bodies displace; we see how with bloodshot fiery
Eyes, they gaze at the shore as they approach,
Licking their hissing mouths with their quivering tongues.
The blood drains from our faces at the sight,

As we shrink back. They reach the shore and dreadful they
Move without swerving toward Laocoön.
Then first each one of the two enwraps the little   320
Body of one of his two sons in its
Enfolding embrace, and pastures upon its limbs.
And then, as Laocoön is rushing, armed
To try to come to the aid of his dying children,
They seize him and bind him in their giant coils,
Twice coiling around his waist, then twice again,
Their scaly coils coiling around his throat,
Their heads and necks held high, victorious;
He struggles with his hands to get himself free
From the knots they wind around him; his priestly fillets   330
Are drenched in his bloody gore and the serpents' black venom.
The clamor of his horrifying cries
Rises to the stars like the loud bellowing
Of a bull, half-killed, who has broken away from the altar
And from the misjudged blow of the ritual axe
Aimed at its neck. And then the pair of dragons
Slither away and seek the shrine of fierce
Tritonia, and shelter there beneath
The feet of the goddess and her circle shield.

Then, when the people see this, there is a strange   340
Terror that shudders through all their hearts and they
Turn to each other and say that Laocoön
Deserved what the serpents had done to him, because
Of what he had done when he hurled his infamous spear
Into the body of the sacred oak,
And so profaned it. This is the general cry:
'We must take the effigy to the goddess's shrine
And supplicate her divinity for forgiveness.'

And so we open up the city walls
And expose the battlements, all working together   350

To make this happen, fastening gliding wheels
To its giant feet, and ropes around its neck,
As halters with which to draw it to the shrine.
The fatal machine, pregnant with arms, begins
To climb our walls. Around it there are boys
And unwedded girls, joyfully singing hymns
And joyfully touching the ropes by means of which
The Horse begins to move. It climbs up through
The opening walls, and, this once done, it rolls
Menacing into the central city—O   360
My country, O my Ilium, home of the gods,
O all-protecting glorious battlements
Of Troy! Four times as it is moved, it halts
At the city gates, and four times then there is
Within the Horse the sound of armor clashing,
Yet blind with fury and not knowing what
It is that we are doing we keep going
Until we have enshrined the monstrous Thing
In the citadel itself. Cassandra is there,
And even then cries out in prophecy   370
Of the doom that was right now coming on upon us,
But by a god's command her voice was never
To be believed by Trojan ears. And we,
Unhappy people, on this our final day,
Festoon the town with celebratory garlands.

>   >   >

And now the heavens move and night comes in,
And covers with its darkness earth and sky,
And the tricks of the Myrmidons. Throughout the city
The Trojans, wearied by joy, lie fast asleep.

And now the Greeks set out from Tenedos,   380
Their ships in ordered formation, under the silent

Stillness of the moon, making their way
Quietly toward the shore they know so well;
And when the lead ship's beacon light is shown,
Sinon, protected by the complicit fates,
Furtively opens up its wooden side,
And frees the Achaeans from the Horse's womb.
The Horse releases them to the open air
And joyfully they come out. First come the captains,
Thessandrus, and Sthenelus, and dire Ulysses,   390
Lowering themselves to the ground by means of a rope,
And Acamas, Thoas, and Neoptolemus of
The house of Peleus, and Machaon the prince,
And Menelaus, and Epeus, he it was
Who built the Wooden Horse. They enter the city,
That slumbers submerged in wine and sleep; they surprise,
And quietly kill, the watchmen, and open the gates
To welcome in their comrades from the fleet,
Letting them in for what they are going to do.

                          ⸞ ⸞ ⸞

It is the hour when sleep by the grace of the gods   400
Steals upon mortals, and, gratified, they sleep.
I fall asleep, and sleep, and suddenly, lo,
Hector is standing there before my eyes,
Grief-stricken, weeping floods of tears, his body
All torn, as it had been, by being dragged
Behind that chariot, and black with the bloody
Muck it left behind, his swollen feet still pierced
By the thongs his legs were dragged along the dirt by.
What sight is this that I was seeing? Oh,
How changed is this from how he looked, our Hector,   410
That day when he returned from the field of battle
Wearing Achilles' armor, or how he looked,
Hurling the firebrands at the burning ships,

His scraggled beard and hair all crusted now
With blood, his body showing all the bloody
Wounds he got in the fighting around the walls
Of the city of his fathers. In my dream
I see myself and hear myself as, weeping,
I cry out to him in a doleful grieving voice:

'O light of Dardanians, hope of Troy,   420
What is it that has kept you from us so long?
Why have you been so long? What shores are those
You come from? At last we see you, Hector, after
So many deaths of those who belong to you,
After so much your city and people have suffered.
We have waited for you so long. What is it that
So shamefully has disfigured that radiant face?
Why do I have to see these terrible wounds?'

There were from him no answers to these questions,
But, drawing groaning sighs from deep in his being,   430
He speaks:

               'Ah, flee from this place, O goddess-born,
You must escape these flames. Troy from on high
Is brought down low. The enemy has her now,
And all her walls. There's nothing any longer
Owed to king or country. If Troy could have
Been saved by the power of any hand, it would
Have been by mine. These are the holy things
And the household gods, committed to you by Troy.
They must go with you to share what happens to you.   440
Carry them to the place where you will build,
After your journeys over many seas,
The city it is your destiny to build.'

Thus Hector says, and brings forth potent Vesta,
The holy wreaths, and the ever-burning fire.

, , ,

Meanwhile the city's turmoil is everywhere.
Although my father's house is deep secreted
Within the protection of surrounding trees,
The shuddering horror of the noise of arms
Grows greater, nearer, clearer every moment.   450
I shake myself free of sleep and climb to the roof
Of my father's house and strain to listen. It is
As when the furious South Wind brings down fire
Upon a grain field, or a mountain torrent
Rushes down on the crops and lays them low,
And ruins all the oxen's labor, and fells
The forest trees, and high on a hill the shepherd,
Stupefied stands there hearing the roar, and I
Know at this moment that this is what it is:
Thus is the treacherous ambush of the Greeks   460
Revealed. All is made clear. The Fire God towers
High up above the fallen-in great house
Of Deiphobus, and now Ucalegon
His neighbor's house is burning and the light
Reflected off the burning houses shines
On broad Sigeum's surface. The shouts of men
And the blaring noise of clarions grows louder.
Frantic, I seize my arms, though in my mind
I think, what could these weapons possibly do?
Frenzied with the desire to find my comrades,   470
And get to the citadel, my heart's on fire
With fury and the wanting to die with glory.

Then suddenly, at the door of my house, is Panthus,
The son of Othrys, who was the priest at the shrine
Of Apollo on the citadel. He carries
The sacred things and images from the shrine,
And holds his little grandchild by the hand.
'Panthus, tell me, tell me, where should we go,

Where should we go to fight?' I could scarcely get
These words out, when, groaning, he answered me thus: 480

'Troy's last day has come; this is the end
Of everything for us; the Trojans are finished;
Our Ilium is utterly undone;
The glory of the Teucrians is gone;
Jupiter, enraged, has taken all,
Everything we had, away to Argos;
The Greeks are now the lords and masters of
The city they are burning; the Horse stands high
In the midst of things, within the city walls;
Armed men are pouring out from within its insides;   490
Sinon, insulting victor, scatters fire;
The gates are open wide and through them come
Thousands of enemy, as many as ever
There were when first they came here from Mycenae;
In serried ranks they block the narrow street,
The glittering points of their weapons eager, avid,
Hungry to kill; our guards at the gates resisted
In blinded futility and were overwhelmed.'

Impelled by the will of the gods and by the words
Of Panthus Othryadas I hasten to be   500
Among the flames and the clashing weapons and where
The black fury and shouting and roar of battle call;
And there, under the light of the moon, I find,
Gathered together, Rhipeus and mighty Epytus,
Hypanis, Dymas, and Mygdon's son, the youth
Coroebus, who had come to Troy because
He was mad with love for Cassandra and had come
To help her father Priam's nation survive,
Unlucky youth whose love for the prophetess
Had made him deaf to what she prophesied.   510
When I see them standing close-ranked there together,

The cohort battle-ready and ready to hear me,
I say these words:

        'Brave hearts, though brave in vain,
If what you want is to follow me to the end,
You know what is our fate. All of the gods
By whom our kingdom was upheld have left
Their shrines and altars, and all of them are gone;
The city you wish to save is all in flames.
Therefore let us die together and rush   520
Desperate together into the enemy midst,
Clarified by despair.'

        Their young hearts roused
To fury by these words of mine they're like
Ravaging wolves whose ravenous bellies' needs
Have driven them forth in rage in the misty darkness,
Their children waiting with famished jaws for what
They can bring home to them. We make our way
Through arrows and swords and enemies toward death.
Black night is a cavern of darkness all around us,   530
And we get ourselves to the center of the town.

Who is it who could tell about such carnage?
Whose tears could be equal to what has happened here?
The ancient city, so long the queen, has fallen.
Dead bodies lying everywhere on the streets,
Among the houses, on the doorsteps, on
The holy portals of the gods. It isn't only
Trojans who have paid the price with blood.
Sometimes some of them, when they could, fought back,
And there are many conqueror Greeks who fell.   540
Dire woe is everywhere, everywhere terror,
Everywhere there are images of death.

Then there's Androgeos before us, with
A company of other Greeks, and he,
Thinking us in the darkness also Greeks, cries out
To us as to fellow soldiers he thought we were,
'Hurry, comrades, why have you been so long?
All of the others are busy at the work
Of pillaging and plundering Pergamum.
Where have you been? Are you just off the ships?'   550
And as he says this, his voice dies back, because
He hears no familiar answer, and suddenly
He knows he is among the enemy,
Steps back, confused and scared, like one who has
Put down his confident foot on a brambled path
And there's a snake unseen in the rough ground cover
That rises up and swells its purple neck,
Enraged, and strikes at him. And so we strike,
Surrounding them in the darkness with our weapons,
And they, unsure in this unfamiliar ground,   560
And shocked and frightened by our sudden ambush,
Are slaughtered. Thus Fortune favors us this time.
Coroebus, exalted, excited by success,
Cries out, 'Oh comrades, Fortune shows us the way!
Let's follow her. Let's put on the armor of these
Dead Greeks, and let us change our shields for theirs.
Honorable or trickery, what matter?
In warfare, what does it matter? Our enemies
Have given these gifts to us.' So then Coroebus
Puts on Androgeos' plumed helmet and takes up   570
His shield with its beautiful emblem and takes hold
Of Androgeos' Argive sword. Rhipeus does
The same, and Dymas too, and all the other
Young warriors, delighted, each of them clad
In the spoils of the Grecian warriors they have killed.

And so we go on, through the unseeing night, among
The enemy and under the cover of
Alien gods, and engaging in many fights
And sending many Greeks down there to Orcus.
Some flee to the ships to get away to safety,   580
And some of them in terror climb back up
On the giant Horse, and hide themselves away
In the familiar darkness of its womb.

It's folly to think the gods are dependable,
When they are not. For suddenly there's the sight
Of Priam's daughter, the virgin Cassandra, being
Dragged away by soldiers from the shrine
Of her Minerva, dragged away with her hair
Disheveled, streaming, and her burning eyes
Looking up vainly at the heavens above,   590
Her eyes, because her tender hands are bound
Behind her back, and Coroebus, who is driven
Mad with fury at the sight of this,
Throws himself to his fate against her captors,
And all of us all together follow him.

Then, from the roof of the high temple above us,
There is a rain of stones thrown down upon us,
By our friends up there in their confusion because
Of our Argive weapons and helmets, and the Danaans
Down in the streets are raging because we're trying   600
To rescue the maiden Cassandra, and more and more
Of the Greeks then come together against us and charge us,
Ajax the fierce, and the two Atrides, and
The whole Dolopian force. It is as when
A great storm bursts, and the violent winds contend
With one another, the West Wind and the South Wind
And the East Wind and his oriental steeds.
The woods are moaning and Nereus rises up foaming,

Bringing the sea up from the lowest deep.
Then there comes in the remnant of the Greeks   610
We had first encountered and fooled in the dark of the night
And scattered before us along the streets of the town.
They recognize the armor that we're wearing,
And the emblemed shields we carry, and they know,
By our voices, that we are foreigners to them.
So we're outnumbered, and Coroebus is slain
By Peneléus in front of the altar of
Minerva, goddess of war, and Rhipeus who
Was the most righteous, most reasonable and just,
Of all the Trojans (but heaven rules against him);   620
Hypanis, too, and Dymas, in the confusion,
Are killed by what their own countrymen hurl down;
And neither his piety nor the fillet wreaths
Of the priesthood of Apollo can save Panthus.

                              ⸲ ⸲ ⸲

O ashes of Troy! O flames of the doom of my people!
Witness that had I died by the will of the Fates
At the hands of the Greeks I would have earned that death.
There was no hazard that I did not face.

                              ⸲ ⸲ ⸲

Now we are forced from that place by the tide of the battle,
I, and together with me, old Iphitus, and   630
Pelias, whom Ulysses had lamed in the fighting.
The clamor from Priam's house summons us there.
And when we go there it is as if it is
The place and nowhere else where the God of War's
Let loose, there is such havoc, there is such death.
Some of the Greeks are protected as they fight,
Holding over their heads their shields, to make

A giant moving tortoise-shell cover protecting;
Others are swarming up on ladders to
The palace's roof, their left hands holding up   640
Their shields against the debris that's raining down,
Their right hands clutching the ladder rungs. The Trojans
Up on the roof are tearing down the towers
And gables of their palace to use as missiles—
They see the end has come and yet defend
Themselves against the death they know is here.
Over the edge they pour down on the Greeks
The gilded splendors that their fathers built
To ornament their pride. And other Trojans,
Down below, are closely joined with ready   650
Desperate swords to guard the palace doors.
Seeing all this our hearts are roused to bring
What help we can to the palace of our king
And augment the last-ditch ranks of those defending.

There is a secret entrance to the palace,
That opens into a private corridor,
By which, while still the Trojan kingdom stood,
Andromache would go, alone, without
Her retinue, to visit her husband's parents,
And take Astyanax to see his grandsire.   660
I enter in this way, and get myself up
To the top, the highest point of the roof, from which
The Trojans are throwing down on the Greeks below
Their ineffectual missiles. There was a tower,
On the edge of this roof, rising up toward the stars.
You could see all Troy from there, and the ships of the Greeks
And the Achaean camps. We use our weapons
To batter it and shake it where it is weakest,
Where its supporting columns meet its floors,
And we break it down and push it over the edge,   670
The wreckage of it; thundering it falls,

With a crash heard far and wide, upon the Greeks.
Yet more Greeks still come up and still we throw
Debris of the palace down on the enemy heads.

◦   , , ,

There in the vestibule of the royal palace,
And at the very doors, there's exultant Pyrrhus,
Shining in the glitter of his armor;
It's as when winter's cold is over and
A serpent having nourished his poisons on
The underground herbs he ate while he lay waiting   680
All winter long for spring to make its return,
Comes forth and sheds his skin, and he's youthful again,
Youthful and shining, his old skin sloughed away,
His crest erect, his menacing breast held high,
His fluent body wreathing and coiling, ready.
Gigantic Periphas is there beside him,
Automedon too, his armor-bearer and
The charioteer of the horses of Achilles,
And behind them their troop of young Scyrian warriors,
Close in to the building and hurling their firebrands up   690
To the roof above. Pyrrhus himself, the leader,
Seizes a battle-axe and tears away
The hinges from the brass-bound portal doors
And bashes a huge hole in the solid oak
And opens up to sight the inner chambers
Of the house of Priam the king and of the ancient
Kings who had lived in the house before him, and thus
The enemy has come to the very threshold.

Inside the palace there is the noise of chaos,
Screaming, shrieking, ululating sounds   700
Of the grief and terror of the Trojan women.
The woeful clamor rises to the stars;

From vaulted room to room of the vast palace
The women wander not knowing where they are going,
Some in their distraction clinging to walls,
Kissing the very doors. And on comes Pyrrhus,
In all his father's power, coming in;
No thing nor person can hold out against
His coming. The great front gate of the palace falls in
Under the battering of the battering ram;   710
Force makes its way, unstoppable; the Greeks
Pour slaughtering in, so many of them, filling
The palace halls with the conquering entering foe.
The force of it and the fury is greater even
Than a foaming flooding river bursting through
All that would hold against its whirling waters
Insanely overflowing and carrying off
Whole herds and their stables with them across the plains.

I witnessed Pyrrhus there, insatiably killing;
I saw the two Atridae there; I saw   720
Hecuba, the queen, and her hundred daughters,
And Priam there between the altars, his blood
Polluting what he himself had sacralized;
The fifty bridal chambers and the great
Hope of progeny, the beautiful doors
Adorned with the pride of conquered barbarian gold,
All brought down low, all fallen, all of it, all.
Where the fire had not yet burned, the Greeks were there.

And if you wish to hear what was the fate
Of Priam, I must tell you. When he sees   730
How the city has fallen and how the doors of his palace
Are smashed and broken into, and how the Greeks
Are in the innermost chambers of his home,
The aged king takes up the royal armor
So long unused by him, and puts it on

His trembling old man shoulders, and girds himself
With his useless sword, to send himself to death,
Helpless old man, against the crowding foe.
In the atrium in the middle of his palace,
That was open to the vault of the heavens above,   740
There was a great altar, and over it, leaning,
An ancient laurel tree that with its shade
Embraced protectively the household gods.

Here's Hecuba and with her are her daughters,
Huddled together like doves sheltering in vain
From the black winds of the storm that drove them there,
And clutching in their hands the sacred icons.
But when she sees her husband Priam wearing
The armor he had worn when he was young,
Hecuba cries out to him, 'My husband,   750
My poor husband, what are you thinking of,
That you have put on this armor and carry these weapons?
Even if Hector were here, this is no longer
A time for such as these. Come here, with me,
Take shelter at this altar. It will protect us.
If not, this is the place where we will all,
All of us together, die together.'

These were her words as she drew him close to her,
And helped him to a seat before the shrine.
But suddenly there's one of Priam's sons,   760
Polites, fleeing through a hail of arrows
From Pyrrhus's slaughter, and running through the halls
And empty courtyards of the palace to
The atrium where Priam was, and Pyrrhus
Hot on his heels, and hot to butcher him,
And going to do so now; and Polites falls
And his life pours out of him in streams of blood
Before the eyes of his father and his mother.

And though already in the hands of death
Priam cries out in rage in his old man voice:

'If anywhere there's righteousness in heaven,
May the deities pay you back for what you do,
Your obscene crime, polluting a father's face
With what it has to see, his own son's slaughter.
Achilles, whose son you pretend to be, did not
Behave like this. He paid the due respect
To a father's supplication and sent back home
The body of Hector to its tomb, and sent
Me home unharmed.'

                    And, saying this, with all

His strength he hurled his spear at Pyrrhus, and
It made its harmless way toward Pyrrhus's shield
And struck with a tinkling sound, and bobbing hung
Purposelessly from the boss of the shield; and Pyrrhus
Says to him,

            'Then go down there below,
And take this news about me to my father,
And be sure to tell him all about his son,
Degenerate Pyrrhus, and his despicable deeds.'

And as he says these words he drags old Priam,

Trembling and shaking and slipping in the blood
That was pouring out of the body of his son,
To the high altar; and there he clutches him by
The hair with his left hand and with his right hand
Raises his glittering sword, and plunges it in,
Up to the hilt, into his side.

                This is
The way the fortunes of Priam came to the end

That was fated for him—fated to see the fires
Consuming his Troy, and the Pergamum fall down,   800
He who had been the monarch of Asia, the ruler
Of so many lands and tribes, a huge, headless,
Body upon the shore, a nameless trunk.

                              ، ، ،

Everywhere there's horror everywhere.
I saw the old king gasping his life away,
And the image of my beloved father, old
As the king was old, appears before my eyes,
And the image of my Creusa, left alone,
And my ruined house, and Iulus, my little child—
What was his fate? I turn and look for those   810
Who had followed me, and all of them are gone,
In their weariness and despair deserting me,
Leaping to death from the burning palace roof
Or giving their bodies to death in the flames up there.
The fires of the burning palace gave me the light
To see, as I looked around, the empty scene.
I was alone.

                    Then, suddenly, there, I saw
Helen, Tyndaris, who was concealing herself
In the deserted shrine of the goddess Vesta,   820
Where, terrified of the Trojans' rage against her,
For having caused the fall of the Pergamum,
And the Grecians' wrath against her for causing the war,
And her husband's wrath because she abandoned him,
She hid herself away beneath the altar,
And huddled there.

                    Fire blazed up in my heart,
The desire to make her pay for what she'd done,
And avenge my fallen country. 'Is it that she—

Will she go back a queen, a queen in a triumph,   830
Unpunished, and see her Sparta once again,
And Mycenae her native country? Is it that she
Will go back to join her husband, her parents, her children,
With a train of Phrygian captives and Ilian matrons
Waiting upon her? Is this what Priam died for?
Is this what Troy was burned for? Was it for this
That the Dardan shore so many times was soaked
With blood? It shall not be! There is no glory
From vengeance on a woman, and no honor
As if it were in battle. But to extinguish   840
Vileness and make it pay for what it did
Will merit praise, and I'll rejoice to fill
My heart with the fire of exacting justice and
Satisfy the ashes of my people.'

These were the words I said as my enraged
Intent for vengeance was rushing me on. But there,
There was my beautiful mother, Venus, she,
Like light in the night sky shining, she, herself,
As the gods in heaven are, when they're in heaven.
She took me by the hand, restraining me,   850
And from her roseate lips she spoke these words:

'What is this unleashed fury for, my son?
Where is your care for me? Before all else,
Must you not find your father, aged Anchises?
Must you not find out whether Creusa your wife,
Or Ascanius, your little boy, are alive?
If by my love they had not been protected,
The river of flames would have carried them away,
Or the thirsty sword would have drunk their blood.
The Greeks are all around them. Understand this: it is not   860
The fault of her whose face you hate, the woman,
Tyndaris of Laconia; it's not
The fault of Paris. It is the gods who bring

This wealth and power down and burn the topless
Towers of Ilium. Follow your mother's guidance;
Obey your mother's injunctions. I'll clear away
The clouds and mists by which you are surrounded.

Behold! Here, where nothing is to be seen
But the smoke and dust that rises from the rubble
Of rocks piled upon rocks, there's Neptune, who   870
With his mighty trident brings down the walls and rears
The foundations up and with great surges heaves,
And upsets, and overturns, the entire city.
There's Juno, who's the cruelest of them all,
Commanding the invasions, holding open
The Scaean Gates and in her armor of steel,
Furiously summoning soldiers from the ships.
And now, look up at the highest towers and see
Tritonian Pallas holding out her shield,
Her threatening Gorgon aegis, and, behind her,   880
The lurid clouds of tempests still to come.
My father himself is giving strength to the Greeks,
And giving them courage, arousing the gods against
The Dardanian arms. Flee from this struggle, my son.
I will not abandon you, and I will take you
To the threshold of your father's house.'

                              She spoke,
And disappeared within the shades of night.

               , , ,

There were demonic shapes around me, beings,
Numinous haters of Troy, moving about . . .   890

Then truly I saw that Ilium was sinking
Down into the flames and Neptune's Troy capsized.

It's as when a gang of woodsmen, high on a mountain,
Are trying to bring a giant ash tree down,
Hacking at it again and again with axes,
And it stands there still, on the verge of falling down,
Its leaves shaking and its great head rocking
Back and forth from side to side, and then,
At last, with a loud sound of its grief, the great
Tree falls, its great base pulled up out of the earth.   900

, , ,

I leave the ruined palace and find my way,
With the help of my weapons and guided by the goddess,
And get past enemies and fires around me
And reach my father's house. And when I get there,
The home I was brought up in, my first desire
Was to carry my father to safety in the hills,
But he, since Troy had fallen, would not agree
To exile or to live out his days any longer.
He said, 'Since you are young and strong, you must
Take flight. If the gods above so willed for me,   910
They would have spared my house. It is enough
That I have already seen one fall of Troy,
And I survived it. But you must leave me now,
And say farewell to me as if my body
Lay here prepared and ready to be buried.
When the enemy comes I will find a warrior's death,
When they in pity treat me as a warrior
And seek my spoils as if on the field of battle.
The loss of the burial rite means nothing now.
I, hated by the gods, have for so long   920
Lived out my life in uselessness, since Jove,
The Father of the Gods and the King of Men,
Sent down his thunderbolt of fire upon me,
For what I boasted of.' And so he spoke,

And would not change his mind, and we, my wife,
Creusa, and Ascanius, my son,
Hearing him, wept, and pleaded with my father
Not thus to make our fate still worse for us
Than it is going to be. But he persisted,
Saying he would not alter what he'd said,   930
Nor leave his home.

                    In misery I make ready,
Longing for death, to fight again—for what
Was else to do, what other chance was left?

'My father, did you think that I could ever
Leave you behind? How could a father ever
Utter such a thought as this? If it
Is what the gods desire, that nothing survive
Of what was Troy, and if it is your will
To add yourself and yours to the sum of ruin,   940
The gate is open through which the ruin comes.
Pyrrhus will soon be here, with Priam's blood
Still dripping from his sword, Pyrrhus who butchered
The son whose father had to watch it done,
And then he butchered the father at the altar.
O gracious mother, was it for this you saved me,
Among the swords, among the fires, to see
The enemy come into my house, and see
Ascanius, and my father, and my wife,
Slaughtered here, each in each other's blood?   950
No! The last light remaining to me is a summons.
Though we shall die we shall not die unavenged.'

I took up my sword once more in my right hand,
Once more took up my shield on my left arm,
And was leaving my house on my way to die in battle,

But there on the threshold my wife was kneeling before me,
And holding up little Iulus to show him to me.

'If you are going forth to die,' she cried,
'Then take us with you to share what fate might be,
But if you have some hope in what your weapons   960
Can do, because of what they have done before,
Then wear your armor to guard this house, your home.
For whom are you abandoning your child,
And your father, and her whom once you called your wife?'

Her moaning cries filled up the house with their sound,
When suddenly there was an astonishing sign.
Iulus was there between his unhappy parents,
Who tenderly were hovering around him, when,
Between their hands and faces, as close as that,
We saw a little visionary flame   970
Playing about the head of the little child,
And gently licking his curls and harmlessly
Pasturing on his forehead as it played.
We were alarmed, trembling with awe and fear,
And, as fast as we could, extinguished the sacred fire
With water and by brushing away the flames.
But my father Anchises looks up to the stars on high,
And joyfully raises up his palms and cries,

'All-Powerful Jupiter, hear me, hear my voice!
Look down upon us and if we merit it,   980
Give us your help and validate this sign!'

No sooner had he spoken than there was,
Suddenly, on the left, a peal of thunder,
And overhead a star came down from heaven,
And with tremendous speed went sliding across

The brilliantly suddenly lighted up nighttime sky.
We saw its tail of fire as it passed above
The palace roof and buried itself in the forest
Of Ida, leaving behind a trail of light,
And the odor of sulfur was everywhere around.   990

My father, overcome, exalted, rose,
And raised his worshipful eyes to the holy star,
And to the gods in the heavens, and urgently spoke:

'Aeneas, we must leave now, we must leave now;
Wherever it is you go, I'll follow you;
Wherever it is you are, there I will be.
You gods of my fathers, save my house and save
My grandson! Oh, you have sent us the omen that
Now Troy is saved and protected by the gods.
My son, I yield, and I will go with you.'   1000

As he spoke we could hear, ever more loudly, the noise
Of the burning fires. The flood of flames was coming
Nearer and nearer.

                        'My father, let me take you
Upon my shoulders and carry you with me.
The burden will be easy. Whatever happens,
You and I will experience it together,
Peril or safety, whichever it will be.
Little Iulus will come along beside me.
My wife will follow behind us. And you, my servants,   1010
Listen to what I say: Just as you leave
The limits of the city there is a mound,
And the vestiges of a deserted temple of Ceres,
And a cypress tree that has been preserved alive
For many years by the piety of our fathers.
We will all meet there, though perhaps by different ways,

And, father, you must carry in your arms
The holy images of our household gods.
I, coming so late from the fighting and the carnage
Cannot presume to touch them until I have washed   1020
Myself in running water.' Thus I spoke.

I took up the tawny pelt of a lion and
Covered my neck and my broad shoulders with it,
And bowing down, I accepted the weight of my father;
Iulus puts his hand in mine and goes
Along beside me, trying to match my steps
As best he can, trying his best to keep up;
My wife follows behind us, at a distance.
So we all set out together, making our way
Among the shadows, and I, who only just   1030
A little while ago had faced, undaunted,
Showers of arrows and swarms of enemy Greeks,
Am frightened by every slightest change in the air
And startled by every slightest sound I hear,
Fearful for whom I walk with and whom I carry.
And just as I had almost come to the gates
And thought that I had almost gotten us free,
I thought I heard the sound of many feet,
And my father, peering intently into the shadows,
Cries out to me, 'Get away, get away, my son,   1040
My son, they are coming! I see their shining shields,
I see the glow of their weapons in the dark!'
I am alarmed, and I don't know what happened
But some power hostile to me distracts my wits,
And I am confused, and I lead us away by ways
That I don't know, and off the familiar streets
That together we are following, and so,
O God! some fate has taken away my wife,
Creusa, my wife, away from me. What happened?
Did she wander from the way that we were going?   1050

Did she fall back, having to rest some place
Back there, and so we left her? I did not know.
I never saw her again, and as we went,
I never turned to look behind, and never
Thought of her until we reached the mound
And Ceres' ancient place. When all of us,
At last, had gotten there, we all were there,
But she had vanished and she wasn't there.
Gone from her people, gone from her child, and her husband.

, , ,

What men or gods in my frenzy did I not   1060
Cry out against? What worse sight had I seen?
I left Ascanius and Anchises and
The household gods in the care of my companions,
And I found a secluded place deep in a valley
For them to hide, and I myself took up
My shining weapons and sought the city again,
Determined, no matter what, to look for my
Creusa everywhere in Troy. I find
My way along the walls and to, and through,
The shadowed gate I'd left the city by;   1070
Carefully, step by unseen step, in the dark,
Backward the way I came I make my way;
Everywhere as I go fills me with terror;
The very silence around me fills me with terror.
I make my way to my home, in case, in case,
She's gone back there. The Greeks had invaded the house
And set it on fire, and through the house the fire
Rolled up on the surge of the wind to the very roof,
And the flames tower high above the burning house,
And the heat of the burning pours up into the sky.   1080
And so I go on, and once again I see
The palace of Priam, and the citadel,

And in the empty courtyard of Juno's shrine
There's Phoenix and dire Ulysses, guarding the treasures
Taken from everywhere from the shrines that the Greeks
Had set fire to; the golden bowls, the holy
Altar tables, the stolen holy vestments;
Boys and trembling matrons stand around.

I wander in the streets, in my desperation
Calling her name, Creusa, Creusa, calling   1090
Creusa, Creusa, over and over again.
And as I went among the ruined buildings
And through the streets of the ruined city, lo,
Suddenly there rose before my eyes
The strange, magnified, image of my wife.
I was stupefied; my hair stood on end; my voice
Caught in my throat. Then she spoke to me and said
Words that altered everything for me:

'Beloved husband, what use is it for you
To persist in this insanity of grief.   1100
What has happened here has happened not without
The will of the gods. The high lord of Olympus
Does not permit Creusa to go with you
To be with you on your journey where you are going.
Long exile will be yours, plowing across
Vast seas until you come to Hesperia,
Where Lydian Tiber gently flows between
Rich husbanded fields and where you will be happy,
A king, and wedded to a royal wife.
Give up your weeping now for your Creusa;   1110
I, a Dardanian woman and the spouse
Of divine Venus's son, will never have
To see the scornful homes of the Myrmidons
Or of the Dolopians, and never have
To be the scullion slave of some Greek matron.

The Mighty Mother keeps me on these shores.
Farewell and may your care protect and love
Your child and mine.'

              And having spoken thus,
The image of her receded into air,   1120
Leaving me weeping, with so much still to say.
Three times I tried to embrace her and to hold her;
Three times the image, clasped in vain, escaped
As if it were a breeze or on the wings
Of a vanishing dream.

              , , ,

              And so, the night being over,
I returned to my companions where they were.
When I got there I was amazed to see
How many others, women and men, had come,
Wretched survivors of the fall of the city,   1130
To join us in the exile and the journey,
A heartbreaking company come from everywhere,
Ready in their hearts and with their fortunes,
To follow me wherever I was going.
And now the morning star was rising over
The highest ridges of Ida, bringing in
The day that was beginning; the Danaans held
The city behind the gates that they had locked.
There was no hope of further help. And so
I acknowledged this, and taking up the burden   1140
Of my father once again, I sought the hills."

Book Three

"The wealth of Asia and Priam's guiltless race
Having been overturned by the will of the gods,
After proud Ilium fell and the smoke from the rubble
Of Neptune's Troy rose up from the desolate ground,
We are, in accordance with the auguries
Of what the gods ordained, sent forth to seek
What places we could find in deserted lands
In which to spend our exile. At the foot
Of the mountain range of Ida, and near the town
Antandros, we constructed a fleet and gathered   10
Our people together, not knowing where the Fates
Were going to take us to, to be our home.

It was the very beginning of summer when
My father Anchises bid us set sail to go
To wherever it was to which we were fated to go,
And so I departed, weeping, leaving my own
Familiar havens and shores, and the plain where Troy
Had been, and was now no more, and I set forth
From there upon the seas, an exile, with
My cohort, and my son, and carrying with me   20
The Penates of my country and my household.

, , ,

Far off there is Mavortia, the land
Of Mars the god of war, whose great wide plains
The Thracians plowed. Warlike Lycurgus was,
In better days, its king and a friend to Troy;
The gods he worshiped were the same as ours.
I sailed there with my fleet and there I built
The first town that I built, to which the Fates
Were hostile, and I gave its people my name,
Aeneadae. Seeking the favor of   30
My mother, Dione's daughter, and the other
Gods, for the labor I was undertaking,
I was in the act of offering a shining
White bull as sacrifice to the god who is
The king of all the gods there are in the heavens;
It happens that, nearby, there was a mound,
And on it, growing, javelin shafts of cornel,
And myrtle branches bristling as with spears.
I went over to this mound, endeavoring
To tear up out of the soil some of the plants,   40
To obtain green foliage with which to dress
And decorate the sacred altar, and,
As I began to do so, suddenly,
There was a wonder! A terrifying portent!
For when I pulled up out of the ground the first
One of these shrubs, drops of black viscous blood
Were leaking from the roots, staining the earth
I pulled it up from. Cold terror shuddered through me.
In fear I pulled up a second plant, in order
To find out why it was that this had happened,   50
And a second time black blood leaked out from it.
From my troubled heart I prayed to the nymphs of the woods
And to Gradivus, the Getae's *genius loci*,
To bless the omen and to make it good.
But when, on my knees, I strained to pull up a third
Out of the sands that resist me—can I tell

Of this or not?—I heard from within the mound
A wretched groaning voice speaking to me:
'Oh, misery, Aeneas, why rend me so?
Leave me untouched, unhandled, where I'm buried.   60
Spare your pure hands from being defiled. I am
One whom you know of, of Trojan blood, nor are
They lifeless, these sticks from which this blood leaks out.
Flee from this place of cruelty and greed.
My name is Polydorus. A crop of spears
And iron javelins burgeons and covers over
My torn body here.' My hair stood on end, dread filled
My mind. What was to be? My voice lodged in my throat.

At the time when Troy was under siege from the Greeks
And Priam was losing faith in Dardanian arms,   70
He sent young Polydorus to be raised
By the king of Thrace, and sent much treasure with him.
When Fortune turned against her, and Troy had fallen,
The Thracian king broke every vow he had made,
And allied himself with the victorious arms
Of Agamemnon, and so killed Polydorus,
And seized for himself the gold he had brought from Troy.
Insatiable avarice, there's no crime, is there,
That you won't drive men to, in your lust for gold?

When I had somewhat recovered from the shock,   80
And my terror at the sight that I had seen,
I returned and told my father about the portent,
And after him told the leaders of my people,
And asked them for their judgment. All agreed
That we should leave this wicked place where the laws
Of welcome were so transgressed, and trust our ships
To the winds. For Polydorus we performed
A solemn funeral rite. The mound was piled
High with earth we'd freshly dug to form it;

Two altars to the dead were adorned with black   90
Ribbons and cypress leaves; and Ilian women,
Their hair let down and streaming, stood beside,
Mourning in the customary way;
Bowls of foaming tepid milk were offered,
And cups of the blood of sacrificial victims;
And together with loud voices we cried the farewell.

Then, when we saw that the sea was to be trusted,
And the winds were peaceable, the South Wind gently
Whispering its summons to the deep,
My company came down to the shore together,   100
To launch the ships. So once again our fleet
Put out to sea, the land and the towns upon it
Receding behind us and slowly disappearing.

                    , , ,

Out there in the ocean a blessèd island is,
Much favored by the Nereids' mother and
Aegean Neptune. Once upon a time,
It wandered past other shores and coasts until
The archer god in gratitude for his birth
Tied it to lofty Myconos and to Gyaros,
So that, despite the winds, it lies unmoving.   110
I sail to this island, where there is peaceful welcome
To all our weary people. We disembark,
And perform the ritual veneration to
Apollo's town, the town where he was born.
Anius, who's the ruler of its people,
And also Phoebus's priest, comes forth to greet us,
Wearing on his brow a wreath of laurel,
And he recognizes Anchises, his old friend;
And so we clasp each other's hands and enter
Under the kindly roof of Anius' house.   120

I worship at the temple of the god there,
At the altar made of stones as old as time,

'Give us a home of our own, O god of Thymbra,
A place for this my weary company
To rest in and at last to be a people,
Within our own enduring city walls,
A second Trojan Pergamum for us,
The remnant who alone survived what they,
The Greeks and pitiless Achilles, did.
Where is it we should go? Whom should we follow?   130
Where is it we should make our home? O Father
Give us a sign to give us hope and courage.'
No sooner had I spoken than everything
Suddenly began to shake around us,
The doors and their lintels, the laurels of the god,
The whole hill on which the temple was, was shaking;
From the holy tripod there was moaning as
The door to the shrine shook itself open wide.
We fell to the ground, prostrate, and heard a voice:
'You sons of Dardanus, who have suffered so much,   140
And for so long, the land from whose first growth
Your parents came will welcome your return
To her fruitful bosom. Return to your ancient mother.
Aeneas's house will have dominion over
All other lands, and it will be thus for the house
Of his children's children and all who are born from them.'

Thus Phoebus spoke and there was a shout of joy,
And great excitement in the crowd, and many
Voices asking one another, 'Where
Can it be, what are the walls, where are they, that   150
The voice is telling us we must return to?'
And then my father, rehearsing in his mind
All he could think of that he knew about

The ancient days of the people of our race,
Spoke thus:

                'You princes, listen to what I say,
And discover where your hopes are. There's an island,
Jupiter's isle, in the middle of the ocean,
The island of Mount Ida, and our birthplace,
A fertile place, with a hundred teeming cities.   160
Teucrus, our first forebear, came from there,
So goes the story, and founded on our shores
Rhoeteum his kingdom. This was before
Ilium and the Pergamum's towers were built;
Men lived in the lower river valleys there.
From Crete there came Cybele and her secret
Mysteries, and the Corybantic cymbals,
And Ida's grove, and the lions yoked to her car.
So let us go where the god has told us to go.
Let us solicit the winds and sail for Cnossus.   170
If Jupiter favors us the way is short;
Our fleet should reach the Cretan shores upon
The dawning of the third day of our voyage.'

It was thus he spoke, and then performed the rites,
And upon the altars slew a bull to Neptune,
And another bull to beautiful Apollo,
And a black sheep, to the god of storms, and a white,
To seek the kindness of the favoring winds.

                        ꜚ ꜚ ꜚ

We had heard that King Idomeneus had left
The country of his fathers, forced into exile,   180
And that the shores of Crete were now deserted,
The houses empty of any who would have been
Our enemies. We leave the port of Ortygia
And fly on the wings of our sails across the seas,

Past Naxos and its Bacchantes roaming the hills,
Past green Donysa, Olearos, and Paros
White as snow, and the scattered Cyclades,
And making our way through clusters of crowding islets.
The sailors compete with one another in shouting;
The cheering cries are heard from ship to ship,   190
'To Crete that is the country of our fathers!'
A strong tail wind propels us as we go,
And at last our fleet comes in to the ancient shores
Of the Curetians, where I labor to build the walls
Of the town I meant to establish for us there.
I call the town I was building, Pergamum,
A name which fills my company's hearts with pride,
And I encourage them to love their hearths
In this new dwelling place to which they've come,
And I tell them to raise a lofty citadel there.   200
And so our ships being now upon the shore,
Our keels aligned upon the sands, and safe,
Young people were getting married; there was a beginning
Of tilling of the land, and I was busy
Promulgating laws and assigning homes
For my people to live in.

               But suddenly there came,
From some infected region of the sky,
A pestilence bringing death and misery
To the trees and the crops and to the human beings.   210
Some of us gave their sweet lives up to death;
Others were left to totter about, upholding
Their wasted feeble bodies as best they could.
And the scorching heat of Sirius the Dog Star
Dried up and withered the grain we were trying to grow.
There was almost nothing left for us to eat.
It was my father's urging that we go back
To Ortygia and the oracle and ask
Apollo to tell us what will become of us,

As weary as we are in our distress. 220
What should we do to help ourselves survive?
Where is it in the world that we should go?

Night came and every living thing in the world
Lay fast asleep, and I too in my bed
Lay fast asleep. The Phrygian Penates,
The images of the gods I'd carried with me,
Away from the burning fires of fallen Troy,
Were there before my eyes, clear in the light
Of the bright moonlight that streamed in through the windows.
Their voices spoke to me with words that brought 230
Relief from what was troubling me. They said:

'Apollo utters here, and sends us here to tell you
The things he would have uttered at Ortygia
If you had come to speak to the oracle there.
When Dardania was burned we came with you
And journeyed with you across the surging waters;
We shall exalt your children yet to be born
And grant imperial power to their city.
You must accept the long labor of exile
And prepare for them the mighty walls of their future. 240
And you must leave this place. These shores are not
The shores that Apollo of Delos sent us to;
This island, Crete, is not the place the god
Ordained for you to find, to be your home.
There is an ancient land, called by the Greeks
Hesperia, famous and powerful both in arms
And in the abundance that its soil brings forth.
The Oenotrians were its first inhabitants,
And then, so we are told, there came a people
Who called it, after their leader, Italia. 250
There is our proper home; it was the land
Of Dardanus and father Iasius, the first
Begetters of the race that we belong to.

Arise and go to your aged parent and tell him
The joyful news that without doubt your home
Is Corythus and the Ausonian lands,
For Jove denies the Dictaean fields to you.'

I was overwhelmed by the sight of the gods and by
Hearing their voices as they spoke to me.
This wasn't a dream—I was seeing them face to face,   260
Their filleted hair, their living presence there,
Before my eyes. I rose from my bed in haste,
In a cold sweat of awe, and raised my voice,
And turned up my hands in reverence, and offered
Gifts to the gods on the hearth, of the purest wine.
And after I performed this ritual,
I went to my father joyfully and told him
Everything that had happened. He recognized
The ambiguities of our dual descent,
And his consequent error concerning where it was   270
That was our primal home, and thus he spoke:

'My son, I now remember that Cassandra,
Distressed by Ilium's fate, foretold all this,
Speaking the words "Italia," "Hesperia."
But who would have thought it was Hesperia
To whom the Teucrians should return? And who
Would then have believed the prophecies of Cassandra?
Let us yield to Phoebus and go the better way,
Warned by the god to do so.'

                    Thus he spoke   280
And we obeyed, and did so joyfully.
And so it was that, leaving some few behind us,
We departed from this home, and with sails outspread,
Our ships set forth over the empty sea.

                ✦ ✦ ✦

After all sight of land had dropped away,
Around us nothing but sky, nothing but sea,
A great dark rainstorm cloud rose up above us,
Impending over us with night and tempest,
And the sea began to agitate with darkness,   290
And soon the winds impel the waters before them,
And they rise and roll and surge, and we are thrown
This way and that before them in their whirling.
Storm clouds have wrapped themselves around the day;
The rain at night has taken away the sky.
Violently we're blown off course and wander
Blindly through boiling waves. Palinurus, even,
Cannot tell night from day nor knows which way
Is the way we go upon the shuddering waters.
Three days, three nights, we wander without stars   300
In the misty dark that shrouds itself around us.
But on the fourth, at last, there's the sight of land;
There are mountains to be seen from far away,
And curling smoke. We lower our sails; the sailors
Take to the oars, and we sweep along toward shore.

⸗ ⸗ ⸗

Having survived the storm, I landed safe
Upon the shores of one of those islands in
The Ionian Sea—the Greeks call them the Strophades—
Which are the place where dire Celaeno and
The other Harpies settled, after they   310
Were frightened away from Phineus' tables and
His house was closed to them. There are no monsters
Fouler than they; there is no filthier plague
Or infestation sent by the rage of the gods
That ever came up and ever issued from
The waters of the river Styx than they.
They have the faces of maidens; disgusting filth

Falls from them as they fly; their pretty faces
Look pale and famished; the hands they have are claws.

As we came into the harbor of the island,   320
Behold, we saw a joyous scene of herds
Of cattle browsing, and goats untended cropping
The lovely grass. We rushed in with our swords,
Calling the gods, even Jove himself, to join us,
And on the winding shore we set out couches
And spread the meal, and were banqueting on the feast,
When suddenly with loudly clanking wings
The Harpies came flying down from the hills and swooped,
Leaving their loathsome excrement everywhere,
Screaming and stinking. We moved ourselves away,   330
To a secluded place, deep hidden behind
A protecting rock, in the shade of sheltering trees
And their whispering leaves, and then again, this time,
From another place in which their nests were hidden,
They came again. They hovered over the tables,
Their claws hung down and with their filthy lips
They defiled the food again. I told my soldiers
To hide away their swords and shields in the grass,
And when the birds came swooping and screaming down,
The brass horn of Misenus sounded alarm   340
And my soldiers attacked, and there took place a strange
Battle in which the birds sustained no wounds,
Nor felt them, but they soared away from the scene,
Leaving their filth, and half-eaten food, behind.

One of the birds, Celaeno, malevolent
Prophetess, flew down from the sky again,
And alighted on a high rock out in the water,
And cried out shrilly,

                    'Would you make war on us,
Having invaded our fields and slain our cows   350

And bullocks, you sons of Laomedon, and are you
Trying to drive us guiltless Harpies away
From our fathers' kingdom? Listen to what I say,
And listen well. Here's what the Father God
Omnipotent told to Phoebus Apollo, and what
He told to me, the eldest of the Furies,
And what I tell to you: you'll sail the seas
And invoke the winds and get to Italy
And enter the harbors there. But you will not
Be able to build the walls of your city there 360
Until what you did to us, and your terrible hunger,
Will make you franticly gnaw with your ravenous teeth
On the very tables you eat on.'

                       She spread her wings,
And was carried aloft, and fled away to the forest.
The blood of my fellows went cold with sudden terror;
Crestfallen they begged me to give up fighting and begged me
To plead for peace, with prayers and vows to them,
The Harpies, whatever they were, if goddesses
They were, or foul obscene dire birds of omen. 370
Anchises, my father, stood upon the beach
And raised his hands and called the mighty gods
And spoke the ritual sacrificial words:
'O gods, prohibit the things they threaten us with
From harming us. Protect your guiltless people!'
Then he commanded that our people untie
The hawsers from the moorings, and loosen the sheets
So the sails are filled with air, and the South Wind blows,
And the sails open wide and over the foaming water
We fly, directed by the helmsman and the wind. 380

                    , , ,

Now, out at sea, first, forested Zacynthus,
Dulichium, and Same, and the cliffs

Of Neritos; and then the rocks of Laertes'
Kingdom, Ithaca, and as we pass
We curse the place where dire Ulysses was born;
And soon, beyond, we see the storm-cloud-shrouded
Peaks of Mount Leucatas, and then, on high,
Phoebus Apollo's shrine that mariners fear.
We make our way to shore near the little town
And its beach, and secure our ships, anchors cast down   390
Into the waters from the rows of prows,
The rows of sterns aligned upon the sand.
Unknowingly we had reached a place of safety,
And our company came to shore to celebrate,
Lighting the fires at altars, to offer up
Our vows to Jove, to purify ourselves.
Our young men stripped, and oiled their naked bodies
For the wrestling matches of our Ilian games,
Here played upon the foreign Actian shore,
Thankful that we in flight had made our way   400
Unharmed past many foes and Argive towns.

Meanwhile, the sun is carried round upon
The great wheel of the year, and icy winter
Agitates the waters with its gales.
And I affix a shield of hollow brass
Great Abas carried long ago in battle
To the columns at the entrance to the town,
Placing this verse upon it, that we were there:

THESE ARMS AENEAS TOOK FROM THE
CONQUERING GREEKS   410

After then I told my people to leave this port
And take up the oars and compete with one another
To sweep across the waters and away.

, , ,

Soon we could not any longer see
The lofty Phaeacian mountains, and we passed
Along the shores of Epirus and entered into
The harbor of Chaonius, and made
Our port close under the high town of Buthrotum.
And it was in this harbor that we heard
A story that was incredible to our ears: 420
That Helenus, who is a son of Priam,
Is now the ruler of these Grecian cities
Of Epirus, because when Pyrrhus, who was the son
Of Achilles, was killed, he'd come into the possession
Of Pyrrhus's kingdom, and of his wife, and so
Andromache is once again the wife
Of a Trojan husband. I was astonished. My heart
Was inflamed with desire to speak to him and hear
How these things happened.

                                    ⸙ ⸙ ⸙

                              I was coming up from the port,   430
Leaving behind the ships at their landing place,
When suddenly, by chance, I saw, in a grove
Before the town, by a river that looked like the river
Simois but was not, that it was she,
Andromache! Herself! She was setting out
Her annual offerings and mourning gifts
To the dead, in ritual seeking to call up the ghost
Of her lost Hector from his empty tomb,
The mound on whose green turf she had raised two altars,
Thus making sacred a place to weep for him.   440
She saw me coming, and she saw that I
Wore Trojan armor and carried Trojan arms,
And she was amazed, undone, by the sudden sight
Of what she saw. She tottered where she stood,
And almost fell; her blood turned cold, and it

Was long before she could bring herself to speak,
And when she did, she said. 'Is it? Are you?
Can you be real? O goddess-born, are you?
A messenger sent to me? Are you? Alive?
Or if the light of being alive is gone,   450
Where is my Hector? Where is it that he is?'
She wept a flood of tears and the sound of her weeping
Was everywhere about us. I could scarcely
Bring the words out in answer to her frenzy,
And deeply disturbed I opened my mouth to speak
And only could speak in broken gasping phrases:
'I live, and I make my way, through life, through all
Extremities . . . but do not doubt it, what
You see is what you really see . . . oh! . . . What
Has become of you since such a husband was lost?   460
What fortune has been restored to you that's worthy
Of Hector's Andromache? Or must you still
Submit to servitude as Pyrrhus's wife?'
Softly, then, and with lowered eyes, she said,
'Oh she, the virgin daughter of Priam, was
The lucky one, beyond us all, who was
Commanded to die, under the walls of Troy,
At the enemy's tomb, she who was not forced
To undergo the casting of the lots
And be chosen for a conquering foreigner's bed.   470
I was carried away, a slave, far over the seas,
To be submitted to the arrogance
Of Achilles' son in all his youthful pride;
And after that, because of his desire
For a Lacedemonian marriage with Leda's daughter
Hermione, he transmitted me, a slave
To a slave, to Helenus; and Orestes, inflamed
With passion for the bride whom Pyrrhus was taking
Away from him, caught Pyrrhus unwary at
His father's altar, and beheaded him,   480

And Helenus by Pyrrhus's death received
His part of Pyrrhus's legacy that was owed
To him as bondsman, and so it came to pass
That a son of Troy called all this land, now his,
Chaonia, and on the height he built
An Ilian citadel, a Pergamum.
But what can the fortune be, what winds are they,
That have carried you this way, what god is it
Who has driven you, who were ignorant that we
Were living here, to land upon our shores?   490
What of the boy, Ascanius? Did he
Survive, and does he feed on the living air.
He who was there, oh, was there when Troy . . . ? Oh, has he
Nevertheless retained some care for her,
The mother he has lost? And have Aeneas,
His father, and Hector, his uncle, excited
In him their examples of manhood's ancestral virtue?'
Thus Andromache spoke, lamenting, weeping
A flood of tears.

              But then from the walls of the city   500
The son of Priam, Helenus, appeared,
And with him a company. He recognized
At once that we were of his kinship and
Joyfully he welcomed us to come
In through the gates of the city, and he wept
Freely, hearing everything we told him
Of our story. We go into the city and
We see that they have built a diminutive Troy,
With a simulated citadel, and a dry
Little stream that they call by the name of Xanthus,   510
And gates that resemble the Scaean Gates of Troy.
The hospitable welcoming king received us in
His colonnaded palace, where we were offered

Libations to drink from bowls of wine and where
Our feast was served to us on golden platters.

Day after day went by and with the new
Season the breezes summon the sails to be filled
With the new South Wind. I went to Helenus,
And questioned him thus: 'O you, the son of Troy,
Interpreter, and privy to the tripod   520
And the laurel of the oracle of Clarus,
And you know what is told by the tongues of birds and by
The auguries of the flying wings, tell me—
For all the manifestations from on high
Have spoken with favor of my quest and have
Encouraged me on my way to Italy
Through foreign lands; but she alone, Celaeno,
The Harpy, prophesies monstrous peril and famine.
What are the dangers I will undergo?
What are the first of them? How shall I plan   530
How to encounter these troubles and survive?'

Then Helenus, having sacrificed the bullocks
According to the ritual, invokes
The blessing of the gods upon it, and
Unbinds the sacred fillets from his head,
And takes me by the hands and leads me to
The threshold of your presence, Phoebus Apollo,
And then from his priestly mouth there issue these words
Of prophecy:

                    'O goddess-born, the gods   540
Have made it manifest that you will go
Upon your journey over the deep, enjoying
The favor of those on high—for thus it is
Allotted by the king of all the gods,

Who turns the wheel of changing Fates; such is
The turning cycle. In order that you may
More safely cross the seas I will be able
To tell you only a few of the many things
That could be foretold for you; the Fates prohibit
Helenus to know more, and Saturnian Juno   550
Has not yet chosen to speak. First, I must tell you,
That Italy, which seems to you near at hand,
And whose ports you are prepared to enter soon,
Is kept apart from where we are by a long
Long path that is not a path, far over the seas.
First your oars must strain themselves against
The heavy surging waters of Sicily,
And then you must get your ships across the vast
Expanse of the salt Ausonian sea, and past
The infernal lakes and Circe's island Aeaea,   560
Before you find the place where it is safe
To build your city. But I will tell you of signs:
When you have come ashore, anxious, dismayed,
And find, lying beside a sequestered brook,
A white sow who had just then given birth
To a litter of her babies, white as she,
And busy at her teats, there is the place
Of respite from your troubles, the place for your town.
And do not fear the gnawing of the tables.
Apollo will hear you when you call for him,   570
And the Fates will find a way. However, you
Must avoid these lands around us, and keep away
From the hither coast of Italy that our own
Sea ebbs and flows upon, for malignant Greeks
Inhabit all those towns. The Locri of
Narycia built a town there; the soldiers of
Lycian Idomeneus are encamped
On the plains of Sallentinus; Philoctetes,
The leader of the Meliboei, has built

His little fortified mountain town Petelia.   590
And, when you in your ships have crossed the sea
And anchored on the shore, and when you then
Set up your altars to make your vows to the gods,
Cover your heads with a purple mantle, so that
No hostile face will be seen among the sacred
Lights of the altar fires, disturbing the omens.
This is the manner in which your people and you
Must always perform the rites; you must hold to this,
And your children and their children must hold to this,
In the discipline of this manner of behaving.   590

But when you depart from there and when the wind
Has carried you toward the shores of Sicily,
And as you approach, and as the channel opens,
Keep to the land and sea on the left, no matter
How long it takes to go that way, and avoid
The land and sea on the right. There was a time,
A long time ago, it is said, when these were joined,
One thing together, and suddenly, by some great
Convulsive power they were broken apart—
Such things can happen as the ages pass—   600
And the sea came in between them, keeping apart
Hesperia and Sicily with the waters
Flowing between the cities and the fields
On either side. On the right is where Scylla is,
And on the left is where Charybdis is,
Who swallows down huge waves one after the other,
Three waves at a time, sucking them all the way down
To the bottom of the abyss of what she is,
And then regurgitates them, throwing them up
To splatter upon the very stars on high.   610
But in the dark recesses of a cave,
Scylla extends her mouths from her hiding place,
And pulls ships in, to perish on her rocks.

She's human down to her waist, and under that
A monster sea thing, bellied like a wolf,
And with a dolphin tail. It's better to take
The longer way, around the Pachynian headland
And doubling back on Sicily's other side,
Than ever to see the hideous sight of monstrous
Scylla in her underwater cavern   620
Or the rocks that echo echo with the barking
Of her sea-green hounds. And moreover, goddess-born,
If my prophetic seeing can be believed,
And if Apollo fills my heart with truth,
There is one thing among all other things
That I have told you that I must tell you again,
And again, and again: adore the mighty goddess
Juno first of all. Adore her with your praise
And with your prayers; in chorus joyfully chant
Your vows to her, and supplicate her favor   630
With many gifts. This being done, at last
You will leave Sicily behind you and
Then enter into Italy in triumph.

After you have been brought there you will come
To Cumae with its specter-haunted lakes
And Avernus with its murmuring woods, and there
You'll see the manic maiden Sybil, who sits
In a deep cavern of rock and sings of the Fates,
Writing on leaves in symbols what she sings.
She sorts out what she has written and puts the leaves   640
In order and finds a place for them to lie there
Motionless, and they lie there undisturbed,
Until, one day, if a hinge in the door is turned
And the door is opened and a breeze comes in,
And the leaves are scattered fluttering everywhere
In the rocky cave, the maiden does not care,
And she makes no effort to put them right again,
So the verses could not make sense; and those who came

Inquiring leave unsatisfied, unanswered,
Loathing the cave to which they came inquiring. 650
No matter how your companions urge and scold,
No matter how the wind blows tempting fair
And urges you to let your sails be filled
To set forth on your voyage, do not let
Any thought of delay keep you from staying,
Persisting in your visits to the seer
And in your prayers that she herself should sing
The oracles and willingly unlock
Her lips to prophesy. If you attend
Upon her with such reverence, then she 660
Will tell you of the tribes of Italy,
And what the wars will be, and how you must
Confront each test of you or find the means
To make your way around it, safe and sound.

The goddess being thus propitiated,
You will succeed. These are the things my voice
Is allowed to tell. You must go now and bring
Troy once again to greatness by your deeds
In the clear light of heaven.'

       , , ,

                  And, having spoken 670
These gracious words he ordered that the ships
Should be stored with gifts of weighty gold and ivory,
Silver, and heavy cauldrons from Dodona,
A triple-woven breastplate with golden hooks,
And a beautiful plumed helmet, Pyrrhus's arms.
Gifts also for my father, horses, and armor,
Arms for our soldiers, and men to augment our crews.

Meanwhile my father Anchises commanded us
To raise our sails to take advantage of

The favoring winds. And the interpreter   680
Of Apollo spoke to him respectfully:
'Anchises, whom the gods have cared for, you,
Judged worthy to embrace in wedlock Venus,
You, twice survivor of the fall of Troy,
Look, over there that I point to is the hither
Italian shore. Set sail and take for yourselves
The lands that will be rightfully your lands;
But when you leave here do not land upon
The hither shore. Go to the farther side,
Far, far beyond are those Ausonian lands   690
That Phoebus Apollo reveals will be your lands.
Go, father, blest in the piety of your son,
Go forth. But why should I with longer speech
Delay your setting forth as the winds arise?'

Andromache, too, came forward then, in sadness
Because she knew this was the final parting.
And she, with ceremony due, brought gifts
Of gold-inwoven robes and other things
The loom has richly made, and a Phrygian scarf
For the boy Ascanius, to whom she says,   700
'O you who are the image that survives,
The only one, of my Astyanax,
Accept these gifts from me, into your hands,
In testimony of Andromache's love,
Of Hector's wife, the mother of his son.
Such were the eyes of my Astyanax,
And such his hands, his face, the face of my child,
Just such he would have been had he been able
To grow into his years as you have done.'
I wept as I heard these words, and I said to them,   710
In parting: 'May you be as happy as those
Whose fortune has been brought to its completion.
We are called to seek our fate by different ways,
One way, and then another way, and another.

But you have achieved your resting place; you have
No need to wander on the sea, no need
To look for lands receding before your eyes.
Here, with your own hands, you have made for yourselves
Another Xanthus and another Troy,
More fortunate and safer from the Greeks.   720
If I should reach the Tiber and the Tybrian
Fields through which the river flows, and if
It comes to pass that I should look upon
The walls of the city promised to my people,
Then our two cities, Hesperia and Epirus,
Will be one Troy together, we who are
One people, Dardanians by descent, and we
Who share the story of Troy, and of its fall.
So may that oneness be the trust entrusted
To our children and their children after them.'   730

We hastened along the waters, close by the hither
Ceraunian cliffs, the shortest distance from where
We were to Italy. Evening meanwhile
Was coming on, the sun was setting, and
The hills were shrouding in darkness. We came ashore
And after the allotment of the oars
Of the rowers for the next day's voyage, we,
Scattered here and there along the beach,
Laid our bodies down so dewy sleep
On the lap of the welcoming land could bring us rest   740
And refreshment to our weary limbs. Not yet
Had Night the Hours were driving on her journey
Gone halfway toward the Dawn, when Palinurus
Awaking rose from where he was lying down,
To ascertain how was it with the winds
And with the stars, inquiring into every
Slightest stirring breeze and studying every
Constellation across the silent sky
As it moved and toward tomorrow made its way,

Arcturus, rainy Hyades, the Bears,   750
The Twins, and Orion in his golden armor clad.
Seeing that all was well and the sky serene,
He called out loudly from his helmsman's seat,
And so we woke, broke camp, and went aboard,
And spread our sails and set forth on our way.

                              ⸙ ⸙ ⸙

Aurora the dawn was just beginning to blush,
The stars were fleeing away, and then, far off,
Though only dimly to be seen, there were,
Along the horizon lying low, the hills
Of Italy. Achates saw them first   760
And cried out joyfully, 'It's Italy!'
'It's Italy!' his fellows cried out joyfully,
And father Anchises, standing high upon
The stern of our ship, the lead ship of our fleet,
Held up a wreathèd bowl, brimming with wine,
And uttered this prayer to the gods: 'You gods of the sea,
And of the earth, and storms, now favor us
With gentle winds and with an easy voyage.'
And then the wind stands fair, the wind we'd hoped for,
And it was not long until we saw the entrance   770
To a harbor opening up before us, and,
High up above, the temple of Minerva.
Our sails are lowered, our prows turn toward the shore.
The harbor bends to the East protected by
Projecting reefs on which the salt spray scatters;
Twin walls of rock descend from towering cliffs
And hold the port in their embracing arms;
The temple stands behind, away from the shore.

It was here I saw an omen, the first I saw:
Four snow-white horses pasturing on the grass.   780

Then father Anchises said: 'O land that receives us,
There's import of war in this, these chariot horses
Are geared for battle; and yet sometimes such horses
Are harnessed to chariots thus in times of peace,
So peace here might be hoped for.' And so we offer
Our prayers to the sacred power of Pallas, she
Whose armor rings with the clashing sounds of strife
And was the first to welcome our votive chants.
We cover our heads with Phrygian mantles and bow
Before the altars, and perform the ritual   790
Sacrifice and vows to Argive Juno,
As Helenus had commanded us to do.

Then, having performed the rituals of our vows,
We turn the yardarms of our sails away,
And toward the open sea, leaving behind us
The untrusted fields and the nearby places where
They live who are of the Grecians by their birth.
The next sight that we see is Hercules' town,
If so they say is true, Tarentum, and
Its bay. Opposite, on the Lacinian cliff,   800
There rises upon our sight the temple of Juno,
The citadel of Caulon and Scylaceum
The breaker-up of ships. And then, afar,
Coming up out of the seas, Trinacrian Aetna
Is to be seen, and from a great way off
The giant ocean moaning is to be heard,
The enormous broken pulsing of the waves
Against the rocks and shattering on the shallows
And mingling with the sands. Then father Anchises
Cries out: 'This must be Charybdis, these must   810
Be the cliffs, these must be the terrible threatening rocks
That Helenus warned of! My comrades, get away!
And side by side rise up upon the oars!'
At once they did what he commanded as

Palinurus turned the roaring straining prow
To the left, into and upon the waves; and all
Our fleet turned left as he did and with all
Our might our oars contested with the wind;
The waves high rising carried us up to the heavens
And when they fell they carried us plummeting down 820
To the place where the Manes are. Three times we heard
The crying aloud of the caverns down below,
Thrice saw the sea-spray dripping from the stars,
And then at last when the sun went down the wind
Also went down and failed us, and we drifted
Wearily toward the Cyclopean shores,
Not knowing where we were.

                   , , ,

                           We came upon
A harbor large enough for our ships to enter,
Protected from the wind; but close to us 830
Was dreadful thundering Aetna, a cloud of smoke
And fiery ashes boiling up to the heavens,
Carrying up great globes of flaming stuff,
High as to lick at the stars; and from the lowest
Deep inside of the mountain its viscera,
Roaring and belching, vomit up rocks and molten
Slag as high as high can ever be. They say
The giant Encèladus was struck down by
A bolt of lightning and the whole enormous weight
Of Aetna lies upon him, and fire breathes forth 840
From all her broken chimneys, and every time,
In anguish he turns from one side to the other,
All Sicily shakes, and the sky is covered with smoke.
All the night long we hid ourselves in the woods
And endured our awareness of monstrous things abroad,
Not knowing what the sounds were coming from.

There were no stars to be seen, no light from them,
Nor any from the moon; mists covered the skies;
In the dead of the night the moon was held in a cloud.

                    , , ,

And now the very first star of the morning was   850
Visible as Aurora began to disperse
The dewy shadows of the night before,
When suddenly, coming from the woods, there is
A stranger, miserable-looking, filthy, wildly
Bearded, emaciated, wearing only
A rag of a garment held together with thorns,
And he held out his hands to us imploringly.
We stare at him in wonder at what we see.
It is a Greek who had fought at Troy. When he
Sees who we are by our dress and our Trojan arms,   860
Afraid, he stops, then, hesitantly, comes
Toward where we are, then suddenly rushes headlong
To the shore, weeping and beseeching, crying out,
'By the stars, by the gods who live up there, by the light
Of day and the air you can breathe, you Trojans, help me,
Take me away to anywhere but here!
It's true that I am a Greek from the Grecian fleet
And that I fought against the Trojan gods.
For all the wrongs I may have done to you,
Scatter the parts of my body on the waves,   870
Throw me into the sea. If I die this way,
At least I will have died by human hands.'

He falls down to the ground and grovels there,
In desperation clinging to our knees.
We ask him who he is and where he comes from,
What is his tribe, and what has happened to him,
And my father Anchises unhesitatingly

Shakes hands with him and pledges his safety, thus
Assuaging his fear so he can tell us his story:

'Achaemenides is my name. Ithaca is   880
The island where I was born. My father is poor,
So I joined Ulysses' army and went to Troy
—Would I had stayed home safe and sound from this.
My fellow soldiers heedlessly left me here
In the vast cave of the Cyclops when, in terror,
They got themselves through his doorway and ran away.
His enormous cave is dark, slimy with gore,
And with the leavings of bloody gorging, and he
Is immense, towering high as high as the stars—
Oh, gods, take this monster away from this earth we're on—   890
The sound of his voice unbearable to hear,
The sight of his body unbearable to look at.
He makes his meal of the flesh of miserable men,
And of their black flowing blood. With my own eyes
I saw it happen, when lying there taking his ease
At dinner time, in his enormous hand
He picked up two of our soldiers and broke them open
By smashing them on a rock, and the gore was spattered
Everywhere around. I saw him crunching
Their bloody dripping quivering arms and legs   900
Between his jaws and teeth as he ate his dinner.
This did not go unpunished. At such a moment
Ulysses knew that he was still Ulysses,
For when the monster had his monstrous fill,
And having drunk himself into oblivion,
Lay with his monstrous length stretched out throughout
The giant cave, and throwing up in his sleep
Vomit of gore and gobbets of human meat
All mixed with blood and wine, we said our prayers
To the gods and chose our parts, and gathered around   910
On every side of him, and with the point
Of a weapon drilled a hole in the giant single

Eye that was there like an Argive shield or the lamp
Of Phoebus underneath his monstrous brow.
And so we had the joy of taking revenge
For our fellows he had eaten.

                                    But you must flee,
Unfortunates, untie your mooring ropes,
And get away. For it isn't only huge
Polyphémus, keeping his woolly flock   920
In his cave, pressing their udders to milk them. There are
A hundred other huge monster Cyclopes, living
Along this winding shore and wandering,
Monsters together, along these mountain ridges.
The horns of the moon have filled with light three times
Since I have been here alone in the frightening woods,
Day after day, dragging my life out, living
On nuts and berries I scrabble from trees and bushes,
And green weeds that I pull up out of the ground,
In woods where wild beasts have their nests and lairs,   930
And sometimes in a hiding place on a cliff
Seeing huge Cyclopes there and hearing the sound
Of their heavy feet and hearing their voices bawling.
One day when from my hiding I was looking
Everywhere to see what I might see,
I saw the fleet of ships come in to the beach,
And so I sent myself, no matter what,
To give myself up to you. No matter what,
To have gotten myself away from the monster crowd.
Better that you should take my life away   940
Than what the monsters would have done to me.'

He had hardly finished speaking when, there, we saw,
All of us saw, high up on a mountaintop
The monster shepherd Polyphémus, huge,
Blind, enormous horrifying body
Moving slowly among his flock of sheep,

And slowly making his way toward the shore with which
His eyesight formerly had been familiar.
He had a torn-up pine tree in his hand
To guide him and to steady him as he went, 950
His fleecy flock beside him and around him,
The only pleasure he had, his only comfort
In his misfortune. As soon as he got himself down
To the water's edge and felt the touch of the breaking
Waves of the sea, he washed the leaking blood
From the socket of his blind eye into the brine,
Gnashing his teeth and groaning all the while;
And then with giant steps he walks out into
The deeper water; so tall he is, that most
Of his towering body is dry because unreached 960
Above the highest waves. We're terrified.
We take on board with us the suppliant so
Deserving of our rescue and we loose
Our mooring lines as quietly as we can,
And bending to our desperate oars, we sweep
Across the waters eager to escape.
The monster heard, and turned himself to the sound
Of our splashing oars, but when he knew he had
No power to lay his hands on us, no longer
Follow us farther among the Ionian waves 970
That were coming in against him, he let out a roar.
The ocean and all its billows shuddered and shook,
And Italy, hearing it, was terrified
To its most inland self, and Aetna bellowed
Through all its winding caverns underground.
And the Cyclopean race, aroused by their brother's roar,
Came rushing out of the woods and from the high mountains
Down to the shore of the port, and stood there, glaring,
Dread gang of helpless one-eyed Aetnean brothers,
Heads high as tall as the sky, like a congress of 980
Great oak trees standing upon a mountaintop,

Or a congregation of coniferous cypress,
Or like a grove of Diana or forest of Jove.

⟩ ⟩ ⟩

Fear made us open our sails as fast as we could,
Striving to catch whatever wind we could,
And in whatever direction there was that we could.
I remember Helenus' warning to keep away
From the narrow passage between Charybdis and Scylla,
On either side of which there's death. And so
We go back, avoiding the way where the North Wind blows   990
Through that narrow Pelorian channel, and sailing past
The living rocks at the mouth of the river Pantagias,
The bay of Megaera and low-lying Thapsus. These
Were the shores that luckless Ulysses' soldier,
Achaemenides, had come along before.
There is, against the wave-washed headland of
Plemyrium, in Sicily, an island
Called from ages long ago Ortygia.
They say that Alpheus the river god,
In love, had made his secret fluent way   1000
Beneath the ground and under the sea from where
He was in Peloponnesian Ilia
To where your fountain, Arethusa, is,
And mingled there himself with Sicilian waters.

As we were told to do, we venerate
The deities of the place, and then sail on,
Past Helorus with its rich marsh soil, and past
Pachynus's rocks and cliffs, and Camerina,
Whom the Fates ordained should never be disturbed;
And, stretching far, the Geloa plains, and Gela,   1010
Named for its tumultuous river; then
The great high walls of Acragas, where once

They bred those famous marvelous horses; and,
With favored winds the gods had granted me,
I leave Selinus's palms behind, and pass
Lybeis's shoals and treacherous hidden rocks.
And then I reach Drepanum's mournful shore,
And here it was that I, whom so many storms
Have beaten upon, alas, I lost my father,
The solace of all my troubles and my cares.   1020

'O best of fathers, you have left me here,
Abandoned, weary, rescued from so many
Perils undergone, now all for nothing.
Helenus the seer, who foretold,
In prophecy, so many horrors to be,
Did not foretell this sorrow, and dire Celaeno
Told nothing of this grief that was to come.
This was the final trial, since I began,
And now the god has driven me to this place.'"

                              , , ,

Thus father Aeneas, alone before them all,   1030
Who were intently listening, told the story
Of his long wanderings, what it was
The Fates had ordained for him. And so the story
Came at last to a close, and he was quiet.

Book Four

But the queen has been wounded by love; hour by hour
The life-blood in her veins keeps nourishing
The hidden fire within her; thinking of
The glory of the hero race he comes from,
And how he speaks, and the things he has spoken of—
At night her body's longing cannot rest.

⸬

In the morning when Aurora has scattered the dewy
Shades of the night before, and Phoebus's light
Has begun to traverse the sky, she speaks to her
Who was one with her in her heart, "Anna, my sister,   10
The dreams I have been dreaming all night long
Fill my mind with strange feelings that disturb me.
Who is this man who has entered into our house?
How noble he is in the way he looks, in bearing,
So brave, so strong. I know without any doubt
That he must be a descendant of the gods.
I know it without any doubt. Those who are fearful
Prove by their fears that they are ignobly born.
What troubles there are that the Fates have confronted him with!
How terrible the long continued struggles   20
Of the wars his story has sung to us about!
If it were not that I have been determined,
Unchangeably so, since my first love betrayed me

By dying, not to commit myself again
To the bonds of love and marriage, and if it were not
That I am so weary of thoughts of the marriage bed,
I might have yielded to these thoughts I have,
For, Anna, I confess that since the death
Of my poor husband, murdered by my brother,
Destroying our household, only this person has   30
Disturbed my sense of who I am, and made
My purpose totter in uncertainty.
I have to tell you, I feel the amorous fire
Stirring, that I thought had been put out.
Rather than yield to that, I pray that the earth
Would open its jaws and swallow me, or may
The Father use his thunderbolt to throw me
Down among pale shades and in the profound
Dark night down there of Erebus, before,
O Chastity, I violate your laws.   40
He, who joined my heart to his and took it
Away with him to the grave, I pray that he
Will keep it where he is and guard it there."

And saying these things, she was overcome with tears.
Then Anna says, "My sister, I love you more
Than I love the light itself—why, so alone,
Do you spend your youth in mourning, and without
The rewards of love, and the knowledge of what it is
To have sweet children? Do you think the dust gives any
Thought at all to any of these things?   50
The Manes, wherever they are, what do they care?
I know you've turned away all suitors, here
In Libya, and, before we were here, in Tyre,
None of them able to sway you from your mourning.
Iarbas you turned away, and others, also
Famed in war and power, in Africa.
But now, why struggle against what pleases you?
Have you thought about your situation here?

Among what lands you are? The Gaetulians,
Invincible in war, the Numidians   60
And their bareback cavalry, the hostile Syrtes,
On the one side pressing themselves against your borders;
On the other side the barren waterless desert
In which the wild Barcaeans roam and rage;
And what about the threats of war from Tyre,
The menacing signs of what your brother intends?
It is my belief that it was by the gods' approval
And by the agency of Juno that
The Ilian ships were blown here by the winds.
Imagine, my sister, the city that will arise   70
Because of such a union, you and he;
Imagine what the Punic glory will be,
Abetted by the arms of the Teucrians.
You must seek the favor of the gods and make
Due sacrifices to secure the omens;
Be yet more welcoming to the Trojans; weave
Arguments, with your welcome, to keep them here,
While Orion's drenching rains pour down and under
Intractable skies the winter winds are raging,
And the broken ships still lie here unrepaired."   80

                        ⹁ ⹁ ⹁

Thus with what Anna said, she inflamed the fire
Already smoldering in the breast of Dido,
And strengthened hope to her uncertain mind,
And loosened the constraints of chastity.
The two of them began to visit the shrines,
Praying for the blessings of the gods.
Offering yearling sheep to Ceres, she
Who gives the laws, to Phoebus Apollo and
To Father Lyaeus, and most of all, to the goddess
Juno, guardian of the marriage bonds.   90
And every day most beautiful shining Dido

Moves with ritual slowness, bearing the cup
Among the laden altars of the gods,
And pouring for them the ritual libations
Between the white horns of a chosen heifer.
Daily she renews her sacrificial
Offerings to the deities, and gazes
Intently into the victims' opened breasts,
Endeavoring to see in there whatever
The throbbing viscera will have to tell her.   100
Alas, how blind are seers! Vows and shrines,
What do these innards say to those maddened with love?
Meanwhile the wound lives silently within her,
And passion eats the soft marrow of her bones.
Hapless Dido burns and wanders through
The streets of her own city—she's like a doe
In the Cretan woods who has been mortally
Wounded by an arrow by a hunter
Unknowing of what he did; and she, in flight
Bewildered, stricken, wanders through the trees,   110
This way and that, taking Aeneas with her,
Showing him her Sidonian fortress walls
And the city she is building, and as they go
Sometimes she is about to speak, and doesn't.
And as the day becomes the evening she
Longs in her delirium to be
At that same banquet where she heard the tale
Of Ilium's trouble, longing to hear it as
It came from the lips of him who was the teller.
And later still, when she finds herself alone,   120
And the light of the moon has gone, and the setting stars
Acknowledge that it is the time for sleep,
All by herself in the empty hall she mourns,
And lies upon the couch that he has left,
Hearing him and seeing him, although
He is not there; sometimes she holds the boy
Ascanius on her lap, embraces him,

Entranced with the likeness of him to his father,
Mimicking the love she cannot speak of.
The towers of the city are left unfinished;
Young men no longer practice their martial arms,
Nor work to reinforce the gates and ramparts;
All the works of building are at a standstill;
A crane machine stands high, against the sky
It almost reaches up to, looking over
The massive, boding, uncompleted walls.

, , ,

As soon as Jove's beloved Juno knew
That Dido was possessed by such a passion,
And reputation could not protect her from it,
Saturn's daughter spoke these words to Venus:
"Your victory is splendid, rich the prize
You two have won, yourself and that boy of yours—
Great, indeed, and worthy to be remembered,
An instance of the power of the gods,
Two gods who by their tricks defeat one woman.
I am aware of your suspicion of
Carthage and its high houses, and your fear
Of its success. But what will all this come to?
What is the point of all this contention between us?
Why should we not together bring about
An agreed-upon marriage and a lasting peace?
You have won all you wanted in this matter:
Dido burns with love and the madness of it
Has made its way into her very marrow.
Let's be in common the rulers of these people,
She serving the Phrygian husband she desires
And bringing you her Tyrians as her dowry."

Venus (who understands what Juno's purpose
Was in what she pretended it was—to keep

The empire away from Italy and keep it   160
In Libya), replied to her: "Providing
That Fortune really favors what you propose,
It would be madness to refuse an offer
Such as this, to wish to contend with you
In hostilities. But the Fates make me uncertain
About what it is that Jupiter really desires,
Whether the Tyrian city and the Trojan
Wanderers should become one city together,
To be one people bound in trust and union.
You are his wife: it is for you to persuade him.   170
Proceed in this and I will follow you."
Saturnian Juno replied to what Venus said:
"I'll undertake the task. Now, listen to me.
I'll tell you briefly what I plan to do.
Aeneas and Dido are hunting tomorrow morning;
They will go to the forest as soon as the sun comes up,
And the morning light begins to undo the darkness.
The hunters will be busily running about,
Draping the glades with nets, and I will bring
A black torrential rainstorm down from the heavens,   180
Mingled with hail, with thunder, and with lightning;
All the people will scatter under the storm,
And they will all be covered in opaque darkness.
Dido and the Trojan chief will come
Into the same cavern, seeking shelter there.
There I will be, and, with your blessing, I
Will bring them together in the bonds of wedlock,
Thus making her his own, this wedding day."
The Cytherean, consenting to her plan,
Smiled at the trickery she had thus learned about.   190

                        ,   ,   ,

Aurora rose, leaving the ocean behind her,
And with the coming forth of the new day's light,

A band of young men carry hunting nets
And webs and broad-tipped spears, the hunting gear;
A mounted troop appears, Massylians and
Their horses and their strong-nosed hunting dogs,
All ready for the day. The Punic nobles
Wait for the queen at the doorway to the palace,
And, harnessed with silver and gold, her horse waits too,
Stamping his feet upon the ringing pavement,   200
Tossing his head, and champing eagerly
At the foaming bit. And then at last it is
That Dido the queen appears, with a great crowd
Of her retainers; she wears a Sidonian cloak,
Bordered with embroidery vividly colored;
Gold is the quiver of arrows that she wears,
And gold the fillet with which her hair is caught;
The buckle of her purple cloak is gold.
There is a Phrygian company in her train,
And Iulus with them, happy at the day.   210
Aeneas then steps forth, more beautiful
Than all, to join his company with hers.
It's as when winter is over and Apollo
Leaves Lycia and the stream of Xanthus to visit
Delos and his mother, and there renews
The annual festive dance, while all together,
Around his altars the Dryopes and Cretans
And the painted Agathyrsians dance and shout
Their frenzied anthems to him while he upon
His birthplace hill of Cynthus walks in beauty,   220
His flowing hair adorned with springtime leaves,
And twined with threads of implicated gold,
The quivered arrows rattling on his shoulders.
As beautiful as Apollo is he is,
Aeneas, shining, radiant as the sun.

When the hunting party came up into the high
Places of the mountain where the untracked

Haunts of their prey might be, startled wild goats
Run down along the ridges of the cliffs,
And deer in crowds in clouds of dust race down   230
And across the open fields to get away
From the hills and get away; and in the valley
The boy Ascanius, on his excited pony,
Gallops past this one, past the next one, hoping
That in among the herd maybe there'll be
A foaming wild boar he's been looking for,
Or a tawny lion come down from the mountain.

And then, in the sky, all of a sudden, there's
A great intermingling noise of roar and murmur,
And following there is rain and there is hail.   240
The Tyrians and the Trojan youth and Venus's
Dardanian grandson scatter, flee, and seek shelter
Wherever it may be where they can find it.
The storm pours down upon them from the sky.
Dido and the Trojan chief find shelter
In the same cavern, alone together, and
Apart from all the others. But primal Earth
And matron of honor Juno are there, and they give
The sign; flashes of lightning in the sky
Were witnesses, and on the mountaintop   250
There was the ululating of the nymphs.
That day was the cause of the death to come, the cause
Of calamity, for Dido was no longer
Inhibited by the restraints of keeping her love
A secret from others; she covered over her shame
By calling the deed they did together a marriage.

՚ ՚ ՚

And Rumor, the swiftest of all evil plagues,
Spread through all the cities of Libya, gathering
Strength and speed by her gathering strength and speed,

Timorous, small, at first, and very soon   260
As high as the sky, her feet on the ground, her head
Hid in the clouds as she goes, who was the daughter
Of Mother Earth, who got her, they say, in wrath
Against the gods, the youngest sister of
Coëus and Enceladus, she, enormous
Monster fleet of foot and fleet of wing,
Feathered all over and under every feather
An eye, unwinking, ever vigilant, and,
A tongue in a mouth, mouthing, whispering, and,
A pair of pricked up, ever-listening ears.   270
At night you can hear her screeching as she flies
Through the darkness, gliding exactly midway between
The heaven above and the earth beneath, and sits,
Nightwatcher, on the ledges of roofs, or on
The towers of cities, and calls down on the ones
Below, her frightening mingle of truth and lies,
Rhapsodically singing about them in the darkness,
And all the people hear what she is singing,
How there's a man of Trojan blood, Aeneas,
Whom beautiful Dido has thought fit to join with,   280
In wedlock while all winter long they spend in
Disgracefully pleasing each other with their bodies,
Forgetting every thing about their duties
To the people that their governance is owed to.
These are the stories this filthy goddess spreads
Upon the lips and talking tongues of men,
And then she takes her crooked flight aslant
Across to where Iarbas is and with
The tales she tells him fills his mind with rage.

Iarbas, the son of a Garamantian nymph   290
Who had been ravished by his father Ammon,
Established in his realm a hundred great
Temples to Jupiter, a hundred altars,
And burning before them ever-burning fires

Witnessing his homage, the ground around them
Rich with animal blood; the portals were hung
With garlands of many flowers. They say that Iarbas,
Disturbed and angered by the stories he heard,
Came to the holy altars and raised his hands
To Jupiter in fervent supplication,   300
Saying these words: "Almighty Jove, O Thou,
To whom, upon our painted divans we
Have at the feast raised high our Bacchic cups,
Have you beheld what has been happening?
Is it for nothing we tremble when you hurl
Your bolts of lightning crashing down upon us,
And your terrifying fire shakes in the clouds?
That woman came to us and sought to buy
Permission to build her little city here,
And we granted this and granted her long-term rights   310
To lands along the coast of Libya,
To use as plowlands. I offered that woman marriage:
She spurned me, and took Aeneas as her lord.
This Paris with his perfumed hair and his Phrygian
Bonnet tied with a ribbon under his chin,
And his sissy band of eunuchs, took it all.
Meanwhile we worship you at all our altars,
And are left bereft to tell you our empty story."

                    , , ,

This was what the pleader pled to Jove,
Anxiously holding fast to the altars, and when   320
The Omnipotent heard him and looked down upon
The royal city, where the two lovers, forgetting
Everything else, were held transfixed in love,
He turned to Mercury and said, "My son,
Glide down upon the zephyrs on your wings
To where the Dardanian chieftain is, who's now

In dalliance at Tyrian Carthage and
Forgetting what cities the Fates had promised him.
Glide down upon the winds and tell him this:
What he is doing is not what his beautiful mother   330
Promised that he would do, nor is this why
She saved him twice from death at the hands of the Greeks.
It is he who was to conquer Italy,
Land full of warfare and contending powers,
And to establish there a dynasty
Of royal Trojan stock, and bring the whole
World under the rule of law. If he does not
Aspire to such a glory for himself,
And if he is unwilling to undertake
The labor of such a task, is he, the father,   340
Willing to deny the towers of Rome
To Ascanius, the son? What is it that
He plans to do? What is it he's hoping for,
Lingering here in the midst of an alien people,
Forgetting Ausonia and the Lavinian fields?
Tell him, set sail. This is my message to him."

He spoke and Mercury at once prepared
To do what his father commanded him to do.
He puts on the golden wingèd shoes that carry
Him with the speed of storm winds high above   350
All lands and oceans. He takes up the wand with which
He summons pale ghosts to come up from Orcus and
With it sends others down to the lowest deeps
Of darkest Tartarus; and as he flies
He sees the peak and perpendicular sides
Of Atlas, who with his laboring strength holds up
The sky above himself, his great head wreathed
In darkest clouds and forests of mountain pine,
And buffeted by rain and wind, his mighty
Shoulders covered with snow, and rivers pouring   360

Down in torrents from his ancient chin,
And his hoary beard, stiff with encrusting ice.
Here Mercury glided down on his even wings,
And paused, and then he dove straight down to the waves
Of the sea below, and then he was like a sea-bird
Skimming just above the waves over near
The sea cliffs where the waters teem with fish.
Thus, cutting across the winds, Cyllene's child,
He flew to Libya's sandy shores to do
The errand he had promised to perform.   370

As soon as the soles of his wingèd feet touched ground,
He saw, beyond the huts, where Aeneas was
Building towers and houses; he carried a sword
Embellished with fiery stars of golden jasper
And from his shoulders there hung a glowing Tyrian
Purple cloak inwoven with threads of gold,
A gift to him from Dido's treasure of riches.
"So is it that you are, for the sake of this woman,
Building a beautiful Carthage, forgetting about
The city that is your destiny? The god   380
Whose power is over the gods and earth and heaven
Has sent me down to you from shining Olympus.
What are you doing? What are you hoping for,
To waste your time like this in these Libyan lands?
If the glory of your fortune does not inspire you,
And if you do not wish to undertake
This labor for the sake of your own fame,
Think of Ascanius, your growing son,
And of the promise made to him, your heir,
To rule Italia and the Roman world."   390
These are the words Cyllenius said to him,
And in the saying he faded from his sight
And vanished far away into thin air.

Aeneas was struck wordless, in terror, his hair
Stood on end, his voice got caught in his throat.
Dumbfounded by the gods' rebuke he burned
With the desire to get himself away
And leave this dulcet country as the gods
Commanded him to do. Ah, how to do it?
What will he say to her, to assuage her fury?   400
What will his first words be? How to begin?
And as, in a panic, he tried, in a panic, to think
Which way to choose and what to do, and how,
It came to him, as he turned this way and that,
That what he must do is this: he summons to him
Mnestheus and Sergestus, commanding them
To make the fleet ready, and do so quietly,
And arm the ships and bring the crews to the shore,
And to dissimulate the reason for this new plan.
Meanwhile, since Dido will be ignorant   410
About what's going on, and since she will
Be unsuspecting that a love as strong
As theirs might ever be broken, he will have time
To find the soothing words, and the moment to speak them.
His people joyfully listened to what he told them,
And hastened to carry out what he commanded.

But the queen (for how can one who is in love
Be kept deceived?), having already been
Fearful when there was nothing to be feared,
Divined his secret plan, becoming aware   420
Of this activity that was underway;
And heartless Rumor whispered to her the news
That the fleet was being armed and prepared for sailing.
The news was maddening; Dido was like

A Thyiad undone, aroused, on fire,
In frenzy, by the sound of the emblems shaking
In rage in the dance around the city, burning,
Inflamed by the noise of the Bacchic orgy and
The clamoring on Mount Cithaeron in the dark
Of the night. These are the words she spoke to him,   430
Accusingly: "O faithless! Did you think that you
Could hide this deed from me, and steal away?
Cannot our love keep you from doing this?
Cannot your plighted word keep you from this?
Cannot the thought of the death you would leave me to,
Keep you from this? Now you are making ready
Your fleet to go out on the winter seas in the teeth
Of the Aquilonean storms. O cruel! If Troy
Were still unfallen, and you, if you were not
Seeking for alien fields and unknown places   440
To make your dwelling in, you would not, would you,
Set sail from Troy with your Trojan fleet in such
Tempestuous seas?—But is it I that you
Are fleeing from? I, by my weeping, and by
The promise made by your right hand and by
Our marriage and our vows, and if there was ever
Anything that I deserved from you
By any sweetness that I brought to you,
And if there is any room for prayer, I pray,
Abandon this that you are about to do.   450
It is because of you that now I'm hated
By the Libyan and the Numidian lords, and by
The Tyrians turned against me. I have been shamed,
And I have lost my honor, the fame that was
To be carried up to the stars. To what am I
Abandoned, dying, by this alien guest?
For guest is the name that is all that's left of husband.
Why am I staying here? Until my brother
Pygmalion takes my city? Until Gaetulian

Iarbas takes me captive? If at least before   460
You left you had left a child with me—if only
An infant Aeneas, whose face would remind me of yours,
I would not feel so deserted and overthrown."

She was silent. As Jove commanded him he did
Not look at her in response; he looked at the future
He was required to look at, and resolutely
Suppressed the anguishing sorrow in his breast.
After a time, he briefly replied, and said:
"As long as I have to live and to know myself,
As long as there is breath in this my body,   470
I will never forget and never regret Elissa;
All you have said you have deserved of me.
About the way I have behaved I have
But this to say: it was never my intention
To abscond from here in secret, do not think that;
I never held out the bridegroom torch to you,
Nor did I plight the wedding troth. If fate had left me
With power to follow my own free will and put
My cares in order, the first would be my Troy
And its dear surviving remnant. Troy would still stand,   480
Would still be there; and I would raise up again
A new Pergamus to protect my vanquished people.
But Grynean Apollo has ordered me
To go to Italy, the Italy of
His Lycian oracles, and take possession.
That destiny, that country, is my love.
If you, a Tyrian, are inspired by
The sight of Carthaginian towers here
In Libya, which you came as aliens to,
Why should not we seek out a dwelling place   490
In foreign lands? Each night when the dewy shadows
Have covered over the earth, and the stars on fire
Have risen up in the sky, my father's ghost

With agitated terrifying gestures
Appears before my eyes, admonishing.
And I think of my dear child Ascanius,
Whom I defraud of his Hesperian kingdom
And the promised fields that were foretold for him.
And now the messenger of the gods, whom Jove   500
Himself has sent to me, has come down here
Upon the blowing winds—I swear, it happened—
It was full daylight when I saw him coming
Toward me, coming through the walls, and with
My very own ears I drank in what it was
That the messenger of Jove was sent to tell me.
So you must cease your protestations now.
I go not to Italy of my own free will."

She stares at him, and looks him over and over,
The man who was before her, all of him,
Silently while she gazed and gazed at him: 510
"It was no goddess who gave birth to you.
And, faithless, you are not of Dardanus' line.
In Caucasus's cold stony cliffs there was
That cave that gave you birth. You suckled at
The udders of Hyrcanian tigresses.
What words are they I should not use, to save them
For things to come to me for me to say?
He did not look at me, he did not sigh, when I
Was weeping, and he did not weep himself,
In pity for me and for my love of him.   520
What shall I say? What *is* there for me to say?
Great Juno's eyes do not look at this with justice.
The eyes of Saturnian Jupiter do not.
There is nowhere where faith is kept; not anywhere.
He was stranded on the beach, a castaway,
With nothing. I made him welcome. Insanely, I,
Gave him a place beside me on my throne.
I made his companions safe and saved his fleet—

The fire, oh, the fire rages around me!
First augur Apollo and then the Lycian oracles, 530
Then Jove himself has sent his messenger down,
To bring this dreadful message through the air.
Is this then what the gods do when their quiet
Has been disturbed? I'll hold you here no longer.
I do not dispute what you have said to me. Go.
Let the winds take you across to Italy.
Seek out your kingdom there across the seas.
But if the gods have justice, you will drink
The cup of vengeance halfway there and call out,
Dido, Dido, over and over again, 540
And when cold death has separated soul
From body my shade will come to you from far,
With sooty brands, and haunt you, wicked one.
You will be punished. The story of it will come
To me in the Underworld and I will hear it!"
She breaks off what she was saying, in the midst
Of what she was saying, and turns away, distraught,
And flees away from the light and from his sight,
And he was left in hesitancy and fear,
With so much still to say. And in the arms 550
Of servants she is carried fainting to
Her marble chamber, and laid upon her bed.

⸝ ⸝ ⸝

But pious Aeneas, groaning and sighing, and shaken
In his very self in his great love for her,
And longing to find the words that might assuage
Her grief over what is being done to her,
Nevertheless obeyed the divine command
And went back to his fleet. There, all the Trojans,
All together all along the shore
Set busily to work to launch their ships 560
Into the water, the fresh-pitched keels afloat;

Avid to get the voyage underway,
Sailors were bringing from the woods new leafy
Branches of trees to be fashioned into oars.
Everywhere you could see them hastening
Away from the town and down to the port and the ships.
It's as when ants, knowing that winter's coming,
Carry back into their house huge piles of corn,
To store it for their use, the long black file
Of workers moving steadily through the grass,   570
Bearing the plundered forage as they go,
Some straining under the weight of the big grains
Upon their tiny shoulders, and others sternly
Marshaling them as they go along the way.

What was it you were feeling, Dido, when
You looked down from the fortress heights and saw
How the labor of their readying the fleet
Seethed with their eager fervor to be gone?
O implacable Love, what is there that
You will not drive men to? Once more she must   580
Submit herself to her weeping and her pleading;
Once more she must bend her pride to submit to love;
To leave nothing at all untried before her death.
"Anna, you see what's happening down in the port;
The Trojans have come together from all around;
The unfurled sails are calling for the breeze,
And, look, the exulting sailors have garlanded
The sterns of the ships in which they will all depart.
If I could foresee such heartbreak, sister, I
Will be able to survive it, now it has happened.   590
Anna—our enemy was your friend and he
Confided his inmost thoughts to you—so you
Will know how best you can approach him—go,
Speak to him humbly for me, and tell him that
I never joined at Aulis with the Danaans
To obliterate the Trojans; I never sent

A fleet against the Pergamus; I never
Violated his father Anchises' ashes
To make offense against his father's Manes.
Why has he shut his pitiless ears to what   600
I want to say to him? Where is he going,
That he leaves for in such haste? Ask him to give
One final gift to her who suffers so,
Because of her love for him? Plead with him to
Delay his parting till the winds will be
More favorable and the parting easier.
No longer do I hold him to be faithful
To the ancient marriage bond he has annulled.
Nor do I ask him to relinquish his
Desires for his fair Latium and his kingdom.   610
I only petition for a little time,
Repose for my frenzied spirit, overcome,
Till I have learned from fortune how to grieve.
This last being granted—pity your sister—I
Will pay for it in full to my death moment."

This was her prayer, and her unhappy sister
Carried the message of these tears to him,
But he could not be moved by them, for he could hear,
But he could not hear, the words she brought.
Fate stands in the way and heaven stops up his ears.   620
It's as when high in the Alpine mountains the boreal
Winds assault an ancient strong oak tree,
Contending how, this way, now that, to fell it.
There is a groaning, the great trunk shakes and rocks,
Its wind-shattered foliage scattered on the ground,
But it holds to where it is upon the mountain;
As far as its crown extends to the high heavens,
Its roots reach down as far, to Tartarus;
So he, though shaken in his grieving heart,
Buffeted this way and that by what he heard,   630
Still stood unmoved; the tears that fell are nulled.

, , ,

Then, truly, wretched Dido, overwhelmed
By knowledge of the fate that has come upon her,
Prays for death; she is weary of looking at
The overarching sky. And to make sure
That what has been begun will be completed
And that she will depart from the light, she saw
As she set out her ritual offerings
Upon the incense-burning altars, how—
The horror!—the holy water darkened and   640
The wine was changed to an excremental slime.
She said nothing about this, no, not even to
Her sister. Furthermore, within her palace
There was a marble chapel devoted to
Her husband who had died and which she had
Wonderfully and faithfully maintained,
Adorning it with leaves and snow-white garlands.
At night, when night possessed the world, she heard,
When she was there, noises that sounded like
Her husband's voice, words calling to her, and too,   650
She heard the gloomy sound of the owl alone
Upon the city roofs, in long-continued
Wailing lamentation; sometimes she heard
The voices of old sayings of the prophets,
Speaking to her in her head their terrible warnings.
And in her sleep savage Aeneas himself
Drives her before him in her madness, or
Always alone along some vacant street
Unendingly unaccompanied she seeks
To find her Tyrians in an empty land—   660
It's as when Pentheus, demented, sees
The Furies and, seeing double, sees two suns,
And sees two Thebes, two cities, or as when
Agamemnon's son Orestes flees from his mother,

Who is brandishing fire and writhing snakes, and there
In the doorway the Dirae crouch, and patiently wait.

, , ,

Therefore, when, utterly subjected to
Her misery, she has received her madness
Into herself, and has decided to die,
And to choose the time and manner of the doing,   670
Concealing from her the plan that she has made,
She speaks to her sister, her countenance serene,
As if her unhappy heart were filled with hope.
"Sister," she says, "I have discovered a way
(Be happy for me, sister) to bring him back,
Or else to free me of my love for him.
Near where the sun goes down and Ocean ends,
There's Ethiopia, most distant place,
Where the heavens and their adorning stars are turned
On Atlas' mighty shoulders. There is a priestess,   680
Of the Massylian people, brought to me,
Who superintends the temple in the Garden
Of the Hesperides, and feeds the dragon
Delicacies there, and tends the sacred
Boughs of the trees that grow there, sprinkling their leaves
With honeydew and sleep-inducing poppy.
She promises that with her incantations
She can, if she wills, unbind the hearts of those
Long pent in their obsessions, and imprison
Others in their own cruel, blinding, cares;   690
She can arrest a river in its flowing,
And turn the stars back in their heavenly courses, and she
Can bring the nighttime Spirits from below;
Can make you feel the shaking of the earth,
And hear its rumbling underneath your feet;
And she can summon ash trees down the mountain.

It is against my will, I swear to the gods,
And too, dear heart, my sister, you, that I
Am arming myself with instruments of magic.
In the atrium of the palace, under the skies,   700
You must build a pyre, my sister, and bring the arms
And all the clothes that he, the faithless, left,
And bring the marriage bed that was my ruin,
And pile them up upon it. I want to destroy
All that reminds me of that impious person—
And this is what the priestess tells me to do."
Having said these things she is silent, and she stands there;
Her face is stricken pale. But Anna has
No thought that her sister conceals her death behind
These occult rituals, has not conceived   710
That this is madness, nor is she brought to fear
That any of this is worse than when her husband
Sychaeus died. So she performs the tasks
As Dido has directed her to perform them.

After the pyre she called for had been made
From ilex boughs and pine boughs piled up high,
In the palace's inner courtyard, under the sky,
The queen hung garlands and black funeral fronds
Around the place, and, on the bed they'd been in,
Laid out his sword, his picture, and the clothes   720
He left behind as if he were coming back.
Around this courtyard there were altars placed,
And the African priestess stood there, calling out
In a thundering voice invoking Erebus,
And his father Chaos, and threefold Hecate,
And triple-headed triple-faced Diana.
She sprinkled water that seemed to be the water
Brought from the Underworld from Avernus' springs,
And herbs were brought to what she was doing there,
Full of the black milky sap of venom, mown   730
By brazen sickles under the light of the moon,

And the birth-growth love-charm from a newborn foal's
Forehead was brought before its dam could eat it.
Dido herself was there, her robe ungirdled,
One foot unshod, assisting at the altars,
Holding out the ritual offerings of salted
Meal, and calling to the gods and to
The stars, to bear their witness to the death
That is before her, and praying to whatever
God there may be who is kind to unfortunate lovers.   740

Now it was night and all across the earth
All living beings were harvesting their sleep;
The wind in the trees and the waves that had been wild
Had quieted down—it was the time when the stars
Were halfway through their journey through the night,
When everything was still, where far and wide
All beasts and painted birds, around the lucid
Waters of the lakes, or hidden in thickets, were
Asleep beneath the silent sky of night.
But she, in her distress, the Phoenician queen,   750
Cannot receive the darkness of the night
Into her eyes or heart. She cannot sleep.
Love rises up once more in her in a surging
Raging wave of fire. In this state, in herself,
Floundering, talking to herself, she says:
"What am I going to do? Must I resort
To the mockery of those Numidian suitors
I scorned to marry? Follow the Ilian ships
And be a Trojan slave? And would they take me,
Hating me as they do, or if they did so,   760
Would it be only for the kindnesses I did
To them in the past, or would they, in their pride,
Remember these? Oh, I am lost! Oh, lost!
Do you not understand yet, do you not know,
How treacherous they are, these people of
The tribe of Laomedon? What should I do?

Go all by myself to follow those sailors as
They joyfully depart? Shall I take all
My Tyrian people with me after them,
Protecting me from them? How could I ask   770
My people to open their sails to the winds of the sea,
When I could hardly get them to leave their Sidon
To go with me? The only thing left is to die,
And put an end with the knife to all this pain.
My sister, my tears persuaded you to be
The first to load me down with all these evils.
You were the first to throw me into the hands
Of the enemy. If only I could have been
A creature like some creature in the wild,
Unwedded, innocent, unknowing. I   780
Have not kept faith with the ashes of Sychaeus."

Such were the cries of the anguish of her heart.

⸱ ⸱ ⸱

High on the stern of his ship Aeneas, having
Prepared for his departure from the city,
Was seizing the opportunity to sleep,
And suddenly a shape appeared before him,
Form of the god who had come to him before,
Radiant young golden-haired Mercury, saying
To him as he lay there sleeping, "Goddess-born,
How can you lie there sleeping when all these dangers   790
Are all around you? Are you out of your mind?
Do not you hear that there's a fair wind stirring?
She wants to die and her mind is billowing with
All sorts of wickedness and tricks because
Of her waves of madness frenzy. Leave this place
And go, as fast as you can, while you still can.
If you linger here till morning, the sea will be
Teeming with ships, blazing with threatening torches,

Your whole fleet burning on the shore. Go now.
Woman is changeable and unknowable."   800
As he spoke he was vanishing into the blackness of night.
Aeneas suddenly woke, and terrified, roused up
His sleeping Trojans from their sleep, "Wake up!
Get to your oars! Open the sails! Get going!
It was a god who spoke to me in my sleep!
It was a god came into my sleep from on high,
Telling us to cut the ropes and go!
We will follow you, O god, whoever you are,
And joyfully once again obey. Be with us;
Set favoring stars before us as we go."   810
As he spoke he snatched his sword from its scabbard and
It flashed like lightning as he cut the mooring
Ropes that held his ship to the shore, and by
The ardor of all his men aroused to ardor
Like his, the shore was emptied, and the water
Was almost not to be seen under so many
Foaming oars as the fleet set forth to sea.

﹐ ﹐ ﹐

And now, as early Dawn began to arise,
Departing from Tithonus' saffron couch,
And scattering pale light upon the earth,   820
Dido, looking down from her high tower,
Saw, as the morning light began to brighten,
That the fleet was moving steadily away,
Under open placid sails, and that the oars
Had rowed away and gone, and the harbor was empty;
She tore at her golden hair and three times, four times,
Struck her beautiful breast, and cried, "O god!
Is he really going away? Can it be true
That this alien is making fools of us?
Can't our people arm themselves and from   830
Everywhere in the city swarm to chase them?

Can't they tear loose our ships from the docks and chase them,
And keep them from getting away from us? Bring fire!
Bring weapons! Man the oars! Go after them!—
Where am I? What am I saying? What is it,
That's happening in my head? Wretched Dido,
See what your wickedness has done to you—
It was that moment when you offered the crown
To him, who pledged himself and gave his word,
And carried his household gods into our country,   840
And bore his agèd father on his back.
Could I not then have torn his body into
Pieces and scattered the pieces on the waves?
I could have put them all, all of them, all,
To the sword, and yes, little Ascanius too.
And served him to his father for his dinner.
But who knows who would win the fight with them?
And yet, what matter, what *of* it, what would I have
To be frightened of, already going to die?
I should have torched his camp, I should have filled   850
The decks of his fleeing ships with fire, I should
Have exterminated father and son and all
The whole race of them, I should have thrown myself
On top of them. You Sun, whose fiery brightness
Shines upon all that happens here on earth,
And Juno, mediatrix, you, who witness
All of my trouble, and Hecate, you, whose name
They ululate at the crossroads in the night,
And you, avenging Dirae, and the gods
Of dying Elissa, I pray that all your powers   860
Will listen to hear my prayers, and heed them as
The evils that have happened to me deserve.
If it is fated that that monstrous person
Will get to where he is going and be able
To swim his way to shore—if this is what
Jove has decided and the goal is reached—

Let him be harried in battle by the weapons
Of audacious enemies and driven from
The place where he has settled, let him be wrenched
From Iulus's embrace, call pleadingly for help,   870
And have to watch his guiltless people die.
And when the need for peace has brought him to
Ignominious terms of truce, may he
Not live in the light to take pleasure in his kingdom,
But let him die before his time, and lie
Somewhere unburied on a lonely beach.
This is my prayer. I pour it out with my blood.
O Tyrians therefore with my ashes make
Offerings of your hatred for his people,
Now and forever after. Never must   880
There be love or treaty between our nations, so,
Arise from my bones, whoever it is you are,
To pursue the Dardanians with sword and brand,
When you have gathered strength to do it, now
Or later, whenever it will come to pass—
Shore against shore, sea against sea, arms
Against arms! War on them and their children's children!"

                        ❜ ❜ ❜

This is how she spoke. Her mind was whirling,
Seeking how and how quickly to end the life
That was her enemy. She said to Barce,   890
The childhood nurse of her dead husband Sychaeus
(The nurse who was her own nurse in her childhood
Was ashes now in the country she had left),
"Dear nurse, bring Anna my sister here, and tell her
To sprinkle purifying river water
Upon herself and bring the ritual
Offerings of atonement, and the victims.
Let her come here thus ready, and you yourself

Must bind your forehead with a pious headband.
I have begun the rites of Stygian Jove   900
And now it is my intention to complete them,
To put an end to my cares and give to the flames
This pyre of what there was of that Dardan creature."
She spoke. The nanny hastened away in her
Old woman way to do the errand. But Dido,
Trembling, her wandering eyes bloodshot and rolling,
Her cheeks blotched red with burning blood, and pale
With the pallor of the death she was going to,
In the throes of what was happening, and resolved,
Impelled herself into the inner courtyard   910
And out of her wits climbed high upon the pyre
And drew from its sheath the Dardanian sword that had
Been given to her, but not for this. And when
She saw the bed she knew so well, and saw
The Trojan clothes, weeping she looked at these things
And threw herself down on the bed and said her last words:
"O relics that I loved while fate and the gods
Permitted that to be, O take my soul
Along with you and let me be released now
From my sorrows. I have lived my life. I have   920
Completed the journey that fortune has put me upon,
And now my image will go with dignity
Beneath the earth. I was the builder of
A famous city. My eyes have seen its walls.
I have avenged my husband and I have
Punished my brother for his enmity.
Happy, too greatly happy, if the Dardan
Keels had never touched upon our beaches."
She spoke, and bent to the couch, and kissed it, saying,
"I will die unavenged, but let me die,   930
Thus—thus—it is right that I go into the dark.
And may the eyes of the cruel Dardanian drink
These flames that they will see upon the deep

And may he carry with him ever after
These omens of the death I go to now."

She spoke her last words thus, and as she did,
Her women see her fall upon her sword,
They see the blade of it foaming red with blood.
They see the blood running down upon her hands.
Their screaming rises high in the palace walls,   940
And Rumor rages through the shock-struck city.
The palace shudders with the lamentation,
And the wailing echoes back from the wailing skies
That ululate above, as when the foe
Comes in on falling Tyre or Carthage and
The flames flood over the roofs of men and gods.

Her sister rushes through the shrieking crowd,
Wild with terror and distraction, tearing
Her own face with her frenzied fingernails,
Beating her breast with her fists, and crying out   950
To the dying one, "Was this what you were doing,
Sister? Were you deceiving me? Was this
The reason why you made me build the pyre,
Set up the altars, and prepare the fire?
Lost as I am, what should I first bewail?
Why is it that you scorned to have your sister
Go with you to death? The sword, it should
Have taken us both, the two of us together.
Did my own hand construct this pyre and call
Upon our gods—oh cruel!—so I should be   960
Away from here, while you lie here like this?
You have destroyed us, you and me, and all
The people, and the senate, and the city.
Oh let me wash the wounds she has with water,
Oh let me with my lips catch what of breath
There still may be from hers!" Crying out thus,

She climbed the high steps to the top of the pyre
And weeping cradled her sister's dying body,
And tried to staunch the dark blood with her robe.
And Dido, trying to keep her heavy eyes open,   970
Failed to, again, and the infixed wound in her breast
Made its horrible noise; three times she tried
To raise herself on her elbow and thrice fell back
On the bed; her wandering eyes looked up to find
The light of day, and found it, and she groaned.

All-powerful Juno then, in pity for
Her protracted difficult suffering, sent Iris
Down from Olympus to free her struggling soul
From the body that was keeping her from going
Away from her life. Because she had not perished   980
From happenstance, or fate, nor earned her death
By heroic deeds, but in her misery
And madness died before it was her time,
Persephone had not yet taken the lock
Of golden hair consigning her to Stygian
Orcus, Iris, her saffron dewy wings,
With a thousand shimmering variegated colors
Glimmering as the sun shone brightly through them,
Flew down from heaven, and, hovering over her, said,
"I take this offering, sacred to Dis, as I   990
Have been commanded, and free you from your body."
She cut the lock of hair, and all the warmth
Of her body glided away and Dido's life
Vanished into the winds. . . .

Book Five

Aeneas and his fleet, far out at sea,
Were steady on their way, and the North Wind
Was darkening the waves beneath their going;
And looking back they saw the funeral fires
On Elissa's walls. They could not know
The meaning of the flames, yet in their hearts
There were distressing auguries caused by the thought
Of what a woman is capable of when so
Maddened by her passion's desecration.
As the ships sailed farther on, and there was no longer   10
Any land to be seen, around them only
Sea and only sky, a great black cloud
Gathered above them, and the waves arose,
Blackening more and shuddering beneath them
As they went before the storm. From high on the stern
The pilot Palinurus called out down:
"Why are these storm clouds around us everywhere?
Father Neptune, what are you preparing?"
He tells the crew to tighten the lines and bend
Their bodies over the oars, and fix the sails   20
Athwart the blowing winds, and says to him,
"Great-souled Aeneas, not even if we went
Under the guarantee of Jupiter,
I could not hope to get to Italy
In such a storm as this that's gathering now.
The winds have turned and are coming from the West,

And are roaring across our way. The air is all
One black storm cloud; there's nothing we can do
Against the force of this, and so, since Fortune
Prevails this way upon us, we must submit,   30
And go where she is telling us to go.
If I remember rightly how I read
The stars that led us here before, I think
I can find our way to Sicily and safety,
On the friendly shore where your brother Eryx dwells.
It is not far." Pious Aeneas replied,
"I too have seen what the winds require of us,
And how they frustrate all your skill. Change course.
Could there be any other land I would
Prefer to bring my weary ships for shelter   40
Than this which is the dwelling place of my
Dardanian friend Acestes and which holds
In her embrace the ashes and the bones
Of my father Anchises?" Having said these things,
They turn and seek the port that they desire.
The zephyrs favor them, and they are borne
Swiftly over the waters and, after a time,
They have joyfully returned to the well-known shore.

From a high hilltop Acestes, wondering, sees
The coming into port of these friendly ships,   50
And he hastens down from there, wearing the furs
Of a Libyan she-bear's pelt, and bristling with
The hunting javelins he carries—Acestes,
Son of the river god Crinisus and
A Trojan mother. Mindful of who he is,
He rejoices with his kin on their return,
And, welcoming them, consoles their weariness
With gifts his farms and orchards could supply.

When, early in the morning, day's bright light
Had put the stars to flight, Aeneas gathered   60

All his fellows from all along the shore,
And from the mound of a hill he spoke to them thus:
"Great scions of the race descended from gods,
The months as those go by have reached the number
Completing the year since we put down the ashes,
Here, into the earth, of my father, divine Anchises,
And consecrated here these altars of sorrow.
We are upon the day, if I am not
Mistaken, which, according to your will,
O gods, I'll keep forever as the day   70
Of honor and the rituals of grieving.
Wherever I was, whether it was among
Syrtian sandshoals in Gaetulia or
Adrift in Argive seas, or captive in
Mycenae's town, I would fulfill my vows
Annually in solemn memorial,
And place due offerings on the holy altars.
Now, carried here into this welcoming port,
We stand in the very place where my father Anchises'
Ashes and his bones lie in their tomb   80
—And this, I think, is not without the gods'
Intention and design. So let us all
Together celebrate the joyful rites,
And pray for favoring winds, and pray that he
Vouchsafe that when my city has been founded,
We'll celebrate the sacrifice each year
In temples we will dedicate to his name.
Acestes, who is of our Trojan blood,
For every ship will give a pair of oxen,
And you must bring to the feast your own Penates   90
And those our host Acestes venerates.
After nine days have passed, if Aurora's light
Spreads for mortals across the waking world,
I will command that there be festive contests,
Trojans competing with Trojans: first, the swift ships,
Footraces then for those who are best at running,

Then he who glories in his strength to show
His skill in the flight of javelin and arrow,
And he who dares to challenge in the fight,
With lead-wrapped rawhide gloves—let those
Who seek to win the victor's prize step forth.
Be silent now, and wreathe your brows with leaves."
Having said this he placed upon his head
A wreath of myrtle sacred to his mother.
So Helymus did also, and after him
Mature Acestes, and then Ascanius,
The boy, and after him, the other youths,
Following suit. And then Aeneas went,
Accompanied by many thousand people,
An enormous crowd of which he was the center,
From the place where they had gathered, to the tomb,
And there, according to the ritual, he poured
Two cups of unadulterated wine,
Two cups of milk, freshly obtained, two cups
Of the blood of victims sacrificed at the altars;
And he scattered flowers upon the ground, and said,

"Hail once again, my sacred father, hail,
You ashes and you spirit and you shade
Of my father who was carried here in vain!
It could not be that I could go with thee
To the foretold fields of Italy or,
Whatever they are, Ausonia and the Tiber."

These words he spoke, and as he finished speaking,
From under the shrine a serpent slithered out,
His long body coiling sevenfold behind him,
Coil after coil as placidly he flowed
Among the altars and circled about the mound,
His beautiful back spotted with blue, and his scales
On fire with blazing gold, their rainbow colors
Shimmering in the sunlight's implications.

Aeneas was astonished by what he saw.
The serpent, then, flowed on among the cups
And the bowls, and tasted a little from all that was offered,
And after that, it glided, harmlessly,
Back down below the shrine, from where it had come.
Aeneas, not knowing whether this had been
The genius of the place or if it was
His father's attendant spirit, begins again
The filial ritual of commemoration.
As was appropriate, he slays two sheep,   140
And after that two swine, and after that,
Two black-backed heifers; he pours out wine
And calls upon the shade of great Anchises,
Set free from Acheron. His fellows, then,
Bring gifts to offer from what they have to give,
And place them on the altars, and slay the steers;
Others bring out the cooking pots on the beach,
And light the fires with coals, and roast the meat.

The ninth, the long-awaited day, had come,
And Phaëthon's horses carried Aurora up   150
Into the cloudless light of the morning sky.
The name and illustrious fame of Acestes excite
The people who gather in crowds along the beaches;
Some of them were there only to see
The Aeneadae, and some were there to contend,
Themselves, in the games. The prizes that are to be won
Are spread out to be seen upon the field:
Sacred tripods, green wreaths, and branches of palm,
Purple regalia, arms, gold and silver talents.
From a central mound the trumpet loudly sounding   160
Signals that the games are about to begin.
Four ships, four equals chosen best of their class,
Four heavyweights in oarage and in bulk:
Fast Pristis, Sea Dragon, Mnestheus in command,
Who would become Italian Mnestheus,

Patriarch of the people called the Memmians;
Then the enormous trireme, the Chimaera,
As big as a city, three tiers of rowers, three
Ranks of young Dardanians with their oars
Impelling her through the water, Gyas the captain;   170
Next came the giant Centaur of Sergestus,
He from whom the Sergestia take their name;
And finally in his sky-blue Scylla came
Cloanthus, from whom the Roman Cluenti descend.

There is a rock, far out in the waters, but still
In sight of the foaming beaches, that when the Northwest
Winds are hiding the stars, the surging waves,
Upswelling, break themselves over, and it's submerged;
But it rises up when the sea is calm and silent,
And its surface is a welcome level place   180
For gulls, who love the sun, to be upon.
Upon this rock Aeneas with ilex branches
Has marked out a goal, where the ships must make their turn,
And then come back on the other side of the course.
They choose by lot the placement at the starting,
And the captains, clad in shining purple and gold,
Mount high upon the stern decks of their ships;
The heads of the youths at the oars are garlanded
With wreaths of poplar; their naked shoulders shine
With glistening oil. Side by side at the thwarts,   190
Arms stretched out at the oars, ready and waiting,
Listening for the signal, their hearts are pounding,
Thrilled and fearful in their desire for glory.
Then when the loud sound of the trumpet came,
Off they went from the starting; the shouting of
The sailors rose to the skies; as the rowers' arms
Move forward and then back, forward and back,
The waters foam, the ships abreast break through
And across the furrows of the waves before them,
And the waters open wide in convulsion caused   200

By the oars and by the plunging beaks of the ships.
The rush of the two-horse chariots as they burst
Out of their stalls and race across the fields
Is nothing to this, the sight of the charioteer
Wildly shaking the reins and bending to lash
The horses' backs is nothing so wild as this.
The forest rings with the sound of applause and the cries
Of the crowd as they urge their favorites on, and the beaches
Around resound and the cliffs shout back the noise.

In all the din and uproar Gyas goes   210
Gliding ahead of all the others, and
After him in hot pursuit Cloanthus,
Whose big ship has more rowers, and so, more power,
But his bulky bigness also inhibits his speed.
Following after these two, Dragon and Centaur,
Equidistant behind, competing for
The lead, one over the other one, so first
The Dragon has it, then the huge Centaur has it,
And then the two go racing along together,
Side by side and neck and neck their prows,   220
Plowing like twins the salt flood with their keels.
And now they all were getting near the rock
Where the turning is, when Gyas, who still was first
At the halfway point, shouted out to his helmsman,
"Menoetes, why are we so far to the right?
Change course, this way, this way, get closer to
The rocks, and let our oar blades touch them as
We get ourselves just by them on the left.
Let the others play it safe!" But Menoetes feared
The hidden rocks, and so he turned the prow   230
Still farther rightward toward the deeper water,
So Gyas shouted again, "Why so far off?
Menoetes, head for the rocks!" and, saying that,
He saw Cloanthus close to him and heading
Closer in to the rocks than where he was.

Cloanthus steers between Gyas's ship and them,
And just scrapes past, and passes the leader, leaving
The rocks behind him as he gets away,
Safe and sound and free and ahead of them all.
Then Gyas's shame and fury burns through to his bones;   240
Tears well up in his eyes, and forgetting all
About the decorum of ships and the rules of safety,
He pitches his sluggish pilot Menoetes right off
The high stern deck of his ship, down into the sea,
And takes the helm, both pilot and captain, he,
And exhorts his crew, and turns the tiller toward home.
But then when old Menoetes rises up
From the bottom of the sea and slowly gets
His heavy soaking weight up onto the rock,
Dripping wet in body and in clothes,   250
And sits him down where the rock is flat and dry,
The Trojans all laugh at the sight of him falling in,
And frantically splashing out, and climbing up,
And sitting there, regurgitating salt water.

The hope of being able to get past Gyas,
Slowed down as now he was, rose up in the hearts
Of Mnestheus and Sergestus, the two behind.
Sergestus seizes the lead and heads toward the rocks,
Ahead, but not by a whole boat's length ahead;
The prow of the Dragon is there along his side,   260
And, moving back and forth amid his crew,
Mnestheus urges them on: "Rise to the oars,
O you who fought with Hector, you, who when
Our Troy was falling I chose to bring with me
As my companions. Show that courage and strength
You showed among the quicksands of Gaetulia,
And upon the Ionian Sea, and in the surf
At Cape Malae. I do not any longer
Seek to be first—Neptune, let them conquer,
Those to whom you've granted victory—   270

But help us be spared the shame of being last.
My comrades, let us keep the place we have
And save us from disgrace." His men, inspired
To do their utmost in the struggle, bend to the oars.
With their powerful strokes the brazen Dragon trembles;
The ocean floor slides backward underneath them;
Their bodies shake with their gasping shuddering breathing;
The sweat streams down their limbs. But it was chance
That brought the glory that they desired to them.
Headstrong Sergestus drives his prow headlong   280
In near the rocks, and suddenly collides
Upon an up-jutting spur; the rock cries out,
His oars are shattered, the bow of the ship hangs pent.
The sailors shout, dismayed at being so balked,
Pick up whatever they can, sharp-ended poles
And iron pikes, and their broken oars fished out
Of the swirling water. Mnestheus was overjoyed
By what had happened to the others and
With skillful oars and praying to the winds
Heads round them, and on the smoothly flowing waters   290
Glides down toward home upon the open sea.
It is as when a dove, whom something has startled,
Flies up and away from where her nest and children
Are hidden in some secret place in the cliff,
And off and over the fields, making a loud
Noise flapping, but after a while she sails upon
The quiet air on still unmoving wings,
Just so Mnestheus, just so the Dragon, with
Unlaboring sails is free on the final stretch,
And speeds along by her own self's speed itself.   300
Sergestus, left behind, is high on the rocks,
And stranded in the shallow water around him,
Crying for help and trying to learn to make
His broken oars compete again. And then,
Mnestheus catches up to Gyas's huge
Chimaera, which, with a helmsman lost, must cede

The race to him. Now, almost at the goal,
Cloanthus was the only one still ahead.
Mnestheus heads for getting close to him,
Trying as best he can. The shouting rises, 310
Everyone rooting for his favorite;
The noise is fracturing the sky. They know
That at this moment they'd give their lives to win
The glory that they think belongs to them.
The better they do the stronger it is they feel;
Their strength is in the strength they know they have.
And maybe they would have won, for now the prows
Are side by side, if Cloanthus had not stretched
His hands up to the gods of the sea, beseeching:
"You gods whose kingdom is the sea my ship 320
Is coursing over, I will joyfully slay
In gratitude at your altars a snow-white bull
And fling its offered entrails into the flood,
And pour out offered wine into it too!"
He spoke, and under the waves the Nereids heard,
And Phorcus too, and the sea nymph Panopea,
Portunus too, the father, god of ports,
Heard and with his huge hand took the ship
And impelled it swifter than the wind or an arrow,
And sent it welcome home into the harbor. 330

Then by Anchises' son's command they all
Were assembled together and the herald loudly
Sounded the note declaring Cloanthus was
The victor, and the green laurel wreath was placed upon
His triumphal head. Each ship was given wine,
A talent of silver and three bullocks and
The captains of the ships were each given gifts
According to their placement. The victor was given
A military cloak with gold enlaced;
Inwoven roundabout in a double meandering 340
Line of Meliboean purple was

The story of the eager royal boy,
On foot pursuing on leafy Ida the tiring
Stags in flight from him, and the weapon-bearing
Eagle of Zeus catching the boy in his talons
And carrying him away, and, stretching up
To the stars the palms of their hands imploring,
His aged guardians, and the sound of the dogs'
Surprised savage barking rising up.
He gave to the one who won the second place   350
A breastplate, coat of mail, with triple golden
Hooks, the armor that he himself had stripped
From the body of Demoleos whom he had beaten
Upon the banks of the fast-flowing river Simois,
Under the walls of Troy. Such was this breastplate,
The servants Sagaris and Phegeus together could hardly
Carry the weight of it on their straining shoulders,
But it was wearing this breastplate that Demoleos
Freely running pursued the scattered Trojans.
The third prize was a pair of great brass cauldrons   360
And goblets made of heavy silver, graven
With rough designs.

        Now all who had won their prizes
And had been given their gifts, were leaving, proud
Of what they had done and the gifts that they had earned,
When Sergestus came in, in his laughed-at unglorious ship,
Free at last of the cruel rocks that held it,
Having lost its oars and a row of the rowers' seats.
It's as when a snake, run over in the road
By a wagon wheel, or left half-dead by the blow   370
Of a heavy rock some passerby had thrown,
Trying to get its mangled body away,
Wriggling in its desperation, part
Of it blazing eyes, and hissing neck upraised,
Defiant, the part where the stone had struck
Holding it back, struggling in its coils,

Getting itself all tangled in itself—
Laboring in like this with such maimed oarage
The ship moves very slowly but somehow
It's under sail and gets itself into   380
The port at last. Aeneas, happy at least
That the ship is saved and the crew brought back alive,
Awards a prize to Sergestus, as had been promised,
A woman-slave whose name was Pholoë,
A Cretan. She is good at Minerva's work,
And she has two infants at the breast, twin boys.

This contest over, Aeneas then proceeded
To a place encircled all around by many
Wooded hills, and then, below the hills,
Deep in the valley that the hills surround,   390
A theater for the running of the race.
Here, on a seat raised high, Aeneas sat,
Many thousands around him, and thus he spoke,
Welcoming all who wished to compete in the footrace,
And telling them what the rewards and prizes would be.
Sicilian and Trojan youths together came
From all sides, eager for the contest. First,
The famously beautiful youth, Euryalus,
And Nisus with him, he who loved him so;
Diores next, a prince of the family   400
Of Priam himself; Salius and Patron next,
Salius an Acarnian, Patron born
In Tegea in Arcadia; then two
Sicilians, Panopes and Helymus,
Acestes' men; and many others, whose names
Have now been lost in time's obscurity.
Aeneas said, surrounded by them all,
"Listen, and be gladdened. Not one of you
Will leave without a gift. I'll give
Each one of you two arrows, polished steel,   410
Made at Cnossus, and a battle-axe,

Two-edged, inscribed with gleaming silver casing.
Each of you who runs will be given these,
And there will be prizes for the first three winners,
And pale-green olive wreathes to crown their heads.
The first will be rewarded with the gift
Of a horse with a beautiful medallioned harness;
The second an Amazonian quiver filled
With Thracian arrows, and, for carrying
The quiver, there's a wide gold shoulder belt   420
With a buckle studded with gemstones; and the third
Will be awarded the gift of this Argive helmet."

When he had finished speaking, all took their places,
And then, when the signal sounded, all burst forth
Like a storm cloud driven before a storm wind, all
Intent upon the goal. The first is Nisus,
By far ahead of all the others, faster
Than the wind or than a bolt of lightning is;
Salius next, though at a distance behind;
Euryalus is third, some space between them;   430
After him Helymus, and on his heels,
And pressing upon his shoulder—and if they weren't
So near the goal, maybe he'll pass him or maybe
Be neck and neck. And now, as gasping and panting,
They're almost, almost there, almost at the goal,
Unlucky Nisus falls down flat on the ground
Soaked and slippery with the blood of steers
That had been sacrificed before the games.
Here, just as he was joyfully about
To win the prize, he could not keep his feet.   440
He staggered and slipped and fell right down in the dung
And the sacrificial blood. Nevertheless,
He didn't forget his love for Euryalus.
As he got himself up he threw himself down again
In front of Salius, who doubled up
And fell down in the muck. Euryalus,

Thanks to what his lover did, raced past,
And came in first, as the people yelled and cheered.
Helymus now is second, Diores third.
Then Salius, outraged, standing in front of the seats   450
Where the elders are, fills the whole theater with
His loud protesting voice, as he cries out
That trickery had deprived him of the prize.
Euryalus is favored by the crowd,
Because, although with tears in his eyes, his manly
Bearing pleases all of them, and all
The more because he is so beautiful;
And Diores cries out loudly in his support,
For he himself had won third prize, but he
Would lose his place if Salius were restored.   460
Then faithful Aeneas said to them: "Young men,
No one will change the order of the prizes.
What you have won are yours. It is for me
To recompense a friend for what mischance
Befell him without his fault." Having said this,
Salius is given the shaggy golden-clawed
Magnificent pelt of a Gaetulian lion.
Then Nisus said to Aeneas: "If you have shown
Such pity for mischance and this is what
The defeated one receives, then what do I   470
Deserve who would have had first prize had I
Not been unlucky, just as Salius was?"
And he shows himself to him, his face and limbs
Covered with filth and blood. The kindly father
Smiles at him and orders that a great
Shield made by Didymaon, that the Greeks pulled down
From Neptune's temple's doorway, be brought forth
And be awarded to the deserving youth.

The races now being over and the prizes
Having been given out, Aeneas says,   480
"Let him who's brave enough for the fight lift up

His arms and hidebound hands to show that he's ready."
Then he displays two prizes: for him who wins,
A steer whose head is wreathed with golden ribbons
And sacerdotal fillets; for him who loses,
A sword and a noble helmet to assuage him.

Huge Dares at once arises and in his strength
Comes forward through the murmuring of the crowd,
And displays himself, who was the only contender
With Paris in the boxing rink, and who   490
In enormous power walked toward Butes once,
Champion of Amycus' Bebrycian race,
And struck him down so that he, dying, lay
On the yellow sand near mighty Hector's tomb.
This is that Dares, he who stands, head high,
And showing off how broad his shoulders are,
And ready for the fight, left arm and right arm
Punching, counterpunching, battering
The empty air with terrifying blows.
But not a single challenger in that   500
Great crowd came forward; there was nobody there
Who dared put on the gloves and go against him.
So he, triumphant, sure that the prize was yielded,
Defaulted to him, stood at Aeneas's feet,
And with his left hand taking the bull by the horn,
Said, "Goddess-born, how long must I stand here?
No one has challenged me. So let me lead
The prize that I have won away with me."
All the Danaans roared out their approval,
Shouting as one that he be given the prize.   510

Acestes spoke in a stern rebuking voice
To Entellus, who was sitting next to him,
In the grass beside his seat, "Entellus, you
Were once the bravest of our heroes, now
No longer so. Are you content to sit there

And let such gifts be taken, without a fight?
What has become of the glory of your master,
Godlike Eryx, where has it gone to? Where
Is your fame throughout Trinacria, and
The prizes hanging from your house's rafters?"   520
Entellus replied: "It is not cowardice.
It isn't that I've lost my love of glory.
It's that the blood in my body has been made sluggish,
Chilled and dulled by age; my body's strength
Is dissipated. If I still had what he,
That boaster there, is glorying in, if I
Still had my youth, it wouldn't be for steers
Or other some such prizes that I'd fight.
It's not for such things that I ever did it."
Having said this, he threw into the center   530
A pair of enormous heavy boxing gloves,
The ones brave Eryx used to wear in the matches,
Binding his hands and arms with the leather of seven
Oxhides heavier still with deadly slugs
Of iron and lead sewn in. The crowd was amazed,
And Dares, stupefied by what he saw,
Drew back, as if recusing himself from the fight,
And Anchises' son, wondering at the gauntlets,
Turned them over and over in his hands.
Entellus spoke directly from his heart: 540
"What if any of you had seen the gloves
That Hercules had worn that fatal day
In that fight that took place here in this very place,
On this shore beside the sea? These are the gloves
Your brother Eryx wore; see them, brain-spattered,
Blood-stained, see. He wore these when he fought
Against Alcides. And when my blood was richer
And I was stronger, before the rivalrous years
Had snowed upon my head, these were the gloves
I wore in my fights. But if this Trojan, Dares,   550
Has backed away because of them, and if

Aeneas, the judge, and Acestes, my patron, give
Their approval to this, let all the odds be even.
I will abjure the boxing gloves of Eryx.
Free yourself from your fears, and you yourself
Strip off your Trojan gloves." Having said this,
He throws off his double mantle from his shoulders,
And bares himself to show his mighty body,
Great arms and thighs, and stands gigantic in
The middle of the arena to be seen.   560

Then father Aeneas, Anchises' son, brought out
Two pairs of boxing gloves that weighed the same
And bound their hands so they were armed the same;
Each stood, undaunted, raising up undaunted
Challenging hands to the sky, heads high and back.
And fist against fist, the fight begins, the younger
Quicker, more agile, cleverer on his feet,
The other massive in his powerful bulk,
Yet moving slowly on unsteady legs,
Knees wobbling, and his huge frame painfully   570
Gasping and shaking. Many blows get missed,
But many don't. The sound of body blows
Rings out, the pounding on chests and bellies and sides;
The hands are jabbing at ears and brows and jaws,
Punching and feinting, parrying, counterpunching,
Uppercutting, hooks. Entellus stands still,
Watchful, fending off blows with his great solid
Body's defenses, blocking, warding, and it's
As if the other man is attacking some fortress
High in the mountains, artfully skillfully trying,   580
This way, that way, every which way he can,
And yet not getting in through the castle defenses.
And then it is that Entellus's body somehow
Seems to become still bigger and taller and larger.
He raises up his giant arm, and the other
Sees that the blow is coming down upon him,

Quickly slips out from under and is away.
Entellus's strength goes out from beneath him as
His blow falls only on the air and his
Enormous weight and power falls heavily down.   590
It is as when a great hollow pine tree falls
Uprooted on Mount Ida or Erymanthus.
The Teucrians and Trinacrian youth rise up,
Wildly excited; the din of their excitement
Goes up to the heavens; Acestes in great concern
For his old friend runs to him but Entellus,
Unhindered and unfrightened by his fall,
Empowered and inflamed by rage and shame,
And consciousness of his manhood, gets up and drives
Dares headlong under his blows, redoubled   600
And redoubled, now right, now left, across
The whole arena, no stopping him—as when
The hail from a great hailstorm pounds down upon
The roofs of a city, such are the crowds of blows
Which he hailstorms battering down on Dares's head.

Then father Aeneas, unwilling to let this rage
And Entellus's brutal fury go on any longer,
Spoke gently to Dares, in order to save his life,
"Unlucky man, why should this madness continue?
Do you not know that the gods have turned against you?   610
The power is elsewhere. You must accede to the gods."
Thus he ended the fight. The faithful companions
Of Dares were bearing him off to the ships, his legs
Dragging behind him, head swaying and spewing
Vomited blood and broken teeth from his mouth.

Then they were called back to receive the sword and the helmet,
Leaving the palm and the steer to the victor Entellus.
He, glorying in the victory and the prize,
Cried out, "O goddess-born and O you Trojans,
See what strength I had when I was young.   620

And witness the death you rescued Dares from!"
He turned to the steer that was standing waiting there,
And raised his mighty gauntleted arm and with
A single blow between the horns broke into
Its skull and shattered its brains; the steer, its lifeless
Body quivering still, lay stretched on the ground.
He stood above it and poured out from his heart
These words: "Eryx, in place of Dares's death
I offer this better life, and in victory here
I now give up this gauntlet and my art."   630

Right away after this, Aeneas invites
Anyone who might want to contend for the prize
In the contest of swiftly flying arrows to do so,
Declaring what the winners' prizes will be.
With his powerful hand he raises up the pole
That was, in the ship race, the mast of Sergestus's vessel,
And suspends, tied there by her feet, a fluttering dove,
High up on the mast to be the arrows' target.
The contenders come together, their lots are thrown
Into a brazen helmet, from which to be drawn.   640
The first lot goes, to enthusiastic applause,
To Hippocoön, Hyrtacus' son; the next
Is Mnestheus, wearing an olive wreath,
He who had just now won in the race of the ships;
Eurytion's lot was third, the brother of
The celebrated Pandarus, he whose arrow
Broke the truce between the Greeks and Trojans,
And thus began the war; and finally, from
The bottom of the helmet basin was drawn
The lot of Acestes, testing himself to see   650
What his elder hand could do against these youths.
Then all of them, with all their strength and skill,
Draw back their curving bows and from their quivers
Bring forth their arrows, and first Hyrtacus' son's
Arrow flew off from the strident twanging string

And through the air to the target mast and struck it,
And hung in place in the wood of the shaking pole;
The terrified dove wings fluttered and flapped; the place
Was filled with the sound of the crowd's applauding hands.
Then brave Mnestheus, bow bent and aiming   660
Skyward, eyesight and arrow together fixed
Upon the target, fired the arrow, and hit,
But not the bird herself, cutting the cords
By which her feet were tied, and free away
She flew off toward the black clouds to the South.
Immediately Eurytion, his bow
Already tense and ready, his arrow drawn,
And calling on his brother with his vows,
Sighted the dove as clapping her wings she flew
Exultantly below the dark South clouds,   670
And hit her; she fell down dead upon the waters,
Leaving her life up there among the stars,
And bringing down in her body as she fell
The arrow that killed her. Acestes now was left,
And the prize was gone, but he, aiming his bow,
Drew the string taut, and fired his arrow off,
And showed them all what skill the veteran has,
And what the sound was of his sonorous bow.
Then there was suddenly shown to their wondering eyes
A mighty portent, that after many years   680
The seers would read and tell the meaning of,
As auguries of great events to come.
For as it flew off through the cloudy mists, the arrow
Burst into flames and as it went it flamed
Away into nothing, vanishing among
The winds, as sometimes shooting stars fly free
On their disappearing way across the skies,
With streaming hair behind them as they go.
The Trojans and Trinacrians stood, amazed,
Transfixed, saying their prayers to the gods. Nor did   690
Aeneas fail to respond to the wonderful sign.

He turned to joyful Acestes, embraced him and said,
"Acestes, father, take these gifts, for the mighty
King of Olympus has shown us that though the prize
Was lost these honors are deserved by you.
Here is a gift of what belonged to aged
Anchises himself, a figured bowl that Thracian
Cisseus once gave to him as a pledge of his
Fidelity and love." Having said this, he binds
The temples of Acestes with a wreath   700
Of green laurel to show he was first above
All others in the contest; Eurytion
Was not aggrieved, though it was he who brought
The bird down falling from the skies. And he,
Whose arrow cut the hampering cord, was next.

But father Aeneas, even before the contest
Of archery was done, summoned the faithful
Epytides, who was guardian of his son,
And said to him, "Go tell my son, if he
And the other boys have practiced their horsemanship,   710
And are ready to show what they can do in arms,
To bring them out, in honor of his grandsire."
He tells the huge crowd there to move to the sides
Of the field and leave it clear. In glittering
Parade the boys appear, and on their bridled
Horses pass before their fathers and
The murmuring throng of Trinacrians and Trojans.

Each of the boys is carrying two spears,
Fashioned from cornel wood and tipped with iron;
Some of them on their backs wear shining quivers;   720
According to custom, each boy's hair is trimmed,
And crowned with a garland; each of them wears a chain
Of stranded twisted gold around his neck.
They comprise three troops of horses, and riding in front
Of each of the troops, capering to and fro,

There's a young captain before them, being their leader;
Twelve boys behind each captain, and beside
Each troop as it passes by the admiring crowd
In orderly elation, its trainer rides.
Of the three young joyful captains capering by,   730
One is little Priam, whose name brings back
Into the world the famous name of his grandsire—
Polites, he is your illustrious seed,
By whom the Italian race will grow. The Thracian
Horse he rides is dappled with patches of white,
White pasterns flashing as it steps along;
Its brow white too, noble, and high. The second
Captain is little Atys whom Iulus loves
With boyish love. From his descent will come
The Atii in Italy. Then, third,   740
Most beautiful of all, Iulus rides,
Upon a Sidonian horse that Dido gave,
To show her faithful love. The other boys
Ride on Sicilian steeds from Acestes' stables.
The Dardanians cheer the nervous little boys
As they come riding in, and they delight
In seeing in their faces the faces of
Their fathers who were lost when Troy fell down.
After they had joyfully ridden past
The whole assembly and their kin, they halted,   750
Waiting, until Epytides cracked his whip
And shouted out the signal to begin.
At this the troops, all together in perfect order,
Galloped down to the end of the arena,
There, turning left and right, divided in two,
And galloped back along the sides, and when
The order was given, turned and faced each other,
Each column charging the other with menacing spears.
Next in the lists they move this way, then that
Alternative way, weaving in circles around,   760
Encircling, circling round, mimicking war,

Now laying bare their backs as if in flight,
Now pointing their spears as in attack, now riding
Together as in a congenial making of peace.
It is as when, high up in Crete, there was
The Labyrinth maze, blind walls in the dark, in which
By bewildering art the signs of how to go
Were broken and obscured before you as
You went there; thus the little sons of Troy
Entangled how they went this way, then that,   770
In a game of playing flight and playing battle,
Like dolphins sporting in the Carpathian or
The Libyan waters, gamboling in the waves.
Thus it was that Ascanius, grown, who built
The walls of Alba Longa, taught the early
Latins to celebrate these martial rites
Of horsemanship, as in his childhood he
Had done along with his fellow Trojan boys.
The Albans taught these games to their own children;
From them the mighty Romans learned them, and   780
Today across the years they play the game,
Ludus Troiae, to honor the sacred sire.

Then Fortune turned her face another way.
While the dedicated games were going on,
Near Anchises' tomb, Juno, Saturn's daughter,
Thinking many things, not having relinquished
Her ancient grievances, sent Iris down
On breezes she breathed to waft her through the skies
And to the fleet below. Iris goes running
Down along the many-colored rainbow,   790
Nobody seeing who this maiden is.
She sees the people watching the solemn games;
She looks upon the fleet, and upon the shore,
And sees the harbor empty, and the ships
Devoid of crew. But at a distance, on
The deserted beach there stood the Trojan women,

Weeping as they gazed at the boundless sea,
And weeping because of Anchises' death. They cried out,
All in one voice, "Alas! What waters there are,
And what empty seas for those who are so weary." 800
They pray for a city, a dwelling in which to be.
The effort of all of this is too much to bear.
Then Iris, knowing how mischief can be done,
And becoming Beroe, the aged wife
Of Doryclus of Tmarus, she who once
Had had a family, a home, and children,
Interposes herself among the mothers,
Putting aside the clothing of a goddess:
"O miserable women, whom the Achaeans
Did not crush to death beneath our walls, 810
Unhappy people, what will become of us?
The seventh summer is passing now since Troy's
Destruction, and we have been pursuing something
That flies away before us as through foaming
Seas and dangerous rocks and unwelcoming stars,
And from land after land we've measured out our journey,
Tossed on the deep. This is the country of
Our brother Eryx; this is the land of Acestes,
And he has shown us hospitality.
What is to keep us from raising up walls, and building 820
A city here, to give to our people to live in?
O our country, our Penates, O!
We're carried away from the hands of the foe for nothing!
Will there never be a city again called Troy?
Will I never see again a Simois or Xanthus,
The rivers of our Hector? Come, let us burn
These unlucky ships! The image of Cassandra,
The prophetess, has come to me in my sleep
And held out fiery brands to me, and said,
'Here is the Troy you seek; here is your home.' 830
Now is the time to act. These omens say
The time to do it is now. Behold, four altars

To Neptune are here at hand—the god himself
Is offering us the flames to do it with,
And the courage and the will with which to do it."

And saying this, she was the first to take
Hold of a blazing torch from an altar fire
And raised it high, and brandished it, and then
She hurled it. The Trojan women stand, astonished,
Stupefied; they don't know what to think.   840
Then Pyrgo, eldest of the women, spoke
Out from the crowd, she who had been the nurse
Of Priam's royal sons: "This isn't, mothers,
Beroe, Doryclus's wife, this isn't she!
See how divinely beautiful she is;
See how she looks when she walks, how graceful she is;
Witness the brightness of her fiery eyes.
Beroe's back there, I saw her myself just now;
She was ill, and unable to be here paying Anchises
The honor that she wished to pay to him."   850
But the women stood there, looking across at the ships.
And torn between their love of where they were,
And the promised kingdom ever calling beyond,
When, suddenly, the goddess herself rose up
On her soaring wings and cleaved the huge rainbow in
The sky above beneath the covering clouds.
Amazed at this marvelous sight and aroused to frenzy
By what they saw and by their own confusion,
The women cried a loud cry. Some of them seized
And snatched up brands of the altar fires, and others   860
Stripped the altars bare, and others fed the fires
With leaves and twigs and branches, and Vulcan caroused
Among the painted hulls and oars and the wooden
Benches that the rowers sit to row in.

Eumelus brings the word to those in the seats
At the theater and by Anchises' tomb,

Of how the ships were on fire; and they themselves
Could see the black ash floating upward in
A cloud of smoke, and Ascanius, who had been
Joyfully leading his equestrian troop   870
Of boys in the gallant show, was the first—his breathless
Trainers chasing after him—to spur his horse
And gallop to where the conflagration was,
And crying out to the women as he got there,
"What is this madness? What are you doing,
My poor sad countrywomen? This
Isn't the camp of the Argive foe. This is
Your future. I am your own Ascanius."
And he cast down on the ground before him the empty
Helmet he had been wearing in the game   880
Of simulated war. Aeneas and his Trojan
Followers had rushed there too. But the women
Scattered and ran away from the shore, and hid
Wherever they could find, in woods or caves,
A hiding place to hide in from the light,
Hating what it was that they had done,
Once again knowing who their people were,
And shaking Juno from their hearts. But this
Did not prevent the flames from burning on
Indomitably. Beneath the wet oak of   890
The beams and planks the tow was smoldering
Alive and vomiting smoke; the heat was slowly
Eating at the bottoms of the ships,
A plague that was making its way all through, and nothing
The heroes' strength or the water they frantically poured
Could do any good. Then pious Aeneas tore
The shirt from his shoulders and lifted up his arms,
Invoking the gods: "Almighty Jupiter,
If you do not yet utterly detest
Every last Trojan that there is on earth,   900
If still you have your ancient pity for us

And for our troubles, save us Trojans from
The ruin of our last hopes, oh save our ships!
Or if I deserve it, may the thunderbolt
From your right hand bring down to final destruction
All that is left." He has hardly finished when
Thunder suddenly shakes the hills and fields,
And a dark storm pours its flooding showers down,
The blackest South Wind tempest filling the ships
With rain, extinguishing the smoke and fire,   910
And all but four of the Trojan ships are saved.

But father Aeneas was shocked by what had happened,
And his mind was confused, this way, then that, between
Contending thoughts of what he ought to do,
Whether to stay in the fields of Sicily,
Forgetting what the oracles foretold,
Or strive to find his way to Italy.
Nautes the sage, then, who was renowned for knowing
The way to summon Tritonian Pallas so
That she would answer, telling him what the wrath   920
Of the gods portended, or what was fated, what
Its course would be, spoke these words in order
To steady Aeneas and encourage him:

"Let us follow, goddess-born, wherever the Fates
In their spinning draw us on to go; whatever
It is that happens, we must endure and survive.
Trojan Acestes is here, born of a god;
Let him join with you; ally him in your counsels;
Trust him to shelter those whose ships were burned,
And so are left without one; and shelter those   930
Grown weary of your venture and its fortunes,
The old men who've already lived their lives,
And the women who are so tired, and hate the sea,
And all the others who wish to shun the dangers

That lie ahead, and let them have their city.
If so permitted, let it be called Acesta."

Aeneas's heart was excited by what was said
By the ancient sage, but his soul was still divided
By all its cares. And when black Night was carried
Up into the sky in her chariot, and all   940
The world was dark, the image of Anchises
Suddenly seemed to glide down from the heavens,
And spoke to him:

              "My son, more dear to me
Than life when I was living, you, my son,
So burdened by the fate of Ilium,
Jove, who from on high had pity on you
And drove the flames away from your burning ships,
Has sent me here to tell you, follow the wise
Counseling old Nautes gives to you.   950
You must take with you the bravest of your youths.
In Latium there are those, formidable tough,
Fighters raised to be so in their tribes.
With these you must contend, and you must win.
But first you must descend through Avernus to
The halls of Dis below, and seek me there,
My son. I am not held among the gloomy
Shades of impious Tartarus; the place
I dwell in is Elysium, in the company of the blessed.
The chaste Sybil will lead you there, induced   960
To do so by the copious blood of black
Sheep shed in sacrifice. There you will learn
The story of your people and of the city
That will be built by them. And now farewell.
Now dewy Night has reached her halfway course,
And she has turned her chariot back again;
I feel the panting breath upon me of
The horses of the rising East." And thus,

He finished saying what he said and vanished
Like smoke into the air.   970

                    "Where are you going?"
Aeneas cried. "Where are you hastening to?
Who is it you are fleeing from? What keeps us
From embracing?"

                    Saying these things, he stirs
The embers of the fire, and venerates,
With perfumed censer and with holy meal,
The Lar of Troy and ancient Vesta's shrine.

And then Aeneas summons his comrades together,
Acestes first, and tells them what it is   980
That Jupiter has commanded and what his dear
Father has told him to do, and how he is now
Himself determined and entirely resolved.
His fellows, and Acestes, are in accord,
The women are made welcome to the town,
And so are those who do not feel the need
For glory, and who wish to be set ashore.
This leaves a band of heroes that is small
But vitally alive for war and glory.

They make new benches for the rowers' seats,   990
And install new beams for those the fire has charred,
And refit the ships with new riggings and new oars.
Aeneas marks out with a plow the town's design,
Showing where the houses will be built,
And where the fields will be. The town he builds
Is called by the name of Ilium, and the fields
Surrounding the houses are called the Troad.
Trojan Acestes who is overjoyed
With his new realm to govern, establishes
A court of law and a constitutioned senate.   1000

High up near the stars on the Hill of Eryx,
They found a shrine to Venus Idalia, and
Around the tomb of Anchises, they plant a sacred
Grove of trees, with an attendant priest.
And then for nine days there is feasting and
Offerings at the altars to the gods.
The winds are gentle and the seas are quiet,
And all the while the breath of the South Wind calls,
Urging them to come back to the deep; and yet
They linger still a night and a day beyond.   1010

But after that, along the shore there's wailing,
As at the parting time they all embrace.
Now those, the mothers and those others who
Had found the sea intolerably cruel,
Are ready to venture out again and share
The peril and the exile, but kind Aeneas
Says consolatory things to them, and weeping
Commends them to the care of his kin, Acestes,
Commanding that three steers be offered to Eryx
And a lamb be sacrificed to the Tempestates.   1020
And then, his brow enwreathed with olive leaves,
He stands apart from all the others, on
The prow of his ship, and flings the offered entrails
Into the sea and pours the votive wine
Upon the waters. A rising breeze behind them
Follows the fleet as on its way it departs,
His rowers contending with their strokes as they
Lash the waves and sweep along out of the harbor.

⸢ ⸢ ⸢

Venus, however, speaks from her heart to Neptune,
Fervently expressing her distress: 1030
"Juno's immitigable rage and her
Implacable animus causes me to lower

Myself to plead, O Neptune, with all my heart:
No matter what time goes by, no matter what
Piety renders to her, her fury is not
Quieted down, no, not by Jove's command,
Nor by the stipulations of the Fates.
Her fury is unslakeable. It's not
Enough that she has utterly brought down
The Phrygians' city to ruin, down to the last   1040
Rubble of Troy. Her hunger for destruction
Pursues them to their very bones and ashes.
She alone knows the causes of her rage.
You know yourself how she suborned Aeolus,
To raise up that storm that brought the Libyan ocean
Up to the sky and brought the sky down to the ocean,
And dared to do this in your jurisdiction.
And now, inciting the Trojan mothers, she
Has burned the fleet and made them leave their comrades
To linger on unknown shores. I pray that you   1050
Will grant that those who still go forward will
Get themselves safely across the seas to where
Laurentine Tiber is. I ask this if
It is right to do so, and if the building of
Those city walls they are going there to build
Is granted by the Fates."

                    The son of Saturn,
The ruler of the sea, replied to her,
"You have every right to ask. You are born from the sea.
And I have earned this too. I have often calmed   1060
The raging of the waters and the sky;
And Xanthus and Simois also witness
That I have had Aeneas under my care
On land as well. When raging Achilles was sending
Thousands down to their deaths and hurling the panicked
Down from their walls, and when the groaning rivers
Were choked with the dead, so that the river Xanthus

Could not flow because he was clogged with the bodies,
It was I who hid beleaguered Aeneas away,
In the cavity of a cloud, outdone as he was,   1070
In strength and in the favor of the gods,
Facing Peleus's overwhelming son.
I did this for him, although it was my desire
To heave up and to bring down the walls I built,
Of Aeneas's perjured city. My purpose is still
The same. Do not be fearful any longer.
Your prayer is answered. He will in safety go
To Avernus's haven. There will be only one
Who, lost in the sea, will not be found among them—
One life given for the lives of all the others."   1080

                              ❦ ❦ ❦

And after he had charmed the goddess's heart
With the words he spoke, and having made her glad,
Father Neptune yokes his wild horses with
Their golden harnesses; their foaming bits
Are in their mouths, and loosely in his hands
The flowing reins; in his azure chariot
He skims along the surface of the water;
The surge beneath his thundering wheels smooths out,
The clouds absent themselves from the sky around,
And all his retinue in all their forms   1090
Then follow—huge whales, Glaucus and all his ancient
Fishy crew, Ino, Palaemon's son,
The Tritons and the company of Phorcus,
And Panopea and Spio, Melite and Nesaea,
And Thalia and Cymodoce too.

Aeneas's anxieties of mind
Now in their turn being quieted, the joy
Of resolution courses through his soul
And he is ready. He orders that the masts

Be quickly raised and that the sails be spread.   1100
All his people together obey at once,
Together unfurl the sails, and all together
Turn the yardarm ends this way and that
Till the breeze is caught and all the sails are full
And bellying out. Leading them all on their way
Is the helmsman Palinurus. All of them know
That they must follow where he steers his ship.

Now dewy Night has come to its halfway place,
High in the sky; the sailors all, relaxed
In placid slumber, on their hard benches lie   1110
Stretched out beneath their oars, when lightly Sleep
Slides down through the dark, slides down from the stars above,
Passing through shadows, parting them as he comes,
Looking for you, Palinurus, and where you are,
And bringing you bad dreams, O innocent one.
The god sits there beside you on the high
Ship stern, disguising himself as Phorbas, and
Playing this part pours forth these words to you:
"Iasidës Palinurus, listen to me.
The sea all by itself carries the fleet   1120
Forward along its way; the breeze is breathing
Steadily as we go. It's time for rest.
Lay down your head and rest your weary eyes.
I will take over your task for a little while."
But Palinurus, scarcely looking aside,
Replies, "Are you telling me to shut my eyes
To the sea when all is calm and the waves at peace?
Are you telling me to trust this monster? Should I,
Whom a cloudless sky has tricked so many times,
Entrust Aeneas to the treacherous winds?"   1130
He tightened his grip on the tiller, not letting go,
And raised his eyes up to the stars and, steadfast,
Fixed his gaze on them. But then Sleep shook
Over his temples a branch dripping with Lethe's

Soporific Stygian dew, and so,
In spite of all, his swimming eyes began
To close. And then they closed. But weariness,
So suddenly come upon him, had hardly begun
To cause his limbs to relax, when, leaning above him,
Sleep seized his body and threw him headlong down   1140
Into the flowing waters of the sea.
He fell, and with him the rudder, torn away,
And a piece of the stern, and he called out for help
Over and over from where he was, unheard.
The god himself flew off on his wings up through
The thin air high above.

                        Nevertheless
The fleet went on, unknowing and unafraid,
Safely under the promise of Father Neptune.
And as it went on it was carried toward and near   1150
The dangerous cliffs of the Sirens, white with the bones
Of what had happened there of old to men.
The hoarse sound of the waves breaking upon
The sea cliff rocks could be heard from far away.
When the leader knew that the fleet was wandering on,
Without her pilot, he took the helm himself,
And steered the vessel through the waves of night,
Stunned and grieving, crying, "O you, Palinurus,
Who trusted in the calm of sea and sky,
You will lie naked on some unknown shore."   1160

Book Six

And this is what Aeneas, grieving, cries,
Then gives their reins to the fleet, and together they glide
Across to the shores of Euboean Cumae where
They turn their ships about, prows seaward, and
Align the curved sterns all along the beaches;
The teeth of their anchors fasten them where they are,
And then the young men eagerly leap from the ships
Onto the shores of Hesperia at last,
Some of them searching for flint, because they know
The seeds of fire are hidden there; some ravage   10
The woods for the hiding places of game; some look
For new freshwater streams, and find them. But pious
Aeneas seeks the hill where Phoebus Apollo
Sits enthroned in his temple, near which there is
The enormous cavern, the secret place of the dread
Sybil into whose being the Delian seer
Breathes a soul and mind that are the telling
Of what it is that is going to come to pass.

Aeneas and his captains now pass through
The grove of Diana Trivia and under   20
The golden roof of the temple of Apollo.
The story goes that Daedalus, escaping
From Minos' Cretan kingdom, dared to entrust
Himself to the sky on his swift-flying wings,
And in this unheard-of way he glided northward

Toward the cold, and finally alighted
On the Chalcidian Hill. Having come down,
Safe to the earth, he dedicated the wings
That had carried him aloft, to you, Apollo,
In a beautiful marble temple that he built there.   30
Upon the doors is shown the killing of
Androgeos, who was the son of Minos,
And the punishment for this of Cecrops' children:
Seven young men to be sacrificed each year.
The urn, with the lots already drawn, is shown there.
Opposite this on the doors is the island of Crete
Arising from the sea; and there's the story
Of Pasiphaë and the trick of the mating of her
To the bull's cruel love, and the biform mongrel that she
Gave birth to, the Minotaur, the product of   40
The vile coition; also depicted there
Is the house of inextricable wandering,
But Daedalus, in pity for Ariadne,
Untangled the tangled strings, showing blind feet
The way to follow along their bewildered way.
And Icarus, you, had grief allowed it to happen,
Would have been figured there to tell your story.
Twice, your father's hands were raised to try
To fashion the gold to show your fall from the sky;
Twice, his hands fell back; he could not do it.   50

The Trojans' fascinated eyes would still
Have kept on studying all the stories that
Were fashioned upon the doors, but now Achates,
Who had been sent ahead, came back, and with him
A priestess of Apollo and Diana,
Glaucus's daughter, Deiphobe, who said:
"It is not now the time to view these things.
It is the time to offer seven bullocks,
And seven chosen ewes, in sacrifice."
Thus she speaks to Aeneas; nor are the Trojans   60

Slow to obey her holy instruction. And then
The priestess calls them into the sacred temple.

>   >   >

The huge Euboean hill is hollowed out
Into a cave with a hundred grotto mouths,
And out of these a hundred voices utter.
The voices come from the grotto openings
When the virgin damsel cries, "It is the time!
The oracles! The god! It is the god!"
Crying out this before the grotto mouths,
She is changed in looks, in color, her hair is wildly   70
Disheveled, her frenzied bosom heaving; she's
Suddenly taller than she is; her voice
Is not the voice of any mortal being;
The breath of the god is breathing in her body.

"Trojan, are you ready to make your vows?
Aeneas, will you not pray? Until you pray,
The mouths of the cavern will not open and speak."
Thus the Sybil said, and then was silent.
Cold shivering went through the Trojans' bodies,
And from the inmost being of their leader   80
The prayers and vows poured forth: "Phoebus, who always
Showed pity for the troubles of the Trojans,
And guided the arrow from the bow of Paris
That struck the body of Aeacus's scion,
It is you who guided us across so many
Seas and to and past so many lands,
The lands of the Massylian tribes and of
The quicksands of the Syrtes. Now we have come
To the ever-retreating shores of Italy;
Let this now be the end of our long journey.   90
You gods and all you goddesses to whom
The glory of the Dardanians and Troy

Has been anathema, at last you may
Release us from your hatred; and, O sacred
Prophetess who can tell what the future knows,
You know that I ask for nothing more than what
Is mine by what the Fates allow to me.
Grant that at last we Teucrians can bring
Our wandering tempest-tossed household gods to Latium,
And in our city I will build a marble   100
Temple to Diana, and one to Phoebus,
And establish festal days in Apollo's honor.
For you, most gracious maiden, there'll be a shrine
Whose inner room, guarded by chosen sages,
Will be safekeeping for your oracles
Of what will come to pass. Do not now let
The wild disordering wind scatter your leaves,
But you yourself descant the prophetic song."

Then he was silent. The prophetess, not yet
Subdued to Phoebus, still wildly raved and gestured   110
Within the cavern, seeking to shake herself free
From the mighty god within her, and the more
She raves the more the god is wearying her,
Is quieting her, is taming her wild heart.
The hundred mouths of the cavern all of them suddenly
Open and through the air there come the words:
"Though you have survived the great sea-dangers, there
Are more and greater troubles, upon the land.
The Dardanians nevertheless will come into
The country of Lavinia—dismiss   120
Your fears that this is not to be—but it
Will not be as they wish. I see dire wars.
I see the foaming blood in the Tiber streaming.
There will be another Xanthus in your future,
And another Simois, and a Grecian camp.
Even now a new Achilles has been born,
In Latium, goddess-born like you, while Juno,

Wherever you go, will follow you—and you,
Among what races and cities will you not,
In your dire need and hunger, cry for help?   130
The cause of all this trouble for the Trojans:
Once more a foreign bride, a foreign marriage.
Do not give in to the woes that are to come,
But all the more bravely you must go forth to face them,
As far as Fortune will allow you to do.
The way to safety will, to your surprise,
Be opened to you first by a Grecian city."
These are the words in which the Cumaean Sybil
Chants in her inner shrine, her dreadful riddles,
In a voice that booms through the cavern, wrapping truth   140
In what obscures the truth—it is thus that Apollo
Shakes the reins and goads her resisting sides.

When the Sybil's raging subsided, and her raving
Lips were silent, then hero Aeneas spoke:
"No kinds of woe come to me unforeseen.
That such as these are going to be, O virgin,
My mind has known and anxiously thought upon.
One thing I pray for. It is said the gate
To the kingdom of the Underworld is here,
And in the gloom there is the swamp that is   150
The overflow of the river Acheron.
I pray that it may be granted that I may
Go down to see the dear face of my father,
And be in his sight. Open the sacred gates.
Show me the way to go. I carried my father
Through flames and through a thousand showering spears;
I carried him to safety on my shoulders;
Weak though he was and old, my father was
My comrade as we went across the seas,
Through all that the menacing ocean and sky could do.   160
It was he who entreated me to come to you,
And cross your threshold, and ask your pity for

Both son and father. You have the power to grant this,
For Hecate has given you superintendence
Of Avernus's sacred groves. Did Orpheus not
Have power in the music of his lyre
To summon from below the shade of his wife?
Does Pollux not, returning and departing,
By dying once again return to that place,
Taking his turn to share his brother's death?   170
And there are Theseus and the mighty Alcides.
I too have my descent from most high Jove."

Those were the words he, at the altar, prayed,
And the prophetess replied in these words, saying:
"Offspring of gods, son of Anchises of Troy,
The way to Avernus is easy, the door is open,
Night and day, down to the darkness of Dis.
But how to come back, how to retrace one's steps
And return to the upper air, that is the task,
That is the labor. Only a few have been raised   180
Up to the heavens, because their virtue earned it,
Or because, sons of the gods, Jupiter loved them,
And granted them special favor. Down there are the woods
Of the Underworld, and folding itself around them,
The swampy river Cocytus. But if your love
And your mad desire is such that it is your will
To swim the Stygian lake two times, two times
To see black Tartarus, you must do this:
There is a tree that's hidden in the mists
Of shadows in the dark of the valleys there,   190
And growing upon that tree there is a bough,
Swaying upon its stem, with golden leaves.
Its golden fruit is sacred to nether Juno;
No one can pass beneath earth's hidden places
Who has not plucked the golden fruit to take it
To the beautiful Proserpina, whose command

Is that this fruit be brought to her as a gift.
Another one will be there in its place,
As golden as the first, and new leaves also,
As golden as before, will be there too.   200
Look up to find it, and then reach up to pluck it.
If the Fates are calling you, it will be easy.
If not, then there is nothing you can do,
Neither by hand nor knife, that will allow you
To separate it from its tree. But, oh!
You do not know it yet! While you stand here,
Upon our threshold seeking our guidance, there lies
The dead body of your friend, infesting your whole
Fleet with the impurity of death.
The body must be carried to its place,   210
And buried in its tomb. Black cattle must
Be sacrificed as offerings of peace.
This done, then you will see the Stygian groves,
And the kingdoms that the living may not go to."
The lips of the Sybil closed and she was mute.

, , ,

Aeneas walked slowly away, out of the cavern.
His troubled gaze was fixed upon the ground,
Thinking about these dark things that the Sybil
Had said to him; loyal Achates walked
Slowly beside him, thinking of these things too,   220
The two together, trying to understand.
What dead friend was it she had spoken of?
Whose dead body was it that they must bury?
And as they walk, suddenly they see
The body of Aeolus's son, Misenus,
Haplessly dead, washed up from where he had drowned,
Lying there on the dry beach, he, whose trumpet
Summoned the heroes to the battlefield,

And with its sound aroused the god of war.
He was great Hector's soldier, brave in battle,   230
With spear and trumpet alike, and then when Hector
Was killed by Achilles, he, not choosing to choose
Anyone lesser than what his chieftain had been,
Joined the comitatus of Aeneas.
But then there came a day, one day, when he
Chancing upon a conch shell, picked it up,
And with it, madman, caused all the sea around
To ring with the sound of its clangoring bugling music,
Challenging what the gods could do with it,
And jealous Triton, according to the story,   240
Caught hold of him and dragged him into the foaming
Waters among the rocks, and so he drowned.

Therefore all his fellows, pious Aeneas
Foremost among them, with loud lamenting cries,
Together mourned around him. Then, weeping, they,
Obedient to the Sybil's commands, made haste
To set about the task of gathering trees,
With which to build the altar of his tomb
And raise it high. They enter the ancient woods,
Which are the wild beasts' haunts; the pine trees fall;   250
There is the sound of axes striking the ilex;
They split ash logs and oak logs with their wedges;
They roll great manna ash trees down the mountains.
Nor was Aeneas less than first among them,
Doing this work, using their weapons like them,
Urging them on, encouraging them, and in
His grieving heart, thinking over and over
About what was next to come: "In this immense
Unending forest, if only the golden bough
Would show us where it is; for what the seer   260
Told us of you, Misenus, was all too true."

, , ,

No sooner had he spoken these words than, there,
As if it was just happening by chance,
Two doves came fluttering down from the sky above,
And alighted together, before his eyes, on the grass.
Then the great hero saw that these birds were
His mother's birds, and he joyfully prayed: "O lead me,
If there's any way to find it, lead me to where,
In a grove somewhere the ground is shaded by,
And made rich by, the fruitful bough is above it!   270
And goddess-mother, O, do not desert me
In this my uncertain journey." Saying these things,
He stood there where he was and watched to see
What signs he might be given by how they went,
Alighting to feed a little, then flying a little,
Alighting a little again to feed on the grass,
Then flying a little way, and alighting again,
Then flying a little again, feeding and flying,
Keeping themselves just far enough ahead
So that they still can be seen by him who follows;   280
And then when they come to Avernus' noisome waters,
Together they quickly rise, and then drop down
Through the lucid air beyond, and settle themselves
Upon a tree they chose to settle upon,
The two of them there, upon the tree, within
The darkness of whose branches could be seen
Glimpses of shining gold. It is as when,
In the dead of freezing winter the mistletoe,
Engrafted from another tree, brings forth
New leaves, strange leaves, yellow flowers and yellow berries;   290
This was what, upon the shadowy ilex,
The golden leafage on the bough looked like,
And this was how the gold-foil leaves were gently
Rustling in the breeze. Aeneas, at once,
Avidly reaches forth, and takes hold of the bough,
And plucks it down from where it clung to the tree,
And carries it back with him to the Sybil's shrine.

The Teucrians on the beach grieve for Misenus,
Performing the final rites to the thankless ashes.
They build a pyre, of rich pitch-pine and oak logs,   300
With interwoven hangings of dark foliage,
And with mourning cypress trees set up in front;
High up, there hangs Misenus's shining armor.
Cauldrons of water are heated on the fire;
They lave and anoint with oil the dead man's body.
There's ritual wailing, and after the wailing ceases,
They lay the body on a funeral bier,
And cover the body with the purple robes
Appropriate to the rite. Some of them then
Perform the ministry—sad ministry—   310
Of lifting the heavy bier upon their shoulders,
And, as their ancestors did, averting their eyes
From what they were doing, lowered their torches to
Light the pyre they built. The frankincense,
And sacrificial viands, and overflowing
Bowls of oil are offered to the flames.
After the ashes collapsed, and the fire died down,
They poured out wine upon the glowing thirsty
Embers of the fire, and Corynaeus
Gathered up the bones and put them away,   320
In a brazen funeral urn. And after that,
Three times he walked around his comrades and
With a fruitful olive branch he sprinkled them lightly
With drops of the pure water he carried with him,
And at the same time he said the farewell words.

But pious Aeneas raised a great tomb there,
With Misenus's spear and oar and trumpet upon it.
The hill that rises above the tomb is called
Misenum, preserving his name for ages after.

Having done this, Aeneas proceeds at once   330
To do the things the Sybil told him to do.
There was the open mouth of a vast cavern
Half-hidden in the shadows of a wood,
And near a dark lake, called by the Greeks Avernus.
No birds could fly in safety over this lake,
Because of the vapors rising from its surface;
And here it was that the priestess sets out four
Young black-backed bullocks, and then she pours,
Upon their foreheads, wine, and then she plucks
A bristle from between the horns of each,   340
And offers the bristles first, upon the fire,
And in a loud voice calls upon Hecate,
Whose power's on high and in Erebus below.
In bowls beneath the altars others caught
The warm blood of the bullocks, whose throats they'd cut.
Aeneas takes his sword and slays a lamb
Whose fleece is black, and offers it to Night,
The mother of the Eumenides, and to
Her great sister Terra; and, Proserpina,
For you he slays a barren heifer. Then,   350
In the darkness he constructs an altar to
The Stygian King, and on the flaming altar
Lays down the offered carcasses of bulls,
Pouring the oil of their fat upon their entrails.

Then, just before the dawning of the sun,
The ground began to shake; the woods began
To shiver in all their ridges; there was the sound
Of howling as of dogs within the shadows,
As Hecate came near. The Sybil cries,
"Depart, depart, all you who are profane!   360
Depart from here who are unauthorized!

And you, Aeneas, unsheathe your sword, go forward!
This is the time to be brave and strong of heart!"
And saying this, in frenzy she went forward,
Into the mouth of the cave, and he with courage
Went in with her, and followed her footsteps as
She went before him into the waiting darkness.

,   ,   ,

You gods who rule the kingdoms of the spirits!
You tongueless shades! You Phlegethon and Chaos!
You silent spreading regions of the dark!   370
By the favor of the gods may I, unharmed,
Be teller of the things that I have heard,
And what is wrapped in the darkness here below!

,   ,   ,

In the lonely gloom of night two figures walk
Through the empty rooms of Dis's empty kingdom,
As if upon a path beneath the uncertain
Meager light of a moon almost not there,
At a time when Jupiter has hidden the sky
In darkness, and black night has taken away
From all things all the colors that they had.   380
Just at the innermost end of the entrance court,
Just at the place where Orcus's jaws are open,
There's Grief, there's unrelenting Cares, where they
Have placed their beds, there's ashen-faced Disease,
Sad Age, there's Fear, there's Hunger, begetter of crime,
There's Destitution, shapes terrible to look at,
There's Death and his brother Sleep, and guilty Desires;
And on the other side of the open door,
There's War, dealer of death, and there the iron
Cells of the Furies, and insane Discord,   390
With bloody ribbons in her snaky hair.

In the midst there is an enormous shadowy elm tree,
Spreading its arms, and false dreams clinging under
Every single leaf of its foliage,
So men say, and also many forms
Of monstrous creatures, centaurs stabled at
The threshold there, and biform Scyllas, and
Briareus, hundred-handed, fifty-headed,
And the strident hissing Beast of Lerna, and
The Chimaera breathing fire, and Harpies, Gorgons,   400
And he, the three-bodied Shade. Aeneas, trembling,
Terrified at the sight, unsheathes his sword,
And turns its edge against them, and he would,
Had not his sage companion told him that these
Were bodiless empty images of life,
Have slashed at fleeting shadows with his sword.

                        , , ,

From here there is a road that leads to where
The waters of Tartarean Acheron are,
And where a bottomless whirlpool thick with muck
Heaves and seethes and vomits mire into   410
The river Cocytus. Here is the dreadful boatman,
Who keeps these waters, frightful in his squalor,
Charon, the gray hairs of his unkempt beard
Depending from his chin, his glaring eyes
On fire, his filthy mantle hanging by
A loose knot from his shoulders. All by himself
He manages the sails and with his pole
Conveys the dead across in his dark boat—
He's old, but, being a god, old age is young.

A vast crowd, so many, rushed to the riverbank,   420
Women and men, famous great-hearted heroes,
The life in their hero bodies now defunct,
Unmarried boys and girls, sons whom their fathers

Had had to watch being placed on the funeral pyre;
As many as the leaves of the forest that,
When autumn's first chill comes, fall from the branches;
As many as the birds that flock into the land,
From the great deep, when the season, turning cold,
Has driven them over the seas to seek the sun,
They stood beseeching on the riverbank,   430
Yearning to be the first to be carried across,
Stretching their hands out toward the farther shore.
But the stern ferryman, taking only this one,
Or this other one, pushes the rest away.
Aeneas cries out, excited by the tumult,
"O virgin, why are they crowding at the river?
What is it that the spirits want? What is it
That decides why some of them are pushed away,
And others sweep across the livid waters?"
The aged priestess thus: "Anchises' son,   440
True scion of the gods, these are the pools
Of the river Cocytus and this the Stygian marsh,
Whose power it is to make the gods afraid
Not to keep their word. All in this crowd are helpless
Because their bodies have not been covered over.
The boatman that you see is Charon. Those
Who are being carried across with him are they
Who have been buried. It is forbidden to take
Any with him, across the echoing waters
That flow between these terrible riverbanks,   450
Who have not found a resting place for their bones.
Restlessly to and fro along these shores
They wander waiting for a hundred years.
Not until after that, the longed-for crossing."

, , ,

Aeneas, child of Anchises, hearing these things,
Stood still, thinking of what the Sybil had told him,

Pitying them in his heart for their hard fortune.
And then he sees there, grieving, homeless, two,
Destitute of the honor that's death's reward,
Leucaspis, and Orontes, captain of   460
The Lycian fleet, they who, together, sailing
From Troy over windswept seas, were overwhelmed
By the whirling East Wind coming down upon them.
All of their ships were lost, and all of the men.
Then lo, there was the pilot Palinurus,
Who, while he was plotting the stars, so lately
Fell into the sea from the helmsman's place on the high
Stern of the ship. When Aeneas at last was able
To make out who this figure was who moved
So sadly in the gloom, he said to him,   470
"What god was it, Palinurus, who took you away
From us and flung you down into the sea?
I have never before this found Apollo false.
Has he this once deluded me? He promised me
That you would make the journey across unscathed.
What of his promise now?" But Palinurus
Replied: "Apollo's tripod did not lie.
It was no god who threw me into the sea.
The helm, which I the pilot was holding fast to,
Steering our course, was suddenly torn loose,   480
And I fell headlong, clutching it to me as
I fell, taking it down with me. I swear
By the violent seas, it wasn't fear of them,
As I was falling, but fear for the ship, that, losing
Both helm and helmsman, it might be swamped, and founder
In the surging waves. Over unmeasured seas
Three days and nights I was driven by the wild
South Wind and then upon the early morning
Dawning of the fourth, I saw, as I
Was carried up upon the high crest of a wave,   490
The coast of what I knew was Italy.
Little by little I swam to reach the shore,

And I was almost safe, just getting my clutching
Hands upon the jagged cliff-base rocks,
When I, weighed down as I was by my sea-soaked clothes,
Was set upon by indigenes with knives,
Who thought that I was prey. And now my body
Moves restlessly in the wavelets of the shallows,
Or it lies, by the wind's impelling, upon the strand.
O by the jocund light and air of day,   500
And by your father and by Iulus's hopes,
O you, unconquered, rescue, rescue me!
Either upon the Velian shore find where
My body is, and cast upon it three
Handfuls of earth, or if your goddess mother
Will show you a way to do it (for I believe
That it is not without the sponsoring gods
That you are seeking to cross the Stygian marsh
And these great streams and get to the other side),
Hold out your hand to me in my misfortune,   510
And take me with you over to there, so I
At least may find in death a place to rest."

Thus he spoke, and then the prophetess said,
"How is it, Palinurus, that your longing
Deludes you so, to make you think that you,
Unburied, uninvited, would be able
To see the other bank of the Stygian waters
And the River of the Fates? Prayer can never
Deflect what it is that the gods have decided upon.
But remember what I tell you, and let your sorrow   520
Be solaced by it: those native tribes, throughout
Their villages will be shown by signs and portents
That they must propitiate your bones and build
A tomb, bring solemn offerings there, and name it,
Forever after that, Palinurus, to you."
Hearing these words his cares were lifted away,
And from his anxious heart its sorrow was driven

Off for a little while; he rejoices in
The headland, Palinurus, bearing his name.

⸻ ⸻ ⸻

So, having begun their journey, they went on,   530
And soon came nearer to the riverbank.
But when, from where he was, out on the marshy
Stygian waters, the boatman saw them coming
Through the silent woods and turning toward the river,
He called out, in a scolding accusing voice,
Before they spoke to him, "Who is it who
Comes armed with weapons here, who may you be?
Stop where you are and tell me who you are,
From where you are! This is the land of Shadows,
The land of Sleep, the land of somnolent Night.   540
I cannot carry those who are alive
In the Stygian ferry. It brought me no joy when I
Took Hercules across the lake with me,
Nor Theseus, nor Pirithous, either, though
They were unconquered heroes and sons of gods.
One of them tried to drag our King's watchdog
Trembling away in chains; the others tried
To kidnap our Queen right out of her marital bedroom."

The Amphrysian Sybil replied, "Be not disturbed.
No trickery here; our weapons are no threat;   550
The huge watchdog can scare the bloodless dead
Forever with his barking; the chastity
Of Proserpina is safe in her uncle's chamber.
This is Trojan Aeneas, famous for his valor,
And for his piety. He is descending
Into the shadows of lowest Erebus
To see his father there. If the example
Of faithfulness such as this has failed to move you,
Regard this bough." She draws the golden bough

From where she had kept it hidden in her robe.   560
The swelling rage in his heart subsides in wonder,
When he sees this awful wand, this sacred gift
So long unseen. He says no more and turns
His blue boat back and toward the shore, and there
He expels the other souls who waiting sat
Upon the cross seats of the boat, and clears
The way for great Aeneas to come on board.
The vessel groaned beneath his weight, and marshy
Water poured in, through the leaky seams and floorboard,
But at last it carries the hero and the seer   570
Across unharmed, and lands them upon the slimy
Mud and sedge grass of the riverbank.

Huge Cerberus, crouching there in the dooryard of
The cavern he was watchdog of, made all
The regions round reverberate with the loud
Barking of his three heads. Seeing the serpents
Bristling around his neck, the Sybil throws him
A drugged pellet of meal, drowsed with honey.
He catches it in his ravenous triple gullet,
Wolfs it down, and at once his monster body   580
Relaxed, and he sank down, and lay stretched out
Across the mouth of the cavern that he guarded.
The watchdog lying there asleep, Aeneas
Gets in through the entrance to the cavern,
And leaves behind him the bank of the river that
No one comes back from ever.

                           ʼ   ʼ   ʼ

                              There is the sound
Of voices loudly wailing—it is the wailing
Of little babies whom black day had taken
From their mothers' breasts and overwhelmed in death,   590
On the threshold of sweet life they would never share in.

Nearby were those who were wrongly condemned to die.
Yet not without judgment were they in this place:
Minos presides, and shakes the urn to call
A silent jury together, to consider
What it was their lives had been, what they had done,
What they deserve. In the next region are those
Sad beings who in innocent hatred of
The light of day, had thrown away their lives.
How glad they would be now to suffer want,   600
And the hardest toil, if in the light and air.
But fate bars this. They are imprisoned by
The dismal waters of the swamp, and by
The coiling chains of Styx nine times around them.

Beyond this but not far, and widely spread,
Are the Fields of Lamentation. That is their name.
Here is where those whom desire has wasted away
Are hidden in secret walkways, in myrtle groves;
They cannot give up their longings, even in death.
Phaedra is there, Aeneas sees her, and Procris,   610
And mournful Eriphyle, displaying the wounds
Her son's cruel knife had made upon her body;
And there's Evadne, and Pasiphaë,
And Laodamia walking with them too,
And Caeneus, who was once a young woman, and
After that was a youth, and then, by fate,
What he had been at first. Among these others,
In the great woods wandering, was Phoenician Dido,
The wound she made upon herself still fresh;
And when Aeneas came close enough to know   620
Who this was he was seeing—this form that moved
So dimly among the shadows—it was like seeing,
Or thinking you were seeing, the young moon rising,
In the early days of its month, behind the clouds—
Tears fell from his eyes and he spoke tenderly
And lovingly to her: "Unhappy Dido,

Is it true, what I was told, that you were dead,
And with a sword had brought about your death?
And was it I, alas, who caused it? I
Swear by the stars, and by the upper world,   630
And by whatever here below is holy,
I left your shores unwillingly. It was
The gods' commands which have brought me now down through
The shadows to these desolate wasted places,
In the profound abysmal dark; it was
The gods who drove me, and I could not know
That when I left I left behind a grief
So devastated. Stay. Who is it you
Are fleeing from? Do not withdraw from sight.
This is the last I am allowed by fate   640
To say to you." Weeping he tried with these,
His words, to appease the rage in her fiery eyes.
She fixed her gaze upon the ground, and turned
Away, and nothing was changed in her countenance,
As if it were set in stone or Marpesian rock.
Abruptly, then, she tore herself away,
And went, his enemy, back to the shady grove
In which Sychaeus, the lord of her marriage, was,
Responding to her cares with equal love.
Aeneas, overcome by the knowledge of   650
Her unjust fate, followed her as far
As tears could follow, and pitied her as she went.

꞉ ꞉ ꞉

After that, they made their way with effort along
The road that offered itself before them till
They came to the farthest field, where there were those,
Famous for the deeds they did in war,
Thronging together, apart from the other shades.
Here, to meet him, Tydeus hastens forward;
Here was Parthenopaeus, renowned in battle,

And Adrastus's pallid shade; here, fallen in war,   660
And grieved for on earth above, the Dardanidae.
He groaned to see them in their martial array—
Glaudias, Medon, Thersilochus, the three
Young sons of Antenor, the priest of Ceres,
Polyboetes, Idaeus, still with his chariot,
Still with his weapons. The soldiers stood around,
Congregated in groups, on the right, on the left,
Looking at him eagerly and longing
To walk with him and learn why he is there.
But Agamemnon's soldiers and the Danaan   670
Leaders, when they saw him, with his weapons
Shining in the shadows, turned their backs,
As if to fly, as they had done when trying
To get themselves back to their ships, and some of them shouted,
But the cries from their gaping mouths were faint and tiny.

⸎ ⸎ ⸎

And here he sees Deiphobus, his whole
Body mutilated, and his face
Hideously, cruelly, lacerated,
And both his arms, his hands, and with his ears
Torn from the sides of his head, and with his nose   680
Shamefully lopped off. Aeneas could hardly
Know who it was, there, trembling and trying to hide
The sight of what had been done to him, but he
Cried out to him in a familiar voice,
"Deiphobus, glorious in the fighting,
High-born scion of the Teucrians,
Who did this to you? Who was able to do this to you?
I was told that on that last night you fell down,
Finally weary from killing Pelasgian foes,
Upon a heap of other fallen bodies.   690
As I was leaving the country, I built upon
The Rhoetian shore a tumulus for you;

Your name and your arms depicted guard the place;
And there I cried out three times to your shade;
I could not find your body itself to bury."
The son of Priam replied, "You did everything
That you could do, and that you ought to have done,
For dead Deiphobus, and for his spirit.
My friend, it was my fate, and the mortal crimes
Of the Laconian woman that overwhelmed me.   700
It was she who left me looking the way I look.
You remember that final night, and how, deceived,
In joy, we spent it. You remember how
It was when the fatal horse climbed over the walls,
With the weight of the armed infantry in its womb,
She led a deluded orgiastic chorus,
Not knowing what they were doing, dancing and shrieking
Around the city streets, and she in their midst
Raised up a torch that signaled the Danaans,
From the height of the citadel above the city.   710
I lay asleep in our marital bed, in sweet
Deep sleep, the image of the sleep of death,
While she, the unexampled wife, took every
Weapon that there was in the house away,
Even from under the pillow that I slept on.
She took the sword I trusted, and then she opened
Wide the door and called in Menelaus,
Hoping maybe that that husband would
Forget by this the mischief she had done.
But why go on with the story? He and his fellow   720
Criminal, Aeolus' son, came into my bedroom—
O gods, if you hear my prayer, pay back the Greeks
With suffering like what I suffered there.
But tell me, what has brought you to this place?
Is it your wandering journey that brings you here,
Or is it what the gods have told you to do?
Or what has wearying fortune brought you to,
That you have come here to these sunless places,

This land of unrest?" While they were talking, Aurora
Had in her roseate chariot climbed as high   730
As the mid point of her heavenly journey, and
They might have spent all their time in such discourse,
But the Sybil interrupted them to say,
"The night is coming, Aeneas. We must not spend
All of the time we have in weeping. This
Is where the roads divide. The right-hand road,
Which passes along beside great Dis's walls
Is that which leads to Elysium, where we are going.
The one to the left is the busy thoroughfare
Of punishment. It is the road that takes   740
The wicked to unpitying Tartarus."
Deiphobus replied, "I will depart,
Great priestess; I will complete the roster of
My brigade and then go back into the dark.
Go, you who are our glory, on your journey.
Enjoy a happier fate." And saying so,
Went back to where it was that he had come from.

' ' '

Suddenly, Aeneas, looking back,
Became aware that there on the left, beneath
The overhanging cliffs, there was a great   750
Castle, triple-walled, and around it, seething,
A river of torrential fire, sounding
Upon the rocks. The gate to the castle was huge,
And built within great adamantine columns,
Utterly impregnable in war;
The most powerful army of men there ever was
Could not prevail upon its battlements,
Not even the sons of heaven, and, rising above it,
There was an iron tower, high as the sky,
Where Tisiphone in her bloody gown keeps sleepless   760
Watch by night and day over the gate.

Within, the sounds of groaning, sounds of the cruel
Lash-whipping, sounds of clanking dragging chains.
Aeneas, hearing the sounds, stood still, in terror:
"O maiden, say, what crimes have been committed?
What are these punishments? What is this sound,
What is this sound of wailing on the wind?"
The seer in answer said these words to him:
"Aeneas, famous leader of the Teucrians.
There's no one who is innocent of crime,   770
Who can set his foot upon this threshold, but,
When Hecate made me prefect of these groves,
She conducted me through all these scenes and showed me
The punishments. Cretan Rhadamanthus
Sits in harsh judgment here, hearing the stories,
Exacting their confessions of what they did,
From those who blithely had, in the upper world,
Concealed their crimes from others until they died.
And when the judgment is made, Tisiphone
Vengefully leaps upon them, her left hand   780
Brandishing her scourging whip of snakes,
And calls her band of sister Furies to join;
And after that there is the dreadful groaning
Noise of the turning hinges of the great
Infernal door as it opens to receive them.
Do you know who the sentry is that's sitting there,
In the doorway? Do you know what shape it is?
The monster Hydra, still worse to behold than what
Has been beheld already, with her fifty
Throats wide open, waiting for the guilty.   790
Inside, plunging sheer downward in the darkness,
Twice as far down in darkness than Olympus
Rises high up in brightness to the heavens,
There's Tartarus where, in the lowest abyss, the Titans,
Primordial brood of Earth, are writhing and turning,
Down there where Jupiter's thunderbolt had sent them.
Myself I also saw the Aloides down there,

The Giant twins, who tried with their hands to bring
Jove down, and along with him, his heavenly kingdom.
Salmoneus too was down there paying for what   800
He did, mimicking Jupiter, and miming the throwing
Of bolts of lightning and the Olympian thunder,
Madman in a four-horse chariot riding
Among the Greeks and through his Elian city,
Pretending to be a god, waving his torches
And using the noise of brass trumpets and the clatter
Of horn-footed horses' hooves, when the Father Almighty—
No need for torches nor for the smoky glare
Of pitchy lights—drove him headlong down
With a single thunderbolt and a wild whirlwind.   810
And Tityos, child of Earth the mother of all,
Is there to be seen, stretched out nine acres long,
With a huge vulture feasting itself upon
His immortal rich abundant liver and
His ever-self-renewing viscera,
Nor ever any letting up of this,
The vulture's crooked probing foraging beak,
And the entrails ever growing back again,
And there are the Lapiths, Ixion and Pirithous,
And the one the great cliff slab hangs over always   820
Seeming as if it's just about to fall;
There are the couches decorated with gold,
Before their eyes a splendid banquet offered,
And, reclining at the table, the eldest Fury
Is ready to spring up screaming and brandishing
Her torch to keep their famished hands from touching.
Here there were those who, all their lives long, were brothers
Hating each other, their brothers, and those who were
Abusers of aged parents, and those who got
Their clients tangled in fraud, and those who sat   830
Alone, transfixed by the sight of their piled-up money,
And those who gave nothing of what they had to their kin
(The commonest wrong), and those who were caught and killed

In adultery, and those who followed treasonous
Banners, betraying their leaders heedlessly—
All such, in this prison, wait for punishment.
Too many for you to know what punishment
There'll be for each of them: some doomed for ever
To roll a huge stone endlessly, or hang
Outstretched upon the spokes of the turning wheel;   840
Unhappy Theseus sits there, and will for ever
Sit there; most miserable Phlegyas, witnessing all,
Loudly cries out from where he is in the shadows:
'Be warned, beware, for this is what justice is.
Do not despise the gods!' One sold his country
For gold, and put a tyrant over it, for gold;
Another worked his country's laws around
Being bribed to do so, all for gold;
Another entered by night into his daughter's
Forbidden bed and made an incestuous union.   850
All these dared monstrous acts, and, daring, did them.
If I had a hundred tongues and a hundred mouths
And a voice as strong as iron, I could not tell you
All of the forms of crimes or their punishment."

⸖ ⸖ ⸖

This is what Phoebus Apollo's aged Sybil
Told, and then she said, "Now we must hasten
To finish the task that you have undertaken,
I see the walls the Cyclopes forges raised,
And the porticoed gate, where you must place the gift
It was required of you to give." She spoke,   860
And together they went along the shadowed road
And over the space between where they had been
And where it was that they were going to,
And so came near the gate. Aeneas steps forward
And scatters drops of purifying water

Upon his body, and takes the golden bough
And places it on the threshold, as he was told to.

>   >   >

Having carried out the goddess's commands,
They entered into a beautiful happy scene,
Green lawns and blessèd groves. Over all this   870
The light of their own sun shone, and there were the stars
Familiar to them in their familiar sky.
The generous air was bright. Some who were there
Contended in play upon the yellow sand
Of the wrestling ground; some who were there
Were dancing and singing together while the Thracian,
In his priestly robe, accompanied their steps
Upon his seven-note lyre, now with his fingers,
Now with his ivory quill, touching the strings.
Here in this scene there was the beautiful   880
Ancestral Teucrian throng—magnanimous
Heroes from the earlier happier times—
Ilus and Assaracus and Dardanus,
Founder of Troy. Aeneas, gazing at them
Across the distance, wondered at the phantom
Chariots and phantom gear, the phantom lances
Fixed in the soil, the phantom horses, freed
Of their phantom bridles, browsing on the lawn.
They take the same care, down there, under the earth,
With their horses and their chariots and arms,   890
To keep them glossy, polished and shining, as
They did when they were alive. And others, on
The right and on the left, were picnicking on
The grassy slopes, or in the fragrant groves
Of laurel, and sang in a chorus hymns of praise,
Where Eridanus the ample river flowed
Through the forest upward toward the upper world.

Here is the company of those who suffered,
Fighting for their country, and who died;
And those who in their lifetimes led pure lives   900
As priests or as chaste pious singers whose
Music was acceptable to Phoebus,
And those whose arts, zealously and with care
Pursued, made life be better for others, all
Whose service is remembered with honor, were there,
Wearing white headbands, white as the purest snow.
The Sybil spoke to Musaeus where he stood,
Taller than all the rest, in the midst of that
Vast throng of souls pouring around and past him,
"Tell us, chief of singers, tell us you happy souls,   910
Where can we find Anchises, where does he dwell?
It is to find him that we have crossed the great
Rivers of Erebus." The hero replied,
"None of us has a dwelling place. We live
In the shade of groves and on the riverbanks
And in the meadows where the fresh streams flow.
But if it is your heart's desire to find him,
Come to the top of this hill, and I will show you
The easy way to go." Having said this,
He led them to the topmost of the hill   920
And showed them the shining fields beyond. And so
They left the heights.

                In a green sequestered grove
Father Anchises was reflecting upon
Those souls still held down there in the world below,
Who were destined to return, once more in bodies,
To the light of the world above; and at that moment,
Was telling himself the number of his dear children
And of the belovèd children of his children,
And what they were going to do, how was it that   930

Their lives would be, what was it that would happen.
And when he saw that it was Aeneas coming
Toward him across the greensward, he cried out,
And weeping stretched out his arms to welcome him,
"Is it my son who has come to me at last?
Has what I prayed for finally come to pass,
To see your face and hear your familiar voice?
Day after day I have been thinking of this,
Counting the time, and now it has happened. My son,
What are the dangers that on your journey you   940
Have undergone and suffered from? I have
Been so afraid that you might come to harm
In Libya." Aeneas replied, "It is because
Of your mournful shade, my father, seen again
And again, that I have sought to come to this place.
My fleet is standing on the Tyrrhenian Sea.
Father, let me embrace you, do not withdraw,
Let me hold your hands." This is what Aeneas said.
Tears streaming down his face. Three times he tried
To embrace his father and to hold his hands;   950
Three times the image, clasped in vain, escaped,
As if it were a breeze or on the wings
Of a vanishing dream.

              And then Aeneas becomes
Aware of a grove in this deep secluded vale,
And of thickets with the breezes rustling through them,
And the river Lethe peaceably flowing past,
And hovering along the banks, a crowd
Of men and nations, more numerous by far
Than he could possibly count, as if they were,   960
On a summer's day, unnumberable bees
Alighting on the many-colored blossoms
And swarming around white shining lily flowers,
And all the fields around murmured and hummed.
Aeneas was amazed by what he saw,

And, ignorant of what it meant, he asked,
"What is that flowing river over there,
And who are the people, so many, gathering?"
Father Anchises replied, "They are the souls
Whose fate it is to be given bodies again,   970
And they are there to drink forgetfulness
From the soothing waters of the river Lethe.
Indeed it has, long since, been my desire
To tell the tale of all my seed to you,
So that you will, with me, be all the more
Glad that Italy has been found."

                       "O Father,
Is it thinkable that any spirits go back
From this to the upper world and once again
Into the prisons of bodies? Why do these   980
Poor things long so to go back to the light up there?"
Anchises answers, saying, "My son, I'll tell you,"
And he tells him in its order all the truth.

"There is a spirit that breathes and moves within
And nurtures earth and sky and ocean's wide
Savannas and the bright sphere of the moon,
And Titan's star, the sun; intelligence moves
Through all there is, all things there are, and they
Are constituted by it. From this come all
The races and the kinds of men and all   990
The other beings; it is the life of those
That fly with wings, and those strange creatures that swim
Beneath the marbled waters of the sea.
It burns with its own pure fire in all those beings,
Until the mortality of their bodies clogs
And inhibits it. And so they fear, and they desire,
They grieve, and they delight, and in the shadows
And the blindnesses of what imprisons them,
Their bodies, the light's obscured. And more than that!

When they come here their souls are tainted still   1000
With faults that are so deep inhabiting
And so corroding that they must be punished
To eradicate these faults from them; for some
It is to be suspended upon the winds,
For others, to be washed through with flooding waters,
For others, it is to be subjected to
Eviscerating fire, until at last
Their souls are purified and purged; this must
For each of us be undergone; and then at last,
When the time comes round, we are sent to Elysium.   1010
A few of us there remain, in possession of
The blessèd fields. But after a thousand years
Those others you see are summoned by the gods,
To drink from the river Lethe, so that in utter
Forgetfulness, willingly they will go back
Into their bodies."

       Having said this, Anchises
Led his son and the Sybil into the midst
Of the murmuring crowd and to a place upon
A mound from which they could see the whole parade   1020
Of the thronging souls and look into their faces
And study them as in order they passed by:
"Now I will tell you, so that you will know
Your destiny in my words, who these will be,
Descended from you, and of Italian stock,
To participate in, and bring about, your glory.

That youth you see there, leaning upon his spear,
Was chosen to ascend into the light
Of the upper world to be the first of those
Of Italian blood, Silvius of Alba,   1030
Whom Lavinia, your wife, after your death,
Will bring up in the forest to be a king
And father of kings, when our descendants will reign

In Alba Longa. The next you see is the glorious
Trojan Procas, and after him is Capys,
Then Numitor, and he who will bear your name,
Aeneas Silvius, renowned for piety,
And famous equally for his martial prowess,
If he will ever come to the Alban throne.
Regard them, see how beautiful and how strong   1040
These young men are, wearing on their brows
The oak leaf honors of their nation. These
Are the men by whom Nomentum, Gabium, and
Fidena will be built, and who will plant
The towers of Collatia on its mountain,
And Inuus' fortifications, and Pometia,
Bola, Cora—now not even names,
But famous names hereafter. And there will be,
In his grandfather's time, a son of Mars,
Wearing the helmet with its double plumes,   1050
Romulus, of Asaracus's line,
And child of Ilia. See how he looks!
The look of majesty his father god
Has formed him with already. Rome will be,
Under his auspices, built on seven hills.
Surrounded by a single wall, and blest
With a genealogy of heroes, while
The Berecynthian mother with her turreted
Crown upon her head triumphally rides
Through the Phrygian towns, rejoicing in her long   1060
Descent of sons and grandsons, all divine,
All citizens of heaven, all dwellers in
The high celestial places.

                    Now see, with the gaze
Of both your eyes, all those who are going to be
Your Roman people. Here is Caesar and here
Are all those of the progeny of Iulus
Destined to live beneath that widespread sky.

And there is one, who has been promised to us,
Augustus Caesar, the son of a god, who will   1070
Bring back for us a golden age, in fields
Where Saturn reigned. His empire will extend
Beyond the lands where the Garamantes are,
And where the Indians are, beyond the years,
Beyond the ways of the sun and the zodiac,
Where Atlas bears, upon his shoulders, the turning
Axis of the stars. The Caspians and
The Maeotians shudder when their oracles tell
Of his approach, and all the seven mouths
Of the delta of the Nile tremble in fear.   1080
Indeed, not Hercules himself has gone
So far abroad, not when his arrow slew
The brazen-footed hind, or pacified
The Erymanthian woods, or terrified
The Lernan Hydra; and he has even gone
Beyond victorious Liber holding his vinous
Reins and driving his tiger-drawn chariot
Down from the highest peak of Nysa mountain.
Have we then doubts about showing what we are worth
By what we will do, or any reason to fear   1090
Establishing our home on Ausonian soil?

But who is that who from afar we see,
Wearing an olive-leaf wreath upon his head,
And carrying holy vessels for an altar?
I recognize that he is that king of Rome,
Gray headed, gray bearded, who will formulate
The laws for the early city, he who came
From the little town of Cures and who rose
To mighty power. Next after him will be
Tullus who called to arms and war a people   1100
Long used to peace and long not used to triumphs.
Right after him there's ostentatious Ancus,
Whom the populace loves too well. There also see

The Tarquin kings and Brutus the Avenger,
Who brought the fasces back, and was the first
To be a consul with the power to wield
The cruel axes, and, when his sons rebelled,
It was he, unhappy, who punished them with death,
So great was his love of country and his desire
For righteousness. Look there, there are the Drusi,   1110
There are the Decii, there's Torquatus with
His own cruel axe, and Camillus, who'll bring home
The battle standards. Those two you see there in
Their glittering matching armor, both now at peace,
Together now, while pent in the darkness here—
Alas, when they go up into the light
Of the upper world, what carnage there will be,
What chaos, when the father-in-law comes down
In force from the Alps and from Monaco's height
Upon his daughter's husband's Eastern army.   1120

Do not let civil bloodshed be your custom.
My sons, be merciful, and do not turn
Your valor against the vitals of your country.
Child of my blood, you who descend from the gods
Of high Olympus, turn away your sword.

That one you see, over there, after having destroyed
Corinth, will drive his chariot up to the top
Of the Capitoline, to celebrate in triumph
How many Achaeans he killed. The next you see,
In revenge for what was done to his Trojan forebears,   1130
And for the insult to Minerva's temple,
Will rip up and tear down Argos, and Mycenae,
Agamemnon's town, and will even destroy
One of the progeny of Aeacus's line,
Seed of Achilles, all-powerful-in-battle;
And who could pass over you in silence, Cato,
Or Cossus, you, or the family of the Gracchi,

Or the Scipios, the lightning bolts that brought
An end to Carthage, or Fabricius, you,
Austere in power, or, Serranus, you,   1140
Called to be consul from where you plowed the field.
O Fabii, where are you taking me in this breathless
Telling of the story? Here is that one,
Fabius Maximus, whose tactical art
Of brilliant inexhaustible delay,
Wears out the foe, and so will save our state.

There are those, I know it, who by their shaping art
Will call forth, from the bronze that breathes, the living
Features of the face; and those who by
Their art of eloquence argue and prevail   1150
In courts of law; or those who by their art
Describe with their pointing wands the radiant wheeling
Of all the stars in all the nighttime sky,
And can foretell the moment of their rising.
And Romans, never forget that this will be
Your appointed task: to use your arts to be
The governor of the world, to bring to it peace,
Serenely maintained with order and with justice,
To spare the defeated and to bring an end
To war by vanquishing the proud."   1160

These are
The words that Father Anchises spoke to them,
While they listened to him in wonder. And then he said:

"Look there! Behold! Marcellus comes! See how
He towers over all the others and
Is adorned with the glorious spoils that he will win
When he himself has killed the enemy chief.
When the Roman state is shaken, tottering, he
Will hold it steadfast, pursuing and chasing down
The Carthaginians and uprising Gaul;   1170

And he will offer to Father Quirinus a third
Rich set of spoils victoriously won."

As he was speaking Aeneas saw that there,
Walking beside that hero in procession,
Was a beautiful young man in shining armor,
But his face was without joy, his eyes downcast,
He said, "Who is that, Father, whom I see,
Walking at the warrior's side? Is it
His son or another in the lineage
Of this great family? What presence he has!   1180
What excitement about him there is, in the company
Of the others who walk with him. But see, how night's
Dark mournful shadows play upon his head!"
The tears starting up in his eyes, Father Anchises
Said to his son, "Do not inquire too soon
Into the greatest grief of your people; the Fates
Will let him only be briefly seen on earth,
Only a little while permitted to be.
You gods above, you knew that the gifts that were given
Weren't given to them to have for good and all.   1190
The Romans would have been beyond themselves.
What a sound of the weeping of heroes will there be,
Carried up from the famous Campus to Mars' great city.
What a funeral of lamentation, you,
O Tiber gliding past the tomb they'll build,
Will be the witness of. No other boy
Born of Ilian stock will bring such hope
To his Latin family; Romulus' land
Will never produce again a boy like this.
Alas for his faithfulness, alas for his truth,   1200
Alas for his unconquerable sword.
There's no one who could have withstood him in the battle,
Whether he fought on foot against the foe
Or spurred his foaming steed. Alas, poor boy,
Could it have been that you could have broken through

The confines of your unrelenting fate.
But you will be Marcellus. Oh let my hands
Strew purple lilies on the image of
Him who descends from me; O let me at least
Perform for him this unavailing duty."   1210

Thus as upon the airy plain they walk
Together through the region, observing all,
As Anchises leads his son through all there was
That was to be seen, exciting in his heart
A love and incitement for all the future glory,
And telling him of the wars that there would be,
And of the Laurentine race and the Latin towns,
And what he was to avoid and what to confront.

                    ❜ ❜ ❜

There are two gates of Sleep, one made of horn;
It is the gate through which the true shade may   1220
Make easy departure to the world above;
The other, of shining ivory, is the gate
Through which false dreams go up from the world below.
And as he tells them these things, Anchises leads
His son and the Sybil to the ivory gate,
And ushers them forth from there.

                    Aeneas returns
As soon as he can to his ships and to his comrades,
And then they sail together along the coast
To Caieta's port. The anchors of the fleet   1230
Are thrown from the prows; the sterns of the ships
Are aligned in rows in order along the shore.

Book Seven

Caieta, Aeneas's nurse, here where you died,
Your name brings fame undying to the shores.

And now, when pious Aeneas had performed
The final funeral rites and raised for her
A burial mound, and as soon as the high seas
Lowered themselves, and when they quieted down,
He opens his sails, and the fleet departs from the port.
The wind is steady as the night goes on,
Nor does the shining moon withhold her favor;
The moonlight gleams on the trembling water's surface.   10
They pass close by the shore where Circe, she
Who is the daughter of the Sun, in her
Secluded grove sings on unceasingly,
Her proud house lighting the darkness with lamps of cedar
Shedding their fragrance on the evening air,
As her shuttle shrills upon the web she weaves.
As they pass by they hear upon the shore
The roaring of lions furious at their chains,
And the raging of bristling boars and caged-up bears,
And the ululating howls of enormous wolf shapes.   20
These are the men whom the cruel goddess Circe
Had with her herbs and potions turned into beasts,
Robbing them of their humanness with her witchcraft.
But Father Neptune, so that the Trojans would
Not suffer the monstrous fate they would have suffered

Had they been brought into that harbor and
Had they set foot upon that shore, saw to it
That they were gotten past those seething shallows,
Keeping them safe. Then, as the morning's first
Rays of light were making the waters redden, 30
And high in the heavens in her roseate chariot
Aurora shone in the saffron light, the wind
Dropped suddenly, all the breezes, and,
Propelled only by oars, slowly they moved
Themselves along through the marbled quieted waters.
As they approached, Aeneas, looking toward
The shore from the sea, saw a great forest, and
The eddying waters of the beautiful river,
The Tiber, bursting forth into the ocean
And pouring its golden sands into the waves. 40
All kinds of birds, the kinds that frequent a river
And its riverbanks, were flying above and around,
And in the groves delighting the skies with their songs.
Aeneas told his cohort to change their course,
And turn their prows to land, and so they entered
The tree-shaded river.

, , ,

O Muse Erato, help me. Who
Were the kings, who were they, what was it like,
Back then when the strangers came to Ausonian shores?
This is the story, the story of the battles 50
That then took place, and the story of how it all started.
Muse, come to the aid of your singer. The history I
Will tell is of the terrible wars and those
Whose great hearts' courage urged them to their deaths,
Etrurians and Hesperians in arms,
In action on the fields. Here in this poem
A greater ordering of things is being told;
I enter here upon this greater story.

Now agèd, the king, Latinus, had governed his country,
His towns and fields, for many peaceful years,   60
He was, it is said, the son of Faunus and
Marica, the Laurentine nymph. And, Saturn, the claim
Is that the father of Faunus, Picus, was
Your son and so you are the founder and
Original of the family. Latinus's son,
His masculine offspring, was, by the gods' decision,
Fated to die while still in the bloom of youth,
And so Latinus's daughter was left to be
The one to carry forward and preserve
The family lineage. She was of age   70
To marry now, to be a bride, and there
Were many in all Ausonia and Latium
Who sought her hand. But of them all the most
Beautiful and of noblest parentage
Was Turnus. It was he of whom the queen
So powerfully wished that he should be
Their son-in-law in union with their house.
But there were alarming portents from the gods,
That stood in the way of this. Deep within
The royal house, in the highest inner court,   80
There was a laurel tree, with its sacred leaves,
Venerated there for many years.
Latinus himself, it's said, had planted the tree
In honor of Phoebus Apollo when he built
His house and raised his towers, wherefore his people,
For ever after that, were called Laurentes.
High up in the topmost branches, wonderful,
Loud humming carried across the liquid air,
And, pendant from the leafy laurel boughs,
Hanging with feet entwined, a swarm of bees!   90
A prophet, seeing them, cried out at once,
"There is a stranger coming, and with him many

Others swarming from where it is he comes from,
Seeking the place he comes to, and will reign
High up among the towers of this town."
While speaking thus he takes the sacred torch
To light the altar fire. The maiden, Lavinia,
Stands beside her father there, and (oh!)
They saw her long hair (horror!) caught ablaze,
They saw her ornate headdress caught afire,   100
Her hair on fire, and the garland that she wore
Upon her head, and the yellow light of the fire
Scattering as she ran through the palace halls.
And when this wonder was known it was said by those
Who heard it that the light of her fame was glory,
But it boded war that was coming upon the people.

Father Latinus was much concerned by this,
And so he sought the oracle in the great
Grove beneath the high mountain, the place where was
A sacred fountain from whose sounding waters   110
Mephitic vapors breathed. It was the place
Where those whose anxieties sought for aid had come,
Italians, and from all Oenotria,
And where the seer, at night, lying upon
The fleece of sacrificed sheep, sought dreams, and in
His sleep the dreams would come, in which he spoke
To those below in the Underworld, along
The rivers there; and he in converse spoke
To Acheron in deep Avernus. And when
Latinus came to the oracle's place, he slew,   120
By the ritual prescribed, a hundred sheep,
And lay upon their slaughtered fleece, and dreamed,
And in his sleep he heard, from deep within
The surrounding grove, a voice that cried, "Do not
Let her be married to one who is born a Latin.
O progeny, the marriage bed is not
Prepared for such. Strangers are coming here

To be your sons, and you by them will be
Exalted to the stars, and as the sun
Looks down upon the oceans as it passes   130
From where it rises up, to where it sets,
So will your people, like the sun, look down
Upon the kingdoms they rule, turning below them."
Latinus did not keep from the ears of others
What was told to him, and therefore Rumor, flying
Everywhere through Ausonia, already
By the time the ships of the sons of Laomedon
Had come upon the grassy shore, had told it.

                        ⸲ ⸲ ⸲

As Aeneas and his companions and beautiful
Iulus, his son, were reclining under the high   140
Trees of the grove, and had spread, as Jupiter
Advised them to do, their simple meal of fruits
Upon wheaten cakes, the gifts of Ceres, and when
These fruits were not enough to satisfy
Their hunger, with voracious teeth and jaws
They devoured the wheaten cakes, profaning the fateful
Circles and quarter-circles, not sparing even
The broad green leaves the cakes were set upon,
Little Iulus laughingly said, "Oh ! Look!
We're eating the tables too!" When he said this,   150
And said no more, their wandering was done.
Stunned by what the will of heaven was saying,
Father Aeneas cried out, "Hail promised land!
Hail faithful gods of Troy. This is our home.
My father, Anchises, now I remember it,
Bequeathed to me this mystery of the Fates:
'My son, when you have gotten to a place
Where you are so hungry, so little to eat, that you
Devour the very plates you're eating on,
That is when you will know that you are there   160

Where you have hope that you have found a home.
Now you must build, and build with your own hands,
Though they are weary, your dwelling places there,
Protected by a mound for battlement.'
This is that hunger that was prophesied;
This is the last ordeal awaiting us;
This is the limit of what we had to suffer.
So, joyfully when the morning sun comes up
Tomorrow, let us see what places there are,
What people in them, what is their principal town,   170
And from the harbor let us explore, this way
And that, discovering where it is we are.
But now, pour from your cups a libation to Jove,
And call in prayer upon my father, Anchises.
Set out before us again the votive wine."

And then he garlanded his temples with
A leafy branch, and prayed thus to the gods,
First to the genius of the place, and next
To Tellus, the Earth, first of the gods, and then
To the nymphs and to the rivers as yet unknown,   180
And he prayed to the Night and to its orbs that rise
When the darkness comes, and to Idaean Jove,
And to the Phrygian Mother, all these in order;
And to his mother and father, the one on high
In the heavens, the other below in Erebus.
Then Jupiter thundered thrice, in a clear sky,
And with his own omnipotent hand shook forth
A golden shower of incandescent rays.
Thus through the Trojan host the news was heard,
That the day had come for building the city that had   190
Been promised to them, and so, because of this
Great sign, in their joy the feasting was renewed,
And the bowls and the garlanded wine set out again.

, , ,

As soon as day arising began to carry
Her lamp across the sky, the Trojans set out
To explore the towns and countryside and shores,
Here seeing the pools the river Numicus sprang from,
There the Tiber, and there where the dwellings were
Of the brave Latins. And then the son of Anchises
As emissaries chose three hundred men,   200
Who represented every Teucrian order,
Commanding them to go to the august royal
Town of the king, each of them to carry
A branch in his hands of Pallas Athena's olive,
Swathed in wool, and there to seek to secure
A peaceful welcome from Latinus the king.

They hastened to obey and moved off quickly
To carry out their embassy. Meanwhile
Aeneas dug a shallow trench to show
With an outline where the walls were going to be,   210
Doing the work himself of preparing the ground,
And marking there on the coast what was the first
Settlement of the Trojans, made like a camp,
Around it a trench and the walls of a battlement.

                        ʼ ʼ ʼ

Now those he had sent before them were approaching
The city, and saw, rising before them, its high
Roofs and towers, and so they came near to its walls.
Here there were boys and young men in their flower,
Improving their riding skills and practicing
Driving their dusty chariots back and forth,   220
Hurling their whirling javelins through the air,
Throwing sharp darts, challenging one another
To race, or to box—when suddenly a scout
Came galloping up with news for the old king's ears,
That a number of men in unfamiliar clothes,

Big men, were coming near. The king commanded
That they be brought into the hall, where he
Seated himself upon his ancestral throne.
The palace, huge, imposing, hundred-columned,
At the highest point in the town, in a sacred grove,   230
Had been the royal palace since Picus's time.
It was the place where the succeeding kings,
From the beginning took up the scepter and rods
That symbolized their kingship office, and where,
After the ritual slaughtering of a ram,
To be their meal, the elders sat in council
At their accustomed places at their tables.
And on the porch, one after another, in order
Were images of the rulers from the beginning.
Italus was there, and Father Saturn, the vintner   240
With his curvèd pruning knife, old Saturn, and
Doubled-faced Janus, and all the ancient kings.
And there were images too of those who'd suffered
Wounds in brave defense of their fatherland;
And hanging from the doorposts of the temple
Were trophies from the battles of the past,
Chariots, curved axes, great bolts of iron
Taken from the gates of alien cities,
Spears, and shields, and broken beaks, the prows
Of enemy ships. And there was the image of   250
Picus himself, horsebreaker, in his short
Quirinal robe, white-mantled, and in his left
Hand holding his crooked augural staff, and in
His right his little oval battle shield,
Picus, whom Circe, his bride, lusting for him,
Had struck with her golden rod, and with a potion,
Changed him into a bird with colored wings.

This was that sacred temple where Latinus,
Upon the throne of his gods, called in the Teucrian
Envoys to his presence, and with a placid   260

Countenance spoke first, and gently, to them:
"Tell me, Dardanians—we are not unaware
Of who you are; and the journey you've been making
Across the seas is not unheard of by us—
What are you seeking? What is it that has brought you
Across the cerulean waters to our shore?
Is it that you have lost your way, or was it
Tempests acting upon you (for we are told
That this has happened to many upon the deep),
That you have entered in, between our river's   270
Banks, and harbored your fleet within our port?
Do not refuse our welcome. Remember that we
Latins are of the race of Saturn, who
Following in the ways of our ancient father,
Need no external laws to obey or be
Forbidden by; we act of our own free wills.
I seem to remember, though the old story grows
Fainter and fainter as the years go by,
That the Auruncian elders said that Dardanus
Was born here, and that he left his Etrurian town,   280
Corythus, to go to Phrygian Ida and then
To Thracian Samos, now called Samothrace,
He who is now admitted to the golden
Palace among the stars, his altar added
To the number of the altars of the gods."

When the old king had finished speaking, then
Ilioneus said these words: "O king, illustrious
Descendant of the line of Faunus, it wasn't
A black storm of winter nor was it surging seas
That drove us this way, nor was it that we mistook   290
A reading of the stars or of a coastline.
We came of our own free will, having been driven
Out of our kingdom, the greatest in the world
That the sun, looking down from Olympus, could ever see.
We are, from our beginning, of Jupiter's line;

Dardanian soldiers rejoice at knowing this;
Our king, Aeneas, is of this highest descent,
And it is Aeneas the Trojan who has brought us,
Here to your shores. How terrible was that storm
That came from savage Mycenae and raged across   300
The fields of Ida, and we have sailed over many
Desolate seas, seeking a simple place
To come ashore and make our dwellings there
Where the air and the water are open and free to all.
We bring no harm to you, nor any shame,
And the glory of your acceptance will never grow dim.
Ausonia will never regret that we
Have come and have been welcomed. I swear it by
The right arm of Aeneas, who by so much
Has been tested, and been found true, on the battlefield.   310
Do not scorn us that we come here bringing garlands,
Petitioning. There are many lands which have sought
To be allied with us. But the gods have willed
That these your lands are the place that we must come to.
This is the land from which Dardanus came.
Apollo calls us here; he has decreed that we
Must return to the banks of the Tuscan river Tiber
And to the spring of Numicus. These poor relics
Of what his fortunes were, father Aeneas
Offers, saved from the fires that burned down Troy: 320
This is the golden cup from which his own father,
Anchises, poured libations at the altars;
This is the vesture Priam wore when he
Sat in assembly to give out laws and make
His proclamations; this is his scepter, and this
The diadem, the sacred headdress, woven
By Ilium's daughters."

                    Latinus's head was bowed
As he heard these words; he sat there motionless,

But scanning intently, reading his inward thoughts.   330
Though he was moved to see the richly woven
Purple regalia of King Priam, he
Was moved still more by his thoughts of his daughter's marriage,
Her marriage bed, and the promises of Faunus.
This must be the one, the prophesied one, this must
Be the one declared to come from another place
To share in the power, and by his glorious deeds
To bring out future generations to rule
Over all the world. At last he speaks, with joy:
"I hope that now the gods are prospering   340
What we have wished for, and they have prophesied.
We freely grant what you have asked for, Trojans,
And we are glad to accept the gifts you offer.
May your leader come here, if so he wishes, that I
May welcome him and touch his sovereign hand,
That peace may be with ceremony pledged.
So now, return to him, bearing these words.
I have a daughter, of whom, by the oracles
Who spoke in my father's shrine, and by many signs,
It was made known to me that I must not   350
Wed her to any son of our own race;
Strangers will come from far away, whose blood,
They sing, will raise our fame to the stars: and I
Believe, and willingly believe, that this
Is he whose coming is promised by the omens."

When he had spoken thus the king commanded
That from their high stalls in his stables three hundred
Glossy-coated horses, hooves as rapid
As rapid-beating wings, caparisoned in purple,
Their champing mouths fitted with golden bits,   360
Bridle reins hung with dangled golden chains,
Should be brought forth and given to the envoys
In ordered courtesy, and, for Aeneas,

A chariot, in his absence, to it yoked
A pair of steeds, their nostrils breathing fire,
Whom clever Circe bred from a mortal mare
And an immortal stallion stolen from
Her father's stables. The envoys mounted high,
With Latinus's words and gifts, carrying peace.

〃〃〃

But Jupiter's fierce wife, borne on the air,   370
Was coming back from Argos, Inachus' town,
When from as far away across the sky
As Pachymus, over in Sicily, she saw
Joyful Aeneas and the anchored fleet
And the roofs of houses that were being built.
And she knew that the Trojans had occupied the land,
And that the ships were empty there on the beach,
Because they had come ashore. Shaking her head,
Full of anger, her heart congested with rage,
She spoke these words and said: "This cursed people!   380
How is it that their fate is so obverse
To what I destined it to be? Why could
Their bodies on the Sigean plains not lie
Forever overcome by force? When Troy
Was on fire, why weren't they all burned up?
Through all those spears and fire they made their way,
They found a way. Now do they think my power's
Spent? Or that my rage has exhausted itself,
And that it has quieted down? I've dared to oppose them
By sea, and from the sky, and everywhere,   390
And what good have they done, have the Syrtes done,
Has Scylla done, has Charybdis's vortex done?
There they are, safe and sound in Tiberside,
Just as they wanted to be. Mars destroyed
The powerful Lapiths, and the sovereign god

Himself conceded the Calydonians to
The anger of Diana. What had the Lapiths
Done to deserve what happened to them? What had
The Calydonians done? But I, the wife
Of Jove, have been defeated by Aeneas,   400
And everything I have tried has turned against me.
But if my goddess power is not enough,
I'll look for help elsewhere than from above.
I'll look below, to Acheron. The Fates
Have decided that Aeneas is in Latium,
And he will have Lavinia for his bride,
But I will make them pay. Father-in-law
And son-in-law may come together but
The cost will be the blood of both their people.
Virgin, your dowry will be the blood of Trojans   410
And the blood of Rutulians; and Bellona,
The goddess of war, will be your matron of honor.
It wasn't only Hecuba, Cisseus' daughter,
Who dreamed that when she was giving birth to Paris,
She was giving birth to a flaming torch. Venus, too,
Gave birth to another torch, another Paris,
Who'll be the torch that burns down a second Troy."

                            ʼ ʼ ʼ

Then terrifying Juno flew down to the earth,
And from the shades below she stirred up she,
Allecto, where she was, among the dire Furies,   420
She, bringer of grief, who has in her heart all rage,
Distress of war, vile obloquy, and plot.
Pluto, her father, hated his monster daughter,
Her sisters in Tartarus hated their monster sister,
So many writhing mouthing changes in
Her savage face, and black snakes sprouting from
Her head and crawling there. It is to such

That Juno spoke to her: "Virgin, begotten
Daughter of Night, do this for me, what you
Can do for me, what you know how to do.   430
See that my fame, my honor, be not damaged,
And that Aeneas not win Latinus's favor
For this marriage. See to it that the Trojans
Will never find their dwelling place and home
In Italy. You know the ways to do it.
You can make brother living in harmony
With brother in concord turn on each other and bring
Their house in hatred down around their heads.
You know the way to bring the funeral torch.
Your ways to hurt have a thousand different names.   440
Your heart is full of possibilities.
Shake them all loose at once. Do all of them.
Tear peace to pieces. Sow the seeds of war.
Make all the young men mad to take up arms."

                              ❧ ❧ ❧

Filled with Gorgonian poison Allecto now
Seeks Latium and Latinus's high halls,
And sits on the quiet doorstep of Amata,
Who was already burning with distress,
As a woman would, because of the incursion
Of Teucrians, and what was happening to   450
The marriage of Turnus. And as Amata was there,
And Allecto on the threshold, Allecto pulled
A serpent-tress that grew upon her head
And put it upon Amata's unknowing body;
It got itself to where her heartbeat was;
It slithered between her snowy breasts; it breathed
Into her mouth; it moved upon her flesh
Where it would go; and it became a golden
Necklace of twisted strands that curled around
Her throat; it was a long ribbon, binding her hair   460

And hanging down behind; it wandered smoothly
Upon her body, gliding everywhere.

As yet unknowing, and not yet fully enraged,
The infection not yet having made its way
Sufficiently through all her veins and burning
Around her bones as it would do, she spoke
To the king still gently and as a mother would,
Distressed by the prospect of a Phrygian marriage,
And tearful because of it. She said to her spouse,
"Is it true that our daughter is to be given away   470
To one of the Teucrian exiles, to take her home
As a wife? Where is your pity for her, or for
Her mother, when, just as soon as there will be
The first North Wind, this treacherous stranger will carry
Our hapless plundered virgin away with him?
Was it not this that the Phrygian shepherd did,
When he entered Lacedemonia and carried
Ledean Helen away to the Trojan cities?
Where are your sacred vows? Where is your ancient
Obligation to what has been promised to Turnus?   480
If it is true that Faunus commanded that she
Be married to one from elsewhere, and if this must be,
Then all those tribes around not subject to us
Are elsewhere, free, other than us; and Turnus's
Own origins are from Inachus and Acrisius,
Deep in the realm of faraway Mycenae."

As soon as she perceived that her words had not
Succeeded in changing her Latinus's mind,
The poison of the serpent suddenly had
Its full effect upon her, and within her,   490
Penetrating everywhere, flowing into,
And seeping through, her viscera; and then
This unhappy, frenzied woman, who was aroused
To madness by the monstrous images

She saw in her head, or that she thought she saw,
Raged crazily throughout the town. It's as
When boys, at play, excited to see the sight,
Have sent a whiptop, struck by the cracking whip,
Spinning and flying across a courtyard, they
Gaze in dumbstruck wonder at the top   500
And what it's doing as it sweeps around
The curving empty atrial space; they gaze
Transfixed by what the whirling top is doing
And what the whip has done to make it do it;
Like this, like such a top, her fury whirled
And agitated all the proud towns of Latium.
Then she became as if she were a maenad,
And in her madness performed more shocking and
Impious acts, and she took her daughter away,
And hid her from sight in a leafy mountain forest,   510
In order to take the marriage from the Trojans
And keep the wedding torches from being lighted,
Screaming "Evoe Bacchus" and crying out,
"It is only you the virgin is worthy of,
To carry your torch, and only for you she carries
The thyrsus in your chorus, only to Bacchus
She consecrates her unbound hair." The fame
Of this spreads wide, and burns in the hearts of mothers;
Aroused to frenzy like hers, they leave their homes,
Looking for other places to lay their heads;   520
They bare their necks, let loose their hair to the wind
And the weather, they fill the air with their howling cries,
They wear the skins of fawns, they carry spears,
And in their midst bloodshot Amata sings,
Wielding a blazing pine torch, fervently sings,
The wedding song of her daughter and of Turnus,
And cries out to the others, "Wherever you are,
You loyal Latian mothers, if you have any
Pity for me, if you know the rights of mothers
And if the knowledge gnaws at your hearts, come join   530

The orgiastic rites, let loose the fillets
That bind your hair." And thus it was for the queen,
Out there in the woods among wild animals,
Goaded to this by Allecto's Bacchic rapture.

⸎ ⸎ ⸎

Then, when Allecto was satisfied that she
Had disrupted all of Latinus's plans and turned
His household upside down, she went aloft,
And on her dusky gloomy wings she flew
To the high walls of the brave Rutulians, where
Danae, when the South Wind brought her there,   540
Had founded a town for her Acrisians to dwell in;
The ancients called it Ardea, "bright shining,"
"Ardea" still its wonderful name, though fortune
Has left it behind. There, under this roof, was Turnus,
Sound asleep in the quiet of the night.
Allecto changed her looks, while Turnus lay there
In deep unknowing. Instead of her detestable
Face and dreadful Furial limbs she looked
Like Calybe, old woman priestess of
Juno's temple, her face all agèd wrinkles,   550
Her white hair tied with a ribbon and secured
With a sprig of olive leaves, and thus she appeared
Before young Turnus's sleeping eyes, and said,
"Turnus, do you not see that all your hopes
Are lost? Latinus has changed his plans and he
Is giving away what he owes to you, and what
Your blood has earned, to the foreign intruders. He
Is giving away the dowry and the scepter
Promised to you, and he has sought for a stranger,
An alien from a foreign land, as heir.   560
You have been treated with scorn. Rise up! Confront
What's happening! Demolish the Trojans! Scatter
Their broken swords and shields upon the field!

This is what Saturn's daughter tells you to do,
As you lie here in the darkness of the night.
Call up the armies, have them make ready, bring them
Out through the gates of their towns and into the fields!
Destroy those Trojans, who have put down their anchors
Here in our waters! Destroy their captain and
Burn their painted ships! You must obey   570
The commands of the gods above; and if Latinus
Refuses to give you the bride, as he has promised,
Confront him with yourself in the armor of war!"
Then Turnus, laughing at her, replied, in his sleep,
"The news of their arrival in our waters
Has scarcely failed to reach my ears; nor is there
Anything to fear. Juno has not
Forgotten us, old mother. You are old,
Old worn-out creature, fooling around with false
Prophecies and worries. Go back to dusting   580
The effigies of the gods in the temple. Leave
Matters of peace and war to us men who know
How to deal with them."

                    Infuriated by
These words Allecto blazed enraged and he
Recoiled, his whole body shook, his words died away,
His eyes were paralyzed by what he was seeing
Revealed to him, the sight of what she was,
The snakes writhing upon her head and the writhing
Countenance of what it was she was,   590
Her rolling eyes, the cracking sound of her whip,
And he fell back in the faltering of his words.
She pulled from her snaky head two serpents and said,
"Old woman am I, withered am I, worn-out
And fooling around am I, did you say, with false
Omens and prophecies? Here I am! I come
From where down there the Sister Furies are,
And in our hands we handle death and war!"

Into his sleep she hurled a flaming torch
Ablaze with infernal darkness, into his breast.   600
Unholy dread possessed him utterly;
Sweat poured from everywhere upon his body;
In the bedroom everywhere he looked for weapons;
Everywhere in the house he lusted for
His sword; and he became his ecstasy
For glory and war. It's as when the sticks and branches
Beneath a huge cauldron of water are set on fire,
And there's the stirring, and then the bubbling, and then
The seething, then the boiling, then the foaming
Boiling wave uprising and the black   610
Smoke as it all pours up and out and over.

Despising peace he orders all his captains
And all their people to arm themselves and march
Against the alien foreigners and Latinus.
"Defend our Italy; expel the strangers.
I am enough, against the both of them,
The Latins and the Trojans!" He calls upon
The gods to hear him swear what he will do,
And all the Rutulians, hearing him, incite
Each other to war, aroused by Turnus's beauty,   620
Or by the thought of his ancestral race,
Or by his glory in arms.

                    〟 〟 〟

                              Then, satisfied
With what she had done to stir up Turnus and
All of his people, she flew on dusky wings
To where the Trojans were. There, by the shore,
Lovely Iulus was setting out hunting traps,
And there the Fury roused up the hunting dogs,
Exciting them by means of the scent of a stag
She made their noses know about and be   630

Made rabid by. This was the cause of how
The hearts of those in the fields were inflamed by war.
The stag they scented was a magnificent creature,
Beautiful to look at, his head adorned
With a great panoply of curved forked antlers.
He had, when a foundling fawn, been brought to their home
By the little sons of Tyrrhus and been cared for
By Silvia, their sister, who petted it,
And combed its hair, and fed it with milk, and bathed it
In the pure clear waters of a fountain, and   640
Garlanded its horns with pretty ribbons,
So, utterly accustomed to his mistress,
And tamed, the stag would wander in the fields
By day, just as he would, and then at night
He'd come back home and enter into the house,
No matter how late it was, and be at peace there.
But Ascanius' dogs discovered the wandering stag
Where sometimes it liked to swim, in the heat of the day,
Cooling itself in the river's downstream flowing,
And sometimes resting itself on the verdant bank;   650
And little Ascanius, eager to be the best
Hunter among his fellows, pointed his arrow,
And drew back to tightness the strings of his bending bow,
And let it go, and the goddess corrected the arrow's
Wobbling flight and with a great hissing sound
It struck the animal's flank and went into its belly.
The wounded creature fled for refuge under
The roof of the house, the house that it knew so well,
And sought its familiar stall, where it lay down,
Beseechingly weeping and weeping and calling out.   660
The house was filled with its pitiful woeful noise,
And Silvia, when she saw it and saw what had happened,
Cried out for help, beating her arms with her hands
In her distress and calling the farmers, who
As if spontaneously and unasked for (for

The fiend already was there in the silent woods),
Came running and shouting, with clubs and poles and knot-holed
Limbs of trees shaped into weapons. Rage made them
Find for weapons whatever there was they could,
And Pyrrhus, who had, with a wedge, been cleaving the trunk 670
Of an oak into fours, his great chest heaving, shouted
With fury for all of his shepherds, and took up an axe.

When cruel Allecto, from where she was, caught sight
Of what was happening, she saw that there
Was a fresh new opportunity for harm.
She flew to the very top of the farmhouse roof
And on her curved war trumpet sent forth a blast,
A signal, in a Tartarean voice that sounded
All through the countryside and far beyond,
A sound unceasing that caused all the groves to tremble, 680
And was heard in the deepest inwardnesses of woods;
Its sound was heard as far as Trivia's lake,
And Nar's white sulfurous waters, and as far
As the Velinian Fountains, and fearful mothers,
Hearing it, clutched their children to their breasts.
And then, in truth, obedient to the dire
Sound of the hellish trumpet that they heard,
They all came hurrying from where they were,
The farmers with whatever weapons they found,
And the Trojan youths, in aid of Ascanius, pouring 690
Out through the open gates of the Trojan camp.
The battle lines were drawn, and now the two sides
Faced each other, no longer armed with clubs
Or poles or limbs of trees, but double-edged
Steel weapons. Now in the cornfield there is a dark
Forest of swords to be seen and there is a glinting
Of brass in the sun, reflecting light to the clouds,
As when, at sea, when the wind grows strong, at first
The water begins to whiten, then little by little

The waves grow high and higher and higher and higher,   700
Until at last the whole sea heaves itself up
In surges from the lowest depths to the highest
Reaches of the sky. Then the young Almo,
Tyrrhus's youngest son, was struck by an arrow.
It got him in his throat, filling with blood
The path of breath and speech. Among the many
Fallen bodies was old Galaesus's body,
Slain while trying his best to keep the peace,
Galaesus, who was the most just of them all,
And the richest, with five herds of his coming home   710
From the fields at night, and five flocks bleating, and
A hundred plows of his plowing the soil of his farm.

                              ⸔ ⸔ ⸔

When the goddess saw how the battle was going on,
And the two sides evenly matched in deadly conflict,
She, leaving Hesperia, flew up high in the sky
To where Juno was, and there she said, in tones
Of satisfaction about her accomplishment,
"Lo! here is what I've done. I've caused dire war,
Bringing them all together against the Trojans.
Now they have shed the first Ausonian blood.   720
And if you say I can do it, I will do more.
Carrying everywhere rumors of war, exciting
All their hearts with unanimous lust for blood.
I will sow all the land with blood!" But Juno said,
"Deceit and terror abound. It is established.
Face to face they fight, and now the weapons
That they at first took up by happenstance
Are stained with crucial blood. This is how they,
Venus's pride and joy, and King Latinus,
Will celebrate the matrimonial feast.   730
It is not Olympus's ruler's will that you

Should wander freely in the upper air.
Whatever is still to be done, I'll do myself."

The monster lifted up her hissing wings,
And flew away to seek her home down there
Beside the river Cocytus. There is a place
In Italy, high up, famously called
Amsanctius Vale, still higher hills above it,
And with a great forest crowding around a river
That swirls and roars and crashes upon its rocks;   740
And in this place there is a horrific cavern,
From which the dreadful breath of Dis breathes forth,
And there's a gorge where Acheron spews up,
And there it was that the horrible Fury hid,
Relieving earth and heaven when she went.

                    ⸼ ⸼ ⸼

Then Saturn's daughter took matters into her own
Hands and put the finishing touches on
The mischief. The shepherds all together came
Back from the fields where the fighting was, and bringing
Young Almo's body with them, and the body   750
Of old Galaesus, its face atrociously mangled.
The shepherds came calling out to the gods and to
Latinus, calling on him for justice, and Turnus
Was there in the midst of all of it, crying out
Against the killing, and so his rage's fire
Exacerbated the raging of the shepherds:
"The Trojans have been called in, into the kingdom.
Our blood will be mingled with theirs. I've been expelled
From the house!" And then it was the mothers, those
Who danced in ecstatic orgiastic dance   760
To Bacchus in the pathless woods (it was
Amata's example that brought them to it). All

Of these people came together calling for war.
Importuning they gathered before the house
Of Latinus. He was as a cliff unmoved by the force
Of the howling waves that dashed themselves against it,
Eddying, boiling, sea-weed flung back and forth
In the violent incoherence of the ocean.
When he saw that nothing could be done against
The blind unhearing stubbornness of their rage,   770
And that savage Juno's rage was having its way,
He called on the gods and the empty winds to witness,
And cried, "The Fates have broken us. The storm
Has swept us away. My miserable people,
You are going to have to pay for what your poisoned
Sacrilegious blood is making you do.
Wicked Turnus, you'll pray to the gods too late
To escape the punishment that's coming to you.
As for myself, I have come to the end of my days,
To the quiet there, but at the portal all   780
Hope of the happiness of the end is spoiled."
Having said this he said no more, and went
Into his palace and shut himself away,
Letting the reins of governance fall from his hands.

                              ❛ ❜ ❜

There was a custom in Hesperia,
In Latium, later adopted as a custom,
And a ritual, by the people of Alba, and
Still later by the still greater city of Rome:
When the leaders of the city have decided
Upon a course of war, whether against   790
The Getae, the Hyrcani or, still farther,
The Indians, the Land of the Rising Sun,
Or the Parthians to bring back the martial standards,
There are twin gates, which are called the Gates of War,
And are sacred to the god; they are secured

By one hundred bolts made from the strongest iron,
And Janus, gatekeeper, never leaves his post.

Here, when the Fathers in their Council have
Decided upon the course of war, the Consul,
Dressed in the Quirinal toga and Gabinian   800
Sash of office, approaches the Twin War Gates,
And opens their locks; slowly they open as
They turn in their shrieking iron sockets, and then
The Consul cries out to the people that war is declared.
Immediately the brazen trumpets loudly
Sound their raucous agreement that it is so.
But when old Latinus was urged to open the gates
Of war in this way, he refused to perform this hateful
Ministry, and would not touch the bars,
And hid himself in his house, unseen in darkness.   810
Therefore the queen of the gods came down from the sky,
And with a powerful hand she pushed the doors open,
The doorposts turning slowly in their sockets.
Ausonia had been peaceful; now it was not.
Some of them readied themselves to be foot soldiers,
Others high on their horses getting ready
To be the cavalry, the dust rising up
From the hooves of excited steeds; the people were busy
Making shields and polishing them with lard
Into brightness; javelins too were shining;   820
Axes were sharpened, one side and then the other,
Against the whetstone; there was a general outcry
Calling for weapons; it was a joy to see
The banners waving and hear the sounding trumpets.
Five towns set up anvils and forges to help in the work,
Ardea, Crustumerium, mighty Atina,
Proud Tibur, Amtemna with its towers, they all
Were busy hollowing helmets to make them fit
For the heads of heroes, framing new shields, breastplates
Of bronze, greaves fashioned of ductile polished silver.   830

No longer do they honor the pruning knife
Or the plow; in their furnaces they turn their plowshares
Into swords. The trumpet sounds, the sign
For war. A soldier yokes his trembling horses to
His chariot, excitedly takes his helmet down
From the rooftree of his house, picks up his shield,
Puts on his breastplate, triple-woven gold,
And buckles on the sword he will rely on.

⸰ ⸰ ⸰

Now is the time to open Helicon,
O goddesses, and sing the roster of   840
What kings have been aroused to battle, and who
Are those who in their train have followed, filling
The beautiful land with armies, and to sing
Of heroes flowering in their shining armor.
O goddesses, O muses, it is you
Who have it in your memory and can tell
The story; the music of it as I try
To hear it sounds but faintly in our ears.

⸰ ⸰ ⸰

The first to take up arms and bring his army
From the Etrurian coast into the war   850
Was he who held the gods in such contempt,
Mezentius the cruel, and riding by his side,
Lausus, his son, who is more beautiful than
Any Laurentian except the beautiful Turnus,
Lausus, horse tamer and famous wild-beast hunter,
Deserver of a better father than this.
One thousand soldiers marched with the fated son.

There's Aventinus in his chariot
Festooned with palm tree leaves and drawn by its

Battle-victorious horses, Aventinus, 860
Glorious son of glorious Hercules;
He carried his father's famous shield, which had
The emblem on it of the Hydra head,
The Hydra and its hundred writhing snakeheads;
His mother, the priestess Rhea, bore him in secret,
The son of a god and a woman, and brought him into
The light on the high hill of the Aventine,
When Hercules came back to Laurentine fields,
After he killed and did away with Geryon,
And bathed his Iberian cattle in the Tiber. 870
Aventinus's soldiers carried pikes
And javelins and Sabine curved-edged spears;
And he himself was wearing a lion's pelt
That swayed its frightening mane around his shoulders,
As he walked in what his father wore, the lion's
Face, with its terrible gleaming teeth, on his head.

Next, two brothers, twins, coming down from walled
Tibur, the city named from Tiburtus, their brother,
Catillus and Coras, fierce Argive youths, undaunted
To be foremost in the missile-showering warfare, 880
Down the mountainside like Centaurs born
Among the clouds they come, as if from Othrys
Or down from snow-capped Homole, crashing their way
Through brushwood or past broken or bending branches,
Down through the hillside woods to join the fight.

Nor was Praeneste's founder absent from
The list, who was, they say, the son of Vulcan,
Found in a burning hearth, or so the story
Goes from ancient days; Caeculus was
A king and a shepherd too, and with him came 890
A host of men, recruited from far and wide.
Some were from high Praeneste, others from Juno's
Gabii, from Henreica, or from Anio's

Streams that scatter their drops like dew upon
The river rocks, and others from rich
Anagnia, and Amasenus's fields.
Not all of them have clanging shields, or swords,
Or rattling chariots; some of them fight
With slingshots throwing lead balls, and others carry
Darts in their hands; still others with hunting spears,   900
Two of them, in one hand; each of them wears
A yellow wolfskin cap to cover his head,
The left foot bare, the right in a rawhide shoe.

But Messapus next, horsebreaker, Neptune's son,
Whom neither swords nor fire could overcome,
Has suddenly roused a people up, who were
Unused to fighting, to take up arms again.
Here were Fescennium's men, and those from Aequi
Falisci, from Mount Soracte, Flavina, from
Ciminia's mountain lake, and Capena's groves;   910
They march in regimented order singing
Of their king who was born of the sea, and who is now
Leading them into war. It is as if
A flight of snow-white swans were passing above;
High in the liquid air their choral song,
Issuing from their long swan throats, was heard
As far as Asia's fens, as coming home
From pasturing on the sea, together they sang.

Behold, there's Clausus, of ancient Sabine blood,
With a great army of men, himself an army,   920
Whose Claudian name now spreads through tribes and peoples,
All throughout Latium, ever since the joining
Together of the Romans and the Sabine
People, so many marching with him now,
The Amiternians and the first Quirites,
The marchers from Eretum and the olive
Orchards of Mutusca, from Nomentum,

From the Rosean plains of Lake Velinus, and
From rocky Tetrica and Mount Severus, and
Casperia, and Foruli, and Hermus's banks,   930
And those who drink from the Tiber river and
Its tributary Fabaris, and those
Who are sent from frigid Norsia, and from Orta,
And from the oldest Latin tribes there are,
And from the lands that are divided by
The river Allia, ill-omened name; they were
As many as the ocean waves that come
In onto the Libyan shore as savage Orion
Hides himself in the winter sea or as
The scorching sun smites down on the thousand ears   940
Of corn in Herminus' or Lycia's yellow fields.
Earth trembles beneath their feet as they march past;
The clanging sounds of war gear everywhere.

After them came Halaesus, who had been one
Of Agamemnon's men, and hated the very
Sound of the name of Trojans, bringing with him
A thousand fierce warriors, those whose work at home
Was turning with their hoes the soil of vineyards
Where the felicitous grape called Massic is grown.
Others whose fathers had sent them down to the fight   950
From the high Auruncian hills, and with them others
Who came from the neighboring Sidicinian plains,
And others from Cales or else from where the river
Volturnus runs along its shallow course,
And marching with them were the Oscans too,
And the tough young men who came from Saticula.
Their javelins were strapped to their backs with thongs,
Small shields to protect their left sides, curved swords ready
For the man-to-man close combat they were made for.

Nor would you go unsung in these our songs,   960
Oebalus, whom the nymph Sebethis bore

To Telon, now an old man, when he was king
Of Teleboean Capri. His son, they say,
Was not content with the patrimony he
Inherited, but ruled far wider, over
The people of Sarrastria, and the plains
The river Sarnus waters, and the fields
Of Rufra, and Celemma, and those orchards
Rich with apples, as close nearby as Abella
Looks to the hand of him who throws them. Their hats   970
Are made of cork-bark; their bronze shields shine,
Their bronze swords shine in the sun as they march along.

And Ufens, you, famous warrior, who
Came from mountainous Nersa, and, marching with you,
Your grizzled Aequicoli comrade mountaineers,
Famous too as hunters in those forests,
And for their war gear as they work to turn
The hard soil of their fields, ready to take
Whatever they can take as highway plunder.

Next there came Umbro, a priest from Maruvium,   980
Who knows, by spells, by chants, by the magic of touch,
How to teach the viper and hydras how to abate
Their anger and fall asleep, and by his soothing
Arts to heal their bites; but there was nothing
The knowing in his sleep-inducing chanting,
Or his gathering of herbs on the Marsian slopes,
Could do to medicate against the sharp
Bite of a Trojan spear; therefore, Umbro,
The groves of Angitia weep, for you the pools
And the glassy waves of Lake Fucinus weep.   990

Then after him was Hippolytus' beautiful son,
Whose name was Virbius, the remarkable youth
Sent by his mother Aricia; he grew up
In Egeria's humid groves beside the lake

Where an altar was that was pleasing to Diana.
The story goes that Phaedra, Hippolytus' wicked
Stepmother, saw to it that his frightened horses
Suddenly bolted, his chariot overturned,
And he was killed. And this was the punishment
His own father had willed. But Diana, and   1000
The nymphs of Diana, took pity on him,
And by the arts of herbs and tender care
He was brought back to life under the stars
And the gentle winds of the heavens; but Jupiter
Was enraged that any mortal being should be
Brought back from the infernal shadows down there,
And with his thunderbolt therefore struck down
Asclepius the Healer, son of Apollo;
But Diana hid Hippolytus away,
In Egeria's grove, to live his life unseen,   1010
And changed his name to Virbius; after that,
Horn-footed horses were banned from being near
The temples of Diana in the grove,
Because on the beach beside the lake they'd been
Suddenly terrified by the sight of monsters,
And in their terror violently shied
And overturned the chariot and he died.
But now his son in a chariot goes by,
Driving his fiery horses toward the war.

And then, among the leaders, there is Turnus,   1020
Taller than the rest, and wearing a helmet
Triple-plumed, on which a Chimaera was
Breathing forth fire as if it were from Aetna,
Hotter and more fierce the hotter the fighting,
And the hotter and fiercer the fighting the hotter the fire
Spilled forth; and on the shield the big image of Io,
Horned already, changed already, into
A bristle-backed cow, and Argus, guarding her,
And, pouring the water from an urn, her father,

Inachus. And, behind Turnus, like a great cloud,   1030
A storm coming on, armies of armed men with
Their spears and armor, Argives, Auruncans, and,
From their ancient hills, the Rutuli and the Sicani,
The Sacranae troops in marching order, and
The Labicians with their painted shields, the men
Who plow the fields beside the Tiber and
Along the sacred river Numicus, or
Those who plow the high Rutulian hills
Or near the mountain Circaeus, or those whose fields
Lie under the protection of the mountain   1040
Of Jupiter of Anxur, or the groves
Whose verdure is the goddess Feronia's joy,
Or the black Saturan swamps, where the cold river
Ufens makes its way through its lowland valleys,
And disappears at last into the sea.

And finally there was the marvelous
Camilla of the Volsci, not of Minerva's
Distaff and her wool and wicker basket,
But bellatrix, a virgin warrior, who
Could outrun the very winds themselves across   1050
The nodding heads of the crop of this year's grain,
Leaving them all intact, or skimming over
The swelling waves of the sea, untouching, free.
The young men all came out from the fields, and all
Their mothers came out, astonished, from their houses,
To see her riding by; they're open-mouthed
With wonder at how her royal purple scarf
Flows back from her lovely smooth white shoulders, and
At how her fair hair flows through its golden clasp,
And her Lydian quiver of arrows and her myrtle   1060
Shepherd's staff, tipped with the sharp point of a spear.

Book Eight

When Turnus raised his banner of war above
His Laurentine citadel, there was the shock
Of the raucous noise of the trumpet's sound, the sound
Of horses snorting and neighing and the sound
Of rattling arms and armor, and all the people
Were swearing their allegiance to his cause,
All the youth of Latium going wild,
Coming together, aroused and raging for bloodshed.
The leaders that day were Ufens, and Messapus,
And Mezentius, the disrespecter of gods;   10
And the fields were wasted and emptied because the leaders
Had taken the farmers away from the work they were doing.
And Venulus was sent to Diomedes,
At his great city, seeking his aid, and telling
How the Trojan, Aeneas, has come with all his fleet,
And bringing his homeless defeated Penates with him,
Settles himself in Latium, and declares
That Fate declares that he's a king; and there
Are many tribes that are joining with him, and
The name of this Dardanian, this Trojan,   20
Is being heard more loudly every day,
Reverberating everywhere in Latium.
What he is up to, what he is hoping for
From the warfare underway, if the Fates are with him,
Greek Diomedes will be able to tell,
Better than King Latinus, or King Turnus.

That's how it was in Latium. And while all this
Was happening, the hero, Laomedon's heir,
Was all at sea in his mind about what to do,
Thinking about the war and what it is,   30
What was the plan, what were the dangers, how
Was it to go, thinking about these things
Over and over, looking this way and that,
As when the light on the trembling surface of water,
In a bronze bowl in a room, in the dark, reflecting
Perhaps the light of a ray of sunlight, or
Maybe a ray of moonlight coming in
Through a window of the room, is fleetingly seen
To touch and show itself on this or that object,
Or else on this or that place on the walls of the room,   40
And sometimes high above on the ceiling panels.
It was nighttime, and the time when all the creatures,
The wingèd ones and all the beasts, were weary,
And ready to go to sleep and rest their bodies,
And Aeneas, still disturbed about the war,
Laid himself down.

              After a little while
He dreamed, and into his troubled dream there came
The aged god himself of the beautiful Tiber,
Rising up from among the poplar leaves   50
That floated upon the water; his garment was
Thin-linen-woven, gray; his head was crowned
And shaded with a wreath of river reeds;
He came to help Aeneas, and his words
Brought resolution to perplexity,
And quieted his disquiet, dispelling his cares:
"Seed of the race of the gods, you have brought back
Past enemies, our Troy to the Latin fields,
And the Laurentine soil waiting for you.

This is the dwelling place for your Penates—   60
You must not take your gods away from here;
Don't be afraid of the menacings of war;
The wrath of the gods against you is now subsiding,
And this is not the figment of a dream—
A giant sow in a grove of ilex trees
Along the shore has given birth just now
To thirty offspring of her milk-white body—
White sow reclining now upon the ground,
White newborn young being nourished at her teats.
This is the place where your city is going to be,   70
The place of rest from all you have undergone.
Here in this place, after the passing of thirty
Years in their turning, Ascanius will build
A city called, in glory, 'Alba,' 'White.'
This prophecy is not uncertain; you
Must listen as I tell you in few words
How you will come, victorious, through all
This present circumstance. There are a people,
Who, following the flag of their king, Evander,
Came from Arcadia, descendants of Pallas,   80
Who when they chose the place upon the hills
Where they would dwell, and built their city there,
They named it Pallanteum in their forebear's honor.
They and the Latins are locked in incessant war.
Stretch out your hands to them, make them your allies,
Bring them into your camp, swear fealty together.
I'll show you how to go, upriver, to find them,
Rise up from your bed, O goddess-born, when the stars
Are setting and the day begins, and say
Your prayers to Juno, with supplicating vows   90
To win her favor and appease her wrath.
I will receive from you, when you are victor,
Your full payment to me of your vows and tributes.
I am that river that grazes between the banks
Of the rich fields, touching them tenderly,

I, cerulean river, most favored by
The heavens looking down. This is my home,
High cities witness my majestic flowing."
He said these things and plunged into the pool,
Seeking the deepest reach of the river water.   100

, , ,

Night and sleep departed from Aeneas;
He rose up from his bed and looked to the east,
Toward the rising sun and its ethereal light,
And then he went to the river and took water into
The hollows of the upturned palms of his hands,
And raised them up, according to the rite,
In offering to the deities of the place,
And spoke these fervent words in ecstasy:
"You nymphs, Laurentine nymphs, who dwell at the sources
From which the rivers flow, and Father Thybris,   110
Thou and thy sacred river, accept Aeneas.
Protect him from the dangers that will come,
Wherever you are in the pools, or in the streams,
Whatever the source you flow from in such beauty,
Pitying us for our troubles. Our offerings
Will honor you forever, divine horned god
Of Hesperian waters. Be with me now, and by
Your presence show that you give us your assent."
Aeneas thus in liturgy spoke these words.
And then, making ready, he chose two ships from his fleet,   120
Biremes, and chose the most skillful crews, and armed them,
Preparing them for the journey up the river.

Then, suddenly, there was a wonderful portent.
Upon the green bank of the river, in
A grove of verdant sheltering trees, there lay
A white mother sow with her newborn young, all of them
Of the same white color as she; and father Aeneas,

While his chosen comrades witnessed at the altar,
Sacrificed them as an offering to you,
Great Juno, in honor of you. And all that night   130
The swelling waters of the river were
Quieted by Thybris, the current reversed,
And all was almost as if it were a pond,
And the way upriver upon the changed current was easy.
And so the journey, long ago begun,
Continued as with glad cries together they went,
And as they went the waters they went upon,
And the woods along the riverbanks, were full
Of wonder, seeing the unfamiliar sight
Of gleaming shields, and men in painted boats,   140
As they came around a wooded river bend,
Cutting across reflections of sky and trees
In the placid water. The sun had mounted to
His halfway place in the sky when there, before them,
The Trojans saw a little scene of walls,
A scattering of roofs, and a citadel.
It was a scene that, later, Roman power
Exalted to the skies; but now it was
The humble town and kingdom of Evander.
The Trojans turned their prows to the riverbank.   150

> > >

It happened that on that day the Arcadian king
And all his men and his little senate were
Carrying out the rite of honor to
The son of Amphitron; the fragrant smoke
Was pouring from the altar. But when they all
Suddenly were aware of high boats coming,
Seeing them as they came, parting the leaves
That hung down low from the branches of the trees,
Quietly being rowed in toward the shore,
They stood up in alarm, the ritual   160

Interrupted. But Pallas, unafraid,
Ordered his people to continue the rites,
And he himself, alone, took up his spear,
And went toward them, and from a little distance,
Standing upon a hillock, spoke to them:
"Why, warriors, have you come by these unknown ways?
Where is it you are going? Who are you?
Do you bring peace or war with you?" From his ship
Aeneas held out toward him an olive branch,
And replied, in a peaceable tone of voice, "We are   170
Of the Trojan people; we come in friendship armed
Against the Latins, who in their insolence
Have sought to drive us away from where we were.
We, chosen leaders of the Dardanians,
Have come to speak to Evander and to offer
Alliance with him in the war." Pallas was
Astonished by what he said, and by the word
"Dardanians," and so he said to him,
"You must come under our welcoming roof, and speak
Directly to my father." He held out his hand   180
And grasped the hand of Aeneas, and together they
Proceeded away from the river and into the grove.

                              ⸗ ⸗ ⸗

Aeneas spoke to the king respectfully:
"Most honored of the Greeks, Fortune has willed
That I should come, entreating, and holding out
To you these branches swathed in woolen fillets.
I come not out of fear of you, a leader
Of Greeks, and an Arcadian, nor because
You are of the blood of Atrides' sons, but because
Of who it is I am, and what I have done,   190
And because of the holy oracles of the gods,
And because I share with you, whose fame is known

Throughout the world, an ancestry in common,
That links me to you. And therefore it is that I
Come willingly in obedience to the Fates.
Dardanus, Troy's first father and author, was
The child of Electra, and she was the child, as the Greeks
Have told us the story, of mighty Atlas, who holds
The stars in the heavens above upon his shoulders;
And you descend from Mercury, who was   200
Conceived and born of radiant Maia, upon
The cold summit of Mount Cyllene, and Maia,
If we believe what we have heard, was daughter
Of Atlas, the very same Atlas who carries the stars.
It is thus we share the same blood, thus we are kin.
This gives me confidence. I am not here
With artful tricks and stratagems of persuasion.
I am here before you, myself in my own body,
I am here as I am and here as what I have done,
A supplicant now at the threshold of your house.   210
The Daunians have brought cruel war upon us,
As they have done to you. They think that, once
They have driven us away, they will yoke all
Hesperia, and thus possess the seas
That wash the shores above, and the shores below.
Accept our friendship. Our hearts are strong in war;
We have been tried and tested in the fighting."

Thus Aeneas spoke, and while he was saying these things,
The light of the gaze of the other to whom he spoke
Was studying, for a long time, studying the eyes,   220
The whole body, of Aeneas, and at last he said,
"I recognized you at once. I welcome you
With delight. I remember your father's words, his voice,
His face, the way he looked. I remember a time
When Priam, Laomedon's son, had traveled to
Salamis, to visit his sister, Hesione,

And then went on to cold Arcadia,
Where I, in the bloom of youth, marveled to see
These Trojan grandees, and marveled to see the son
Of Laomedon, but most, to see Anchises   230
Walking there, tallest of all. I yearned
In my ardent youthful heart to speak to him
And shake his hand. I approached him eagerly,
And soon I was his guide in Pheneus' city;
And when he left he gave me a beautiful quiver
With arrows in it, a handsome woolen cape
Interwoven with gold, and also a pair of golden
Bridle bits, which my son Pallas has now.
Here is my hand in fellowship and faith.
Tomorrow morning when the light returns   240
Back down to the earth, we'll send you forth, happy,
Accompanied by an escort of troops, and with
Stores of materiel to support your mission.
Meanwhile, since when you came we were performing
An annual rite we cannot defer, we ask
The favor of having you join us in the worship,
And after that to join our family feasting."

Having said this, he commanded that the feast
Should recommence and that the drinking cups
Should be brought out again; he saw to it that   250
The Trojans were seated well upon the grass
And that the guest of honor, Aeneas, was led
To a maple throne with a cushion of a lion's
Shaggy hide. Aeneas and his Trojans
Dined well upon the sacrificial viands,
And when the communal feast had been concluded
And everyone's hunger was satisfied, the king,
Evander, said: "You must not think that this
Ritual, this customary feast,
By which our people pay honor to a god   260
To whom we owe our gratitude is but

A local superstition that ignores
The reverence that is due to the ancient gods.

Look at the cliff that overhangs us here,
With all its pending rubble of huge stones
Fallen down in chaotic ruin. This once
Was an enormous cave, with its inner chamber
Recessing as far far back as could be thought.
It was the dwelling of the semihuman
Monster Cacus. He lived there in the dark   270
Beyond what any rays of the sun could reach;
The ground back there in the blackness reeked with blood;
And hanging high upon the doors to the cave
Were pale deliquescing faces of human beings.
This monster was the child of Vulcan, and,
Like son like father, out of his mouth black fire
Spewed as he moved his giant bulk around.

In time help came. It was a god who came,
Just as he was returning from his glorious
Triumph over the triple Geryon monster,   280
Driving before him huge bulls and the oxen he'd won.
Cacus was raging out of his wits at what
Was happening, and trying in his mind
To think what it might be he could do about it,
To commit what crime or wicked stratagem
That never had been done before. And so
He went to where they were stabled and took away
Four bulls, outstanding in their beauty, and
Four heifers that were as beautiful too, and hid them
In the darkness of his cave. But he did so   290
By walking each one of them backward by pulling it
By its tail, so that whatever signs of what
He had done would seem to be the tracks of cattle
Going away from and not going toward
The entrance to the cave. But when Alcides was

Driving his cattle forth to go on their way,
Their bellowing and their mooing filled all the grove
And echoed back from the hills. But from the cave
There came a plaintive lowing, replying from
Deep in the cavernous dark. And so the monster   300
Cacus's cattle-rustling plan was spoiled.
When Hercules heard the heifers' plaintive call
He was enraged. He took up all of his weapons
And his heavy knotted oaken club, and raced,
On fire with fury, up to the top of the mountain.
This was the first time that our people ever
Saw fear in the eyes of Cacus, who fled, as fast
As he could go, fast as the wind, fright putting
Wings on his flying feet, to hide in his cave,
And once he got there, in a rush he broke   310
The iron chains by which an enormous rock
Had been suspended by his father's art,
And the rock came down behind the mighty doorposts
And blocked with its size and weight all entrance in.
Then Hercules arrived, huge in his anger,
Looking everywhere for how to get inside.
Three times he walked in fury around and around
And around and over the Aventine, in rage.
Three times he tried to break into the cave,
To force his way by forcing the giant rock   320
That blocked the entrance to the cave to move
Enough to let him get himself by, and he failed.
Three times he sat, exhausted, defeated by what
He was trying to do and what he was failing to do.
But there was a leaning spar of flint-rock rising
Up from the cavern roof, rising up higher
Than all the rest, a place suitable for
The foul nests of the carrion birds of the place.
It leaned over toward the river, and Hercules
Took hold of it, and with his might he wrenched it,   330
And bent it back, and suddenly its roots

Tore up, and the river in shock sprang back, and the sky
Thundered and Cacus's kingdom and all his realm
Down there below were suddenly revealed.
It was as if the whole of the Down Below,
All of the things that were hateful to the gods,
And its pale ghosts, the terrified Manes, were
Exposed to the scaring light. And there was Cacus
Bellowing in the unexpected sunlight.
Then Hercules from above bombarded him   340
With everything there was to bombard him with,
Great limbs of trees, and stones as big as mill wheels,
And everything; and Cacus, caught in the sunshine,
Walls on every side of him, without any
Way to get out, knowing that this was final,
Bellowed as he had never bellowed before,
Wonder to say it, vomiting forth a great
Darkness laced with fire, and Hercules,
Nothing stopping him leaped down into the darkness
And through the flames, and seized the monster by   350
His hairy throat, throttling him until
His eyeballs came out of their sockets and his throat
Was drained of all of its blood. Then Hercules
Quickly freed his cattle imprisoned there,
And dragged the hideous semihuman body
Out into the light, and there was no one who
Could leave off gazing at the terrible
Empty sockets of the creature's eyes,
And the fur that grew so thick on his beastly chest,
And at the scorched-out drained-out throat of this thing   360
That lay there dead at last."

>   ,   ,   ,

                         And after that
There was a rite of gratitude led by
The priest Potitius, he who was the first

To initiate the Herculean rites,
And by the Pinarii, custodians
Of the altar called by us, and which will be
Forever called, the Ara Maxima,
"For Hercules the Mightiest is the hero.
He is our god." And then Evander said,   370
"Warriors, hold out your cups in your right hands."
His hair was garlanded with the green and silver
Poplar leaves, colors of Hercules,
And in his hand he held the sacred goblet.
The others poured out libations at the altar
And offered their prayers to him who is their god.
As evening and its star were coming nearer,
The priests, led by Potitius, appeared before them,
Carrying torches and dressed, as was the custom,
In animal skins, bringing offerings of   380
A second feast; gifts were heaped upon
The altar as the Salii, wearing branches
Of poplar upon their heads, and singing as—
A choir of youth, another of old men—
They moved in dance around the fire-lit altar.
Their songs were songs of praise of Hercules
And of his deeds; of how he strangled those
Two monstrous serpents his stepmother set upon him;
And how he brought two cities down to ruin,
Troy and Oechalia, both of them famous in war;   390
Of how he carried out those hundred labors
He was fated to be put upon at the cruel
Behest of the goddess Juno by King Eurystheus,
"Unconquered, you were the one who slew Hylaeus
And Pholus, the cloud-born half-men Centaurs, and
You killed the prodigious monster-bull in Crete,
And the lions under that cliff in the Nemean desert;
The trembling Stygian lake was terrified
Of you, the guardian dog of Orcus, too,
Lying there in his cave, with his bloody half-eaten   400

Bones scattered around him; whatever Shapes, however
Terrible, confronting you, you did not lose
Your courage, not even when it was Typhoeus,
Tall as the world itself, towering above you
With all his weapons; you did not waver when
The many venom-fuming snakeheads of
The Lernaean Hydra were hissing around you, hail!
Truly the son of Jove, worthy addition
In glory to the gods, come to us now,
Be present at our rites." Thus ended their song   410
With, finally, and above all, what he had done
To the fire-breathing monster there in the cave.
The woods and hills were echoing with their song.

                              ＞ ＞ ＞

Then, when the altar rites had completed themselves,
Aeneas, Evander, and Pallas, Evander's son,
Walked together back in the little town,
And walking slowly because of Evander's age.
Aeneas was captivated by the charm
Of what he saw of the town, and by Evander's
Narration of how things were, in the olden times—   420
Evander who founded the citadel of Rome.
"These woods were first inhabited by nymphs
And fauns and by a people who were born
Of the trunks of oak trees, people who had no culture,
No habits or methods of work, who didn't know how
To yoke their oxen, or how to plant crops, or how
To save anything they had against the future.
They lived by what happened to fall down from the trees
Or what they happened to kill when they were hunting;
Hunter-gatherers merely. Then Saturn came   430
From Olympia, in flight from Jupiter.
Saturn gave laws and established customs for these
Undisciplined peoples dispersed among the high hills,

And called the region Latium, from 'to hide,'
Because he had hidden himself in refuge within
The region's boundaries. What he established
Was what men call today the Golden Age.
There, for a very long time, he ruled in peace.
But little by little there was degeneration;
Lesser people came, war lovers and greedy.   440
The Ausonians came, the Sicanians came, and the same
Condition of what it had been in Saturn's day
Faded away. Then cruel hard kings succeeded,
One of them Thybris, for whom the river was named,
Losing its old true name, which was Albula.
I came to this land, sent by all-powerful Fortune
And ineluctable Fate, and the warnings of
My mother, the nymph Carmentis, and by the divine
Authority of Apollo."

        Soon after he said this,   450
They came to an altar and to the gate the Romans
Later called Carmental, in honor of
The nymph Carmentis, she, who long before,
Predicted the greatness of Aeneas and
Pallenteum's glory. He showed him that huge wood where
Old Romulus, the tough, made a refuge; and told
Of the cold Lupercal cave beneath the cliff—
The Parrhasians called it the cave of Lycaean Pan.
He showed the grove of the Argileti and said
That this was the very place where Argus, when   460
He was a guest of Arcadians, was killed.
He took him to the Tarpeian Rock and to
The Capitoline, which is golden now, but then
Was only a tract of scrub and thorn and trees;
The natives here were terrified and awed
By the Rock and by this wild wooded place. He said,
"There's a god that lives on this leafy hill; we don't
Know who it is, what god it is. The Arcadians

Believe it is Jupiter himself, and think
That they have sometimes seen him with his right   470
Hand shaking his aegis and bringing on dark clouds.
Moreover you can see the remains of two
Old towns, the relics of the earlier people,
The towns Father Janus built, and Saturn built,
Saturnia and what was the Janiculum."
Conversing in this way they made their way
Down toward Evander's humble dwelling, and
On their way they saw the browsing cattle
In the fields that would one day be the Roman Forum
And the fashionable Carinae, and heard their mooing;   480
And when they came to his house, Evander said,
"When Alcides in triumph came to this place he stooped
To go in through this doorway. He knew this house
Was a palace. You are my guest, Aeneas. You must be
Scornful of wealth; you must be worthy of
The example the god has set. Enter my house
And do not look down upon what we have to offer."
He spoke, and huge Aeneas went in under
The narrow sloping rooftree of the house,
And lay down on a bed of leaves and under   490
The cover of a Libyan she-bear's pelt.
And after that the night came on, enfolding
All of the earth in the dark embrace of her wings.

＇　＇　＇

But Venus was, as a mother, disturbed by what
Was going on in Laurentium, the menacing tumult.
She went to find her husband and met him in
Her golden matrimonial bedroom, and
She poured these words into his listening ear
In amorous tones: "When the Pergamum of Troy
Was being devastated by the gods,   500
And the fated towers were falling, I never asked

For any help from you, I never asked
Anything of your art to come to my aid,
No matter what I owed to the sons of Priam
Or the tears I wept for Aeneas, my son, in distress.
I did not, dearest husband, wish to ask for
Labor of you that would have been labor in vain.
But now my son is here on Rutulian soil,
By Jove's command, and I, a suppliant,
Am asking you, the god I adore, to make   510
Arms for my son to keep him safe in battle.
Nereus' mother's tears could persuade you to this,
And the weeping of Tithonus's wife could do so.
How many nations now are gathered against me
And sharpening their swords against my people."

Having said this, she embraced her husband and took him
Into her snow-white arms and fondled him,
And fondled him again. All of a sudden,
Vulcan began to feel a familiar feeling,
The heat of the desire coursing everywhere   520
Throughout his trembling body and into the very
Marrow of his bones. It's as when a clap
Of thunder speaks and suddenly a streak
Of lightning runs through the clouds. Venus was pleased.
She knew what it was that was happening to him;
She was fully aware of her game and of her beauty,
When Vulcan said, "Where has your faith in me gone to?
Why do you think you need to ask, my queen?
Had you but wanted this so urgently,
Back then, neither the Fates nor Jupiter   530
Would have denied to Priam ten years more.
If war is what you are getting ready for,
I will do everything I can to help you,
Whatever it be, arousing fire and breath
To melt the iron and shape what is desired,"
And saying this, in their embrace, desire

Sought and found, in the lap of his wife, completion,
And after that the peacefulness of sleep.

➤   ➤   ➤

It's as it is when the woman of the household
Gets up early, before the night is over,   540
To take up her daily tasks of keeping life going,
By doing the things she was required to do,
The work of Minerva, stirring the ashes and
The sleeping flames of last night's fire, assigning
Their tasks to her maidens, keeping the maidens busy
In order to maintain the chastity
Of the marriage bed; just so with the God of Fire
Who, night having passed its halfway mark, and the deep
Sleep of satisfaction over, got up,
And went about his labor at the forge.   550

➤   ➤   ➤

There is a cavernous island in the sea
That rides between the coast of Sicily and
Aeolian Lipari. Smoke rises up
From its rocks, and you can hear, from deep within it,
Sounds like the sounds that can be heard in the thundering
Caves deep within Aetna, the hammering blows on the groaning
Anvils, the hissing of Chalybian iron.
This is the home of Vulcan and it is called
Volcania, the place the God of Fire
Came down to when he came down from up on high.   560
In the caves down in the depths within the island
There were the naked Cyclopes, Steropes and
Brontes and Pyracmon, working the iron, making
A thunderbolt that would be one of the many
Thunderbolts that the omnipotent Father
Hurls down onto the earth from the sky above.

It was only shaped and polished, as yet, and they
Were adding a twisting pouring down of hail,
Three storm clouds big with flooding water, three
Fires pursuing on the East Wind's wings   570
And, mingling into all of these, the flashing
Of lightning, fear, and terrifying noises.
And in another range of the caverns they
Were eagerly working together fashioning
A chariot with its wingèd wheels for Mars,
With which he'd ride to rouse up cities and
Their populations of men for bloody war.
And somewhere else they were polishing the gold
Scales of the writhing serpents imaged on
The dreadful shield of Minerva, with its Gorgon,   580
Its bodiless transfixing head, its rolling eyes.
"Suspend what you are doing!" Vulcan cries,
"Put all these things aside, and put your minds
To work on this: Make armor for a hero;
Use all your strength and all your mastery
For this, and use your hands to do it swiftly.
Do not delay." And they, at once, together,
Obeying his command, began the labor.
Rivers of bronze and gold flowed in the vast
Furnace as they shaped the wounding steel,   590
And shaped an enormous shield, circle on circle,
Sevenfold circles made, to confront the Latin
Weapons, one against all the other ones.

                          , , ,

While Vulcan was doing his work on his Lemnian island,
Evander arose and came out of his humble dwelling
Into the light of the gentle early morning.
Under the eaves of his house the birds were singing.
He was wearing a simple tunic, and on his feet

Tyrrhenian sandals; a simple Tegean sword
Hung by his side; a panther's hide, slung from   600
One shoulder, and gathered at the other hip.
Two dogs preceded him as he walked toward the guesthouse
Where Aeneas was, and thinking of him and of
The promises he had made the evening before.
Aeneas, who had gotten up as early
As Evander had, was walking with Achates;
Evander's son Pallas was walking with his father.
They met in a space between the buildings, shook hands,
And sat down together in the open air,
And spoke to each other freely. The king spoke first: 610
"We will never concede that Troy has fallen, as long
As the great leader of Teucrians is safe.
The aid we can offer is little compared to our fame.
The Tuscan river confines us here on one side;
On the other side the Rutulians press against us;
Our walls echo back the clangor of their arms.
But now this unhoped-for opportunity
Has shown itself to us, I am prepared
To bring a powerful ally in with us,
And the camps of their twelve kingdoms. It is the Fates   620
That have brought you here. Not far away from here
Is where there was a town, Agylla, on
The Tuscan heights. It was the city of
The Lydians, and for many years it prospered
Until it came to be ruled by a tyrant king,
Mezentius, whose crimes and cruelties were
Unspeakable. May the gods bring down those same
On him and all his ilk. It was his way,
To tie dead men to living men, together,
Hand to hand and face to face, and let   630
The living slowly die in the stench and slime
Of the decomposing bodies they embrace.
But then his people had had too much of it.

They armed themselves against him and attacked
His house and slaughtered his guards and set the roof
Of the house on fire. But Mezentius
Escaped from all this welter and fled to where
The Rutulians were, and there King Turnus took him
Into his household and shielded him from his people.
The furious Etruscans wanted him back   640
To make him pay for all his horrific crimes,
And rising up in rage they had become
A host desiring revenge in bloody war.
But the oracles spoke to them saying, 'Maeonian people,
Mezentius deserves the punishment
You ask him to have. But the Fates ordain that your leader
Must come from elsewhere. Etrurians should not
Be under the command of an Italian.'
And so their army waits for a leader to come,
As prophesied in the words of the oracles.   650
The army is in the field; their biremes' prows
Are drawn up on the shore, ready, but waiting.
Tarchon, their king, has sent me the scepter and aegis
Of kingship, but I am old, my feet uncertain,
My blood too cold for battle. I would have sent
My son, our hope, our Pallas, but he, the child
Of Sabella, is half Italian blood. Aeneas,
It is you who must be our leader, our commander.
And you must take our Pallas with you, our hope
And our solace, so that while he is still so young   660
He will learn by your example the ways of war,
Admiring the work of Mars as he observes you
Going about this work before his eyes.
And here I give two hundred chosen horsemen,
The flower of our youth; and Pallas too,
In his own right, brings the same number with him."

, , ,

And while Evander was telling them these things,
Aeneas Anchisiades and loyal Achates,
Their eyes downcast, were troubled in their hearts
Because of all that they had undergone,   670
When suddenly there was a sign in the sky,
Sent there by Venus. A flash of lightning, Tyrrhenian
Thunder everywhere heard across the heavens.
Again and again they looked up at the sky;
Again and again the thunder sounded, and
In the clear space between two parting clouds
There was armor shining golden red, and also
There were the thundering sounds of clashing weapons.
Troy's hero Aeneas knew what it was, and he
Said to the others, "Do not be surprised   680
At what this is, I know these are the signs
Of my mother fulfilling her promise to me that when
There is the coming of war she would send down
Arms for me from on high, and this she has done.
Now by slaughter the Laurentians will know
What suffering is. Now Turnus will be paid
For what he has done by what I will do to him.
How many shields and helmets and brave men's bodies
Will tumble in the Tiber's rolling waters?
Now let them break their treaties. Let there be war."   690

Thus Aeneas spoke, and then he rose
From his high seat and went to the altar and stirred
The slumbering fires within the ashes of
The rites devoted last night to their humble gods,
The Lares and Penates of the household;
And Evander and the Trojans worshiped together,
With the sacrifice, according to the custom,
Of the chosen sheep. And then Aeneas went
Back to his ships, and from his warriors chose
The most valorous to follow him to war;   700

The others he sent to sail peacefully down
The gentle waters of the stream to carry
The news from his father to Ascanius
Of what had taken place.

⸳ ⸳ ⸳

Steeds were brought forth
For the Trojans going to Etruria;
For Aeneas himself a specially chosen horse
Whose caparison was the tawny pelt of a lion
With its dangling ferocious gleaming lion claws.
Suddenly Rumor was flying through the little   710
Town, spreading the news that there were troops
Of horsemen riding away toward the border of
The territory of the Tyrrhenian king.
Mothers saying prayers for their sons redoubled
Their prayers in fear as the prospect of war came closer;
The image of Mars the god of war grew larger
And larger and larger as their fear increased,
And Evander coming forth took hold of the hand
Of his departing son, and weeping said,
"If only Jupiter would give me back   720
The years when under the walls of Praeneste I,
Victorious, piled up their shields and burned them
And with my right hand sent to Tartarus
King Erulus whose goddess mother had,
When he was born (awful to talk about),
Given the baby three lives to live, and with them,
When he was grown, three sets of armor to
Protect those lives, and I, that day, stripped him
Naked three times of his armor, and took away
All three of his lives, I'd never be torn from this   730
Embrace of father and son, this sweet embrace;
Mezentius would never have been able

To slay so many with his derisive sword;
Nor would so many cities have been so cruelly
Widowed. Almighty Jupiter, have pity,
This is the prayer of the Arcadian king:
If it is the will of the Fates to keep Pallas safe,
And he will return to me, I pray for this,
And I will suffer hardship patiently;
But, Fortune, if you threaten me with some   740
Unspeakable event, then break off the life
In me now, while the signs of what is to come are still
Ambiguous, and while I still embrace
My son, my only joy, in this my age.
If what it is is dire, I do not wish
To know it." This is what Evander his father
Said at the moment of their final parting,
And then his retainers bore him, weeping, away
From there to his humble dwelling.

꙳ ꙳ ꙳

                                The gates of the town   750
Were open and the horsemen went riding out,
Father Aeneas and faithful Achates among
The first, and all the Trojan captains with them,
And in the midst, there was young Pallas himself,
Elegant in his war cloak and painted armor,
Looking like Lucifer, the Morning Star,
Venus's favorite of the stars in the sky,
Whose light dispels the darkness as it rises
Up from the nighttime waters of the Ocean.
The eyes of the trembling anxious mothers watched   760
The departing horseback riders in the far-off
Cloud of dust around them where there was only,
Once in a while, a fleeting gleam of bronze;
You could hear the shouts as the army column forms,

And upon the crumbling turf of the thorn-bush plain
The sounds of the four-footed galloping as they go.

◦ ◦ ◦

On the banks of the cold river Caere there's a great
Dark grove of trees with silver bark, that was sacred
To folk both far and near in ancient days;
The hills behind it embrace it, and, it is said,   770
The Pelasgians, who were the original people
To settle there in Latium, consecrated
The grove to the sylvan god Silvanus, who
Was god of the fields and of the browsing flocks.
A little way away from here was the camp
Of Tarchon and his Tyrrhenians; they could
Be seen from the tops of the hills around, stretched out
Across the wide expanse of valley fields;
Father Aeneas and the soldiers he
Had chosen for the war came down into   780
The camp to rest their horses and themselves.

◦ ◦ ◦

Then there was beautiful Venus, high up in the clouds,
Revealed by their parting, and bearing in her arms
The gift she was bringing; and, looking down, she saw
Aeneas, all alone in a valley, secluded,
Away from all the others, and suddenly she
Appeared before her son and spoke to him thus:
"Here is the gift that was promised, the promise kept,
Made by the skill and art of my husband the god.
With these you need not fear the scornful Laurentians,   790
Nor hesitate to challenge fierce Turnus's sword."
She spoke, and embraced her son, and placed the shining
Armor at the foot of a great oak tree.

Aeneas was overjoyed by the honor of
His mother's gift and by what it was he saw.
He could not take his eyes off all these things,
Taking each in his hands and in his arms,
Turning them over and over, gazing at each
In wonder—the terrifying helmet with
Its plumes pouring forth flames; the sword blade that   800
Brings death; the blood-red huge bronze breastplate, as
From a dark-blue cloud the rays from the setting sun
Blaze forth; the polished gold-and-electrum greaves,
The spear, and then, before his eyes, the shield,
Beyond description, whereon the Ruler of Fire
Who knew the truth of all the prophecies
Of what was going to come to pass in the future,
Told on the shield the story of what would be
The story of Rome and the Roman triumphs, and who
Would be the sons, Ascanius' progeny,   810
And their wars.

       He told how the mother wolf
Would peaceably lie on the floor of Mars' green cavern,
While the little twin boys played fearlessly around her,
Or suckled at her udders, each taking his turn
While she looked back at him, her gentle tongue
Caressing and shaping his body.

       Near this on the shield,
The story of the rape of the Sabine women,
How, at the Great Games at the crowded Circus, they   820
Were violently seized and carried away
By the Romans to be their women, and suddenly
There was new war between old Tatius' Sabines
And Romulus's people. After a time
The warring kings agreed to end the war,
And they stood before the altar of Jupiter,

Still wearing their arms, and offering him libations
Pledged to observe the newly recovered peace,
And sacrificed a sow to seal the pledge.

Then there was Mettus, who should have kept his promise, 830
And when he didn't keep it, Tullus Hostilius
Ordered him tied to four-horse chariots,
Two chariots, one on each side, and sent them off
In opposite directions. They tore him in two,
And Tullus Hostilius carried away with him
The two halves of Mettus's severed carcass, and,
As the halves of him went through the woods, dewdrops
Of blood were scattered upon the leaves.

                              Near this,
Porsenna, he who had sworn to force the Romans 840
To take Tarquinius the tyrant back,
Whom they had overthrown, is shown, with a mighty
Force attacking the city, and the Romans
Are shown, Aeneas' descendants, rushing upon
The enemy swords in the fight for liberty.
You could see Porsenna, blustering, raging, as
He stands there futilely watching Horatius Cocles
Destroying the bridge, and Cloelia, as she,
Free of her chains, is swimming across the river.

And topmost on the shield there's Manlius, 850
Standing before the temple on the Tarpeian
Rock to guard the Capitoline. There's Romulus'
Palace with its rough-thatch roof, and its golden
Portico through which the silver goose
Is fluttering and calling out in its honking
Voice telling the Romans that the Gauls are coming;
And down below in the dark, which is the gift
Of the ending of the twilight, there are the Gauls,
Climbing up through the underbrush, in their golden

Clothes, striped cloaks, and with their golden hair,   860
And their milk-white necks adorned with golden chains.
In one hand each of them holds two Alpine spears,
And in the other each of them holds a long
Shield to protect the whole length of his body.

There Vulcan also showed in sacred procession
The naked Luperci and the leaping dancing
Priests, the Salii, with their conical hats,
And the ancile shields that fell from heaven, and
The honored chaste matrons riding in their covered
Two-wheel chariots to lead the processions.   870

Next, but not near this on the shield, there were
Images of the high doors of Dis, and of
The terrible punishment the guilty suffer
For what they did to deserve it; and, Catiline,
There's you, hanging from the fearsome cliff
And trembling before the faces of the Furies;
And then, apart from this, there's Cato, imparting
The principles of righteousness to the pious.

Between these representations winds an image
Of the sea, depicted in gold, but the foaming waves   880
Pure white above the blue of the ocean water,
And in the sea are silver dolphins playing,
Cutting the waves, beaks first, and coming back up
To feather with their tails the foaming crests.

Then, in the middle, there was Actium,
And all the frenzy under Leucates Headland.
The waves shone golden in the famous scene.
On the one side, in the center, Caesar Augustus
Standing tall, on the high deck of his ship,
Directing the battle action being waged,   890
And the senate and the people of the republic,

And the Lares and Penates, and the great
Favoring gods, and from the helmet on Caesar's
Joyful head two joyful flames stream forth,
And his father's star shines in the sky above him.
On the other side is depicted, leading his fleet
Of warships under the sponsorship of the gods
And the sponsoring winds, Agrippa, upon his head
The beakèd crown of naval victory.

On the other side, too, is depicted Antony,   900
Triumphant as he was upon the Red
Sea shores and over the People of the Dawn,
And Egypt and all the Orient forces coming
With him from as far as Bactria, and
Followed (monstrous) by his Egyptian wife.
All together they come, in all their varied
Armor, the spume and foam convulsive from
Their oars and around their three-beaked plunging prows.
They're heading for open seas; you'd think you were seeing
The Cyclades uprooted from their roots   910
And floating loose upon the churning waters,
Or mountain and mountain collapsing into each other
Before your eyes, all those men hurling down
Flaming torches of tow, and iron missiles,
And the fields of Neptune turning red with blood.

In the midst of this you see the Egyptian queen
Not knowing yet about the asps in the future,
Rattling her inciting brazen rattle,
Calling all kinds and sorts of her sundry gods,
And the barking dog-headed god Anubis, to wield   920
Their weapons against Minerva, Venus, Neptune;
And there was Mars engraved in iron in
The middle of all of this, and the grim-faced Fates
Coming down upon the scene from the skies above,
And exulting Discord, with her torn cloak flapping,

Walking along, and following her, the Goddess of War,
Bellona, brandishing her bloody whip;
And when they saw Apollo drawing his bow
And targeting them they fled, all of them fled,
The Arabs, Indians, Shebans, the Egyptians;   930
The Egyptian queen herself is depicted there,
Pale with the pallor of death in her future; she's
Loosening by herself the lines of her ship
And calling on the winds to come and help her;
And in all the scene of slaughter the god of fire
Depicts her with the winds and waves of panic,
Fleeing toward the sorrowing Nile, who opens
Wide the foldings of his blue-green cloak,
To bring his vanquished people home within
His manifold secret waters where to hide them.   940

But Caesar is depicted as he brings
His triple triumph home to the walls of Rome,
Establishing three hundred shrines as he
Had vowed in homage to the immortal gods;
Three hundred shrines, in each of them a chorus
Of matrons singing, three hundred altars, and
The ground is strewn with the bodies of the steers,
The sacrificial offerings to the gods;
At the threshold of the beautiful white temple
Of Phoebus Apollo sits Caesar himself, receiving   950
The gifts of the people, and these are being displayed
Over the doors within; there's the depiction
Of the long parading lines of conquered nations,
In their various dress and in their various armor,
Speaking their various languages. Mulciber
Is shown there and the Nomads and, in their
Long robes, the Africans; the Geloni with
Their bows and arrows; the Carians, the Leleges;
And the river Euphrates now flowing more mildly, subdued;
The faraway Morini, and the Danae,   960

Wild, untamed; the two horns of the Rhine; the angry
River Araxes and the bridge that yokes it.

                      ˌ ˌ ˌ

These were the scenes on the shield which Vulcan made,
His mother's gift for Aeneas to wonder at,
Admiringly. Although he did not know
The meaning of what he saw, he took upon
His shoulders the fame and fate of his descendants.

Book Nine

As this was going on, elsewhere, Saturnian
Juno sent Iris down from the sky to seek
Brave Turnus where he was, by chance, in the grove
That was sacred to his forefather, the god Pilumnus;
To him from her rosy lips Thaumas's daughter
Spoke and said, "Turnus, what none of the gods above
Would have dared to promise that they would do for you,
In answer to your prayers, time in its turning
Has caused to happen, all on its own accord.
Aeneas has left his city, his comrades, his fleet,   10
And gone to the Palatine town of Evander, its king,
And more than that, he has gone as far away
As Corythus and to the Lydians, to
Raise up if he can, from the fields, armed bands of farmers.
What are you waiting for? Call up your horsemen,
Your chariots, surprise their camp, and seize it!"
Having said this, she flew away and vanished
Through the great rainbow colors beneath the clouds.
Turnus saw who she was, and cried: "Whose voice,
O you who make the sky so beautiful,   20
Has sent you down through the clouds, through the air, to speak
To me thus? How is it that the stormy sky
Is suddenly now so clear? The clouds have parted;
I see the stars as they wander in the heavens,
And I will follow all these signs, obeying
Whoever's voice it is that calls me to arms."

When he had said these words he went to the river,
And, stooping down, took water into his hands,
And standing, raised them up, the upturned palms
Toward heaven, and offered prayers to many gods,   30
And burdened the skies with his ecstatic vows.

, , ,

And now it was that the army moved into the open,
A splendid sight, the horses, and their riders
In their painted armor, and all the gleaming
Bronze of weapons shining. Messapus led
The vanguard as they rode; the sons of Tyrrheus
Were the rearguard, and in the middle, Turnus rode,
Commander of the force. It is as it is
When the seven rivers come together to be
The Ganges, in a great surging flowing forward,   40
Or when the Nile withdraws its waters from
The rich fields it had been flooding and becomes
One concentrated forward river purpose.

The Teucrians became aware of a black
Dust cloud out there, on the horizon, and
That a darkness was gathering on the plain far off.
Caicus, on the rampart, looking out,
Was the first to see what was coming, and he cried,
"What is that great thing rolling toward us, wrapped
In darkness? Get up on the walls! Grab your weapons! Ho!   50
The enemy is coming! Beware!" The Teucrians,
Making a great noise, rushed in, all of them, through
The gates of their camp, and got themselves up on the walls,
Obedient to the commands of Aeneas, the greatest
Of warriors, who'd told them not to engage in fighting
Man-to-man with their swords, nor trust themselves
To the open fields outside the walls of their camp.
Though half ashamed that they couldn't do what their fury

Urged them to do, nevertheless they did
What Aeneas told them to do, and manned the ramparts   60
And waited within their walls for the foe to come.

Turnus, wearing his red-and-gold plumed helmet,
And riding a Thracian piebald steed, flew forward
Ahead of the slower moving troops, with twenty
Young warriors of his choice, and suddenly,
There in front of the Trojan camp, cried out
To his young comrades, "Who's with me now to be
The first of us to get into the fight?"
And saying this he whirled a javelin
High into the air, the sign of the battle beginning.   70
Shaking, excited, the youths responded with
A great horrific blood-hungry cry, and followed.

But soon to their surprise they're left to wonder
At the Teucrians' timidity, who won't
Commit themselves to the level battlefield,
And who are men but men who will not fight
Sword against sword, but huddle down for safety
Inside their walls. Around and around the walls,
And back and forth he rides; he's looking for
A way to get himself in, not finding any.   80
He's like a growling wolf outside a sheepfold,
Looking for any way, while the wind blows,
And the rain falls; and in the fold and under
Their sheltering mother the little lambs are bleating,
Safe and sound. Left out in the night, the wolf's
Tormented by his hunger that has been
So long unsatisfied, and the back of his throat
Longs for the taste of blood so long not there.
How to get in to shake the Teucrians down
From where they are, and onto the battlefield?   90
But hah! The fleet is there, behind protecting
Mounds and beside the flowing river. Turnus

Calls on his cheering men for brands of fire
To set the fleet ablaze, and leads the attack,
With a branch of flaming pitch-pine in his hand.

, , ,

Tell me, Muse, what god was it that turned
The fire away from the ships? Who was it who
Had power to thrust away such flames from them?
The story is old but its truth is guaranteed.
Back when Aeneas on Phrygian Ida sought   100
The means to build a fleet fit for the high
Seas they were embarking upon, the Mother,
The Berecynthian Goddess, came to mighty
Jove who was her son and said, "My son,
Now that you rule Olympus, grant your dear mother
What it is that she asks of you. There was a grove
Of maple and of pine with their dark branches,
A sacred place, to which my votaries
Brought offerings. When the Dardanian warrior
Needed a fleet, I gladly gave him the wood   110
To build it, and now I'm anxious and afraid,
And I pray that these ships be ever kept free from harm
By the pounding seas, or by any other harms.
The ships are born from our woods." He who controls
The stars and how they move, replied to his mother:
"What is it that you call upon the Fates for?
The keel that's made by mortal hands can never
Be made immortal, nor can Aeneas ever
Steer his way with certainty on his
Uncertain course. Not one of the gods has ever   120
Been granted this. Oh why should Aeneas be?
However, when they have reached the Ausonian shore,
And when the Dardanian leader has finally come
To Laurentian fields, I will command that those ships
Which have survived be changed from their mortal forms

To goddesses as Nereid Doto is,
And Galatea, breasting their playful way
Through the foaming waves." He spoke and swore assent
By the black pitchy waters that swirl and seethe between
The river banks of his brother's Stygian river,   130
And at his nod, in response, Olympus trembled.

The day came when the promise was fulfilled;
When the primal Mother was warned by Turnus' attack
That it was time to save the ships from fire,
The Fates did what he'd said that they would do.
So in the East an uncanny kind of light
Appeared and across the sky there came a cloud
And in the cloud were votaries of the Mother,
And there was a terrible voice come down from the sky:
"Trojans, you need not fearfully defend   140
Your ships; you need not take up your weapons; the sea
Will burn to a crisp before Turnus's fire
Will bring its harm to any one of these;
Go free, you ships, you goddesses of the sea.
The Mother commands it." At once the ships break free
Of the ropes that held them fastened to the shore.
And dip their prows, which are like the beaks of dolphins,
And dolphin-like they dive into the deep
And soon, like dolphins, miraculous, come back,
And as goddesses swim away to the open sea.   150

                    ❧ ❧ ❧

The Rutulians were astonished, Messapus himself
Was terrified, his terrified horse was rearing,
And the Tiber's downward flow was shocked, was stopped,
And reversed itself with a loud raucous noise.
But Turnus was unflinchingly himself.
With confident severity he spoke
To his people and said, inciting them: "These portents

Are signs that Jupiter is cutting off
The support he gave the Trojans. No need for them
To await what Rutulian force or weapons would do   160
To do the work of ruin; they have no way
To flee from us, they have no place to flee to,
Their option is taken away, and the land is ours,
We hold it in our hands, and gathering
Against them there are thousands of armed allies
Coming to join us from all Italy.
Nor am I frightened by what these Phrygians boast of,
The responses by the Fates or by the Gods.
What Venus promised and gave was over and done with
Once the Trojans were allowed to get   170
To the fertile soil of our Ausonia.
And I myself have my own fate in mind:
To slaughter with my sword this wicked race
Who ravished her away I was betrothed to.
The Atrides were not the only ones such outrage
Touched nor were the Myceneans the only
Ones with such a cause to take up arms
And go to war. But they have paid for it once.
That's not enough? It would have been enough
If they, back then, had thenceforth stayed away   180
From women and from such outrage once and for all,
These men so confident behind these walls,
These walls that are so thin a barrier
Between themselves and death. Don't they remember,
It was the hand of Neptune that made the walls
That later sank in flames? My chosen men,
Whose sword is ready now to cut its way
Into this terrified camp? I have no need
Of armor Vulcan made, nor do I need
To launch a thousand ships to get at these Trojans,   190
Nor do they need to be afraid that we
Will come in furtively to kill their guards
The easy way and take their Palladium,

Or hide ourselves in the dark of a horse's belly.
Nor will they be able to say that they are dealing
With enemies like the Pelasgians or the Danae,
Held off by Hector for ten long years of siege.

But now the day is coming to its end,
And so, my men, well done; we must rest our bodies,
Preparing ourselves for the fight we'll have tomorrow."   200
Messapus was assigned the task of blocking
The gates of the stronghold and encircling the walls·
With watch fires; fourteen Rutulian captains, each
Commanding one hundred soldiers, all of them wearing
Glittering bronze purple-crested helmets, were
Assigned to patrol the walls of the Trojan ramparts.
And as the evening comes in, the soldiers disperse,
Some to the duties assigned, the others resting,
Lying around on the grass, drinking their wine,
Tipping their upturned bronzen flagons back;   210
The fires burn bright; the soldiers on watch are keeping
Themselves awake in the night by playing dice games.

                    ، ، ،

Meanwhile the Trojan soldiers from their high walls
Looked down at all of this, and, inside, they
Were busy behind the walls securing the inter-
Connecting gangways of the fortress, and
Bringing up weapons and missiles, getting ready;
Each man with the task he'd been assigned to do,
Preparing for the danger that was to come.
Nisus, son of Hyrtacus, bravest of warriors,   220
Consummately skillful with javelin and bow,
Whom Ida the Huntress had sent, because of this,
To be in the comity of Aeneas's men,
Was on this night on guard watch at the gate.
Beside him was Euryalus, a youth

More beautiful in his Trojan armor than
Any of the Aeneadae; his beardless
Face was just beginning to show the signs
Of the bloom of his young manhood. He and Nisus
Loved one another and together went   230
With mutual ardor into the fields of battle.
This night they were together, guarding the gate.
Nisus said to Euryalus, "Is it a god
Who puts this desire into our hearts, or is it
Our hearts that make a god of our desire?
I feel the need to do great things tonight.
I'm disquieted to stay so quietly here.
The Rutulians are so confident and unwary,
Over there where they're resting, taking it easy,
Some just lying around, some of them sleeping;   240
The gleam of their watch fires thinly scattered now;
Everything's fallen silent out there in the night.
So let me tell you what thoughts there are in my mind.
Everybody's anxious, the people are, the elders,
To call Aeneas back; they're planning how
To send men out to tell him what's happening here.
As long as you will have what's promised to you—
The glory is all I care about for myself—
I think I know how to get out though the trench
And make my way to the walls of Pallanteum."   250
Euryalus was stunned by the force of the love
Of glory Nisus's words had struck him with.
He said, "Is it really true that you intend
To go alone without me, into this danger?
I wasn't brought up that way. My father,
Opheltes, taught me to know how it is to be
One whose habit is to go right into
The vortex of the fighting, wherever it is,
Argive terror or the strife at Troy.
It is glory I seek, contemptuous of what   260
Would bargain with death just for the light of day.

The loss of life is worth it if it is lost
For the honor it wins." Nisus replied: "I had
No doubt of that, your being who you are.
And it would be right, if Jupiter brought me back
In triumph; but, as you know, in this there are
So many perils and uncertainties
That if by chance or by some god it happens
That calamity overtakes me, takes me away,
I want you to survive me, by your youth   270
More worthy of longer life, to tend the grave
In which my body will be buried, or,
If it's not returned, by courtesy or by ransom,
Then to pay due honor at an empty tomb,
To pay due honor to the absent dead.
Nor do I want to be the cause of grief
For your poor mother, who was the only one
Of the women who had no wish to stay back there
In Acestes' town, and dared to follow her son
Wherever it was that he was going to."   280
Euryalus said to him, "Your argument
Has no effect at all on my resolve.
Let us go quickly." He summoned those who were
The next to take their turn at guarding the gates;
This being done, Euryalus and Nisus
Then went together to seek the Trojan prince.

⸙ ⸙ ⸙

All other beings in the redoubt were quiet,
Oblivious of their cares, relaxed in sleep,
But the chosen leaders of the Trojans, standing
Together, with their javelins and shields,   290
In the middle of the camp, were deep in discussion
Of what to do in their present situation,
And how to get a message to Aeneas,
When Nisus and Euryalus, the two,

Eagerly sought admission to the council,
Assuring the leaders that their petition would not
Interrupt for long the leaders' conference.

Iulus was the first to welcome them,
Inviting Nisus to speak. And so the son
Of Hyrtacus spoke: "Aeneadae, listen with open   300
Minds to what it is we have to say.
Do not discount it because we are so young.
The Rutulians are submerged in wine and sleep.
I know a way, over there, over near the sea,
Where the line is somewhat broken, where there's more
Of an interval between the watch fires; and
The smoke that rises from them toward the sky
Is blackened. Slaughtering as we go we'd go,
Gathering spoils and making our way to Aeneas
At Pallanteum."   310

                    Then wise Aletes spoke:
"You gods who are protectors of our Troy,
I see that you're not ready to let us be
Abandoned and destroyed, when there are such
Young men as these, wholehearted in their ardor."
And saying this and with tears in his eyes, he put
His arms around their shoulders and embraced them.
"What can we give, what honors, what gifts, to thank you
For your wholeheartedness and courage? The gods'
Approval, and what your own characters are,   320
Are in themselves reward enough, but surely,
When he returns to us, father Aeneas's
Gratitude will be immediate, and
That of Ascanius here will know no bounds."

Ascanius said, "It's true, there are no bounds
To what I owe. My father must come back,

Bring him back home to me. My safety and
The safety of all of us here depends on my father
Coming back. I swear by the Lares and
Penates of Assaracus, and by the white-haired 330
Vestal Virgin in her shrine, my hopes
Are all in what you will do. Bring back my father;
I need to have my father in my sight;
When he comes back, all will be well again.
Two silver cups with fine-worked imagery,
Masterfully inscribed, trophies from where
My father was victorious over Arisba;
Twin tripods, two talents of gold, and an ancient
Wine bowl Sidonian Dido gave to my father;
But if the victory is complete and if 340
The scepter and the rule are fully won,
And there's a distribution of the spoils,
Nisus, you have seen Turnus's war horse
And his gleaming armor and his helmet with
Its crested crimson plumes. Nisus, all these
Will be your share; and more than these, my father
Will give you ample fruitful fields in Latium,
A generous portion of Latinus's kingdom.
And, Euryalus, the boy I venerate,
So near my age, not so much further along 350
In life than I, I take you into my heart
Wholeheartedly in everything I do,
Comrades together in peace and war, for glory."

Euryalus replied, "Nothing I do will be
Unequal in the future to the courage
Required for what I set out to do this night,
However fortune falls, for good or ill.
But there's one thing I beg for, from your bounty,
Precious above all other gifts. My mother
Was born of the race of Priam, the best of these. 360

Neither the land of Troy nor Acestes' walls
Could keep her from following me to be with me.
Now I am leaving her, with her not knowing
The dangers I'm going into. I could not tell her
Because (let night, and your right hand, be witness)
I could not bear to see my mother weeping.
Take care of her, I beg you, comfort her
If she's made desolate by what happens to me.
If you will give me hope that you will do so,
I'll go into the danger all the more boldly."   370

This caused the Trojans, hearing him, to weep,
Especially fair Ascanius, who saw
In Euryalus' filial piety for his mother
The image of his own piety for his father.
He said to him in response, "I promise all
That's worthy of the deeds you go to do.
Except for the name Creusa, your mother will be
My mother, and fully share, no matter what happens,
In all that's promised to you when you return."
Weeping as he said these words, he drew   380
A beautiful golden sword from its shoulder belt—
Lycaon of Cnossus made it, perfectly made it—
And gave it to Euryalus in an ivory
Scabbard it fitted perfectly;

                        Mnestheus
Gave to Nisus a bristling lion-skin cloak;
Trusty Aletes exchanged his helmet with him.
Armed thus, they set forth on their mission; the Trojans,
The young ones and the old ones, all went with them,
Taking them to the gates with their prayers and wishes,   390
Fair Iulus the first among them and the chief,
Already now a man with the cares of a man.
He gave them many messages to his father
(Which as they went were scattered to the clouds).

Then they went out through the trench and into the shadows,
And made their way through the dark and into the enemy
Camp, and what they saw were the chariots,
Unhitched, unyoked, scattered across the fields,
And down among their wheels and hanging straps
Rutulians sleeping, soaked in the wine they'd drunk,   400
And Nisus said, "Euryalus, this is it,
This is the time for daring; this is the place,
And this is the way we sought." He kept his voice quiet.
"You go over there, to the right, and watch that we're
Not noticed by anyone. I will begin
The killing here." And so he went to where
Proud Rhamnes lay, high up on piled-up cushions,
His stertorous body breathing out sleep and wine.
He was himself a king, and Turnus's favorite
Augurer of things to come, and now,   410
Asleep like this, he could not augur his fate.
There were three men of his, lying among
The wheels and hanging harnesses, drunk and sleeping;
And Remus's weapons-bearer and charioteer,
Down at the horses' feet. He lopped off their heads,
And the head of Remus their lord, whose blood poured out
In sobbing pulsations warming the nighttime ground;
Next he slaughtered Lamyrus where he lay,
And Lamus too, and beautiful young Serranus,
Who had played the dice game far into the night   420
—Victim, alas, of Bacchus and Slumber, slain—
Had he played on till dawn he would have been lucky.
Nisus was like a lion famished for food
Who's gotten into a full sheepfold at night,
Tearing the meat from the bodies of the mute
Unbleating terrified sheep, growling and snarling
Through what was dripping down from its bloody mouth;
And over where he was, Euryalus

Was killing too many of them to count, unnamed
And named, in his own furious rage for glory;   430
Herbesus and Fadus, in their sleep, he killed,
And Abaris and Rhoetus; but Rhoetus was
Still awake when it happened, and when he saw
The slaughtering, he hid himself behind
A huge wine jar and Euryalus found him there,
Cowering in terror, and came close to him,
And pierced his body through, all the way through,
The whole length of his sword, and drew the whole length of it back;
And his soul came vomited out in a gushing of blood
And the wine he'd drunk. Having done this, Euryalus,   440
Still in his silent bloodlust rage, went over
To where Messapus's sleeping soldiers were,
And where the horses were peacefully cropping the grass
For their nighttime meal, the watch fires slowly dying.
When Nisus saw him still at his raging work,
And that he was at the height of his slaughter rampage,
He said to Euryalus, "Now is the time to quit.
Now we have done enough. Our vengeance has made
A way for us through to where we want to go.
Daylight is coming and daylight's our enemy."   450
They left much spoil behind, abandoned arms,
And silver-wrought armor, and bowls and beautiful rugs;
Euryalus took Rhamnes' medallions and
His sword-belt with the silver knobs, the one
Caedicus gave to Remulus of Tibur
As a host gift long ago, and when Remulus died
He left it to his nephew, and when in turn
The nephew died, the Rutulians took it as
War booty in some fight. Euryalus slung
The precious sword-belt over his broad shoulder   460
(It was never going to do him any good),
And as they went he snatched up Messapus's
Gorgeous-plumed helmet and put it on his head.

So they left the encampment and sought to find the path
To get themselves out of danger and away.

Just then a troop of cavalry came along,
Sent from Latinus's town to bring dispatches
To Turnus, the prince, three hundred horsemen riding,
Volcens their captain, all of them carrying shields.
As they were nearing the camp and the rampart walls   470
There was a flicker of light, off to the left,
A glimmering ray of moonlight in the darkness,
Reflected from the helmet of Messapus
That Euryalus had forgotten he was wearing;
And so they saw Euryalus and Nisus,
On the road over there, and Volcens, suddenly
Alert, called out through the dark to the two of them, "Halt!
What are you doing, over there on that road?
Why are you armed? Where are you going to?"
There was no reply from them across the darkness.   480
The two were startled and fled into the woods,
Putting their faith in the darkness they fled into.
The horsemen spread out in an orderly way, to watch
At every path at its exit from the woods,
And posting watchers along the pathless sides.
The woods were thick, with brambles, and thorn, and dark
Ilex trees, and inside there it was only
Once in a while a path could be discerned,
And hardly then, little more than animal tracks.
Euryalus in these woods and in the dark,   490
Distracted by his fear and encumbered by
The spoils he was carrying with him, lost his way.
Nisus got through, not knowing how he did so,
Scot-free of the enemy, and in the place
Called, after the town called Alba, "Alban,"
The place where Latinus kept his cattle enclosures.
When he got there he found that his friend wasn't there,

And in his bewilderment, scared, called out to him,
"Where are you, poor Euryalus, where did I lose you?
Where is it that you are? How can I find you?"   500
He went back into the woods, trying his best
To retrace his steps and go by the way he came,
But the paths were never able to tell him the story
Of how he got to where he got to, or
Where he came from, and where Euryalus was.
And all was silent as he went.

                    But then,
He heard the horses, and then, he heard the noise
Of what had happened, and suddenly then he saw
Euryalus, who had lost his way and then   510
Been caught by all the troop, and he was being
Carried away, struggling as he went,
And overpowered. What could Nisus do?
What could he do? What could he do to rescue
His young Euryalus? Hurl himself in
Among the swords and die a glorious death
Trying to save his lover from his death?
Nisus looked up at the moon and, desperate, prayed:
"O moon, Latona, goddess of the groves,
Protectress looking down from where you are,   520
If ever my father, Hyrtacus, at your altars
Has offered gifts, and I, seeking your favor,
Have offered the spoils of my hunting, now from on high,
Help me, guide my weapons to the mark."
And with that he threw his javelin through the night,
And flying through the shadows it struck the Rutulian
Sulmo in the back. The javelin splintered,
A splinter went through his middle from behind,
And Sulmo fell to the ground, rolling over onto
His back, the hot blood pulsing out of his chest,   530
His mouth choking out its rattling sounds as he went
Into the cold. The Rutulians in confusion

Looked everywhere to see where the attack
Was coming from, and Nisus was encouraged
By his first hit's success and so he aimed
Another javelin and sent it off,
And it went hissing through the darkness straight
To its target, hitting Tagus in his forehead,
In his temple, and growing warm as it went there,
Into his brain. Volcens was enraged   540
But he could not see in the dark from where the deadly
Shafts had come or where the assailant was,
And so he cried out to Euryalus, "If I
Don't see the other one you'll pay for both,"
And he pulled out his sword and rushed at Euryalus,
And Nisus, witnessing this from where he was,
And maddened by his anguish and his terror,
Came out of the shadows and revealed himself
And cried out in his grief, "Rutulians,
Turn your swords against me, not against him.   550
It is I whose fault it is. I did these things.
He wouldn't have done these things, I swear by the stars
And the gods above, he did the things he did
Because he loved his unlucky lover so."
But the sword already was thrust full force between
Euryalus's ribs and broke through into
His snow-white chest. Euryalus fell to the ground
Into his death; his beautiful head was lolling
Upon his shoulder; it was as when a scarlet
Flower, say, falls gracefully to the earth,   560
When the tooth of a plow has suddenly cut its stem,
Or as it is when a poppy flower falls,
Under the weight of a sudden summer rainstorm,
Bringing it down. Nisus rushed in, seeking Volcens,
In his fury thinking only of Volcens, and
The Rutulians gathered, protective, around their leader,
And time after time kept Nisus away from him,
But he with his flashing-like-lightning sword kept fighting

His way toward Volcens and finally, dying, thrust
His sword into Volcens' open mouth as it   570
Was open to shout. And after that, he fell,
Stabbed through and through by the weapons of the Volscians,
Upon the lifeless body of him he loved,
In the stillness of death finding his rest at last.

Fortunate both. If my song has any power,
No day will come when you have been forgotten,
While Aeneas's house still stands at the Capitol
And the empire of Rome's father still remains.

When they had won, the Volscians, with the spoils
They had retrieved, rode weeping back to the camp,   580
Carrying Volcens' body. And there was mourning
Over the bloody corpse of Rhamnes and
Serranus, and Numa, and those others who
Had died in the events of this past night.
A crowd gathered to look at the dead and the dying,
The blood still pouring out, still warm and foaming,
From what had been so recently done to them.
They saw what had been recovered at such cost,
Messapus's shining helmet and the medallions.

                    ❧ ❧ ❧

Then Aurora leaving the bed of Tithonus began   590
To scatter her light upon the world, and soon
Sunlight was everywhere, and all revealed.
There Turnus in his armor was urging on
The captains all around to sound the cry,
"Assume battle formation," and soon there was,
In gleaming battle array, the Latin army,
Their fury for battle aroused still further by
The stories about the slaughter the night before.
And, following the battle files, were carried,

Impaled on the points of two uplifted spears,   600
The heads of Nisus and Euryalus.
The tough Aeneades behind their trench
And high up on their turreted rampart walls
(The left wall side, the river protecting the right),
In battle order ready for the onslaught,
Were grieving and shocked at seeing out there the two
Faces they knew, two heads held high to be
Shown to the Trojans, waggled before their sight,
The black gore dripping down from both of them.

And then the flapping wings of Rumor carried   610
The bad news over to be heard by the ears
Of Euryalus's mother. Grief's freezing cold
Took all the warmth away from her very bones.
The shuttle fell from her hands and the threads revolved
Backward. She tore her hair, and ululating,
As a grieving woman does, she went to the ledge
Of the stronghold tower and, out of her mind, she stood,
In front of all the watching army, careless
Of all the danger, careless of everything,

"Euryalus, Euryalus, is it you?   620
Is this Euryalus I'm seeing? Oh,
How could you leave me here, alone, oh cruel!
The only solace of my age? How could you go
Away from me into such dangers without
Giving me any chance to say goodbye?
Somewhere in some strange country your body lies
To be the food for scavenging dogs and birds.
I couldn't even go with you to your grave,
Or close your eyes, or bathe your wounds, or wrap
Your body in that garment I was weaving,   630
Weaving as fast as I could, at the loom, for you.
Where can I go to find your torn-apart body?
How can I find you, my child? Is this that I see

All that's come back to me? For this, for this,
Have I followed you over the lands and over the seas?
Rutulians, have pity on me, kill me,
Or you, the Father of the Gods, send me down
To Tartarus with one bolt of your lightning.
How else can I get myself out of this hateful life?"
This mother's grieving sent a shock through all   640
The Teucrians hearing her, and their resolve
For battle was weakened. Ilioneus and Iulus,
Who was bitterly weeping, bade Actor and Idaeus
To bear her away, and they did so, carrying her
Back in their arms, in under the tower roof.

                  ➣ ➣ ➣

The music of the trumpet suddenly sounded
Its terrible outcry, and a great shout followed;
The sky above redoubled the bellowing noise.
The Volsci, under the moving roof of shields
Upraised and linked together to keep them safe,   650
Went forward then, filling the rampart trench
And hacking at the walls to tear them down,
Or trying to climb them with ladders just where the line
Of defenders up there looked thinnest so you could see
The light of the sky behind them. The Teucrians,
As they had learned to do in their great war,
Hurled missiles down from above, and pushed the ladders
Away from the walls with poles, and, hoping to
Break up that tortoise-back shield, rolled heavy stones
Over the rampart edge to come down upon it.   660
For a while the Rutulians were happy in
Their safety under their roof, but not for long.
The Teucrians rolled over the edge a stone
So huge that it came crashing ruining down
Where the mass of attackers was greatest, and it broke open

The tortoise roof and scattered Rutulian arms
And bodies everywhere. The brave Rutulians then
Gave up caring for fighting blind that way, and pelted
The rampart with missiles; Mezentius, elsewhere,
A frightening sight to see, brandished a great   670
Torch of Etruscan pine, and Neptune's child
Horsebreaker Messapus was tearing at pieces of wall,
And crying out to his men for scaling-ladders.

⸙ ⸙ ⸙

O Calliope, O Muses, breathe upon
My singing as I tell how many men
The slaughtering sword of Turnus sent down to Orcus.
Unroll for me the scroll that tells the story.

⸙ ⸙ ⸙

There was a high-up tower, good for surveying
The countryside around, and this the Italians
Were eager to conquer, dismantle it, destroy it,   680
And the Trojans gathered together on the rampart,
Hurling down stones and missiles through the windows,
Desperate to defend it, keep it from being
Brought down. Fierce Prince Turnus it was who threw
A fiery torch that struck the wall of the tower,
And fixed itself in the wall, and, helped by the wind,
Its flames spread out to set on fire the wooden
Boards and the wooden posts supporting the tower.
All those inside were terrified and all
Clustered together as far as they could away   690
From where the fire was burning, but then the whole
Great structure collapsed and there was a sound as of
The thundering sky being one sound of thunder.
And many fell, dying, down with the falling structure,

Bodies impaled upon their weapons as
They fell upon the wooden shards. Young Lycus
And Helenor were the only ones who lived,
Helenor whose father was the king
Of Moenia and his mother the slave Licymnia.
He was her secret child, and she had sent him,   700
Against the prohibition, to Troy, in arms;
Here he had only his bare unscabbarded sword,
And his inglorious plain white shield, to protect him.
Here he was, in the middle of thousands of soldiers,
Line after line of Turnus's Latins around him;
It was as when a wild beast, caught, surrounded
By a circle of hunting spears, leaps raging upon them,
Knowing full well what it's doing, so the young man
Threw himself to his death upon the spears
Around him and exactly where they were thickest.   710
But Lycus, who was quicker of foot than he,
Ran through and past the surrounding foe and their weapons,
And fled to the rampart wall and desperately
Took hold of the ledge at the top of it and clung there,
His friends up on the rampart ledge above him,
Desperately reaching down to try to help him,
And Turnus, who had been chasing him with his spear,
Cried out, victorious: "You fool, did you
Think you could get away from my hands, did you?"
He tore him away from the wall and tore a great   720
Piece of the wall away with him too. Turnus
Was like Jove's arms-bearer eagle seizing a hare,
Or carrying up to the sky a beautiful swan
In his eagle claws; or else he was like a wolf
In a sheepfold seizing a lamb while its bleating mother
Looks everywhere for where her lamb could be.
Rutulians were shouting everywhere;
They filled up the trench; others flung burning pine
Torches as high as they were able to throw them.

Then Ilioneus threw a huge rock, torn   730
From a mountain, down on Lucetius as
He was getting toward the gate with a flaming torch,
Then Liger slew Emathion, Asilas slew
Corynaeus; one was good with the javelin,
The other good with the arrow shot from far;
Corynaeus killed Ortygius, Turnus killed
Victorious Corynaeus, and after that he killed
Itys, Clonius, Dioxippus, Promolus, and
Sagaris, and Idas, who was standing high
Up at the top of the tower battlement;   740
And Capys was the one who killed Privernus,
Who had been grazed by the spear of Themillas, and
Like a fool put down his protecting shield, so as
To finger the wound he had gotten from the spear,
And so the arrow of Capys winged its way
And struck him in the left side of his body,
Demolishing all the avenues of his breathing.
And there was Arcens' son, handsome and tall,
And wearing an embroidered cloak of several
Varied colors, bright and Spanish dark;   750
Arcens's father had sent him to the war
From his mother's beautiful grove by the river Symaethus,
With its bountiful altars to the Palíci, the Twins.
When Mezentius saw him he put aside his spear,
And took up his slingshot and whirled it around his head,
Three times, and the leaden shot went whizzing through
The air and struck, splitting his skull wide open
And his body lay stretched out, far from his home.

                           ⸳ ⸳ ⸳

As they tell the story, this now was the first time that
Ascanius's swift arrow, which only had   760
Been used before to terrify wild beasts

As they fled from him, brought brave Numanus down.
Numanus was of the Remuli clan and recently
Had married Turnus's younger sister and,
Proud of this new connection with his king,
Puffing out his chest and striding up and down
In front of the army, he shouted out loudly things
Both fit and not: "Phrygians, aren't you ashamed
To be cooped up in there behind those walls
The way you were two times before, with only   770
Walls you were hiding behind between you and death.
Who asked you to come in here to try to take
Our women away from us? What god was it,
Or was it only all by itself your madness?
You won't find any of the Atridae here
Or storytelling Ulysses either. We're
The kind of people who take our babies out
And plunge them into the ice-cold waters of
Our mountain streams to toughen them up for what
Their bodies will endure when they are grown;   780
Our boys unwearied beat the woods in the hunt;
Unwearied they practice their games of horsemanship,
And stretching the bowstring to ready the arrow for flight;
We work the fields and learn to live on little;
Our hoeing shakes and overturns the glebes;
The sound of our warfare shakes the walls of towns;
All of us, all our bodies, are bruised by iron,
The spears we use in the fight, reversed, we use
To goad the oxen as they plow the field.
But when we're old, old age does not surrender   790
To weakness or to compromise our vigor;
Our helmets hide our gray heads in the fight,
But you, look at *you*, you love to dance, you love
To fool around in your saffron-colored or purple
Fish-dyed shirts, in your helmets which are like
Pansy bonnets with ribbons hanging down.

You're not Phrygian men, you're Phrygian women.
Go on over to Mount Dindymus where they've got
Your kind of music, double boxwood pipes
And tambourines those priest castrati are playing   800
Just for the ears of people such as you."

Ascanius could not bear what he was hearing,
The vile insulting words, the ridicule;
He stood there opposite, the horsehair string
Of his bow pulled back and held, high as could be,
In tension with the string and carefully aimed
As he'd been taught; and prayed, making this vow,
Beseeching: "Omnipotent Jupiter, if you
Will nod upon my first attempt in war,
I promise solemn gifts to your temple and   810
Before the altars I will set up a statue,
A young bullock, now grown as tall as his mother,
With glistening golden horns, old enough now
To butt with his horns and kick up the soil with his feet."

Jupiter nods, and in the clear sky there was
The sound of thunder, and then the sound of an arrow,
Delivering death, a dreadful strident hissing
As the arrow flew to the targeted Numanus,
And struck him in the head and then went through
The hollows of the temples within the head   820
And into the brain within. "Go mock the brave
Down there with words like these! This is the answer
To the tough Rutulians from us twice-beaten Phrygians."
The Teucrians shouted with joy; the clamor of it
Rose as high as to the stars above.

It happened that long-haired Apollo heard it,
Where he sat among the clouds, looking down on all
Ausonia and its towns and the battle scene.

He saw what Iulus had done and spoke to him:
"You are the son of gods and you will be   830
The father of gods to come. Under the house
Of Assaracus all wars will come to an end."
And as he spoke the god descended through
The breathing air, parting its whispers as
He went, and as he went, he changed himself
Into the look of old Butes, he who had been
The armor-bearer and faithful doorkeeper of
Dardanian Anchises; in his old age
Aeneas made him companion to his son.
Apollo went to Ascanius, looking like   840
The ancient mentor Butes, in every way—
His face, white hair, his coloring, and the very
Sound of his rattling arrows in their quiver.
He spoke and said these words to ardent Iulus:
"Aeneas's son, unharmed you have faced Numanus,
And you have brought him down. Now great Apollo
Acknowledges the glory of this deed,
And does not deny that you have done so with
A weapon like his own. It is enough;
For now, boy, it is right for you to refrain   850
From the battlefield." As he began to say
These things to the boy the god was shedding his mortal
Simulation and was vanishing
Into and through the tenuous air, and the Teucrian
Chiefs were recognizing who it was
As they saw him vanishing and heard the divine
Rattling of his arrows in their quiver;
Therefore they knew that by Apollo's command
Ascanius was prohibited from the fighting.
And they all, aroused with zeal, committed themselves   860
Full-armed to the battle and all its dangers. The clamor
Was everywhere upon the battlements,
Men everywhere stretching their bows to send off their arrows,

Men twisting the straps of their spears to send them to kill;
The ground was covered with missiles; sounds of the clanging
Of swords and helmets and shields were everywhere,
As everywhere the battle was as when
The storm of hail from the Hyades pours down
And pounds the earth with the dreadful noise of its falling,
And Jupiter brings on the whirling South Wind,   870
And the winter winds of Auster, and from above
His emptying storm clouds bellowing as they burst.

                    ， ， ，

Pandarus and Bitias, who were the sons
Of Alcanor of Ida, and Iaera the wood nymph
Of the sylvan grove of Jupiter,
Were young men of the hills and woods of their country,
And tall like the silver trees they grew up among.
They were so confident of their arms that they
Opened the gate that they had been keepers of,
And so they let the enemy in. They stood,   880
The two of them, one on the right of the gate,
The other on the left, their weapons ready;
They looked like a pair of oaks that you might see,
Maybe, upon the banks of the river Po,
Or standing tall above the beautiful river
Athesis, their high branches nodding in the breeze.
The Rutulians, when they saw that the gate was open,
Come rushing in; the first of them were Quercens,
Aquiculus in his beautiful armor, and
Headlong Tmarus, and Haemon, son of Mars,   890
And all their men, are routed, some of them
Frantically trying to get back through the gate,
Others laying their lives down on the threshold.
Discordant rage rose higher in their hearts,
And Trojans, seeing all this, came gathering

To fight where the gate was open, hand to hand,
And some of them daring to carry the fighting into
The fields beyond.

                    , , ,

                    Turnus was raging, and causing
Havoc elsewhere in the battle, when   900
The message came to him that the enemy
Were lavishly slaying his people over where
The gate was open. Turnus turned at once
And went, his savage fury greater still,
To seek the Dardanian gate and the proud brothers.
But the first he met was Antìphates, who was
The great Sarpedon's son by a Theban woman.
The beautiful lance that Turnus threw was made
Of Italian cornel wood, and it flew toward him
Through the unprotesting air and fixed itself   910
In Antìphates' stomach and traveled up inside
The bleeding cavity behind his chest,
Until it arrived to warm itself in the lung.
Then by hand there was Meropes he killed,
Next was Erymas, and after him Aphidnus,
And then there was Bitias, himself, whose eyes
Were on fire with rage and defensive fury as
He fell, not by a spear (since no such thing
Could be enough to bring down such a man),
But by a great revolving hissing missile   920
That struck him with the force of a thunderbolt,
His double bull's hide shield unable to shield him;
His double golden breastplate could not save him;
His giant legs gave out from under; he fell
To the earth that groaned as his body came down upon it,
His great shield thundering falling down upon him.
It was as it is at Euboean Baiae where
They've made a huge pile of stones and pushed it over

The edge of the shore, into the water to be
The foundation for some great man's villa, and when   930
It falls to the bottom the booming sound of it
Causes Prochyta to tremble; and Ischia,
Where Jupiter buried Typhoeus, the greatest monster,
Under the earth; and in the disturbance of waters
The black sand rises up as if in terror.

                    ❦ ❦ ❦

Then Mars All-Powerful-In-War stirred up
The Latin men, goading them in their hearts
And inflicting on the minds of the Teucrians
Black fear and thoughts of running away; the Latins
Came in from all sides and gathered themselves together,   940
Aware of their advantage, the War God in them.
Pandarus, when he saw his brother's body
Stretched out on the ground, and saw what his fortunes were,
And what his own situation was, went to
The gate and there, with all his shoulder strength,
He moved the gate to turn it back on its hinge,
And so, though letting in some who were running toward it,
Closed it, leaving so many of his own people
Out there, outside the walls, out in the midst
Of the enemy all around them. Madman, he didn't   950
See that he'd closed in the Rutulian king,
A huge tiger there in a hapless cattle pen.

Light blazed in the eyes of Turnus; the blood-red plume
That crested his helmet shook; the sound of his armor
Clashed and rang horrendously; his shield
Shone as with the fire of lightning in it.
The Aeneadae were shocked in disarray
At what they saw and recognized, the face,
The giant form, a terrifying sight.
But big young Pandarus stepped forth, in fervid   960

Rage because of his brother's death, and said,
"Don't think this is the bridal bedroom in
The palace of your mother-in-law Amata;
Don't think you're safe and sound behind the walls
Of your father's house in Ardea. This is
The enemy camp, with no way to get out."
Turnus laughed and calmly said to him,
"If you're brave enough, let the fight begin, and you'll
Tell Priam there was another Achilles here."
Pandarus' weapon was a huge raw wooden   970
Spear, made with its knot and its bark still on it, and
He threw it with all his force at Turnus's body,
But a gust of wind diverted it. Juno had
Turned it aside, and it struck the gate and stuck there.
Then Turnus called over to him and said, "This weapon
I wield is a better weapon than yours; this arm
I have is a better arm than yours. Get ready."
And saying this he raises up the spear
Above his head and throws it and it strikes
Straight through the foredoomed forehead of the boy,   980
Cutting Pandarus's unbearded face in half.
The wound was terrible. His heavy body
Fell crashing down upon the sounding earth;
His limbs collapsed unjointed and moving about,
Askew, as he lay dying; his blood and brains
Poured out upon his armor; each half of his head
Lay bobbing from his shoulders, right and left.

⸻ ⸻ ⸻

The Trojans, terrified, tried to run away;
If Turnus, right then, had thought to force open the gate,
It would have been the end of the war and the Trojans;   990
But he went on, in his ecstasy of slaughter,
Enraptured by what he was doing, first taking out
Phaleris, and after him, then, Gyges,

Slitting his hamstrings as he fled away;
And taking their spears from the dead, he hurled them
Into the backs of the fleeing others, sending
Halys with them, and Phegeas through his shield,
Unknowing Alcander, Halius, Prytanis, Noemon,
Before they knew he was there inside the walls;
Lynceus, calling out for his fellows to follow,   1000
As he came down from the rampart tried to rush
At Turnus and Turnus stopped him in his tracks
As with one single expert swipe of his sword
He severed his head from his body and sent the head
Flying far off from where the body fell.
Next was Amycus, the hunter, nobody better
Than he at the art of using his skillful hand
To smear the arrow point or the point of the spear
With poison to kill the prey; next Clytius,
Then after him the turn of Cretheus who   1010
Was the lover of the Muses and was one
The Muses loved, Cretheus who sang
To the constant music of the cithera songs
Of war and arms and horses and famous battles.

                    ʼ ʼ ʼ

The Teucrian leaders, Mnestheus and brave
Serestus, heard about the devastation
Visited on their people, and so they came
To the scene of what was happening and saw
Their soldiers scattered in such confused retreat,
And Mnestheus cried out, "Where are you going?   1020
O countrymen, where else have you to be?
What other town do you have, what other walls
To protect you? Is it possible that one,
Alone, inside your battlement should do
Such savage harm to you and go unpunished?
That he should send so many of our best

Young men down there to Orcus? Where is your shame?
Where is your pity for your wretched country?
Where is it for your ancient gods? Where is it
For great Aeneas?"   1030

            Hearing these words they were
Aroused and heartened and came together again,
Not scattered now but in close formation, and
As Turnus moved away, little by little,
Toward the river and toward the place where the river
Oxbowed around the edge of the Trojan camp,
The Teucrian soldiers, clamoring, shouting, press
Around him, leveling spears, and he, like a savage
Lion surrounded by many hunters, raging,
Frightened, glaring, backs away, but never   1040
Turning its back, and yet unable to back
Swiftly through the press of the hunters and spears,
Moving slowly, his mind on fire with fury,
But doubtful of his way, backing away,
Though twice he lunges and scatters them so they
Go flying away, but twice again they come back,
And twice again they come together around him,
All of them, all of the camp, gathered against him,
And Juno no longer dared to help him out
Against his enemies, for Jupiter   1050
Sent Iris down from the skies to tell his sister,
In no uncertain terms, that Turnus must
Take his leave of the Teucrian battlement;
And Turnus could sustain himself no longer
Against the barrage of missiles coming upon him;
The bronze helmet protecting his hollow temples
Rang, rang, and rang with the constant sound of blows;
Its bronze was cracked by a rain of stones upon it;
Its horsehair crest was torn away; the boss
Of his mighty shield fell in; like lightning bolts   1060
Striking again and again and again the spears

Of the Trojans and Mnestheus himself
Struck down upon him; the sweat poured out, a river
Of pitch down all of his body, unable to breathe;
Exhaustion shook him in all of his quaking limbs.
And then at last Turnus was able to fall,
In all his armor, into the flowing river.
It carried him away on its yellow waves
And, as it carried him gently along, it washed him
Of all the signs of blood and wounds and brought him,   1070
Jubilant to the company of his comrades.

Book Ten

Almighty Olympus opened its doors to reveal
The gods of the heavens, seated in council, ranged
To the right and the left of the Father of the Gods
And King of Men, who, sitting among the stars,
Looked down the steepness of the sky and saw
All lands and countries that are there below,
The Rutulians' army and the Dardanians' camp.
Briefly he spoke: "Great dwellers in the sky,
What is it that has caused such contention among you,
That has led you to raise, on this side, and on that,   10
These armies against each other? What was it that caused you
To do this in spite of what I have commanded?
You knew I forbade the Latins to interfere
With the Teucrians when they came into these lands;
No need to hurry it, the time will come
When the savage Carthaginians will open
The Alpine walls to let destruction in
Upon the citadels of Rome. That time will be
The time for ravage and for hatred. For now,
Maintain together the peace that I have willed."   20

Then golden Venus replied in words less brief:
"You are that power that rules over all, all things,
All men—who else is it for us to pray to?
Do you not see how the Rutulians mock us,
And Turnus swollen with glorying in his triumphs,

The gate protecting the fortification open,
And can't be closed, the Trojans having to fight
Hand to hand within their own stronghold walls,
The trench around the rampart flowing with blood,
Aeneas not there, and knowing nothing of it?   30
Can you not lift the siege? Troy is trying
Its best to be reborn and now there's a new
Enemy, new army, and a new
Aetolian Diomedes coming from Arpi.
Am I to be wounded again? It is I, your daughter,
Threatened by enemy weapons in the field.
If the Trojans have sought to come to Italy
Without your blessing, without a god's being willing,
They should be punished. But if they have obeyed
Faithfully what they have been told to do   40
By the gods above and the shades below, then why
Are those others able to overturn what you,
Yourself, have commanded? Why are those others allowed
To define a different fate for us than this?
Have you not seen the ships on fire upon
The shores of Eryx's kingdom, my own son's,
And the Aeolian king's tempestuous winds,
And Iris being sent, down through the clouds,
How she was sent to call up from below,
From the only places where you do not rule,   50
Allecto, and the mad Bacchante women
Through all the towns? I will no longer contend
For imperial sway. We hoped for that while still
There was reason for us to hope. But now, I see,
You wanted the others to win and they have won.
If, Father, your pitiless wife will not allow
One piece of ground for those who've come from the smoking
Ruins of fallen Troy, then I must pray
To be granted just one thing, by the smoke that rises
Up from the ashes of the ruined city: 60
Ascanius, my grandson, keep him safe.

Let him survive. Aeneas may be tossed
On the dangerous waters of his enterprise,
However it is that Fortune will deal with him;
But let me protect this child. My palaces,
Idalia, high Paphos, Amathus, Cythera,
Where he can live out the length of his peaceful life,
Under their sheltering roofs, far from the wars
And all their terrible glories, his armor unused
Beside him where he sits and reads his book.   70
By the authority of your command,
Carthage will prevail over Italy.
What has it gotten him to have been taken
Away alive from the plague of war, and through
The Argolican fires, only to suffer
Among the vast wastes and the desolation of
Foreign seas and alien lands, what has it
Brought him to be brought to Latium where
The Trojans seek to find and build a new
Pergamus for themselves? Instead, ought they   80
Not have been left back there, where they were, to settle
Their miserable selves among the smoking
Ashes of what Troy was, and re-enact
Again the story of their history?
Give them back their Xanthus and Simois."

Then Juno spoke, enraged: "Why is it that I
Must give words to my anger, in front of all of these,
Assembled here? What gods or men was it
Who caused these Trojans to take to war, invading
Latinus's kingdom with their troops? It's said   90
That the Fates have brought all of this about. Not so.
It is the raving madness of Cassandra,
Prophesying. Who was it exhorted him
To leave his camp and trust himself to the winds,
Leaving his child in charge, trusting the walls?
Was it us, were we the ones, who got him to go,

To rouse up the Tyrrhenians and their people?
What god was it who led him into this?
Was it some sinister power of mine that did it?
Where's Juno in all of this, and where is Iris   100
Coming down from the clouds to do some mischief?
It's wrong of the Latins, you say, to surround with fire
The walls of this newborn baby Troy. Is it wrong
Of Turnus to stand up for his ancestral land,
Land of his fathers, Turnus whose grandfather was
Pilumnus, his mother the goddess Venilia?
Who was it, who was the one who caused the Trojans
To raise the black torch of war against the Latins,
To seize and plunder the fields that belonged to others,
Felt free to choose what father-in-law to choose,   110
Abducting the bride from the bosom of her mother,
Proffering a hand as if offering peace, from the stern
Of a warship bristling with his weapons of war?
You had the magic to spirit Aeneas away
From the hands of the Greeks, and where there was a man,
There was only a nebulous something in the wind;
You have the magic to turn the ships into
A fleet of dolphin-like nymphs, swimming away;
Is it so wrong to give the Rutulians
What help we can give to them? Aeneas is   120
Ignorant of this and he is absent.
Ignorant and absent let him be.
You have Idalia, high Cynara, Paphos;
What do you have to do with these cities brimming
With warfare and killing? Why do you try the hearts
Of these desperate folk? Do you think that it was we
Who caused the crumbling walls of Troy to fall
Down upon the foundations it was built on?
Who was it made the wretched Trojans fall
Down abased before the triumphant Greeks?   130
Who was it who caused all Europe and Asia to rise
In treacherous war, breaking the faith they swore?

Was it I who sent the Dardan adulterer
To Sparta to steal with the weapons of Cupid your child?
That's when you ought to have taken care of your people.
Now you rise up and hurl these ugly lies
And these accusations."

When Juno finished speaking,

Saying these things, the heavenly gods were stirred,
Some in agreement, some disagreeing; it was   140
As when in a wood there's a quiet stirring in
The leaves of the trees, as if an unseen little
Breeze was in them telling sailors that
Stronger winds were coming, so beware.

Then Jupiter, the ruler of everything, spoke,
And there was a waiting silence in his palace;
The sea was quieted, the winds were stilled,
And the trembling earth attended, the heavens were hushed.
"Now listen to what I say, and take it to heart.
You have been busy preventing the concord that   150
There ought to have been between the Trojans and Latins.
There is no end to the discord you have fostered,
I will not discriminate between the two.
I am the king of all. What happens to them
Is whatever happens to them on the day it happens,
Whether it is the Trojans under siege,
Having come there under false prophecies,
I will not care; nor will I favor the Latins.
The fate of each man will be as the Fates decide."

His nod confirmed this by the pitch-black swirling   160
Waters of his brother's river Styx,
And all Olympus trembled at his nod.
There was nothing more to be said. Jupiter rose
From his golden throne and all the heavenly gods
Escorted him to the threshold of his departure.

While this was happening the Rutulian
Fighters were crowding around the rampart gates,
Lusting for killing and to surround the Trojan
Stronghold with fire. The Trojans, immobilized
Inside the walls, helpless, nowhere to go,   170
Were together high up, where the citadel tower was,
A thin wreath of defenders around the circling
Parapet of the walls of their redoubt.

There was Asinus, the son of Imbrasus,
Thymoetes, the son of Hicetaon, the two
Assaraci brothers, and old Thymbris, and,
In the forefront, next to him, was Castor, and
Among them there, the two brothers of Sarpedon,
Clarus, and Thaemon who had come with him,
Comrades together in the same troop from high   180
Lycia in the mountains, and Lymesian
Acmon, as big and as strong as was his father,
Clytius, or as his brother Mnestheus,
Struggling with his mighty strength to carry
A huge rock, a piece of mountainside, to the edge.
They all were struggling, hurling down great stones,
Hurling down flaming torches, fitting their arrows
To bowstrings, struggling to defend themselves
In the situation in which they found themselves.
In the midst of these was noble Ascanius,   190
Venus's favorite, as he deserved to be.
His head was bare and his beauty that of a gem
In a golden setting shining, or an ivory in
A pendent framed in terebinth or box.
And your admiring comrades witnessed you,
Ismarus, intent on your task, applying the deadly
Poison to the tips of arrows and

Aiming them at the foe, a scion of
A noble family of Maeonia,
Where men were busy plowing and working the rich   200
Soil of the fields along beside Pactolus,
Whose waters watered them with gold; and also there
Was Mnestheus, he, who deserved and won such glory
For having been the one who drove Turnus down
From within the stronghold walls; and Capys was there,
The one who gave his illustrious name to his city,
Capua, which he founded, in Campania.

That is the way the struggle there went on.

⸱ ⸱ ⸱

And the prow of Aeneas's ship cut through the waves
In the middle of the night as he made his way.   210
He had left Evander's town and gone to the king
Of the Etruscans and told him who he was,
And who were the people he was the leader of,
And what he had come to offer and to ask for.
He told him what their situation was,
Their human plight, Mezentius gathering force,
In enmity against him, the violence
That raged in Turnus's heart. Tarchon listened,
And heard him, and responded at once with help,
And with a treaty. Thus the Lydian men,   220
Under the gods' authority embarked
With Aeneas in his fleet, committed to
The leadership of one who is foreign-born.

Aeneas's ship went first, its beak adorned
With two painted Phrygian lions, and above them,
A delight to the eyes of all the Trojan exiles,
The painted figure of their mountain, Ida.

At the tiller great Aeneas sat, considering,
This way or that, what the fortunes of war would be,
And Pallas sat close beside him, questioning   230
About the stars above and about the course
They were taking through the nighttime waters and
What it was Aeneas had suffered, by land and by sea.

Now goddesses of Helicon, tell us in song
Who were the men who came from Tuscan shores,
And with what weapons, and from what places, to join
Aeneas in this journey upon the seas.

                    ، ، ،

There's Massicus, in his bronzen vessel Tiger,
Bringing a thousand warriors with him, who
Came from the walls of Clusium and Cosae,   240
With bows and, in light quivers on their shoulders,
Death-bringing arrows; next was fierce Abas, with
The force he was carrying with him in his ship,
With its golden Apollo image; six hundred youths,
All in their gorgeous armor, skillful in arms,
Whose mother country Populonia sent;
Three hundred more from the island Ilya of
Chalybria, profusely generous
In mineral ores.

                    Then next, the ship of Asilas,   250
Interpreter of gods and men, who reads
Entrails of cattle, and knows what the stars above
Are telling when they appear, and understands
The language of the birds, and what the fire
In the thunderbolt presages when it strikes.
His ship was hastening to war, with a thousand
Men with bristling spears, in battle array.

They had been sent by Pisa, Etruscan now,
But whose origin was Alpheus, Olympia's river.

The next was the ship of beautiful Astyr, 260
With his many-colored weapons, and the horse
He rode and trusted so in the pitch of battle;
Three hundred men, all of one mind and purpose,
He brought to the war; they came from Caerete and
The fields of Minio, and feverish Graesca.

Nor will I, brave Cunaro, be neglectful
Of you and your Ligurians as you pass,
Accompanied in the fleet by Cupavo and
His little band of warriors. High up,
Above Cupavo's head, swan feathers float 270
From the pinnace like a banner, image that tells
The story of how his father, Cycnus, who
(Amor, it was your doing) was in love
With Phaëthon, and sang of his loss of him,
Among the shading leaves of the poplar trees
That had been Phaëthon's sisters, till in his age,
And, in the white plumage of a swan, still singing
Unforgettingly, he left the earth
And singing flew, a swan, up to the stars;
It's his young son who now commands the huge 280
Ship Centaur, bringing with him a band of fellow
Warriors as young as he; as the ship goes by,
Propelled by many oars, the giant centaur
Figurehead as menacing poised as if
About to hurl an enormous rock, from on high,
Down into the waves protesting below, and so
Its long keel cuts an escaping groove in the sea.

Next there was Ocnus, who was the son of the river
Of Tuscany, Tiber, and whose mother was

The prophetess Manto, she who gave her name   290
To Mantua and its walls, Mantua, rich
In its descent but not of one people alone—
Three peoples, and each composed of four different folk,
And each of them with their own separate town,
But Mantua, with its strong Etruscan blood,
The capital of all. (This also was
The place from which Mezentius, in the war
Against himself, was carried with his five hundred
Warriors in their war ships made of pine,
Down to the sea by the child of Lake Benacus,   300
The river Mincius, veiled in gray sedgy reeds.)

Next, heavily coming along, but rising on
The waves in rhythm with its hundred oars,
The churned-up marble waters spuming behind,
Was Aulestes' enormous war ship called the Triton,
Scaring the blue sea with its sounding horn;
Its figurehead down to its shaggy belly was
The belly of a man, a human being;
Down below, in the water, its lower half
Was that of an unknown monster of the sea;   310
Half-man half-beast, it moved along on its way.

These were the leaders of the thirty ships,
Their bronze beaks plowing them through the salt sea waters
To come to the aid of their Teucrian allies.

                          ، ، ،

It was the hour when day was conceding the sky
To gentle Phoebe; the silent hoofbeats of
Her horses on their nocturnal journey beat
As the chariot they are drawing, rising, passes
Halfway past Olympus; and Aeneas,
Unable to rest himself in the night, sat holding   320

The tiller, and tending the lanyards of the sails,
When midway in the voyage, suddenly, lo,
There was a company near him in the water.
It was the nymphs, the nymphs who had been the ships
Whose bronzen prows had once been moored on the beach,
And now they were immortal, nymphs of the sea,
According to the command of kind Cybele.
They had sighted their king, Aeneas, from a distance,
And were swimming gaily round him as in a dance.
Cymodocea, who spoke for them all, approached   330
The ship at the stern, and took hold with her right hand,
And rose up from the waves, while with her left
She quietly rowed, and spoke to unknowing Aeneas,
"Aeneas, are you awake? Aeneas, wake up,
Let loose the sails. We were once your ships and now
As sea nymphs we are once again your fleet.
When Turnus sought to burn us and destroy us,
As we lay moored upon the shore, Cybele
Took pity on us, transformed us, set us free,
And together we swam away, looking for you,   340
Seeking you everywhere upon the sea.
Aeneas, your son Ascanius is surrounded
By the enemy and his weapons. It is true
That Etruscan troops and Arcadia's cavalry
Are trying to come to his aid, but Turnus is doing
All he can to keep them from coming together.
Awake! Hurry to help him! Unless you think
My words are meaningless, tomorrow there'll be
Great piles of Rutulian dead upon the field!"
Having said this, with her right hand she propelled   350
The ship upon its way, swift as an arrow,
While with her left she divided the waters before it.
The other ships followed in order, close behind.

Aeneas, son of Anchises of Troy, was amazed,
Astonished by this, and then, by this, aroused

In spirit, and looking up at the vault of the heavens,
He said this prayer: "O gentle goddess on Ida,
You for whom towered cities are your delight,
And taking in your hands the chariot reins
Of the two yoked lions, lead us, now, we pray;   360
Let the omen be fulfilled, be with the Phrygians
Every step of the way." He said this prayer
Just as the daylight was growing and night was fleeing.
And then he told his fellows to prepare
Themselves in their hearts for what was coming, and follow
His standard in the field of battle tomorrow.

⸪

Aeneas stands on the high stern of his ship
And sees the Teucrians and their camp, and holds
High the shining shield in his left hand,
And when his people on the walls see this,   370
There's a joyful clamor rising to the sky,
And the hope that's engendered is transforming, for they
Hurl their spears, and it's as when, under black clouds,
The Strymonian cranes, as they flee from Notus the South Wind,
Suddenly see the signs that spring is coming
And they are going home; the noise of their joyous
Honking fills the skies. When Turnus and
The Ausonian leaders hear the rising clamor,
They wonder at it, but when they turn to look,
They see how the sea is full of incoming ships,   380
And how from the crest of the helmet on great Aeneas's
Head there is a light like flames uprising,
And how from the golden boss of his shield there's fire
Vomiting forth, as when in the night there's sudden
Flux of blood-red fiery comets, or when
The Dog Star Sirius shows its sinister light
In the dark of the nighttime sky, and it's the sign

Of bad luck coming soon, thirst and sickness,
Coming into the fields of mortal men.

                    , , ,

But Turnus the brave was not diverted from   390
His intention of repelling them from landing.
He cried out to his soldiers, "What you hoped for
Has come to pass. Mars the god of war
Is in what your hands will do. Think of your wives,
Think of your homes, think of the glory of
The deeds of those your fathers who begot you.
We'll attack as their tentative very first steps are taken,
And Fortune comes to the aid of the audacious."
He said this, and in his own mind was thinking about
Which of his troops should go to the shore and which   400
Should remain to besiege the walls of the Trojan camp.

Meanwhile Aeneas's men were getting themselves
Down out of their ships, by gangways and by ladders,
And, some of them, by leaping, some of them with
The aid of their oar blades. But Tarchon, wanting not
To contend either with waves or the undertowing
Backwash of the waves, had his eye on the place
Where there were neither, where the sea washed up
Untrammelled onto the sand, and he turned the prows
Of his ships that way. "My boys, bend to your oars,   410
Pull back and drive, drive hard, bend to the oars,
Pull back and drive, cut your way into
This enemy land. Who cares if we shipwreck if
We make it in there to stay. Let the keels plow through."
The oarsmen on his ships responded to him,
Rising high upon their oars and driving their spuming
Vessels' beaks straight forward onto the dry
Land of Latium, keels plowing the way till they

Settled themselves where they got to, safe and sound—
Tarchon, all ships but yours, caught on a spur   420
In the shoals, and rocking back and forth, impaled.
At last his ship broke up, and all its oars,
And thwarts, and beams, and men, together in
The swirling water pulling at their feet.

Fierce Turnus was quick to respond, massing his forces
Together in battle order upon the shore.
The trumpet sounded. Aeneas was the first
To leap onto the shore, a sign of what
The future was going to be, Aeneas
The first to attack the Latin farmer-soldiers,   430
Rushing against the horde that was massed against him.
The first he brought down was Theron, the tallest of all,
Who dared to be the first to challenge him.
Aeneas' bloodthirsty sword slid through a seam
In the bronze plates of his shield and pierced his tunic,
Crusted with gold, and drank from the wound it made.
Next was Inche, who when he was born had been
Cut free and alive from the womb of his dead mother,
And therefore lived as if he were under the safe
Protection of Phoebus Apollo, the God of Health.   440
How long could this keep him from the weapon's edge?
Next Cissa the tough, and his giant brother, Gyas,
Clubbing down Trojans on the battlefield:
What could the arms of Hercules do to save them,
Or that their father, Melampus, was Hercules' comrade
While he was performing all his famous labors?
There's Pharos taunting Aeneas haplessly,
And Aeneas's javelin whirls at him and gets him
Right in his mouth as he was calling out.
And Cydon, there was lust-besotted you,   450
Pursuing Clytius, your latest beloved,
On whose fair cheeks the first blond signs of a beard
Were just beginning to show. You would have been dead,

Had not the cohort of Phorcus's seven sons
Gathered together to save you, seven brothers,
Seven javelins thrown, and some deflected
By helmet or shield, and one, by kindly Venus's
Guidance just barely grazing Aeneas's body.
Aeneas called out to his faithful Achates, "Achates,
Find me those spears retrieved from the bodies of   460
Those Greeks we killed on the plain of Ilium.
I'll use them now to kill Rutulians."
He picked up one of those great spears and hurled it,
And when, with its great force, it sped to Maeon,
One of the brothers, it shattered his breastplate and
His breast at once. His brother Alcanor raced
To try to help him, holding him up with his own
Right arm, but, dripping blood, Aeneas's spear
Full speed on its way went through his arm, and so
It dangled dying from one shoulder tendon.   470
Then Numitor picked up the spear that had pierced
His brother's body and hurled it at Aeneas;
It missed the hoped-for target and only grazed
The thigh of Aeneas's faithful companion Achates.
Then there was Clausus of Cures, glorying in
The strength of his youthful body, who aimed his stiff
Spear from a distance away at the Trojan Dryops,
And hurled it and it struck him in the throat,
Full force underneath his chin, as he was saying
Something, and so his life and his speaking voice   480
Together went away. He fell to his knees,
His forehead touching the ground, and out of his mouth
Came vomited thick gouts of pulsing blood.
Then Clausus killed three Thracian brothers, sons
Of Ida of Ismarus, exalted Boreans,
And he took their lives each in a different way.
Halaesus with his warriors came to help him,
And Messapus too, the son of Neptune, with
His famous horses. Now this side, now on that,

The two sides at the Ausonian threshold, as   490
When, in a great storm, wind contends with wind,
Wind against sea, and sky, unyielding forces.

Thus was it with the sons of Troy and the sons
Of Latins locked in struggle, man against man.

A ways away from there, wherever a river
Torrent had thrown down rocks and had broken trees
Along its sides, the debris scattered around,
Pallas saw his ignominious warriors
Retreating, on foot, having abandoned their horses
Because of the rough terrain; pursued by Latins   500
And trying to make their way, back to the shore.
All he could think to do was call out to them
In scolding arousing speech: "My fellow soldiers,
Where are you going? Why retreating? Why?
Remember who you are, the courage you
Have had and you have showed, your victories.
Remember Evander and his reputation,
And the glory of your people. Remember me,
Evander's son, and my desire to win
A glory here like his. Can it be that you want   510
To give it all up and go back to what was Troy?
The only thing to do is, turn around,
And go to where the fighting is thickest, and fight!"
And saying this, he plunged into the fray.

First there was Lagus, there by unlucky fate,
Bent over trying to lift up a huge great stone
He was going to heave down the hill at the foe; but Pallas
Hurled his spear at Lagus stooping there,
And it struck him in his spine just where the spine
Divides the ribs on each side of the body;   520
And Hisbo, seeing this, saw young Pallas, who

Was wresting the spear from the backbone where it impaled
The corpse of Lagus, and Hisbo came rushing down
To surprise him in revenge for the cruel way
His friend had been killed. But Hisbo, breathing hard,
Got there too late, for Pallas saw he was coming,
And turned, and hurled, and buried his spear in Hisbo's
Gasping lung. Next he took care of Sthenius;
Anchemolus next, of the ancient Rhoetian line,
Who, with his stepmother, profaned his father's sacred   530
Marital bed; and you, Larides and Thymber,
You twins, you sons of Daucus, you who were so
Exactly alike it amused your parents that
They couldn't tell which one of you was which,
But Pallas's sword could tell which one was which:
Thymber, it cut off your head, and, Larides, it
Severed your hand, and, half-alive, your fingers
Fingered about in the dust and tried to crawl,
Trying to find where was the sword they'd held.
And when the Arcadians saw these glorious deeds,   540
Shame and remorse rekindled their ardor for war.

As Rhoeteus in his two-horse chariot
Was fleeing from you, brave Teuthras, and Tyres, your brother,
His body intercepted Pallas's spear,
Which Pallas had aimed, from a far distance, at Ilus,
So Ilus, by this, had only just that much
Longer to be alive. Rhoeteus, struck,
Fell sideways out of his speeding chariot,
And flat on his back; he died. His frantic heels
Protesting as he died, were drumming on   550
The Rutulian earth.

                    It is as when a shepherd
Has set a few fires in different parts of a woods,
And then with the help of the summer winds the fires

Come together and together become
One great oneness of blazing, all of it, and
The exulting shepherd sits at the top of a hill,
Joyfully looking down at the flames below;
Thus, Pallas, your joy in seeing how your comrades
In the fellowship of courage come together.   560

　　　　　　＇　＇　＇

But then warlustful Halaesus gathered all
His formidable strength and went to meet
The Trojan enemy, and slaughtered Pheres,
And Ladon then, and then Demodocus, and,
After them, with one swipe of his sword, cut off
Strymonius' hand he had raised to protect his throat;
And after that he smashed a heavy rock
Into Thoas's face with such force that the blood,
Mingled with bones and brain, poured out. Halaesus's
Father, warding off fate, had hidden him in   570
The woods to keep his son from war, but when
The father's eyes sealed over in death, the Fates
Saw to it that the son was consecrated
To Pallas's father's spear, Evander's spear,
Which Pallas was poised to hurl, saying this prayer:
"If you will grant this missile, Father Thybris,
Good fortune to go straight into Halaesus's breast,
His armor will be hung from the branches of
Your sacred oak." His prayer was heard. Unlucky
Halaesus was using his shield to protect Imaon,   580
So the missile went straight to his own unshielded breast.

But Lausus, Mazentius' son, in order to
Prevent his soldiers from being overwhelmed
With terror at the sight of all this killing
Done by Arcadian Pallas, desired to set

An example in response to him. First, then,
When confronted by Abas, who was the foremost master
Exemplar of Trojan defensive fighting skills,
He killed him, and then, one after another, he killed,
Systematically, many others, Etruscan   590
Sons, Arcadian sons, and Trojans, you
Whose bodies had survived the fights at Troy.

Two armies, pressed together, leaders and common
Soldiers, so crowded together that neither hands
Nor weapons could be raised, the front ranks and
The rear together, and Pallas and Lausus in
The center, urging their own, the two of them,
Almost the same age as each other, both of them
Beautiful, neither of them to be
Allowed by Fortune ever to get back home.   600
But the ruler of great Olympus on high did not
Permit their final meeting, saving the death
Of each of them for someone greater than they.

                        ⸲ ⸲ ⸲

Meanwhile, when Turnus's sister urged Turnus to take
The place of Lausus on the field, he went
In his swift chariot into the midst of the fighting,
And, seeing his soldiers there, cried out to them,
"Now is the time for you to suspend the fighting.
Pallas is owed to me, and me alone.
I only wish his father were here to see it."   610
His people obeyed his orders and stood aside.
When Pallas heard these arrogant commands,
And saw the soldiers draw back, and Turnus there,
He wondered at Turnus's body, the size of it,
The power. His face was grim and he responded
This way to what the Rutulian hero had said:

"I will win glory today, either by stripping
His armor from my country's enemy,
Or by a glorious death. Whichever way
Its value will be the same for my grieving father.　　　　620
No more insults from you." And he strode into
The arena made by both sides having stood down.

The blood in the veins of the Trojans, watching, turned cold.
Turnus leaped down from his chariot, and went
Rapidly toward Pallas. It was as when
A lion, from some high place, sees in the distance
A bull that's ready for taking. Pallas, maybe hoping
The gods would favor the lesser man for his daring,
Went first, calling out to great Hercules on high,
"By the hospitality of my father to you,　　　　630
When you were a stranger and entered under his roof,
Hercules, help me in this great deed I attempt.
May it be that Turnus will see, with his dying eyes,
Who it is who's stripping his armor from his body,
And taking the glorious spoils."

　　　　　　　　　　, , ,

　　　　　　　　　　　　Hercules heard him,
And groaned and shed a few unavailing tears.
His father, Jupiter, tenderly spoke to him, saying:
"Each man has his fated day, and life is short
When time runs out for each. It cannot be changed.　　　　640
But the hero must validate the time he has,
By the glory of what he does. Many are those
Who fell before the walls of Troy. Sarpedon,
My son, was one of them. For Turnus, also,
The limit of his time has come." Jove spoke,
And then averted his eyes from Rutulian fields.

But Pallas used all his strength to hurl his spear
And drew his shining sword from its hollow scabbard;
The spear went flying at Turnus, and it struck,
But it struck high up at the upper edge of the shield;   650
It made its way in, but only grazed the skin
Of great Turnus's body; and he, in turn, as he
Poised his oaken spear with its deadly spearhead
Above his head, called out, "Let's see if this
My spear goes farther in than that," and hurled it,
And it struck right through the middle of Pallas's shield,
Right through its plates of iron, its plates of brass,
Right through its bull's hide coverings and through
The breastplate, last protection of the body,
And finished, hurtling into his mighty chest.   660
Frantic, he wrenched the missile from the hot wound,
And with the missile his blood and his life poured out.
Pallas fell forward dying on his wound;
His armor rang around him as he fell;
His bloody mouth was mouthing the enemy earth.

Turnus stood over him then and proudly said,
"Arcadians, this message is for Evander.
Here is Pallas your son, sent back to you,
As he deserved to be. Whatever there is
To be done to honor him at whatever tomb,   670
By whatever custom there is, I freely grant.
But you ought not have welcomed Aeneas into your house,
And you will have to pay for having done so."
And with that he put his left foot on the dead body,
And reached across it to strip from it the great
Heavy sword-belt on which Eurytides
Engraved in gold the atrocious story of how,

On their wedding night, fifty young men were slain
By their brides incited by their wicked father.
Men do not know what fate has in store for them,   680
Nor of their exaltation know its end.
The day will come when Turnus will wish that Pallas
Was still alive, and he will hate the spoils
He took from his dead body and gloried in.
But Pallas's grieving comrades placed his body
Upon his shield and carried him away,
And with great honor, to take him to his father:
One day in war was all there was, but he
Left many slain Rutulians in the field.

, , ,

First, rumors of calamity, and then   690
An eyewitness messenger bringing Aeneas the truth:
The line between the Trojans and utter death
Was thin to disappearing, almost gone.
There was a desperate need for help. Aeneas,
Aroused, raged through the ranks of the enemy army,
Cutting a path of death as he went to find
Turnus and Turnus's pride in what he had done.
All he could see in his mind were Pallas, Evander,
The tables they had sat at, the right-hand hand-clasp
Pledges of peace there had been. He seized four sons   700
Of Sulmo, four sons of Ufens, young men whose blood
Would later be poured into the funeral flames
In sacrifice for Pallas at the rites.
Then there was Magus: when Aeneas hurled
His mighty spear at him he ducked it, ducked
Agilely under it, and the spear flew past
Above his head, and Magus, then, was upon
Hs knees before Aeneas, imploring, saying,
"By your father and by your shades, and by your hopes

For Iulus your growing son, I pray, spare my life   710
For the sake of my growing son, and for my father.
Our family has a palace, high up in the hills,
And deep in the palace cellars there are many
Talents of silver incised with legends, and many
Piles of gold, both wrought and as yet not wrought.
Victory for Troy won't be delayed
By one life left to live, so let me live."
"Keep your gold and silver for your son,"
Aeneas said. "The time for bargaining
Was past when Pallas was killed by Turnus. This   720
Is the judgment of my father Anchises' shade,
And of my son, my Iulus." With his left hand
He held the pleading head of Magus back,
And plunged his sword in, to the very hilt.

Not far away was Haemonides, who was
A priest in the sacred rites of Diana and
Of Phoebus Apollo; he wore the white-wool priestly
Headband, and his armor shone with white
Insignia of his priesthood; Aeneas attacked,
And drove him across the field, and when he fell,   730
Aeneas, standing over him, cast a dark shadow
Upon the white battle dress he was wearing, and
Sent him as an offering to the shades.
Serestus carried the armor back on his shoulders,
As trophy spoils in honor of Mars Gradivus.

The fight was renewed by two: Caeculus, fierce
Descendant of Vulcan's race, and Umbro, who
Had come to the war down from the Marsian hills.
Aeneas ravaged the two in raging fury.
His sword had just then severed Anxur's left hand,   740
And with the same stroke he shattered Anxur's shield,
Its oval center useless on the ground—

Anxur—he boasted of his great powers and
He seemed to have believed he really had them,
And promised himself long life and many years.
Tarquitus, next, who was the son of Faunus,
God of the woods, and of Dryope, a nymph,
Exulting in the boast of his glittering armor,
Stood right in the way of Aeneas's scorching rampage.
Aeneas drew back his spear and hurled it at him,   750
And the spear pinned the shield and the breastplate both together,
So what could he do, so helpless, but plead for mercy,
And keep on trying to plead for mercy, as
Aeneas smashed his severed head to the ground.
As his body rolled aside Aeneas stood
Over the body and said to the body, his voice
Full of contemptuous hatred of it, "Lie there,
Pretense of a hero, your mother won't be able
To build a memorial tomb for you, back home.
Let the wild birds have you, or let you be thrown into   760
The sea and be washed away in the waves, and as
Your body tumbles around in the water, let
The hungry fish lick hungrily at your wounds."

After that he went after Antaeus and Lucas, two
Of Turnus's foremost captains, and then, brave Numa,
And blond Camers, the son of magnanimous Volcens,
The richest in fields of all of Italy
And governor of silent Amyclae.
Aeneas was like the dragon Aegaeon,
One hundred arms, they say, one hundred hands,   770
And fifty mouths, breathing out fire, and fifty
Breasts on fire, and fifty swords and fifty
Shields against the thunderbolts of Jove.

Then, look, there was Niphaeus's four-horse chariot,
The big-chested horses confronting him, but when
They saw the hero striding toward them and

They heard him roar, in terror they turned and ran,
Spilling their master out, the chariot
Rumbling behind them as they raced for the shore.

Right after this a two-horse chariot came 780
Into the fighting, in it two brothers, one
Was Lucagus, holding the reins, the other was Liger,
Madly waving his sword, kill-ready, flaunting.
Aeneas couldn't bear this flourishing.
Spear poised he rushed to where the brothers were,
And appeared before them, huge. Liger cried out,
"These aren't Diomedes' horses! It's not Achilles'
Chariot you're looking at! It's not
The plains of Troy you're on! It's here and now,
The end of you and with you the end of war!" 790
Aeneas didn't answer him with words;
But with his whirling spear he answered him.
Lucagus was bent forward, urging on
The horses with the flat of his sword, and with
His left foot, getting ready to fight, extended
Out from the chariot side; the javelin struck
At the lowest border of his shining shield,
And went into the groin; Lucagus was
Expelled from the chariot and rolled across
The sward and as he died Aeneas said, 800
Taking fast hold of the bridles of the horses,
"Don't blame your horses; it's you deserted them;
They didn't bolt away from an enemy shadow;
You bolted away from your chariot and them."
And as he took fast hold of the horses' bridles
The unhappy brother, having fallen out too,
Stretched out his pleading hands, and said to him,
"By who you are, and who it is your parents
Brought you up to be, great Trojan, have
Mercy on me, do not deprive me of life." 810
He tried to go on pleading but pious Aeneas

Said to him: "This isn't how you talked just now.
Brother should not desert brother into death."
With the point of his sword he opened up in his chest
The place which is the hiding place of the soul.

Thus, like a torrent run wild or a black storm wind,
The Dardanian chief on the battlefield was the cause
Of so many deaths, and thus Ascanius,
And the Trojan youths, were freed from within the walls
Of the stronghold where they were penned, and the siege was over.   820

, , ,

Meanwhile, Jupiter said to Juno, his wife:
"Dear sister of mine and dearest wife of mine,
You will already have been told that because
Of Venus the Teucrians have survived, and not
Because of their valor or skill in fighting, nor
Because of their patience or their withstanding the siege."
Juno humbly replied, "Most beautiful
Of husbands, why upset me so with these
Frightening words, when I am worried sick.
If you still loved me as you used to love me,   830
And as you ought to still, then why not grant
What I ask of you, that Turnus be sent home
Safe and sound to the town of his father Daunus?
As things are now, let him die, his innocent blood
A sacrifice to the vengeance of the Trojans.
But remember that Turnus is of the blood of Pilumnus,
God of his household, his great-great-grandsire, and
Your altar has been heavy with his gifts."
Jupiter, king of Olympus, briefly replied,
"If what you ask is for his death to be   840
Put off for a little while, it shall be so.
Go rescue him for now from what is now
Impending. But if there's more in what you ask,

And in the way that you ask it, that this would change
The outcome of the war, or what is willed,
Then what you hope for has in vain been hoped for."
Juno, in tears, replied: "But if your heart
Differs from what your voice is telling me,
Might Turnus be freed from what I fear for him?
As it is now, my terror-stricken fears   850
Tell me that he is under sentence of death,
Though innocent; if these my fears are false,
I welcome mockery; but you are free
To change it, any or all of it, just as you please."

                              , , ,

Having said what she said, Juno the goddess
On her storm chariot came down through the clouds,
And sought the plain between the Laurentine camp
And where the Trojans were, and there she created,
Out of the tenuous air a powerless brainless
Creature made of the airy nothing it was;   860
But freakily it was Aeneas' semblance,
The semblance of his helmet with its plumes,
The semblance of his shield and of his weapons,
A creature speaking words that had no meaning,
Its phantom hand that waved a phantom sword;
And as this image of Aeneas leaped
And gamboled, flourishing and challenging, it
Was like something come back from the other world, or else
Something in a dream the dreamer was dreaming.
And Turnus rushed at the creature, and threw his spear,   870
And the creature fled away, and Turnus, exulting,
Drinking deep from an empty cup of hope,
Pursued it, thinking that victory was his,
And derisively cried out, "Aeneas, come back,
You're going to miss your wedding. The bride is yours.
The land is yours you came across the seas for.

I have it here in my right hand for you."
The winds were scattering what he was saying, as
He ran pursuing the creature where it went.
The figment fled toward where there was a ship,   880
Moored there and tied up to a high rock ledge,
Its ladders lowered and its planks all ready
For King Osinius' troops from Clusium
To come ashore; and simulating fear
It fled on board the ship and hid somewhere.
Turnus, just as fast, raced past or over
Anything in his way, leaped over across
To the high prow of the ship, and just as he did,
The daughter of Saturn cut the cable and
The ship slid back, taking Turnus on it on   890
The ebb tide out to sea, and, aboard the ship,
The airy figment came out of wherever it was,
And rose and blended into the blackness of
A cloud above.

    Meanwhile in the battle fray
The real Aeneas was seeking absent Turnus
To challenge him, and as he fought to do so
He sent many warrior bodies down to death.
And Turnus, whom the bewildering wind had carried
Over the waves to safety, and all at sea   900
About it all, cried out, "What's happening?
What's happening? Where am I going to?
What have I done? Omnipotent God,
What am I being punished for? My soldiers,
What can they do, who followed me into the battle?
I see them wandering on the plain without
The leader who led them there. I see them dying,
I hear them groaning as they die back there.
You winds have mercy on me, blow this ship
On the waves, on the rocks, on the sands, somewhere, somewhere,   910
Anywhere where there's no Rutulians there

To see me so disgraced. Where is their Turnus?"
And so his mind among the winds and waves
Was fluctuating so, this way and that way,
Not knowing whether to take his life with his own
Sword sliding between his ribs, or leap into
The sea and try to swim to the faraway shore
To find the Trojans and to find his own people,
To fight again where he had been fighting before.
But Juno in her pity prevented him   920
From either way, and so he was carried upon
The billowing waves and the favoring currents, home
To the ancient royal town of his father Daunus.

                    ⸙ ⸙ ⸙

But then, at Jupiter's urging, Mezentius
Entered, violent, into the fight against
The exultant Trojans, and they, unanimous
In hatred of him, surrounded him with all
Their weapons; but Mezentius stood there,
Like a great cliff standing out into the sea,
Buffeted by the waves and winds from the sky,   930
Uncaring and unyielding. First he kills
Hebrus, son of Dolichaon, and next,
Latagus, then, Palmus running away;
Latagus with a huge rock fragment torn
From the hillside, smashing his face to pieces; then
He hamstrings Palmus the runaway so that he lies
Dying writhing his no-longer-running legs;
Mezentius gives his armor to Lausus his son
To carry on his shoulders and wear his plumed
Helmet on his head. And then it was   940
Evanthes the Phrygian, and Mimas who had
Been Paris's friend when they were children and
Was brought into the light the very same night
That Paris's mother, Hecuba, Cisseus' daughter,

Dreamed she was giving birth to a flaming torch,
And Paris was the baby she gave birth to,
Priam's son, and Mimas's friend and comrade.
Paris lies dead in his father's burned-down city;
Mimas, unknown, on this foreign Laurentine shore.

Mezentius was like a wild boar driven 950
By snapping biting dogs down from the high
Places on Mount Vetulus or in the reedy
Laurentian forests where he fed, and finally
Cornered between the hunters' nets, stands snarling,
Brave, bristling his mighty shoulders, considering
Which way to turn to attack to defend himself,
And all the men surrounding him don't dare
To run at him or get too close, no matter
How right the reasons they have for hating him;
So from a distance they hurl their spears and shout. 960

And after that there was Acron, the young Greek, who
Had had to come down to the war from Corythus, before
His wedding night had time to have taken place,
And when Mezentius saw him, from a distance,
Ardently embroiled in the hectic fighting,
Dressed in the crimson warrior garb, with the purple
Feathers floating from his helmet crest,
That his promised bride had joyfully made for him,
It's as when a famished lion looks across
The fields and sees a she-goat over there, 970
Or maybe a stag, full-antlered, and the hair
Of the lion's shaggy mane's aroused, and he opens
His hungry desiring mouth; he feasts upon
The viscera of the creature, and the gobbets
Of flesh wash through his bloody mouth. Just so,
Mezentius, delighted, entered the fray,
And dying Acron lay drumming his heels, his blood
Spilling out upon his own broken weapons. Then

Mezentius saw Orodes running from him,
And he thought it beneath his dignity to kill   980
From behind as if he were a robber, so
He ran before him and turned around so as
To kill him man-to-man and face to face,
And when he stood, with his foot upon his fallen
Body, and leaning on his spear, cried out,
"Look, see how I have killed this Orodes, who wasn't
The least of you in war. He stood so tall,
And now does not." Mezentius' joyful soldiers
Cheered, but Orodes, dying, managed to say:
"You have so little time to rejoice for this.   990
The time will come very soon when you, like me,
Will lie here dying." Mezentius, smiling, and not,
Said, "That's for the king of the gods and men to know,"
And he pulled his spear out of Orodes' body,
And iron Sleep closed over his eyes for ever.

Then Caedicus killed Alcathous, and Sacrator
Killed Hydaspes, and Rapo killed Parthenius,
And Orses, famously strong; Messapus killed
Clonius, and Lycaon's son Erichaetes,
The one who had lost control of the horses' reins,   1000
The other on foot; and Agis the Lycian also
Was killed as he came on foot, by Valerus,
Who showed by this he had the family courage;
And Thronius was killed by Salius,
And Salius by an arrow sent from far,
By Nealces who was known to be good at this.

                    ❯ ❯ ❯

Mars impartially deals out grief and death;
Equally they kill and equally die,
Victors and victims alike; the gods look down
From Jupiter's palace above, and pity them,   1010

Sorrowing for the mutual labors of men;
Venus looks down, and opposite her, Saturnian
Juno looks down; and Tisiphone down there rages,
Pale as death among the thousands fighting.

, , ,

Then came Mezentius again, gigantic,
Looking like Orion as Orion's
Mighty feet step after step strode hugely
Upon the floor of the sea through waves that, billowing up,
Couldn't billow high enough to reach his shoulders;
Or he looked like a giant coming down a mountain,   1020
So tall, his head in enshrouding mountain clouds,
And holding an ancient ash tree in one hand.

Aeneas saw him where he was in the long
Line of battle, and, ready for the encounter,
He moved to the confrontation. Mezentius stood
Fearless, as huge as a cliffside, ready, eyeing
The distance between the two of them to gauge
How he would throw his spear, and saying to
Himself, "My god, my right hand, help me now,
As now I take my aim and hurl my weapon.   1030
May the armor, stripped from the body of this pirate,
Aeneas, be worn by Lausus as his trophy."
And then he hurled it, and it went, revolving,
Hissing, shrilling, fast, across the distance
Between himself and Aeneas, and with tremendous
Force it caromed off Aeneas's shield,
Fatally striking noble Antores, between
The groin and the lower flank of him who'd been
Hercules' comrade, and who had come, a stranger,
From Argos to join Evander and to settle   1040
In his Italian town. He died of a wound
Not meant for him, and as he, dying, lay,

Looking up at the sky, there were pictures in
His mind of his sweet Argos he had left.

Then pious Aeneas hurled his spear; it struck
And penetrated three bronze layers of
The orb at the center of Mezentius' shield,
And through the three stitched linen-covered bull-hide
Layers beyond, and pierced, though losing force,
Mezentius' groin, and settled itself in the wound.   1050
Aeneas, at the sight of Tyrrhenian blood,
Excitedly pulled his exultant sword from its scabbard,
And Lausus groaned and wept at what he was seeing,
His father, whom he loved, in such distress.
—Lausus, so men in the far-off future will know
Of what you did, I will ever tell the story;
You are a youth the greatness of whose deed
Is never to be forgotten, the history
Of how you died, trying to save your father—
His father, helpless, entrammeled by the shield   1060
He dragged behind him, the spear still hanging from it,
Was trying to make his way away from this,
Aeneas standing above him and ready to strike,
When the son rushed in between them, and hindered the blow,
And all his comrades shouted, and from their distance
Showered Aeneas with missiles, and so the father
Managed to live, for a little, protected by
The small heroic shield of his young son.

Under this showering onslaught of missiles Aeneas
Had to take cover under his shield. It was   1070
As when a storm of rain and hail comes on,
And all the workers in the fields, and the passers-by,
Must look for shelter somewhere, under the pending,
Say, of a riverbank, or the overhang
Of a rocky cliff, or in a nearby cavern,
Until the storm is over and it's time

For the interrupted work to begin again.
So, after having withstood the hail of missiles,
Aeneas confronted Lausus and said to him, chiding,
"Why, so young, in such a hurry to die?   1080
You're trying to do what you're not yet able to do.
Is filial piety making a fool of you?"
But the youth still exulted in his madness, and
Terminal anger rose up in the heart of Aeneas,
The leader of the Dardanians, and now
It was the time for the Fates to spin the last thread.
His mighty sword descended on the boy,
And went straight through the little shield he carried,
Piercing deep to its hilt in Lausus's belly;
The tunic he wore, that his mother had woven with loving   1090
Threads of gold, was soaked with the blood pouring out,
And sorrowing life departed from his body
And through the air flew away to the place of the Shades.

But truly when the son of Anchises saw
The face, the features of the face, so pale
With the paleness of his dying, he groaned, and with
Mournful pity he stretched out his right hand
As he thought of his own father and his own
Filial pious love that was so like this,
And he said to Lausus's body, "What can Aeneas   1100
Give, O wretched boy, worthy of deeds
Like these that you have done? What is it that
Pious Aeneas can do but send your armor,
That you so delighted to wear, home with your body,
To be with the shades and ashes of your people,
And perhaps it can solace you that they will say,
'He met his death by the hand of the great Aeneas.'"
And then he scornfully called upon the comrades
Of Lausus to venture nearer, and, himself,
He lifted up the body from the ground,   1110
Where the blood has soiled and clotted its beautiful hair.

Meanwhile his father, over by the Tiber,
Was leaning against the trunk of a tree, attempting
To salve his wound with clear water from the stream,
His bronzen helmet hanging from a branch;
His armor lying quiet in the meadow;
His chosen fellows were standing around him where
He sat, bent over, trying to wash his neck,
Gasping for breath, the water streaming down
Through his great beard and onto his mighty chest;   1120
He kept asking over and over for news of Lausus,
And sending orders to him, to call him back,
But Lausus was dead already, and, even then,
Soldiers, weeping, were bearing his body back
Upon his armor, a mighty warrior's body
Slain by a mightier warrior than he.

Mezentius knew what his mind had already known,
As he heard the soldiers weeping as they came;
With his hands he despoiled his hair with dust of the earth,
And raised his hands to the skies, and then flung himself down   1130
Upon the body of his son, and cried out, "Why
Did I want so much to be alive that I
Allowed my child, my son, to rescue me
By putting himself between me and the sword?
Were you, my child, the one who lost your life
By saving the life of the father who begot you?
And the father who soiled the name of the virtuous son?
What has happened to you, and the wound I suffered, for which
You lost your life, has driven home to me
What I have been and what it is I am,   1140
In this exile from what I ought to have been and what
I ought to have done. For my odious crimes for which
My people hated me and drove me away
From them and from my kingship, the scepter and rule

Of my fathers, I ought to have suffered the punishment
That I deserved, but I still live, unpunished,
Here in the light of day, while you are gone.
But I will leave this light, I will." Saying this
He raised himself up, to stand in spite of his weakness
And his wounded thigh, and as if not noticing these,   1150
He called for his horse, the horse he took such pride in,
The horse he had ridden from triumph to triumph in war.
He said to his horse, "Rhoebus, we have lived
Long together, if life is ever long.
Today we will either win together and you
Will take revenge with me on him for what
He did to Lausus my son, and you will carry
Back with me on your back the armor stripped
From Aeneas, and with his head; or if we find
That our way to doing this is blocked, then we   1160
Will fall together. I don't think you will consent
To live to be obedient to some Trojan."

With that he mounted into the saddle he was
So used to, and, wearing his bronzen helmet with
Its horsehair plumes, in both hands javelins,
He galloped, out of his mind with shame, rage, grief,
Onto the scene of battle. Three times he calls
The name of Aeneas out, and Aeneas hears him,
Joyful at hearing him and prays to the gods,
"Let the Father of the Gods, and let Apollo   1170
Be with me now," and moved toward Mezentius,
Threatening him with his great spear, and he,
Mezentius, cried out, "Don't think that you,
You savage, can frighten me. Neither my son
Nor I will bargain with the fear of death,
Nor of any gods. It is my purpose here
To die, but first I have these gifts to give."
And with these words he hurled a javelin, and
Then another, and another, and

Another, and another, and Aeneas's   1180
Great shield withstood them all. Three times
Mezentius circled around and around him, hurling
His javelins, and Aeneas, turning with him,
Withstood them all, and then at last, refusing
To be defensive any longer, and weary
Of plucking javelin after javelin from his shield,
Suddenly broke forward and aimed his spear
At Mezentius' horse and struck it in the hollow
Between the temples of its head, and the horse,
In pain and fear, rose up and with its forefeet   1190
Kicked at the wind, and pitched its rider off,
And fell upon his master so he was pinned
Under the dislocated great horse shoulder.
The Trojans and Latins shouting inflamed the skies.
Aeneas drew his sword from its sheath and went
Rapidly over to where Mezentius lay,
And said, "Where now is that wild animal power
You had, that was your soul?" Mezentius lay there,
Searching the sky with his eyes, and drinking in
The air; and coming back to his senses, said,   1200
"You are my enemy, and you have won.
Why waste your words, threatening me with death.
I had no thoughts of bargaining for life,
Nor did my son when he entered into battle.
It is right that, being the victor, you should kill me.
I only ask one favor from the winner.
My people hate me. Protect my body from what
Their fury would do to it, that it may lie
Together with the body of my son,
Under the cover of earth." Having said this,   1210
In full awareness of what it was he did,
He offered his throat to the sword, and his life poured out
In gushing streams of blood upon his armor.

Book Eleven

Aurora was rising up from the sea, and Aeneas,
Though grieving in his heart for those who died,
First made his vows to the gods and then cut all
Of its branches from a great oak tree, and stood
Its naked trunk on a mound of earth, and put
The dead man's shining armor on it, trophy
To show to Mars All-Powerful-In-War;
And at the top of it he hung Mezentius'
Helmet from which dewdrops of blood dripped down;
In the breastplate that he put on it were twelve   10
Holes his spear had made, and hanging down
From the effigy's neck its ivory-handled knife;
Tied to the left side was the round bronze shield
Mezentius had carried; on the right,
Several bronze spears, broken in battle. This done,
Aeneas spoke to the other leaders, who
Were gathered around him: "Great things have been achieved.
There is no need to fear what the future will bring.
These are the spoils and this is proud Mezentius,
First fruits of war plucked down by my own hands.   20
Next we must go to the king of the Latins and
The walls of his city. Be armed, make ready, give over
All your thoughts and all your hopes to war;
Have nothing in your minds that would hold you back
Or distract you when the signal comes from the gods
To march the army forth to the battlefield.

Meanwhile we must attend to the burial of
Our comrades, whose bodies lie unburied here.
The funeral rite is the only honor that
Is recognized in the region down below.   30
Therefore, go," he said, "and pay what is due
To these noble spirits who gave with their blood their lives,
To save their country. But first let Pallas's body
Be sent to his father Evander's grieving city,
For Pallas was one whose courage never failed him.
But his black day has carried him away,
And death has overwhelmed him."

                                   Thus, weeping, he spoke,
And then returned to his house, wherein there lay
The body of young Pallas, attended by   40
The aged Acoetes, who himself had been
Arms-bearer to Arcadian Evander,
And who, now under worse auspices, kept watch
Over the boy he had been the guardian of.
Gathered around the body where it lay
Were a crowd of Trojan soldiers in attendance,
And Trojan women with their hair unbound,
According to the custom; and when Aeneas
Entered the room the great bellowing sound
Of lamentation rose as high as the stars,   50
And there was beating of breasts in lamentation.
And Aeneas, when he saw Pallas's face,
And in his snow-white chest the open wound
The Ausonian had made, burst into tears,
And cried, "O wretched child, Fortune has kept you
From sharing in the good things that have happened,
And now you will not see us in our kingdom,
Nor ride victorious home to your father's city.
This isn't what I promised to Evander,
When I was leaving Pallanteum with his child   60
To take up my great command, and he embraced me,

And warned me at the parting that we were going
To fight against a dangerous race of men.
And now, back there, enthralled by empty hopes,
He's making vows to the gods, and on their altars
Imploring them with gifts to keep him safe.
But the body we're bringing back to him owes nothing
More to the gods than it has given already.
Is this what it all has come down to? Is this what I
Have trusted my faith to? But the horrific wounds   70
That Evander will see on the body of his son
Have brought no shame with them. Evander is not
One of those fathers who'll have to wish that his son,
Shamefully still alive, had died like this.
What a great defender Arcadia has lost,
And, Iulus, you have lost."

                  And saying this,
He ordered that the body be raised, and that
A thousand soldiers from the army should
Accompany it in the funeral cortège,   80
To share their tears with his father's at the rites,
As owed to the father, although for such a sorrow
The payment is meager. A bier was constructed, adorned
With arbutus and intertwined oak-leaved branchlets,
And shadowed overhead with many garlands.
They placed the body high on its bed of straw.
He looked like a flower a young maiden had picked,
Soft violet, say, or a hyacinth fallen,
Not faded, as yet, as yet not having lost
Its shape, but now, it is true, no longer being   90
Fed and fostered by its mother earth.
Then Aeneas brought out two robes Sidonian Dido,
Happy at the work of doing so,
Had made for him, finishing it with lines
Of threaded gold. His final act of honor
Was to wrap the body in these funeral shrouds,

One of them arranged so as to veil
The hair that will so soon be offered to flames;
On the bier he piled up many trophies that Pallas
Had stripped from the bodies of the Laurentians, and 100
He ordered the captains to carry and display
Still more of the trophies; and in the cortège there were
The horses and spears of those whom Pallas had slain;
And next in the procession were the captives,
Hands tied behind their backs, whom Aeneas had chosen
To be sent down as offerings to the shades,
Their blood to be sprinkled in flames of the funeral fire;
He ordered his captains after that to parade
Tree trunks wearing the enemy armor, with names
Of those whom Pallas had killed affixed to them. 110
Then came, distraught, disheveled, old Acoetes,
Beating his face with his fists, or with his fingers
Tearing at it; he fell, and lay stretched out
In grief upon the ground. Then they led by
The chariots of the slain, with the signs upon them
Of spattered Rutulian blood; and after that
Came Aethon, Pallas's war horse, naked, without
Its saddle and bridle harnesses, and, itself,
Weeping great tears of faithful sorrowing.
Then, finally, long lines of grieving soldiers, 120
Teucrians and Tyrrhenians and Pallas's
Own Arcadians, marching with weapons reversed.
Aeneas halted, and, sighing deeply, said:
"The Fates call us to other, and the same,
Tears of this terrible war. For ever, Pallas,
Great Pallas, hail and farewell." He turned back toward
The high walls of his camp, and went to enter there.

❦ ❦ ❦

Then envoys came from the city, seeking a truce.
They were carrying olive branches swathed in wool.

Dead bodies of Latins lay everywhere around,   130
And the envoys were asking that they be allowed to take
The bodies home, so they could be laid to rest
In their native soil. "The dead," the envoys said,
"Can no longer harm when they can no longer breathe
The air and see the light of being alive.
Spare them, some of them were your hosts, and some
Might have been fathers of Trojan brides one day."
Good Aeneas, without asperity, answered them,
Granting them freely what they were asking for,
And, further, said these peaceable words to them: 140

"How is it that Fortune has gotten you involved
In this unfortunate war, so now you flee
From us who are your friends? You ask us to
Let you bring back the bodies of your dead
To honor them. I tell you that the peace
We grant to the dead we would have freely granted
While they were still alive. The reason we
Are here is only because the Fates have told us
That this is where we must come, to find our home.
I had no hostile intent against your people;   150
Your king was our friend, and now your king has chosen
To put his faith in Turnus and Turnus's army.
If Turnus desires to send the Trojans back,
Then he should not have put these lives at risk,
But only his, with mine, in single combat
Man-to-man, and let the gods decide,
Or our right hands decide, which it should be.
But now, take up your dead and submit their bodies
To the funeral fires and rites that honor them."

The emissaries stood looking at one another,   160
Open-mouthed, silent, because of what he said.
Then Drances, who was the senior of the envoys,
And who had always hated young Turnus and

Opposed him at every turn, had this to say:
"O great in fame, prodigious Trojan hero,
Which praises are the first with which to praise you?
Which object of our admiration is it?
Your wisdom, is it, or what you have done in battle?
We will return to our city grateful for what
You have granted to us, and if Fortune will find us the way,   170
May Aeneas and may our king be friends again,
And may Turnus have to look for other allies.
And more than that, we will join with you to build
Upon their predicted foundations, our shoulders helping
To raise them, the new walls of Troy." He spoke,
And with one voice his companions gave assent.

Twelve days of truce were decided, and for those days
The Teucrians and the Latins worked together,
Harmless to one another, in the woods.
There was the sound of axes felling ash trees   180
And the pines that reached up toward the stars above.
Together they used wedges to split the oaks
And fragrant cedars, and in groaning wagons
Brought logs of the manna ash down the mountainside.

꜊ ꜊ ꜊

Then Rumor, first harbinger of woe, came flying
To the city of Evander and his people—
Rumor, who had only so recently told
Of Pallas's victories on the fields in Latium.
The Arcadians came to the gates of their town, and as
Their custom was, took up their funeral torches,   190
And all along the road, and stretching out
Beyond, along the borders of the fields,
As if to mark them out, there was a long
Processional of grieving flaming lights
Out there in the dark. Out there the weeping cortège

Of soldiers bringing Pallas's body home
Met the weeping procession of citizens of the town;
The matrons came out of their houses and there arose
The clamor of the sorrow, filling the skies.
Evander—no power on earth could keep from this—   200
Came through the crowd of mourners around the bier,
Shaking, weeping, and threw himself down upon
The body of his son, and said to the body,
"Pallas, my son, this isn't what you promised
To your father; you promised him that you'd be cautious about
Not getting yourself too close too early to
The face of Mars. I know too well that when
The young men go too young into the fight
They want to get to glory right away.
Wretched first fruits, gathered of that hard truth,   210
The lesson that you learned. None of the gods
Would listen to your father's prayers and vows,
And you, dear sanctified wife, are kept by death
From the knowledge of what this is that has happened to us,
While I the father am left alone in this life,
Surviving the son. It is I, it is not my son,
Who should have been the one brought home by this
Procession of trophies stripped from the bodies of
These many Rutulians.

                    But Trojans, I do not blame you   220
For this, nor do I regret our clasping of hands
In mutual faith. This death is owed by the Fates.
And if my child has died, so young, his glory
Is that he has killed so many Rutulians,
Helping the Trojans come into their Latium homeland;
And so he deserves this grateful procession brought
By Father Aeneas and his Phrygian warriors,
The Etruscan captains and their men, and our
Arcadian soldiers who were his comrades in battle.
And, Turnus, as for you, your headless trunk   230

Would have been standing naked here in the fields,
If he had had the years to grow to be
As strong as you. But Trojans, why should my
Unhappiness keep you here? Go tell Aeneas,
And do not forget to do so, that all that sustains me
Here in this wretched life, now Pallas is gone,
Is what his strength and his right hand will do.
Turnus's life is owed to the son and his father.
When this is done I will go down to the shades
To tell my child down there that the debt is paid."   240

                        ❟ ❟ ❟

Aurora rose, spreading her pitying light,
And with it bringing back to sight the labors
Of sad mortality, what men have done,
And what has been done to them; and what they must do
To mourn. King Tarchon and Father Aeneas, together
Upon the curving shore, caused there to be
Wooden funeral pyres constructed, and to which
The bodies of their dead were brought and placed there,
In accordance with the customs of their countries.
The black pitch smoke of the burning of the bodies   250
Arose up high and darkened the sky above.
Three times in shining armor the grieving warriors
Circled the burning pyres, three times on horseback,
Ululating, weeping, as they rode.
You could see how teardrops glistened on their armor.
The clamor of their sorrowing voices and
The dolorous clang of trumpets rose together
As they threw into the melancholy fires
Spoils that had been stripped from the Latins, helmets,
And decorated swords, bridles of horses,   260
And glowing chariot wheels, and with them, also,
Shields and weapons of their own familiar
Comrades, which had failed to keep them alive.

Bodies of beasts were thrown into the fire,
Cattle, and bristle-backed swine, brought from surrounding
Fields to be sacrificed to the god of death.
And all along the shore the soldiers watched
The burning of the bodies of their friends,
And could not be turned away until the dewy
Night changed all the sky and the stars came out.   270

Over there, where the Latins were, things were
As miserable as this. Innumerable
Scattered funeral pyres; many bodies
Hastily buried in hastily dug-up earth,
And many others, picked up from where they fell
When they were slain, and carried back to the fields
Which they had plowed and tilled before the fighting,
Or back into the city where they came from;
Others were indiscriminately burned,
Unnamed, and so without ceremony or honor.   280
The light of the burning fires was everywhere.
On the third day when the light of day came back
To show the hapless scene, they leveled out
What was left of the pyres and separated what
Was left of the bones, now cold and among cold ashes,
And covered over the ashes and the bones.

, , ,

In a house high up in Latinus's rich city,
There was transcendently the din of grief
And desolation, outcry of mothers for
Their fallen sons, young wives for their husbands, sisters   290
Heartbroken for the brothers they have lost,
Fatherless children wailing for their fathers;
And there was execration of Turnus for
This war and his marriage claims, Turnus who wants
The kingdom and all the honors for himself;

And Drances weighs in to say, "Yes, all himself;
If it's all himself then he himself alone,
With sword and shield should settle it alone."
But there were others there who disagreed,
And spoke for Turnus, invoking in his support   300
The great name of his promised mother-in-law,
And the fame of his own glorious deeds of war.

In the middle of all of this, while the argument
Was at its height, the envoys who had been sent
To Diomedes returned, with depressing news:
Nothing they'd hoped to achieve had been achieved,
Neither by gifts, by gold, by fervent urgings.
The message from Diomedes was that the Latins
Should look for help elsewhere or else should find
A way to seek to make peace with the Teucrians.   310
The king, Latinus, was deeply cast down by this news.
The Trojans were being favored by the gods,
Who were showing their anger by all the funeral pyres
He and the others were seeing before their eyes.
The king announced he was calling a council together.

                        , , ,

All those whose presence had been invoked streamed through
The streets of the town and entered the palace, where
Latinus sat enthroned in majesty,
First among all empowered for government.
He called upon the leader of the envoys,   320
To tell them all what Diomedes had said,
Leaving nothing out, and Venulus obeyed:
"Citizens, after a long and difficult journey,
We reached the camp of Argive Diomedes,
And clasped the hand that brought Ilium down to the ground,
In his town in the fields near Mount Garganus, in
The kingdom of Iapyx, Argyripa, after the name

Of his father's Argos. After we were admitted
To Diomedes' presence we told him who
We were and offered him our gifts, and spoke   330
Urgently from our hearts, about why we had come,
And the hopes we had for having help from him.
He listened patiently, and gently replied:

'O you of the ancient race of Ausonians,
You fortunate people of the kingdom of Saturn,
Enjoying such peace and quiet, why has your fortune
Caused you to stir up war without knowing why?
Think of our suffering, under the walls of the Troy
Whose fields we violated. Think of how
The river Simois's waters were choked with the bodies   340
Of Grecians slain, think of us scattered around
The world to pay for what it was we did.
Priam, even, would pity us for what
We have become. The gloomy star of Minerva
Has looked at us; Euboea's terrible rocks
Have welcomed us, and vengeful Caphareus;
Menelaus Atrides is exiled where
The Protean columns are; Ulysses at Aetna,
Having to see the Cyclopean monster;
The Locri cast out on the alien Libyan shore;   350
And Neoptolemus, and Idomeneus,
Both of them overthrown, their kingdoms lost:
And even the Mycenean chief, himself,
The conqueror of Asia, home from the wars
And crossing his own threshold into his house,
Murdered by the lover, waiting there,
Of his own venomous wife; and the gods, offended,
Denying to me, in exile here, the sight
Of my wife, my love, and the sight of the lovely
Landscape of my Calydon. And lately   360
I have seen frightening portents, those birds I see,
In the sky over my head, or along the streams,

Or up on the island cliffs, importunate, crying,
My comrades, killed in the action, crying, crying.
And I am haunted too by the madness of
My fighting against the gods and, with my sword,
Wounding the sacred hand of the goddess Venus.
Do not attempt to persuade me to go back
To such a war, do not, do not, do that.
We sacked the Pergamum, and the towers fell, 370
But I don't hate the Trojans, and there's no pleasure
In my remembering what those bad deeds were.
Take back the gifts you have brought me from your nation.
Give them instead to Aeneas. I've seen him fight.
I tell you what it is to have seen Aeneas
Rise up above his shield and what it is
To have seen him hurl his cyclonic whirling spear.
If Ida's ground had produced two more such men
As these, the Trojans would have come to Greece
And would have ransacked the Inachian towns, and Greece 380
Would be lamenting the turn of fates against her.
It was because of Aeneas and Hector, those two,
Great in their courage, great in their skill, and Aeneas
Greatest in filial piety, it was because
Of the two of them that it took ten years before
The walls of Troy fell down. Against such greatness,
Peace, not war, must be offered.'

           Good king, these are
The answers of the king to whom we were sent."

         , , ,

Almost before the envoy had finished speaking, 390
The disturbed voices of those who heard him were like
The noises you hear when a swiftly flowing river
Encounters within its narrow banks the rocks
Of a rapids, and there's the sound of its swirling and

Along the banks the muffled roaring of
Its distress; and then when there was a calming and
The fear in their voices was somewhat quieted,
The king, first bowing to the gods, replied,
Addressing these considered words to his people:
"I would have wished that all of this would have been   400
Settled before there was any need of a council,
With an enemy waiting just outside our walls.
We are fighting a hopeless war. The enemy
Is invincible, untireable, no matter
How near defeat, unbeatably resourceful.
Forget any hope you had for help from Arpi.
The hope for help you hoped for has come to nothing.
Look at us with your own eyes. All that you see
Has fallen down in ruins, all of it, all.
I do not disparage anyone for this;   410
What courage was able to do, it has been done.
Now listen carefully to what I tell you
About what in my doubtfulness of mind
I have been thinking. There is, along the western
Coast, beyond the Sicanian properties,
A tract of land that I am owner of.
Auruncians and Rutulians work the hard
Soil of the lower flanks of its hills, and pasture
Their flocks and herds above, where the soil is thinner.
Let us offer this land, and its forests of pine still higher,   420
To the Trojans if they wish it, with a treaty
That guarantees friendly partnership with them.
Or if it is their wish to depart from here,
We will build, of oak wood from our forests, twice twenty
Ships for them, to help them on their way.
One hundred of our foremost men will go,
Carrying peaceful branches with them, and gifts
Of gold, and ivory, talents, and the imaged
Robe and throne which are the insignia of
My kingly office, to make our peace with them.   430

Consult together, and, I urge you, agree
That this is the way to rescue us from our weakness."

Then Drances spoke, malicious as always, obliquely
Envious of Turnus because of his glory—
Drances, plenty of money, and plenty of words,
Though cold in the things of war. He was, in the councils,
Not ineffectual in argument and
An arguer for discord always. He was
The son of a mother whose family was of
The nobility, although his father came   440
From a family whose origins were uncertain.
When he spoke, the words he spoke were loaded with
Vituperation and anger: "Good king, the way
Things are, what fortune has brought our people down to,
Has been obvious to them, though they were afraid
To speak of it. But now, what you have said,
And our seeing what has befallen us, makes us free
To get past all of his blustering heroics
(I say this in front of this menacing sword of his),
His reckless actions, his threatening the skies   450
With his terrifying gestures, all the while knowing
How to get himself out of it, safe and unscathed.
Look at the consequence, all of these bodies out there,
Lying out there in the violated fields.
Great king, add one more gift to the gifts that you
Are offering to the Trojan. Give him your daughter,
A father's gift to him whose birth and whose
Outstanding worth deserves it. Do so unfearing,
Because it is right to do, and because we will then
Ensure a lasting peace and amity.   460
But if our hearts are still transfixed by fear
Of Turnus himself, then we must urge him to
Appeal to himself to yield his rights, for the sake
Of king and country. Turnus, you are the source,
You are the cause, of all the miseries of

The citizens of Latium. Time after time,
You hurl them into terrible dangers. Why?
All of us Latins are calling on you for peace,
And for the one inviolable pledge
Of continuing peace. There is no safety in war.   470
I, whom you imagine to be your foe,
Come (setting that aside) in supplication:
Have pity on your people, put aside
Your pride, admit that you are beaten, quit!
For we have seen too many bodies dead,
Too many of our fields left desolate.
But if glory is still what moves you, that and desire
For the dowry and the palace, why then, be brave,
Go forth, onto the battlefield, while we,
Whose lives are nothing to be reckoned with,   480
Lie scattered in the fields, unwept, unburied.
But if there yet remains in you anything of
The warrior spirit of your forebears, then
Meet your foe and look him in the face."

Turnus's rage blazed up at what he said.
Snarling from the violence in his heart
As he answered: "Drances, you're so good
At talking big, while you're sitting there safe and sound.
Call up a meeting, you're bound to be right there,
Talking away with your famous windbag blather.   490
Who needs your big talk, big mouth. Call me a coward?
Call me that when you've killed as many Trojans
And gathered as many trophies in the field.
Go ahead, Drances, show us what you can do.
Why are you hesitating? Here's your chance.
The enemy's right there outside our walls,
And blood's about to flow in all the trenches.
You say I'm beaten? You lying nothing, who
Would say that, when they see the Tiber swollen
With Trojan bodies killed by me, or when   500

They see Evander's Arcadian house brought down,
And all his undone army weaponless?
Big Pandarus and Bitias can't say I'm beaten,
Nor any of those thousand men that I,
With my right arm, sent down to the Underworld,
That day when I was trapped inside the walls.
'There's no safety in war.' That's what the twice-beaten
Trojans should take to heart, those people you praise
And try to make us afraid of. And now you tell us,
Diomedes, the Myrmidons, Achilles,   510
Are all of them scared to death of Phrygian weapons,
And the river Aufidus turns around and runs
Up backward from the violent Adriatic;
And Drances says he's scared of violent me.
Drancian trick. Drances, don't be afraid.
This right hand wouldn't condescend to take
Away the life of such a thing as you.
Let it live on hid out in your nothing body.
If we have no hope for what our arms can do,
And if we regard ourselves as utterly fallen,   520
And without hope that Fortune might change its mind,
Then let us sue for peace, holding out drooping
Peace-wanting branches imploringly. However,
What if there's still something left of the virtue that
We used to have? The man I praise the most
Is the one who chooses to fight, and if need be, fall,
Chewing the ground, rather than be a witness
To degradation like this. But if we still
Have warriors and their arms to fight for us,
And if we still have so many cities and towns   530
Of Italy supporting us, and we know
The Trojans have bought this victory with their blood,
And they have had to bury as many as we,
Because the same storm came down on all of us,
Then why should we give up the fight with them,
Disgracefully, before it's even begun?

Why do our knees knock when the war horn sounds?
Many a day, inexplicably, bad luck
Has changed for the better. Fortune plays games,
Knocking men over, then setting them up again.   540
The Aetolian at Arpi refuses to help, so what?
We have Messapus, and lucky Tolumnius, and
All those leaders who have sent their people,
And no small part of the fame will go to Latium,
And to those chosen from the Laurentine fields.
And there's Camilla of the great Volscian nation,
Her cavalry and soldiers in their bronzen
Shining armor. And if the Teucrians
Have challenged me alone, and it is thought
That I am otherwise an obstacle   550
To the common good, victory has not
So despised these hands of mine that I should keep
From daring whatever is so great a hope.
For I will eagerly fight him, whether or not
He is as great or greater than Achilles,
And I will fight him in the armor made,
Like his, by the art of Vulcan. I am Turnus,
Of my forebears second to none in courage, and
I dedicate my life to all of you,
And to Latinus, the father of my bride.   560
Aeneas challenges me? I pray that he does,
And that it isn't Drances, who, by seeking
To pay them off, appeases the gods, but I,
By valor and the glory I will win."

⸙   ⸙   ⸙

While they were arguing all of these things, in such
Confusion, Aeneas was moving his army, and
Suddenly, wild with excitement, a messenger
Ran into the palace hall to tell them all
That a huge number, Tyrrhenians and Trojans,

Were coming along the Tiber valley road,   570
And the plain was filling up with the enemy.
The shock of it was everywhere, in all
Their hearts and minds; and terror roused up anger,
Calling for weapons, the young men calling "To Arms!"
Old men, their fathers, weeping and groaning, because
They knew what was going to happen to their sons;
Dissension and confusion everywhere,
As when so many chattering birds are flocking
Into the tall trees of a grove, or like
The raucous sound of swans in their excitement   580
Over how many fish there are in those
Loquacious ponds there are, near Padua.
It was Turnus who seized the moment and said to the others,
Scornfully, "You sit there praising peace,
While the enemy swords are right outside your walls,
Invading your country." That's all he said to them,
And rushed out of the palace, shouting out orders:
"Volcens! Call up your Volscian soldiers! And
The Rutulians! Messapus, your cavalry!
Coras, you and your brother, mobilize!   590
Get your troops out now, lined up and ready.
Secure the access roads into the city!
Man the towers! Be ready! The rest of you,
Follow me, full-armed, and ready to fight!"

Then all the people from everywhere in the town,
Came out upon the walls. But old Latinus,
Abandoning all the plans he had spoken of,
Retired from the council room, and separated
Himself from all of it, and over and over
Regretting in himself that he hadn't accepted   600
Dardan Aeneas as his son-in-law,
And hadn't accepted him into the city. Meanwhile,
Many men outside the gates were digging trenches
And carrying in on their shoulders great stones and limbs

Of trees to use as weapons to defend them;
The blood-filled voice of the war horn sounded loudly;
A circle of matrons and boys lined up around
The walls of the city, intending to be, themselves,
The last line of defense, if they had to be.
Amata the queen and a crowd of mothers with her,   610
And with Lavinia, too, the cause of it all,
Her beautiful eyes downcast, together they went
Up to Minerva's temple, and at her high
Altar in the smoke of incense prayed,
"Tritonian maiden, our goddess of war, break that
Pirate's spear, stretch his body out,
Supine on the ground in front of our gates!"

And Turnus in the excitement of his rage,
Aroused in the joy of fury, was girding himself
For battle, his red breastplate with copper scales,   620
Yellow and gold; the greaves he wore were golden.
He shone like gold as from the tower he ran
Down on his way to find the enemy;
He was like a young stallion breaking free, away
From the confines of his stable, excited by
The idea of open pastures, where there are mares,
Or maybe a stream he knows of for a plunge,
And as he runs his beautiful mane flows back.

Then it was that Camilla of the Volsci
Came riding to the city gates on horseback,   630
Leapt down from the saddle, and all her cohort, too,
Gracefully followed suit, and she said to Turnus:
"If honor is to be achieved by this,
Why then I dare to do it. I will go first, alone,
With my cavalry, to meet the Tyrrhenians;
And you, on foot, stay here to protect the walls."
Turnus regarded this wonderful maiden with stunned
Amazement in his eyes, and said to her,

"How is it I can thank you? How can I show
My gratitude? For now, I have learned from reports   640
Of scouts that while Aeneas has sent his mounted
Cavalry ahead to shake the plain,
He himself by trickery is moving
Toward the city secretly by crossing
Over the heights of that intervening mountain.
But I am sending armed men to intercept
And block them on the mountain paths that they
Will be coming by. You must stay here with your troop,
In battle array, and join with Messapus and with
The other captains." Having said this, he went   650
Up the high mountain to meet the enemy.

                              ❧ ❧ ❧

Along the side of the mountain there is a narrow
Valley, winding and turning, an excellent place
For warfare tricks and deceits; on both sides of
The valley dense woods slope down, as black as night.
There's only a narrow road into and through
This valley, and above the valley, unseen
To view from below because of the trees above,
There's a little plateau from which, looking down,
You can see how you could stage an attack from above,   660
Or, staying there, how you could roll great stones
Down on your foe. This is the place young Turnus
Chose to go to, to lie in hiding, waiting
To ambush.

                              ❧ ❧ ❧

             High in the heavens, meanwhile, Diana,
Latona's daughter, spoke, and spoke sadly, to
Swift-running Opis, one of the maidens who

Were her companions in her sacred band:
"The war is cruel that Camilla is leading her troops to,
And it will come to nothing. My love for her   670
Is beyond my love for any other, nor
Is it new that this is so. Metabus, her father,
Because of his cruel tyrant ways, was driven
Out of his kingdom by his angry people,
And when he fled from his city, ancient Privernum,
He carried with him his child, his baby daughter,
Camilla, named after the name of her mother, Casmilla.
With the vengeful Volsci in full pursuit they fled,
The father and baby, high in the mountain woods,
Until they came to the furious foaming river   680
Amsenus, over its banks because of the deluge
Pouring down from the bursting clouds above.
The Volscians and their weapons were pressing upon him.
The only way to escape was to cross the river.
But love for the child and fear for her safety made him
Hesitate, and try to think of a way
To get her there unhurt; and so, at last
He thought of the great oak solid-knotted spear
He held in his hand, and he took his baby daughter
And wrapped her in a swaddling made of soft   690
Cork-bark, and tied her tightly to the spear;
And then, with his great right hand, he raised the spear
Up high, and said, to the skies above, these words:
'Gentle goddess, daughter of Latona, who
Dwells in the woods, here is, I make my vow,
A suppliant for your sisterhood, sent by
Her father upon this spear that flies upon
The hazardous winds. Accept her, this I pray.'
He drew back his powerful arm, the muscles tensed,
And sent the missile off; the river roared;   700
Over the rushing waters the baby was flown,
Sent to safety upon the whirling missile.

The great force of the enemy almost upon him,
Metabus dove into the stream, and on the other
Side in triumph found the baby safe,
Tied to the spear, in a soft green tuft of grass,
The child who was his offering to Diana.

No town would take him in inside its walls,
Nor would he, in his wildness, go in there.
He lived his time out on the lonely heights   710
Of mountains, only shepherds there, where he brought
His daughter up in the thicketed brambled woods,
And near the dens of beasts. When she was little,
Metabus nourished the child with wild mares' milk,
Forcing the paps between her tender lips.
From the time she took her own first little steps,
He had her holding in her hand a tiny
Spear, and a quiver hung from her small shoulder;
Instead of a golden fillet on her head,
And a long robe trailing to the ground, she wore   720
A hooded tiger skin. She learned to be
Fluently skillful with her youthful hands
At targeting her whirling javelins or
Whirling the sling above her young-girl head,
Propelling a stone to bring a white swan down
Or a Strymonian crane. Many a mother
In mountain towns who saw her wished her son
Could marry her, but she was faithful to
Diana and her weapons. I wish she had never
Gone against the Teucrians. But Opis, now,   730
Upon your wings glide down to Latium where
The fighting, under bad omens, is, and with
This bow of mine, and drawing this arrow from
Its quiver, see to it that, whoever it is,
Latin or Trojan, whoever it may be,

Who violates with a wound her sacred self,
Will pay for what he did, with his own blood.
Then, in a cloud, I will bear her virgin body,
In the armor that it wore, to her home country
And the burial tomb where she will lie in honor." 740
The whirring sound of Opis's wings was heard
As she flew down through a shrouding black storm cloud.

, , ,

Meanwhile the Trojans and Tyrrhenians were
Advancing toward the walls of the Latins' city,
Their troops of cavalry in marshaled order,
Company by company by number;
There were the sounds of the music of the horses'
Hooves upon the ground, and of the horses'
Whinnying and nickering, rearing and prancing,
Asserting themselves against the governance 750
Of tight-held bridles, turning this way, then that,
Everything getting ready, the whole field shining
With a vast crop of bristling upheld spears,
Blazing with the light of the weapons' brightness.

Then on the other side there came Messapus,
Coras, and Coras's brother, Camilla with them,
And her cavalry, right arms drawn back and holding
Long spears protended toward the foe, the sharp
Tips trembling with their eagerness for the fight.
The Latin forces moved toward the Trojan forces. 760
There was a moment of silent confrontation,
Only a spear's-throw distance between the two,
Spearpoint eyeing spearpoint holding still,
And then, explosion, imbroglio, shouting, horses
Suddenly spurred; then as it does, a blizzard

Of spears from everywhere showering, under an opaque
Sky turned blank with the shock of the beginning.

> > >

Tyrrhenus and Aconteus were the first
To attack each other with spears, and were the first
To go down in ruin, their galloping horses crashing,   770
One into the other, breast to breast, and falling,
And Aconteus was hurled from his saddle, out
Into the air with the force of a thunderbolt,
Or like a stone shot from a catapult, and
His life was shattered away out there in the air.
The Latins in panic disorder turned their horses
Toward their city, and with their shields on their backs
Went racing for home, with Asilas and his riders
Galloping after them in hot pursuit;
But as they get near the city walls the Latins,   780
With a great shout, changing their minds, turn around
And, loosening reins, ride back on attack. It's as
It is when upon the tide the waves boil in
Upon the shore and over the rocks and in
As far as to reach the sand beyond, and then
They turn and rapidly run the other way,
Carrying tumbling rocks in the undertow,
Taking itself away, draining the shallows.
Twice the Etruscans drove the Latins back
To their city walls, and twice the Latins turned   790
And drove the Etruscans in turn, back from the walls,
Their shields reversed to cover their backs, and looking
Over their shoulders as they rode away;
The third time, though, the armies came together,
Man-to-man locked together in deadly closeness,
And there were the groans of the dying, fallen weapons,
Dead bodies covered with blood, and half-dead horses

Gesturing with their upraised hooves, imploring,
Entangled with the bodies of human beings.
And the battle growing fiercer as it went on.   800

Orsilochus, wary of Remulus's skill,
Aimed his feathered spear at Remulus' horse,
And struck it, just below its ear, and the horse,
In frightful pain, rose up, reared back, its front legs
Flailing at the sky, spilled Remulus off;
Catillus then killed Iollas, and after him,
Herminius, great in prowess, spirit, body,
His greatness in its innocence such that he
Was fearlessly unarmored, his golden hair
Unhelmeted, his shoulders bare; the spear   810
Drove through his body and emerged between
His shoulder blades; Herminius, transfixed,
Fell doubled up in agony. Black blood
Was everywhere as in their slaughtering they
Sought in the blood the beauty of glory and death.

                           , , ,

In the midst of all this killing was exultant
Camilla, looking like an Amazon,
With one breast bared, and wearing on her side
A quiver full of arrows, exuberant in
The fighting, showering javelins, or, when   820
She needs to, killing with the doubled-edged
Formidable axe; and on her shoulder was
The golden bow of Diana, ready, and if
Ever there was the circumstance that she
Had to retreat, she skillfully could, as she fled,
Fire backwards with her arrows at her pursuers.
With her were her chosen maidens, chosen by her
To be her helpers whether in peace or war,

Tulla, Larina, Tarpeia shaking an axe;
They're like those Amazons in Thrace, with their painted   830
Weapons and crescent shields, as if they were with
Hippolyta or Penthesilea come back,
Ululating, howling, in her chariot.

Fierce maiden, who was the first of the men you killed?
Who was the last? How many that you brought
Down to lie dying, out there on the plain? The first
Was Eunaeus, son of Clytius. When
Eunaeus turned to face her, Camilla thrust
Her pine-wood spear straight into Eunaeus's chest,
And, vomiting streams of blood, he fell, his mouth   840
Hysterically gnawing the bloody ground,
His body turning and twisting on his wound.
The next were Liris and Pagasus. When Liris,
Whose wounded horse had reared and thrown him off,
And he was unsteadily getting up, and reaching
Confusedly for the reins, and Pagasus
Came hastening over to help him, dropping his weapon
To hold out his hand to help his brother stand,
Both of them, when struck, fell down together,
One on top of the other, into death.   850
And after them Amastrus, Hippotas' son,
And after him, in sequence, Tereus, and
Harpalycus, Demophoön, and Chromis;
And for exactly as many javelins
Spinning away from her virgin hand, exactly
As many Phrygians died. Next was Ornytus,
A hunter riding on his Iapygian horse;
He was strangely dressed for fighting, and strangely armed;
Over his broad shoulders there was a hide he'd stripped
From the body of a bullock, and on his head   860
A cap that was made from the head of a wolf, its huge
Mouth open, jaws wide, its white fangs gleaming;
He carried the kind of little spear, curved-bladed,

That rustics are accustomed to use for hunting.
She saw him from a distance, easy to see
In the midst of all the others riding, because
So big and tall and because so strangely garbed;
And Camilla from a distance brought him down,
And pitiless stood over him and said,
"Did you think you were just out hunting in the woods?	870
How wrong you were to think so, and now you know,
By the weapons of a woman, how wrong you were.
But the name you'll carry down with you won't be nothing.
You can proudly tell your ancestral shades that you
Were sent to them down there by the spear of Camilla."
Next, Butes and Orsilochus, who were
Two powerful brothers, the tallest of the Trojans.
Butes she got when, idle a moment, he
Was sitting on his horse, looking away;
His shield was hanging useless on his side;	880
And where she got him was the place on the back
Of his naked neck whose whiteness shone just where
There was a space between his helmet and
His cuirass; and then she fled from Orsilochus,
And he followed her in a great circle of chase,
But then, with skill, she cut into the circle,
So, in a smaller circle, she was pursuing
Him, pursuer pursued, until she caught up with him,
And while as they rode Orsilochus pleaded and pleaded,
She struck him again and again with her savage axe,	890
Which broke through his armor, and broke his bones, and at last
Broke through his head so his brains poured down his face.
And then there was, astonished and terrified
By what he saw, the son of the liar Aunus,
Ligurian, from up in the Apennines, a place
Where the Fates have allowed them all to get used to being
Good at guile and trickery, so when
He saw he wasn't going to be able
To escape Camilla's attention or his death,

If he stood targeted there, he thought of a trick,   900
And he said, "Well, what's so great about a woman
Putting her faith in the getaway speed of her horse?
Where's the glory in that? Why don't you get
Down from your horse on foot and, man-to-man,
So to speak, let's fight each other as equals.
This way will show how your pretensions to being
Glorious are as empty as the wind."
Of course this made Camilla furious.
Red-hot with anger she got down off her horse,
And handed the reins to one of her companions,   910
And stood there, unafraid, with only a naked
Sword and her small plain cavalry shield to fight with.
When the Ligurian saw her dismount, he thought
His trick had worked, and so, as fast as he could,
He got himself onto his horse and galloped away.
But Camilla, swifter than anything, swifter than wind,
Ran after the man and his horse, and when she ran past them
She turned around, and stopped his horse in its tracks,
And said, "This will show you how empty your boasts are,
The lies you learned to tell from your father Aunus."   920
With that, as quick as the flick of a flame, she seized
The reins of the horse, and exacted expertly
His punishment from the blood of her enemy.
Just as Apollo's bird, the falcon, sees
From his rock that, high in the clouds, there's a dove, and he
Pursues it, catches it, holds it, and with his claw
He tears out its heart as he flies, and feathers and blood
Come floating down from the sky.

                              ❥ ❥ ❥

                                        Nothing escaped
The notice of the Father of Gods and Men,   930
Looking down from where he was seated, high upon
The summit of Mount Olympus. He called up anger

In Tarchon, the Etruscan king, who went
Into the midst of things and roused up war
In the hearts of his wavering army, shouting at them,
Berating them, some of them even by name:
"What are you so afraid of, you so-called soldiers,
You no-good, hang-back, half-ass Etruscans, it's
A woman tearing up your crop fields, it's
A woman making all of you run away.   940
What are the weapons you have in your hands for? Use them,
For gods' sake, use them. Oh, yes, I know,
It's the battlefield of love at night *you* like,
It's wine, it's what the menu is tonight;
You love the crackling sound of cooking and
The crooning voice that tells you dinner is ready,
The feast is ready for you." Having said this,
He suddenly spurred his horse and galloped wildly
Into the battle, at risk for his life, and like
A whirlwind galloped straight at Venulus,   950
And, tearing him off of his horse, went galloping on,
Holding Venulus close to his chest with his great
Right arm, the man and his armor, and riding he broke off
The head of Venulus' spear and probed for bare
Skin to plunge the beakèd spearhead in,
And kill. Venulus struggled, with all his strength,
To keep the searching beak away from his throat;
It was as when a tawny eagle, high
In the sky, has a wounded snake in her claws, her talons
Around its struggling body, the nails of her talons   960
Digging into the serpent's flesh, and the serpent,
Scales erect and bristling, head up-reaching,
Voluminous folds of the sinuous body twisting
And turning, the great hook beak tearing and tearing
The flesh, as the eagle, flapping her wings as she kills,
Flies on; thus Tarchon galloped away with his prey
From the Tiburtine lines. The Maeonians follow Tarchon's
Example and into the battle rush after him.

Then Arruns, so swift and adept at aiming the spear,
More experienced than Camilla in the art,   970
Arruns, whose life is owed to the Fates, begins
To try what Fortune might facilitate,
To circle around her, furtive, secretive,
Following her wherever her footsteps go,
Circling round her, watching her where she is,
Whether she rages in fury in the battle,
Or sometimes, after a victory, she, for a moment,
Retires, he follows her, quietly turning his reins
This way, then turning them that way, circling around her,
Ever attentive. His spear, that makes no mistakes,   980
Is trembling in his hand, excited, ready.
By chance it happened that Chloreus, disciple
Of the goddess Cybele, and having been a priest
In her rituals, could be seen from far away,
In his shining Phrygian armor, spurring along
On his snorting horse caparisoned with a hide
Adorned with a pattern of bronze feathery scales,
And fastened with golden buttons. Himself he was
A sight, as if on fire with indigo
And purple hues, over his shoulders a saffron   990
Cloak whose folds were gathered with a golden
Linen sash; golden the Lycian bow
That hung from his shoulder, and golden too its arrows,
Made in Gortyna; his tunic and his leggings
Were stitched with gold. Camilla saw him, and whether
It was that she wanted to hang up this armor and
These trappings as trophies of war in the temple, or by
A desire to wear this gold while hunting, she went
Straight toward him through the fighting, blind to all else,
Utterly without caution, maybe because   1000
Of a female desire for spoils and especially for
This particular kind of spoils, and at this moment,

Arruns, seeing his chance had finally come,
His excited lance raised high, prayed to Apollo,
"Apollo, high god and protector of Soracte,
We are the first to worship you, for whom
We dare in our ardor walk in reverence through
The burning embers of the pine-wood fire,
Our bare feet deep in them, Father, we pray, give us
The power to abolish this disgrace.   1010
I have no wish to take trophies from her body,
Nor any desire for any spoils at all.
Glory will come to me by other acts.
I only desire that this abomination
Will be obliterated by my bow.
Then I will return to my native town, without
The glory of what I did, and willingly so."
Phoebus Apollo heard him and granted half
Of what he asked. He granted that, as prayed for,
Camilla should suddenly be brought down. That he   1020
Could return to, or ever see, his town again,
He did not grant. A sudden South Wind gust
Dispersed into the air what he desired.

The spear he threw went whistling through the air
And all the Volsci heard it, and saw it, and
They turned their minds and eyes on the queen, who didn't
Hear the sound nor thought of anything
Coming toward her through the air, and the spear,
Accomplishing what it had been sent to do,
Struck home just beneath her naked breast and lodged there,   1030
Drinking her virgin blood. Arruns was more
Terrified than anyone, though his terror
Was mixed with joy; and he got himself away,
Fearing to face retaliatory weapons.
He was like a wolf who, having killed a shepherd,
Or bullock, before any weapons could come to get him,
Immediately flees, through pathless ways

High up in the mountain woods, afraid, and with
His quivering tail in under his belly, and knowing
What he has done, and seeking the woods to hide in.   1040
That is how Arruns went, confused, content
To have gotten away with it, and disappeared
Into the battlefield mêlée.

               Camilla was trying
To pull the spearpoint out of her side, but it stood
Transfixed between the bones of her ribs, and blood-lost life
Was slipping away, sight slipping away
Into cold death. Dying, she called to Acca,
Of all the others the friend most dear to her,
The one to whom she had told her inmost thoughts,   1050
And she said: "I can do no more, Acca, my sister.
The shades are growing darker all around me.
This terrible wound has destroyed me. You must flee,
And take these new orders to Turnus. Tell him that he
Must take my place in the fight against the Trojans
And in defense of the city." Having said this,
Against her will she let go of the reins of her horse,
And slid to the ground, and little by little the cold
Was freeing her from her body; her neck was drooping;
And, yielding her weapons, Camilla, captive of death,   1060
Laid down her head, and life, with a groaning shudder,
Indignantly fled away to the shades below.

When this was seen a tremendous shouting clamor
Rose up to the stars. Camilla having fallen,
The battle raged more furiously still.
The army of the Trojans, the army of
The Tyrrhenian kings, the Arcadian squadrons of
Evander, all rushed in, together, at once.

                    ❯   ❯   ❯

High on the mountaintop Diana's Opis
Sat imperturbably watching the battle scene;   1070
But then she saw, in the midst of it down there,
Camilla's terrible death, and moved by this,
She spoke from deep in her heart, "Camilla, you
Have paid too dearly for your challenging
The Trojans, as you have done. That you have been
A worshiper of Diana, alone in the woodland,
Wearing her hunting quiver upon your shoulder,
Has not protected you from your suffering
And your death. But now Diana will see to it
That your death will not be unknown to all the countries,   1080
Nor will it be unavenged. Whoever it was
Who violated your body will pay for it
With his own."

       High on a mountainside there is,
Shaded by ilex trees, a burial mound,
Of an ancient Laurentian king, whose name was Decennis.
Beautiful Opis flew to this place, and landed
Lightly and stood, looking down from that height, and saw,
On the plain below, in shining armor, Arruns,
Pleased with himself, and she cried, "So far away?   1090
Turn your steps this way, this way, this way,
And come to your perishing, paying the debt you owe
To the dignity of Camilla. So now you will know,
You are to die by the weapon of Diana."
And so she drew a wingèd arrow from
Her golden quiver and drew the bowstring back
To its fullest extent of tension until the curved
Ends of the beautiful bow drew almost together,
Opis's hands in perfect understanding,
The one and the other, the left at the arrow point,   1100
The arrow in perfect intention on its target,
The right hand perfectly drawing the bowstring back,

Touching her breast, to perfect tensity,
And holding; and then there was the hissing sound
Of the arrow, and Arruns heard it as it struck,
And pierced his body at his breast, and Arruns
Fell gasping and groaning his last in the dust of an unknown
Unremembered place as his forgetting
Oblivious comrades passed him by; and Opis
Then flew back to Olympus, where she came from.   1110

, , ,

The virgin cavalry of Camilla were
The first to flee, their leader lost, and then
The Rutulians in confusion and disorder,
Then brave Asilas, and all the other captains
Scattered around the plain, and all their men,
Turning their horses and racing toward the city,
Seeking safety there. There was no weapon
To stand against the Trojans coming on,
And bringing with them death; their unstrung bows
Hang loosely from the shoulders of the Latins;   1120
Their galloping hooves are shaking the dust of the plain,
And a murky black cloud rises up upon the walls.
And the mothers, seeing this, and knowing what
Its meaning is, are beating their breasts and wailing,
And the sound of their voices rises to the skies.
When the first of those who were racing for home broke in
Through the gates of their native city there were galloping
Trojans too, pursuing Latins, coming in through
The gates along with them and so, within
Their walls and in the haven of their houses,   1130
Latins were dying, gasping away their lives,
And other Latins, in panic, got the gates closed,
To keep more Trojans out, and they didn't dare
In spite of their desperate pleadings, to open them
Again for comrades who were left outside,

And miserable mutual slaughtering took place,
Of those whose swords were defending shut gates and those
Who were desperately fighting to get themselves in, and all
This under the eyes of their weeping parents. Of those
Who were left outside, many of them, impelled   1140
By the unseeing weight of the crowd behind them, fell
Precipitously into the trenches and perished,
And others, letting go of the reins of their horses,
Were wildly blindly battering at the gates
That were shut against them. Above, their frantic
Mothers, Camilla their example, were
With their shaking hands throwing down missiles and logs
Upon the pandemonium below.

                    ❜ ❜ ❜

When Acca came to tell Turnus how bad it was,
Camilla killed, the Latins routed, the terrible   1150
Confusion and the pain at the gates of the town,
Turnus of course was enraged, and he gave up any
Idea of ambush, and set out to get down to
The battleground of war on the plain below.

And at the same time Aeneas and his soldiers
Were coming through the pass higher up on the mountain,
Making their own way, down to the battleground.

Each of them saw and heard the other, and both
Were hastening to make the final face-off,
But then there were the signs in the sky that the day   1160
Was coming to an end, and so the two forces
Bivouacked for the night, waiting, preparing,
For the next day's confrontation that was to come.

Book Twelve

When Turnus sees how bad things are, the war
Going against them, the soldiers losing heart,
He knows all eyes are upon him, and he knows
The time has come to keep his promise, and
His heart's courage is roused. It's as when a lion,
Out in the fields, having been wounded by
A hunter's arrow, shakes his mane as if
In joy and raging wrenches the arrow out,
And roars through his bloody mouth—so did it swell,
The violence there was in Turnus's heart.   10

He went to the king and said, in these wild words:
"Turnus is here. Now the weakling Aeneadae
Can't retract. They can't get out of it now.
Turnus is here. Father, ready the rites,
Draw up the terms of the treaty. Turnus is here.
Either with my right arm I'll send the Asian
Refugee down to Tartarus, and while
The Latins watch, erase our country's shame,
Or if he wins, he wins Lavinia!"

Latinus replied to him, gently and sincerely,   20
"O passionate youth, when your ferocity
Of bravery explodes this way, it causes me

To try to think as calmly as possible,
To think things out, considering what there is
In this to be cautious about, and what to fear.
You have the kingdom of your father Daunus;
You have the many towns that you have made
Subject by your skill in battle, and I
Have wealth and benign intentions on your behalf.
In the Latin countryside there are many unwed   30
Maidens, of suitable rank. It is hard for me
To tell you this, and hard for you to hear,
But I must plainly say it and you must take it
Into your heart: I cannot choose for my daughter
Any suitor who is native-born.
The divination singing of men and gods
Forbids that I should do so, and for that reason
I have refrained from uniting my daughter with any
Suitors Italy-born. But overcome
By love of you, and consanguinity   40
Of blood, and by the sorrowful tears of my wife,
I broke the bonds of what I promised. I took
The promised bride from the promised son-in-law,
And entered into impious warfare, and, Turnus,
Now you see what the consequences are:
Two great battles leaving the city almost
Without resources to be Italy's hope,
The Tiber still warm with our blood, and on the wide plains
The bones still whitening. Why have I wavered?
Why have I been so recklessly changeable?   50
If Turnus dies (heaven forfend!), I must
Be prepared to accept an alliance with the victors.
Why not settle these things while Turnus lives?
What will your own Rutulians say, what will
All Italy say, if I barter with your death
While you are asking for my daughter's hand

In marriage? Think of your agèd father waiting
Apprehensively for news of you in Ardea."

But the violence there was in Turnus's heart
Was utterly unchanged by what he said;   60
The medicine of Latinus's calming speech
Only inflamed what it was meant to quiet.
When he was able to speak in reply to the king,
He said, "I beg you to put aside your kind
Solicitousness for me, O best of kings,
And leave it to me to bargain with death for glory.
My right hand knows what it is my spear can do,
And when it strikes the life-blood pours from the wound.
His goddess mother is far away from him now;
She cannot use her feminine tricks to hide   70
Her runaway in a cloud and save him from me."

The queen was terrified by the prospect of
The choice before them. She was weeping as
She spoke to Turnus pleadingly, saying, "Turnus,
It is you I have been praying for. If you
Have honor for me in your heart, listen to me.
You're all I have and all that Latium has.
Do not engage with your body in combat with
The Trojan. I cannot live, a slave, and having
To see this Trojan as son-in-law and master."   80

Lavinia, hearing these words of her mother, wept,
And her beautiful face, bathed in her tears, was like,
In its alternate blushing and pallor a garden where
There are lilies, white, and crimson roses, or like
An Indian ivory painted with blood-red dyes,
And Turnus, by the beauty of this lovely
Virginal face impassioned, is by his passion

Aroused all the more to meet his rival, whom
He has challenged for her bridal hand; and so
He spoke thus, briefly, to Amata: "Mother,   90
Do not, I pray, send me with tears, and with
Such omens as these are, into the hard
Encounters of war. Turnus is not free
To know, or to delay, the day of his death.
Idmon, go to the Phrygian tyrant and
Bring him this message, which will be
Unwelcome to his ears: 'Tomorrow, when
Aurora in her chariot brings the first
Reddening of the morning sky, you must
Not lead the Teucrians into battle against   100
The Rutulians. The two of us, alone,
At the risk of our own blood, will end the war.
He who survives will have Lavinia's hand.'"

                              ʾ ʾ ʾ

Having said this, he went quickly back to his palace,
Where he rejoiced to see his chariot horses,
Neighing and tossing their heads in their excitement
That he was there. These were the fabulous horses
Descended from those Ortygia, wife of the North Wind,
Gave to Turnus's great-grandfather Pilumnus;
These were the Thracian horses, whiter than snow,   110
And swifter than the swiftness of the wind.
The grooms were gathered around, combing their beautiful
Streaming manes, and using the palms of their hands
To pat and pummel their horses' mighty chests,
Getting them ready for what tomorrow would bring.

And Turnus himself got ready, over his shoulders
His leather corselet, gleaming with golden and copper
Armoring scales; and he took up his two-edged sword,
And his shield, and his ruby-crested helmet; his sword

Which the potent-in-fire god made for Daunus his father,					120
Forging it in the seething Stygian waters.
Against a column in the palace was
The spear that was battle spoil of Auruncian Actor;
When Turnus took it up and brandished it,
The great spear trembled in his powerful grasp.

"This is the spear that mighty Actor hurled;
Now it is Turnus's never-failing weapon.
Don't fail me now, when I will with my bare
Hands rip the corselet from this eunuch's body,
And will, with this hot iron of mine, mess up					130
The hair perfumed with oil of myrrh his heated
Curling iron had crimped and fussed with." Thus
Turnus's speech, and his face and his eyes were on fire
With rage, like a bellowing bull, filling his vengeful
Horns with the power of fury, charging at trees,
Striking blows at the sky and at the winds, again
And again and again, pawing the sands, preparing.

                              ❟ ❟ ❟

And fierce Aeneas, too, was getting ready,
Rousing up Mars's fury in his heart,
And joyful that the war was going to end,					140
And going to end by the terms he had proposed.
He solaced his sorrowing comrades and fearful Iulus,
Reminding them of what the Fates have said,
And sending to King Latinus to ratify
The terms of the treaty and of the peace to come.

                              ❟ ❟ ❟

The day was just beginning, the morning beginning
To spread itself across the mountaintops,
The horses of the sun, riding up from the sea,

Their flaring nostrils breathing out rays of light.
In the field below the walls of the city, they all   150
Were getting ready, Rutulians and Trojans,
Working together, measuring the space
Where the single combat between the two would be,
And on grassy plots setting up altars to
The gods the two communities worship in common.
The priests, wearing purple aprons and linen hoods,
Brought pure spring water to the sacred altars;
The Ausonian soldiers, armed with spears, poured out
Of the city gates, an army of disciplined men;
The Trojan forces and the Tyrrhenians came   160
Streaming in, in their variegated armor,
Looking as if about to be called by Mars
To cruel war. And, riding among the thousands,
The leaders too appeared, Rutulian
And Trojan, clad in the pride of purple and gold,
Mnestheus of Assaracus's line,
And brave Asilas, and Messapus who was
The son of Neptune and famous breaker of horses.
The signal was given and each of them found his place,
Their spears pointed down at the ground, their shields   170
Reclining at rest by their sides. Old men and women,
Unarmed, intently watching the scene, were gathered
On all the rampart walls and tops of the gates,
And high on the roofs of the houses in the town.

                    ❧ ❧ ❧

From the high top of a mountain, now Albanus,
But then had neither name nor honor nor glory,
Juno looked down from that height and saw the field,
And both of the armies, Rutulians and Trojans,
Latinus's city and all the gathered people.
She spoke to the youthful goddess, Turnus's sister,   180

Who was now a deity of lakes and streams,
For Jupiter, God of the Heavens, had honored her thus,
In recompense for the virginhood he'd taken;
And Juno said to her, "Nymph, young goddess of ponds
And fountains and rivers, you know that of all those others
In Italy whom all too magnanimous Jove,
My husband, has taken into our marital bed,
You are the one, dear to my heart, whom I
Have welcomed to your place among the gods.
But I must tell you now what will cause you to grieve,   190
And do not blame me for it. As long as Fortune
And the Fates permitted, I protected Turnus
And the walls of your city. But now I see
That this young man, your brother, has come up against
The hostility of his fortune. Decided by
Inimical Fates, his final day has come.
Perhaps, if you help him, things will turn out better.
I can no longer look upon the scene;
Nor can I any longer interfere
With the treaty or its peaceable stipulations.   200
But if you dare to do it, go to your brother,
To see if there's anything you can do to save him.
Go. It is right. No time for tears. You must hurry."

                              ⟩ ⟩ ⟩

Then was the time for the kings to enter. First,
Latinus, in his great chariot, seated high,
His brow shining with twelve gold rays which were
The emblems of his descent from the God of the Sun;
Then, in his chariot drawn by two white horses,
Came Turnus, with two great double-edged spears in his hand;
Then from the camp came father Aeneas, who was   210
The founder and source of the Roman stock, and who,
With his heaven-sent shield and armor, shone like a star;

And beside him was Ascanius his son,
Who was the second hope of the greatness of Rome.
And then came a priest, who was dressed in purest white,
Conducting a yearling ewe and the offspring of
A bristle-backed boar to the flaming altar, where,
After they turn to look with reverent eyes
At the rising sun, the two who are to fight,
Sprinkle the temples of the sacrificial   220
Beasts with meal and salt, and mark with a knife
The foreheads of the offered, and from goblets
Pour at the altar libations to the gods.

Then, drawing his sword, Aeneas began to pray:
"O Sun be my witness, and hear my words, O Earth,
Because in my labors I have endured so much;
And you, Omnipotent God, and you, his wife,
Saturnian Juno, Goddess now more kind,
More kind, I pray, to us; and glorious Mars,
Whose nod determines all in war; you gods   230
Of rivers and lakes, of the high heavens, and of
The vast cerulean waters of the sea:
If it should happen that victory should come
To Ausonian Turnus, it is agreed that all
The army of the defeated will withdraw
To the city of Evander, and Iulus will yield
The fields of battle; nor, after the war,
Will any of the Aeneadae, rebelling,
Return with swords provoking war again.
But if Victory should give the nod to us   240
(As I believe will be the case, and I
Believe that the gods will nod in affirmation),
I'll never order that any Latins be
Subject to the will of any Trojans:
Two unconquered peoples sharing as equals

Their equal laws together. I will bring
The ancestral gods and the sacred rites of worship;
Latinus the father-in-law will rule the army,
And the solemn governance of the polity;
And with my Teucrians I will build our city,   250
To which Lavinia will give her name."

Latinus, after Aeneas, spoke these words,
His right hand raised, his eyes fixed on the heavens:
"All these I here affirm and take my oath,
Swearing by earth, by sea, by the stars, and by
The two deities born of Latona, and by
The two faces of Janus, and by the Infernal
Below, and the holy shrine of implacable Dis.
Let the Father of All, who ratifies all with lightning,
Hear what I swear as I touch his holy altar,   260
Calling on all the gods and on this fire
To witness: No matter what befalls, this is
My promise that will never be turned aside from,
No matter whether earth is brought down into
The flooding sea, or sky falls into Tartarus;
It's as this scepter (for in his hand he held
The royal scepter), which never again will grow
Green leaves upon the bough as it had once;
Now separated from its mother, its
Light leaves no longer shadowing one another   270
On the branch but by the hand of the artist transformed
To bronze, and given thus to royal kings
From ancient times to carry as their rule."

Saying such words, together they sealed the treaty,
In the sight of all the leaders of their people;
And, according to the rites, together they slew
The sacrificial beasts, cutting their throats, and from

Their bodies took the living entrails, and
On laden smoking plates together placed them,
As mutual offering on the sacred altars.   280

⸪ ⸪ ⸪

But in truth the Rutulians watching this spectacle
Had been becoming more and more uneasy,
More and more worried that the contest between
The two of them was going to be unequal;
Seeing the two together they could see
The differences between them in size and strength.
Adding to this worry was how Turnus
Looked when it was his turn to pray at the altars:
Kneeling in supplication, his eyes downcast,
His boyish face and body, pale, unready.   290
When Juturna, his goddess sister, became aware
Of how, in the very ranks of their own army,
People were talking, the murmurings of doubt
In their wavering voices, she took upon herself
The guise of Camers, whose family was famous,
His grandsires and his sire, for valor in war,
And he the most valorous of them all, and in
The midst of the army began to stir and increase
The doubts and fears already in their minds:
"Aren't you ashamed of yourselves, Rutulians,   300
To let one man be sacrificed for all?
Are we not more than a match for them, so few
Of them, the Trojans, the Arcadians,
That little band of Etruscans hating Turnus?
We haven't got enough enemies to go
Around. Our every second soldier won't
End up having anybody to fight.
He who's making his vows at the altars now
Will ascend to the skies and his glory will be told

On the lips of every one of us, but if   310
Our country's lost, then we'll be subjected to
Obedience to arrogant masters, these
Aliens lounging around in our native fields."

Now more and more the murmuring crept its way
From voice to ear and voice to ear throughout
The army and to those who had wished for rest
And safety from the dangers of the fighting.
Their minds were changing, desire was rising up
To take up arms, hoping to break the treaty,
And pitying Turnus.   320

                              Then she did something else,
More powerful still. In the sky appeared a portent,
Nothing there was more potent to confuse
The Latins about what the meaning of it was.
High in the sky was Jupiter's golden bird.
The sight of him was scaring the little birds
Along the shore, and the clamor of their distress
Was sounding everywhere, when suddenly
The eagle plunged straight down to the water and seized
In his cruel crooked talons the noblest and most   330
Beautiful of the swans and carried him off.
The Italians were astonished at the sight,
And their amazement grew as they saw the huge
Flock of panicked birds, which had been fleeing,
Wheel in their flight and envelop the eagle within
The flapping of their wings, as in the darkness
Of a cloud, until at last the eagle, in
The weariness of defending himself against them,
Dropped his burdening prey and flew away.
Then in truth the Rutulians responded   340
With clamorous shouting to what they saw in the sky,
Their enthralled excited hands raised high as if

In salutation to what the meaning might be,
And Tolumnius, an augurer, cried out,
"There it is, why, there it is, it's what
I prayed for, it's what I made my vows for!
I recognize that this is from the gods!
The portent is for me, for me, I'll be
The leader, with my spear! O my poor fellows,
This wicked stranger brought war upon us and we   350
Were weak as birds when he came pillaging
Upon our shores. But come together, all
As one, to fight to rescue our leader, who's
Entrapped inside the terms of this so-called treaty.
When this is done the stranger will sail away,
Seeking the deepest Profound in the Faraway!"

Running he hurled his whirling spear. The sound
Of its screaming whirling flight was heard by all;
The troops drawn up in formal ranks were in
Confused disorder; hearts were aroused for war;   360
The spear was flying toward nine beautiful brothers,
Who were standing together in the opposite ranks.
They were all the sons of Arcadian Gylippus,
And their faithful Etruscan mother, and the missile
Struck one of them, the fairest of them all,
Who was wearing shining armor; it entered where
The belt line was, and went between the ribs,
And into his belly and his life poured out
As he fell upon the yellow sands of the plain.
But his brothers, a phalanx fearless and blind in grief, 370
Ran forward all together, waving their swords
Or brandishing their spears, and the Latins ran
To meet them as they came, and against them came
The Trojans and the men from Agylla and
The Arcadians in their painted armor, embroiled,
One motive in all, to settle this war by blood.

They tore the altars all to pieces, and
The sky was a wild tempest of spears and arrows
And altar bowls turned weapons; it was a storm
Of steel coming down like rain upon the scene;   380
And old Latinus himself retired from this,
The treaty broken, taking his battered gods.
Everywhere, on both sides, men leaping onto
Their chariots, or onto the backs of their horses,
Swords drawn and ready. There was Aulestes, who was
A Tyrrhenian king, wearing his kingly armor,
With all the insignia of his kingship, and
Messapus, in his fervor to break the treaty,
Rode straight at him, and Aulestes, terrified,
Retreating backward, crashed down flat on his back   390
Upon the altar, and Messapus from his horse
Dispatched him with his great spear, as big and long
As a roof beam is, killing him as he pled,
And Messapus said, looking down at dead Aulestes,
"Look, here, here's a better sacrifice for the gods,"
And the Latins ran in to strip from the still-warm body
Of this king the kingly trophies that it wore.
Corynaeus, confronted by Ebysus, seized
A burning torch from off the holy altar,
And used it to set Ebysus's face on fire;   400
His great beard burst into flames and there was the stench
Of burning as it burned. Corynaeus seized him,
By the hair on his head, and threw him down on the ground,
And as he lay there kept him lying there, pressing him
Down with his knee, and drove his rigid sword
Into his body. Podalirius with
His naked sword was chasing the shepherd Alsus
As he ran through the rain of missiles in the rout,
And caught him, and stood over him, ready, but Alsus
Struck him with his desperate country axe   410
In the middle of his forehead and split his face,

Down to his chin, and Podalirius
Was laid to rest by this in iron sleep,
His eyesight gone in everlasting Night.

, , ,

But then Aeneas came forward, head bared, unarmed,
And, holding out his weaponless right hand,
Cried out to all of them in a loud voice, "Why
Are you rushing into this bloodshed? Why suddenly
This violence? The treaty has been made,
And it's agreed that the right is mine alone.   420
Forget your fears. Leave it to my right hand.
The sacred rites have given Turnus to me."
And as he spoke these words, right then when he
Was saying these things, an arrow came whining, whirling,
Gliding at him, and struck him, and nobody knows
Whose hand it was who sent it, nobody knows
From whom or what it came, from chance, or from
Some god, or who, or what Rutulian
Could claim the glory of being the one who was
The one who sent the arrow that wounded Aeneas.   430

When Turnus saw Aeneas leaving the field,
With his comrade leaders so dismayed by this,
Hope was on fire, suddenly, in his heart.
He called for his arms and horses all at once,
And he leaped into his chariot and seized
The reins and went flying into the enemy ranks,
Sending to death how many strong-bodied heroes;
His chariot wheels rolled over how many others,
Leaving behind him the half-dead fallen and as
His wheels went over their bodies he seized the spears   440
From the bodies and sent the spears showering down
On terrified Trojans trying to run away

From what was coming upon them. It was as when
Up there beside the icy Hebrus, bloody
Mavors rattles his shield, and lets the reins loose
On his war-maddened horse, and all Thrace hears the sounds
Of their galloping hoofbeats as they gallop racing
Before the winds, the North Wind and the South,
Accompanied by his galloping comitatus,
Black Terror, Treachery, and Rage; like this, 450
Turnus was lashing his sweat-soaked horses through
The midst of the battle, his chariot scornfully
Riding over the miserable bodies of
The slain, the hooves of the horses scattering
Gobbets of blood and churning the sand with gore.
Sthenelus he killed, getting him at a distance,
Then Thamyrus and Pholus at close quarters,
Then from a distance both of the Imbrasides,
Glaucus and Lades, whose father Imbrasus had
Brought them up in Lycia to be good fighters, 460
And furnished them with armor suitable
For hand-to-hand battle or equally suitable
For riding on horseback faster than the wind.
Seen entering the battlefield was Eumedes,
Named for his grandsire, but, in heart and hand,
He was the son of his father, old well-known Dolon,
Who when he dared to offer to spy on the camp
Of the Greeks, he also dared to ask, as a prize,
For the horses and the chariot of Achilles,
But Tydides gave him a different prize, and he 470
No longer had any wish for Achilles' horses.
Turnus from far off saw him and sent a light
Javelin to him across the distance between them,
And then he went to where Eumedes lay dying,
And leaped down from his chariot, and stood
Above him, his foot on his neck, and wrenched the bright
Flashing sword from Eumedes' dying hand, and plunged it

Deep in Eumedes' throat, and said these words:
"Here you are now in the field you wanted to win.
Trojan, this is the prize I give with my sword.   480
Lie there and measure the fields of Hesperia.
This is the way the Trojans find their land."
Then Turnus with his spear sent Asbytes down,
To keep Eumedes company down there,
And after that came Chloreus, the priest,
And next were Sybaris, Dares, Thersilochus,
And then Thymoetes whose horse, falling down, had thrown him
Forward over its head. It was as when
The Edonian North Wind howls and its sound is heard
Upon the deep Aegean, and it drives   490
The terrified billows fleeing toward the shore,
And the gusts pursue the clouds across the sky;
Just so when Turnus cut his way through the lines,
The Aeneades fled away before him like
Waves receding whichways in their terror,
And he by the purposive force of his shouting rage
Drove through, the plume on his helmet streaming back.
His momentum was unstoppable as he killed,
But Phegeus couldn't bear it, and he leaped
In front of the chariot as it came on, and tried,   500
With his right hand, to turn aside the horses'
Heads by wrenching their foaming bridle bits
Aside, and as he held on, and was dragged along
By the harness, Turnus struck him a blow with his sword,
On his vulnerable side, just grazing the skin
Where the sword cut through his two-plated corselet, and
Phegeus tried to turn his body around,
And with his left hand tried to raise his shield
To protect himself from Turnus's sword, but he
Had to let go, and the wheel and the chariot yoke   510
Buffeted him as he fell and lay on the ground,
And Turnus from where he rode leaned down and got him

With his sword exactly where there was a space
Between the lower edge of his helmet and
The corselet's upper edge, and sliced off his head,
Leaving the trunk of his body in the sand.

                   ❯   ❯   ❯

Meanwhile, while victorious Turnus was dealing out
Death on the field of killing, Mnestheus and
Faithful Achates, and Ascanius with them,
Were helping Aeneas back into the Trojan camp,   520
Aeneas supporting himself for every other
Step on his long spear, and raging, trying
With his own hands to wrestle free from his leg
The broken arrow shaft, and calling on them
To find the nearest way, to take a sword
And cut the flesh around the wound right down
To the bone to free the shaft from where it was,
In its hiding place.

                Then there came Iapyx, whom
Apollo had loved with such passion that he offered   530
To give him all of his powers of divination,
The lyre he wore, and his quiver full of arrows;
But Iapyx, wanting to learn how to prolong
The life of Iasus, his ailing father, piously
Sought the knowledge that humbler arts could give him,
Less glorious than the glorious offerings of
His lover, the God of Arts, and so he made it
His work to study what were the herbs and plants
With power to heal the suffering of the body.
There stood Aeneas, supported as he stood   540
By his gigantic spear; he was furious,
Groaning wth anger, indifferent to the tears
Of his leaders and of Iulus, his sorrowing son.

The old man, Iapyx, wearing the kind of robe
Apollonian healers wore, tried everything,
Working with his hands with every kind
Of Phoebus's herbs he knew, to no avail;
To no avail, trying with his right hand
To solicitate the arrow from the wound;
To no avail the forceps; nothing would work;   550
No prayer to Fortune for help was answered; none
To his patron Apollo was answered either; and
Meanwhile the horrors in the fields grew greater,
And greater, and nearer, and nearer; an enormous
Cloud of dust was standing in the sky;
The enemy cavalry were riding in;
And a rain of missiles was pouring into the camp;
There was the clamor of young men fighting and dying,
Young men under the iron laws of Mars.

⸌ ⸌ ⸌

His mother, Venus, when she knew of this,   560
Was made unhappy by the news of her son's
Injury, undeserved; and, upon the slopes
Of Cretan Ida she sought a remedy,
And found it, and plucked it, dittany, a crested
Plant with purple flowers and downy leaves,
Of which, it is said, that sometimes mountain goats,
Wounded by vagrant arrows, ate and were cured.
Venus, hid in a rain mist, carried it down
To where a river was, and in a shining
Bowl poured in, upon the dittany   570
That she had gathered, juice of ambrosia and
Of fragrant panacea, and steeping it thus,
She made the occult medicine that agèd
Iapyx, not knowing what he did, then used
To bathe the wound, deep in, and made it well.

The arrowhead was freed, and Aeneas was
As utterly himself as he had been.
Iapyx cried out, the first to arouse the others
To what it was that had happened, "Bring him his arms!
Why are you standing there? Aeneas, it wasn't   580
Me! It wasn't my right hand that saved you!
It wasn't done by a human being! It wasn't
My art! It is a god that brings you back
To your great self to do still greater things!"

Aeneas, avid for battle, sheathed his calves,
This leg, then the other, and scorning delay,
Was brandishing his sword, and as soon as they
Fitted his corselet to his back, and as soon
As his shield was fitted to his side, he turned,
In his full armor, to Ascanius,   590
And put his arms around him, and, through his helmet,
Kissed him, and said to him, "Learn, my son, from me,
What courage, and the true labor of courage, is.
Let others by their example show you what
It is to be the mere play thing of chance.
When the years to come have ripened you into your manhood,
Remember what I have said to you, and may
Aeneas, your father, and Hector, your uncle, excite
In your mind the virtue they exemplify."

           › › ›

Having said these things, Aeneas, huge, himself,   600
His great spear brandishing in his hand, emerges
Through the gates of the Trojan camp, and following him
The close-packed troops of Mnestheus and Antheus
Flowed out through the gates; a blinding dust cloud rose
High and darkened the sun; earth trembled from
The heavy pulsing of their tramping feet

As marching in order they moved into the field.
Turnus saw it and heard it from the rampart
Where he was standing; the Ausonians saw and heard it,
And the blood ran cold in their bodies into their bones.   610
The first of the Latins to see it and hear it was
Juturna, Turnus's sister, who fled in terror.
It was as if a great tempest was coming, and
A great storm cloud moved in from where it came,
Far out at sea, and alas the farmers know
In their shuddering hearts what it is that's going to happen—
The trees brought down, the crops destroyed, and ruin
Everywhere. Just so, the Trojan leader
Was bringing in his army like that storm,
Shoulder to shoulder marching together as   620
In wedge formation they came against the foe.

⸎ ⸎ ⸎

Thymbraeus's sword killed mighty Osiris; and
Mnestheus killed Arcetius, Achates
Epulo, Gyas Ufens; Tolumnius too,
The augurer who had been the first to throw
The spear that broke the truce that day, was killed.
The clamor rose to the skies; the Rutulian
Lines gave way and they turned and fled in a great
Cloud of dust in terror back through the fields.
Aeneas himself did not condescend to pursue   630
Any of those who were running away, nor did he
Bother to meet the challenge of any who carried
Spears or sought to challenge him as equals.
It was Turnus he was looking for in the murk
Of the battle, Turnus alone he was searching for.

⸎ ⸎ ⸎

And then the maiden Juturna, shocked and fearful,
Because of what she saw that was happening,
Expelled Metiscus, Turnus's charioteer
From where he was, holding the reins, and left him
Back in the field, while, looking exactly like   640
Metiscus himself, in armor exactly like his,
She took up the reins, which fluttered in her hands
As she drove away; it was as if there was
A black barn swallow flying through the halls
And atria of a rich man's country villa,
Looking for bits and crumbs of food to take
To feed her loquacious younglings in the nest;
Sometimes you'd think you could hear her voice high up
In a column in the portico, sometimes
Somewhere around an atrial pool; just so,   650
Juturna was carried by the chariot flying
Among the fighting everywhere; sometimes
She'd allow a fleeting glimpse of her triumphant
Brother, but only fleeting as she flew
Away, keeping him far from the fighting, and
Aeneas, loudly calling out Turnus's name,
Kept trying to find him and track him in the track
Of the orbiting of his chariot's wing-footed horses,
And every time he saw him and followed him,
Trying to be as quick, and almost was,   660
Juturna wheeled again and flew away.
What could he do, tossing on waters of
Perplexity in his mind like this, not knowing
What to do or how to do it? But then,
Messapus, carrying two spears in his hand,
And taking careful aim at Aeneas sent
One of them whining and whirling, and Aeneas,
Seeing it coming, got down on one knee behind
His shield, but the spear struck the crest of his helmet, and

Tore off the plumes, and Aeneas, enraged, and seeing   670
That Turnus was now too far away to catch,
Invoking Jupiter and the altars of
The broken treaty, rushed into the midst of the fighting,
Like Mars letting loose all the reins on his terrible fury,
The cause of undiscriminating carnage.

What god is it whose song can tell of how
There was such slaughtering on that bloody ground,
And how so many died when these two leaders
Came together to kill; and what were Turnus's
Deeds on that field of battle and what were the deeds   680
Of the Trojan hero? Was Jupiter pleased to see
Two nations in such war with one another,
Who would at last find resolution in peace?

Aeneas met Rutulian Sucro, who
Was the first of them to slow the Trojan advance,
But not for long, because Aeneas's spear
Went easily between his ribs and easily straight
To the place where death comes quick; and Turnus met
Two brothers, Amytus and Diores, unhorsed,
And killed them both on foot; Amytus he killed   690
With his big long spear, as Amytus advanced on him,
And Diores he killed with his sword, and, having done that,
He cut off their heads and hung them dangling from
His chariot, the blood dew-dropping down;
And Aeneas brought death to three, all at once and together,
Talon, Tanais, brave Cethegus, and moody
Onites who came to the war from Echion's Thebes,
Peridia's child; and Turnus killed two brothers whose
Father had sent them there from Apollo's Lycia;
And then he killed Menoetes, who from his earliest   700
Youth in Arcady had hated war
And the things of war, and whose peaceable art was the art

Of fishing the fish-filled rivers and brooks of Lerna;
He was ignorant of the patronage of the rich;
His home was poor, his father a tenant farmer.

The way the two, Aeneas and Turnus, were,
Was as, in a forest, two fires, come in from both sides,
And blaze with a seething noise in the laurels, or as,
From a mountaintop come down, two rivers wildly
Roaring, and as they reach the level ground   710
Bring everything in their way that there is, to ruin.
These two, Aeneas and Turnus, rush into the battle,
Their hearts are bursting with fury, unknowing of
Anything of defeat; and laying waste,
Inspired with rage in the landscape of their killing.

As Murranus was bragging about his grandsires and
All his ancestors and all the kings of Latium
He was descended from, an enormous rock,
Thrown by Aeneas, knocked him down and out,
Under his chariot's reins and yoke, and over   720
His body the wheels of the chariot rolled as the hooves
Of the horses trampled him, and the horses' poundng
Hooves knew nothing of who his ancestors were.
Howling with rage, Hyllus rushed at Turnus, and
Turnus hurled a javelin whirling at Hyllus, and
The javelin went straight through his golden helmet
And fixed itself in his brain; and Cretheus,
You bravest of the Greeks, your brave right hand
Couldn't save you; nor did your gods, Cupencus,
Protect you when Aeneas saw you and   730
Your chest was unprotected because you didn't
Get in behind your shield until too late,
Poor creature. And you, Aeolus, too, struck down,
Flat on your back, for all the Laurentians to see;
Neither the Argive battalions could bring you down,

Nor could Achilles, destroyer of Priam's city,
But here is the measured ending of your life,
Whose lofty home was on the high slopes of Ida,
And now your lonely sepulcher is this field.

Now the two armies were wholly engaged in the warfare,   740
All of them, Latins and Trojans, all in the struggle,
Mnestheus and passionate Serestus,
Messapus, tamer of horses, and brave Asilus,
The Tuscan battalions and the Arcadian
Cavalry of Evander, each army, each man,
Strength striving with enemy strength, without rest, without end.

❧ ❧ ❧

Beautiful Venus, Aeneas's mother, inspires
In the mind of her son the idea that he should turn
His attention now away from the battlefield,
And suddenly bring destruction and panic upon   750
The city itself. Aeneas, who had been looking
Every way, this way and that, for Turnus, searching
For Turnus in the field, saw, over there,
The city in its impunity and calm,
And in his head there was an image of
A greater possibility in the war.

He called his leaders together, Sergestus and
Mnestheus and brave Serestus, and stood
High on a mound of earth, with Teucrian soldiers
Gathered around, a crowd of them, with weapons,   760
Their shields and swords, ready for what he would say.
Standing tall in the midst of them, he said,
"Jupiter's on our side. There will be no
Hesitation, none, though this is sudden,
To act as I command you now to act,
Today, this day. It is this city which is

The cause of war, this city of Latinus
Himself, it is the cause. If they do not
Surrender at once and submit to us as their masters,
I'll burn their houses down to the very ground. 770
Did Turnus think he'd be able to get away
With putting off, again, a second time,
His promised fight with me, promised by treaty?
Citizens, this is what war is all about,
The wicked cause of it all. Bring brands of fire,
We'll sign the treaty with fire!" Aeneas spoke,
And all of them, roused for battle, were all at once
Together with this. They formed a wedge, and together
Moved, a great army, toward the city walls.

                    , , ,

Right away, suddenly, scaling-ladders upraised 780
Upon the walls were seen, and, as suddenly, flames;
Many warriors rushing to the city gates
And cutting down the gate guards posted there;
The sky was suddenly iron dark because
Of so many whirling missiles they were hurling.
In the midst of all this, among his leaders, Aeneas
Stood, right hand upraised, as he called out
Loudly the name of Latinus accusingly,
And called upon the gods to witness that he
Had had to attack the city because the Latins 790
Had shown two times that they were enemies,
And that, the second time, the treaty was broken.
Discord and dismay among the frightened
Citizens of the town, some of them wanting
The gates of the town to be opened wide to the Dardans,
And the king himself was dragged out onto the walls;
Others were looking everywhere for weapons
To help them defend the city. It was as when
A shepherd might investigate a cave

With a burning torch and disturbs a hive of bees   800
With its bitter acrid smoke, and the bees are scattered
Everywhere, this way and that in the cavern,
The black smoke curling in all the crevices
And hiding places and finally blowing away
In the empty air.

⸙ ⸙ ⸙

         The fortunes of the wretched
Latins had fallen away, struck down by blows
That brought the whole city down to its very foundation.
And the queen who saw the walls attacked and brands
Of fire igniting the roofs, and no Rutulian   810
Army there to defend them, and Turnus nor
His soldiers anywhere there, she thought that he
Must be dead in the battle, and in the wilds of grief
Amata cried out that it was she who was
The criminal cause of it all, and she decided
To die, tearing her regal purple robes
In unseemly ways, and tying a rope with a noose
To a high beam in the royal palace; and put
Her head in the noose, and died a frightful death,
Throttled and dangling. When the shocking news   820
Of this was heard, Lavinia was the first,
Tearing her golden hair and rosy cheeks
And uncontrollably weeping, and the palace
Halls reverberated with the sound
Of the maddened grief of the women, and when the news
Spread quickly through the town, it broke the hearts
Of all the people; and there was Latinus walking,
His garments torn and rent, the agèd monarch
Dazed by the death of his wife and his country's ruin,
His shaking hands polluting his head with dirt.   830

⸙ ⸙ ⸙

Out at the edge of the plain the warrior Turnus
Was wandering in his chariot more slowly,
And finding fewer and fewer Trojans to kill,
And more and more reasons not to be exultant
About his horses' glorious performance;
And then the air brought to his ears the joyless
Sound of terrified voices terrified by
Unknown unspecified causes. He strained to hear them,
And knew the joyless sounds came from the city.
"Oh, what is the reason for these grieving noises?   840
What is the reason for the sounds I'm hearing?"
Wildly upset, he pulls on the reins to stop
The chariot where it is, and his sister Juturna,
Who had changed herself into the semblance of
Metiscus, Turnus's charioteer, said to Turnus,
"Turnus, let's keep on bringing down Trojans here,
On this field where you've already brought down so many;
Yes, Aeneas glories in his attacking the city
And causing havoc there, but there are many
There to defend the walls and houses and   850
There's no less glory and honor in what we're doing,
Sending so many Teucrians down to death."
But Turnus said, "My sister, I knew it was you
When you came in, disguised, to disrupt the treaty,
And then went onto the field of battle yourself.
This time again I know you're a goddess pretending
Not to be. What god was it whose will
Has sent you down from Olympus to suffer the mortal
Pain of seeing your wretched brother die?
What can I do? Fortune has no more leeway   860
To keep me safe. With my own eyes I saw
Murranus, no one more dear to me than he,
Fall calling out my name for help. I saw him,
A mighty warrior felled in a monstrous way.
I saw unhappy Ufens die, his armor
In Trojan hands; he died in order not

To have to live to see Turnus's shameful death.
Shall I stand by while the houses of the city
Burn and fall? Shall my right hand not keep
Drances from getting away with what he said?   870
Shall I turn my back and let them watch their Turnus
Running away? Is death as bad as this?
Be kind to me, O Manes, now that the gods
Above have turned against me, when I descend,
Guiltless of any deed unworthy of
My great ancestors there among the shades."

                    ❛ ❛ ❛

Just as he was finishing what he was saying,
Suddenly, on his foaming horse, came Saces,
Saces, wounded full in the face by an arrow,
Desperate, coming through the fighting seeking   880
Turnus, calling his name, imploring, "Turnus,
Turnus, help us, help us, Turnus, you
Are our only hope, our only hope, our last.
Aeneas's armies are striking like thunder and lightning,
Threatening to bring the arches down,
To utterly destroy us and all we have.
The fire brands are burning in the roofs.
The faces of all the Latins are turned to you;
Every eye is looking for you to come;
The king in his distraction doesn't know   890
Wherever to turn, which son-in-law to have;
The queen, who was unfailingly true to you,
Is dead; she fled in terror from the light.
There's only Messapus and brave Atinas holding
The line together, though we're surrounded by
Line after enemy line, like a great nighttime
Crop of bristling weapons risen up
In the fields of corn, while Turnus, here you are,

Driving around in your chariot in the deserted
Grasslands." Turnus stood there, looking at him,   900
Stupid, confused, ashamed, in grief, in love,
In consciousness of his own manhood, dismayed.
And after he came to his senses from these shadows,
These images of his being's situation,
He looked back, out of the burning orbs of his eyes,
At the walls of the Latins' great city in its distress.
Beholding how the flames were whirling through
The upper story of a tower, and coiling
Around the very beams he'd put in place
When he himself was the builder of it, by hand.   910

He said to his sister, "Sister, the Fates are too strong.
The time has come. You must leave me, leave me now.
We must do what the Fates are telling us to do.
I must meet Aeneas in single combat. No matter
How bitter it is to die, I must be willing
To suffer death as willed. Sister, you will
Not see your brother put to shame again.
Let me be mad in the madness I know this is."

⸏ ⸏ ⸏

With this, he leaped down from his chariot,
And rushed away among the enemy,   920
Leaving his sorrowing sister behind, and ran
Through all the enemy files and all their weapons,
To where he was going; it is as when a great boulder,
High on a mountain, loosened by years of wind
And rain or just because of long
Years of eroding soil, suddenly crashes
Down the sheer face of a rocky cliff and bounds
With uncontrollable force and crashes through
The clumps of woods, and flocks, and men, thus Turnus

Rushed through and across the blood-soaked field and under   930
The whizzing noise of so many missiles hurled by
Men at war and reached the city walls,
Where he stopped and with one hand raised high, cried out,
In a loud voice, "Rutulians, you,
And all you Latins, put aside your weapons.
Whatever fate it is going to be is mine.
I am the one who must atone for the treaty,
And be the one who decides it with my sword."
Then both sides stood aside and made room for this.

, , ,

When Aeneas heard the name of Turnus he   940
Was overjoyed and turned his attention away
From the walls and the arches and all those other
Things he was doing, and he leaped into action.
His armor thundered and in the eyes of all
Those who were watching, it was as if they were seeing
The mountain Athos and seeing the mountain Eryx
And seeing beyond even them the highest peak
Of the Apennines and its great tree-covered side,
Rising before their eyes, the snowy summit
Shining with terrible joy; all of them watching,   950
Those who, high on the walls, were trying to save them,
And those, below, who were pounding at the walls
With battering rams to bring the city down.
All of them, watching, now put their weapons down.
And old Latinus was stupefied by the sight
Of these two great warriors here from the opposite
Ends of the world, coming together to settle
Everything with steel.

And they, as the field
Is cleared to make a space for the fight, rushed in,   960

Casting their spears at one another as
They ran, and as they came together their
Great bronze shields resounding, the earth is shaking
Beneath their feet; then with skill and chance in one,
They came together with clashing of swords. It is
As it is when two raging bulls contend
In violent tremendous altercation,
Charging with leveled horns, butting and goring,
The black blood flowing down their sides; their mighty
Bellowing re-echoes and re-echoes   970
From the woods up to the top of the nearby mountain,
On Sila or the summit of Taburnus;
All of the watching herd in fear are silent,
Waiting to know which of the two who fight
Will command the herd, which of the two it will follow.
So it was, between Trojan Aeneas and the Daunian
Hero, the clashing of swords, blow after blow
Repeated and the noise of the clanging shields
Filling the air.

        And Jupiter holds up the two   980
Scales evenly balanced, and puts the fates of each
Upon them to show which one is fated to die,
The weight of his death causing the scale to sink down.

           , , ,

Then Turnus saw his opportunity
And confidently raised his threatening sword—
The shouting around him of the Trojans and
His anxious Latins, both sides watching him holding
High his sword—and then, with all his body's
Strength he struck—and the sword he struck with broke,
And it fell away, and Turnus was left defenseless,   990
The unfamiliar handle of the sword

Was gone, and there was nothing to do but run.
And when he saw what had happened he fled as if
The East Wind were pursuing him. It is said
That when Turnus first was setting out for battle,
Fervent for warfare, in his haste he took,
By mistake, the sword of his charioteer Metiscus.
The mistaken sword worked perfectly against
The scattering of Teucrians out on the plain
Where Turnus killed them. But here when he thought that he   1000
Was using the sword that Vulcan made, it shattered
As if it was fragile as an icicle,
The broken pieces shining on the ground.
Desperately trying to get away he tried
This way then that to get away, but there,
Preventing, a dense closed ring of Teucrian army,
And then there were the high preventing walls
Of the Latin town, and over there then there was
A miry bog impossible to enter.

But Aeneas was not deflected from what he intended   1010
To do though the arrow wound had slowed him down,
Making his walking more difficult for him;
Yet nothing turned him aside from his pursuit;
He was like a hunting dog who had, perhaps,
Seen a stag which had been cornered in the bend
Of a river, or maybe trapped in its own fears
By a red-and-white hunting-scare, and the stag
Terrified by the pursuing barking dog
Is trapped in the terror of where it is, unable
To get away, turning and turning, looking   1020
This way and looking that way and the dog
Pursuing, pursuing, now sometimes seeming
To catch him, now sometimes snapping its open jaws
Now sometimes snapping at empty air. The clamor

Of shouting rose and echoed from river and lake,
And the sky above resounded with a huge
Overwhelming noise, and Turnus in terror running
This way and that way and calling out to his
Rutulians, some by name, to find and get
His familiar sword to him before too late, 1030
And Aeneas, although still hampered by his wound,
Threatening anyone who came near him with death.
And terrifying the crowd with the threat that if
They did not stay away he'd bring the whole city
Down into final ruin. This was no game.
The prize for the winner was the life of Turnus.

It happens that, growing there, there was the stump
Of a tree, wild olive tree, with bitter foliage,
Sacred to Faunus, to which it was the custom
That Laurentine sailors, getting home safe from sea, 1040
In gratitude to the god for this, would bring
As votive gifts the sea-soaked garments they'd worn;
This tree the Teucrians had destroyed, without
Regard for its sacred character; they did so
When they were clearing out the space in which
The ratified single combat would take place.
Aeneas's spear, thrown with tremendous force,
Struck—and got stuck—in the tough roots of what
Had been the tree, and no matter how hard he tried
To retrieve the weapon in order to hurl it at 1050
His fugitive target, he wasn't able to do it;
And Turnus, in the wild distress of fear,
Prayed frantically to Faunus, "Faunus, have pity;
O Earth, I have always honored you, and I fight
Against those Teucrians profaning you,
Hold tight to that weapon; do not let him have it."
He prayed and the gods were listening to him,

For Aeneas's great strength was to no avail;
He could not free the spear from the roots' tight clutch.
Then suddenly Juturna, the Daunian goddess, 1060
Dressed once again as the charioteer Metiscus,
Ran out from the crowd and gave her brother back
His proper sword, the sword that Vulcan made
For their father, Daunus. But Venus, offended by
The audacity of this, plucked Aeneas's spear
From the clenching roots of the tree that held it fast.

Thus both of them, in dignity restored,
One of them trusting to his faithful sword,
The other to his formidable spear,
Were face to face for the fight that was to come. 1070

             ꞌ ꞌ ꞌ

Meanwhile, Jupiter, from on high in Olympus,
Spoke to Juno who was looking down
At the fight from where she was, in a golden cloud:
"What's going to be the end of all of this?
Why are you trying, my wife, to put it off?
You know, and you know that you know, that Aeneas
Is fated to be a god and will be raised
By the Fates up to the high heavens to be so?
What are you doing, what are you thinking of doing?
What hopes do you have out there in those chilly clouds? 1080
Do you think it was proper that the body of
A god was wounded, or that the fated loser,
Whose sword that was snatched away from him was given
Back to him again, and his strength restored?
How could Juturna have done this without your help?
Please, now, give up all you have done to not listen
To all my prayers, and, please, in the future, don't
Let this frustration gnaw at you, and please,

In the future don't show me all the time how you
Are suffering from all of this in silence.   1090
The end of it all has come. Wherever they went
You've persecuted the Trojans, by land, by sea,
Brought houses down in turmoil and destruction,
Brought grief into the joyousness of weddings.
I forbid you to try anymore. Enough is enough."

Thus Jupiter spoke, and Juno answered him,
Bowing her head submissively, and saying,
"Because it is your will that I must do so,
I will leave my Turnus and the earth, although
Reluctantly. If it were not your will,   1100
You would most certainly not be seeing me here,
Up here in the air. I would be standing down there,
In the line of battle, dressed in a garment of fire,
Dragging the Trojans into the bloody combat.
It was I, I confess it, who saw to it that Juturna
Came to the aid of her poor brother, and I
Approved the lengths of daring that she went to,
Trying to help him survive. But I did not
Authorize her to draw the bowstring back
To send the wounding arrow on its way.   1110
I swear this on the source of implacable Styx,
The oath the gods above cannot go back on.
And now I yield and now, with loathing for it,
I turn away from the battle, for good and all.

But I ask of your divine majesty that the Latins,
Their defeat accepted and the marriage accomplished
—And now I wish it well—not be commanded
To call themselves Teucrians; that they be called
By their ancient name, as Latins, and with their own customs,
And with their own dress, and with their own language, and   1120
The Alban kings who have always been their kings.

Let all of them be Romans, for Troy has fallen,
And fallen forever must Troy and its language be."

Jupiter, smiling, all but laughing, replied,
"You're truly Jove's sister and Saturn's other child,
With such familiar surgings of such anger.
But now, put down the anger that rose in vain.
Willingly conquered, I yield to what you wish.
The Ausonians will keep their speech and their ways.
They will not lose their name. The Teucrians   1130
Will blend with them and be submerged into
The one race and its language; and I will give them
Their modes of worship and their rituals;
You will see that arising from this mingling of
Their blood the Ausonian people will surpass
All men and gods in their devotion, and
In honoring Juno no other nation be equal."

Juno nodded, and joyfully changed her mind,
And, departing from her cloud, she left the sky.

                    ❯ ❯ ❯

This having been accomplished, Jove thought to himself   1140
Of something else to do, to separate
Juturna from her brother and his fighting.
It's said that in Tartarean night there were
Twin pestilences who are called the Dirae,
Twin sisters born together enclustered with
A third, the fiend Megaera, the three of them; on
Their backs were growing sprouting coiling serpents,
And each with a pair of wings of wind, they sit
On the threshold of the throne of terrible Jove;
They bring down dread upon terrified mortals whenever   1150
He decides to visit sickness and death upon
Mortal men and bring destruction onto

The roofs of guilty horrified cities at war.
Now Jupiter sends down from the heavens above
One of the sisters to be to Juturna an omen.

Obedient down through the sky on a whirlwind she
Flew like a Parthian or a Cydonian poisoned
Immedicable arrow, shot and flying down
Unseen to the earth below, and when she saw
The Ilian line and Turnus's army there,   1160
Night's daughter suddenly made herself small, like the bird
That sometimes late at night bodingly sings
In the shadows on burial mounds and sometimes on
The deserted roofs of cities. Again and again
The monster flitted back and forth close to
Turnus's face and there was the sound of its wings
Beating upon his shield; his hair stood on end,
His limbs went weak with a strange torpor of dread,
And his voice clung to the inside of his throat.

When unhappy Juturna heard from a ways away   1170
The screaming of the Dirae and the beating
Of their wings, she tore with her desperate nails at her
Disfigured face, and beat her breasts. "Oh what
Can his sister do to save her Turnus now?
What art is there left to keep him in the light?
What can I do against these portents? You
Boding obscene birds, I hear, I hear
The death in the beating of your wings, I hear
The message high-hearted Jupiter is sending.
O do not frighten me so in what I hear,   1180
I hear the sound of it. To be a goddess,
Is this what Jupiter's bargain was, to give me
Immortality in return for my lost
Virginity so that I am unable to die,
So I must live forever not able to go
Down to the shades in the company of my brother?

Is there no deepest place down there for one
Who cannot die to go down there to die?"
And saying this she veiled her head in gray
And plunged, becoming gone, into the deep   1190
Lamenting waters of the flowing river.

                              ＞ ＞ ＞

Aeneas stood before him, brandishing
His huge spear that was as big as a tree, and from
His savage breast brought forth these words to him:
"Turnus, where have you been? Why have you taken
So long to get here, Turnus? This wasn't a race,
Nor is there any way to get away
From what this is. Not by flying on wings
Up to the highest sky, nor hiding away
Deep in the earth. What it comes down to at last   1200
Is this: this is the single combat, this
Is the two of us face to face, with weapons that kill.
Whatever you still have left of courage or skill,
Now get it together, the time has come." And Turnus,
Shaking his head, replied, "It isn't your words
That terrify me, ferocious. It is the gods
And Jupiter's enmity I'm terrified by."
He said no more, and he looked around and saw,
By chance, a huge stone lying in the ground,
Ancient huge stone, a marker of the limits   1210
Of the fields to show the ownership of one
And ownership of the other; it was a stone
So great, as now the bodies of men are made,
It would take the strength of twelve men to lift it up.
But Turnus lifted it up in his trembling hands,
And staggered forward and ran as fast as he could,
And hurled the huge stone toward the hero, not knowing who
Was hurling it, not knowing who he was,
And his buckling knees gave in beneath him and

The stone fell heavily onto the ground and by   1220
The impetus of its own great weight it rolled
And bounced and wobbled its way toward the hero, and stopped
Before it could reach what he had hurled it at.

It's as in sleep, in the quiet of the night,
Our languid eyelids close and in their dream
Won't tell wherever we are nor where we're going
Or trying to go nor can we get there where-
Ever where might be, and who knows who it is
We maybe are, our legs gone weak, no way
To get there where? It was thus it was with Turnus.   1230
Wherever he tried to go, the dreadful goddess,
Up from Tartarus, everywhere in his way,
Turning him back and around; in his head he saw,
Or thought he saw, the Rutulians and the city;
Turnus was shaking in mortal dread at the death
That was coming; he couldn't find the enemy;
He couldn't find his chariot anywhere;
The chariot driver gone, the sister gone.

As in his confusion he was wavering thus,
Aeneas was watching him and ready with   1240
His death-bringing weapon to strike. And then he struck.
It was more than the sound of the catapulted stones
That bring down the walls of cities, more than the thunder
Sound of a black tornado whirling in,
More than the sound of a bolt of lightning smiting
The nighttime sky, louder than any such,
Howling, screaming, straight through the sevenfold shield
And through the lower edge of his body armor.
Great Turnus doubled over as he fell.
The spear transfixed in his thigh, the screaming stilled.   1250
There was a groaning roar from the Rutulian
Watchers, rising up to the heavens above,
And echoing and re-echoing through the high

Side-spreading groves behind them. And Turnus, his eyes
Abased, stretched out his pleading hands, and saying,

"I have done this to myself. I have no excuse.
Do with me what you will. But if you can be touched
By any thought of a father—you had a father,
Your father was Anchises—with pity for fathers,
Have pity for my father Daunus, old.   1260
Send me or my dead body back to him.
You are the victor. The Ausonians have seen
My hand stretched out surrendering to you;
Lavinia is yours. Lavinia's your bride.
Let this be the end and limit of your hatred."

Aeneas stood there, fierce, in his threatening armor,
Rolling his eyes, his right hand on his sword,
More and more hesitant, little by little,
As he heard what Turnus was saying to him. But, then,
Suddenly his eyes saw, high on the shoulder   1270
Of fallen Turnus the fatal sword-belt with
The gleaming studs he recognized—sword-belt
Of Pallas, the boy, whom Turnus had wounded, and when
He lay there dying on the ground, had torn it
Off of his body and wore it now as spoil.

When Aeneas saw it on Turnus's shoulder, shining
Memorial of the dolorous story, and
Of his own grief, the terrible savage rage
Rose up in him, and he said to Turnus, "Did you
Think that you could get away with this,   1280
Wearing this trophy of what you did to him?
It is Pallas who makes you his sacrifice. It is Pallas
Who drives this home!" And saying this he ripped
Open the breast of Turnus, and Turnus's bones
Went chilled and slack, and his life, with a groaning shudder,
Indignant fled away to the shades below.

ACKNOWLEDGMENTS

First of all, I'm deeply grateful to the University of Chicago Press for their care in the publishing and presenting of this book, to Kelly Finefrock-Creed, to Levi Stahl, and to Randolph Petilos. It has been my great luck that Randy has been my guide and editor for previous books of my poetry and now for this one. I wish to thank George Kalogeris, Richard Thomas, and Kenneth Haynes for their sustained and generous encouragement and, when need be, helpfully corrective attentiveness to the work of this translation as it developed. They have brought to their attentiveness the resources of their own deep understanding of Virgil's poem and its context, and I hope I will have demonstrated that there are some signs in my translation that I have learned from them. For the same reasons, I'm very grateful to David Wray for his very helpful reading of my work and to Catherine Parnell for her generous and expert help in the copyediting.

I have consulted two prose translations of the *Aeneid*: the translation by H. Rushton Fairclough, revised by G. P. Goold, in *Virgil: "Eclogues," "Georgics," "Aeneid,"* 2 vols. (Cambridge: Harvard University Press, 1999); and the translation by David West, *Virgil: "The Aeneid"* (London: Penguin Books, 2003). I have also sometimes consulted passages in John Dryden's great seventeenth-century translation of the poem.

I am indebted to the following scholars for their invaluable work: to Michael C. J. Putnam for his *The Poetry of "The Aeneid"* (Cambridge: Harvard University Press, 1965), his *Virgil's "Aeneid": Interpretation and Influence* (Chapel Hill: University of North Carolina Press, 1995), and his *The Humanness of Heroes: Studies in the Conclusion of Virgil's*

"Aeneid" (Amsterdam: Amsterdam University Press, 2011); to W. R. Johnson for *Darkness Visible: A Study of Virgil's "Aeneid"* (Berkeley: University of California Press, 1976); to David O. Ross for *Virgil's "Aeneid": A Reader's Guide* (Oxford: Blackwell, 2007); to Nicholas Horsfall for his edition of the essays in *A Companion to the Study of Virgil* (Leiden: E. J. Brill, 1995); and to Steele Commager for his edition, *Virgil: A Collection of Critical Essays* (Englewood Cliffs: Prentice Hall, 1966). I am most especially indebted to Adam Parry for his article, "The Two Voices of Virgil's 'Aeneid,'" in *Arion* (vol. 2, no. 4, Winter 1963), to K. W. Gransden's edition of book 11 of the *Aeneid* (Cambridge: Cambridge University Press, 1991), and to Richard Tarrant's edition of book 12 of the *Aeneid* (Cambridge: Cambridge University Press, 2012).

I have sought advice, at various times, and received rich responses from a number of friends, among them Robert Pinsky, Sarah Spence, Stephen Scully, Michael Putnam, Rosanna Warren, Christopher Ricks, Timothy Peltason, Lawrence Rosenwald, and Richard Wilbur. And I must reiterate my gratitude to George Kalogeris, for his generous attention to the work, day by day, which made it feel almost like a collaboration, a brotherly relationship.

I am grateful to the editors of the following journals, which have had the kindness to publish passages from the translation: *Arion*, *Harvard Advocate*, *Hopkins Review*, *Literary Imagination*, *Paris Review*, *Persephone*, *Poetry*, and *Raritan*.

Finally, I wish to thank Cynthia Hadzi for permission to reproduce Dimitri Hadzi's *Thermopylae*, and my son Stephen Ferry, the photojournalist, for his photograph of the sculpture. The lines accompanying the image are from the poem "Sculptures by Dimitri Hadzi," from an earlier book of mine, *Strangers* (1983).

ITALY

Adriatic Sea

Tiber River

Pallanteum (Rome)
Trojan Camp

Caieta
Cumae

Temple
of
Minerva

Tyrrhenian Sea

Eryx
Drepanum

SICILY

Harbor
of the
Cyclopes

Carthage

LIBYA

Mediterrane